Praise for *A Front Page Affair*

"A delightfully spunky heroine defies convention as an investigative reporter in this engaging historical mystery. The small factual details of New York life are gems."

—Rhys Bowen, *New York Times* bestselling author of the Molly Murphy and Royal Spyness mysteries

"This first in a planned series is a nice combination of mystery and thriller seasoned by historical facts and a look at women's lives before woman's liberation."

—*Kirkus Reviews*

"This lively and well-researched debut introduces a charming historical series and an appealing fish-out-of-water sleuth who seeks independence and a career in an age when most women are bent on getting married, particularly to titled Englishmen. Devotees of Rhys Bowen's mysteries will enjoy making the acquaintance of Miss Weeks."

—*Library Journal*, Starred Review

A FRONT PAGE AFFAIR

RADHA VATSAL

sourcebooks
landmark

Published by Sourcebooks Landmark, an imprint of Sourcebooks, Inc.
P.O. Box 4410, Naperville, Illinois 60567-4410
(630) 961-3900
Fax: (630) 961-2168
www.sourcebooks.com

Library of Congress Cataloging-in-Publication Data

Vatsal, Radha
  A front page affair / Radha Vatsal.
     pages cm
  (pbk. : alk. paper) 1. Women journalists--United States--Fiction. 2. World War, 1914-1918--United States--Fiction. 3. Murder--Investigation--Fiction. I. Title.
  PS3622.A885F76 2016
  813'.6--dc23

                    2015032577

      Printed and bound in the United States of America.
      VP 10 9 8 7 6 5 4 3 2 1

"History is nothing if not far-fetched."

—Albert O. Hirschman

CHAPTER ONE

*T*his is whom they've sent to cover my party?" Mrs. Elizabeth Basshor was in her forties, plump, and well-preserved. As befitting a queen bee, she was dressed in crisp yellow silk, and the plunging neckline of her gown revealed an ample, bejeweled bosom.

"Hotchkiss?" She turned to her secretary, a boyishly handsome fellow who coughed into his palm by way of reply. Behind them, workers put final touches on the dais for the band, and waiters scurried about, pushing chairs into place and arranging floral centerpieces on tables dotted across the lush lawns of the Sleepy Hollow Country Club.

Mrs. Basshor trained her gaze on Capability Weeks. "Are you sure you are up to this?"

Nineteen-year-old Kitty squared her shoulders. Today's Independence Day gala—held on Monday, July 5, since the Fourth fell on a Sunday—would be her first solo outing as a reporter. In a simple tea dress, her glossy chestnut hair pinned away from her heart-shaped face, her brown eyes sparkling, Kitty felt ready. "Miss Busby wanted to attend, but she sent me because she's indisposed. I've been working for her for the past sixth months."

"I know your Miss Busby." Mrs. Basshor sniffed at the

mention of Kitty's editor at the Ladies' Page of the *New York Sentinel*. "She gives me a nice write-up." Her gaze drifted to the workmen on the lawns. "Too close, too close," she called, frowning and pointing to a string of lanterns, patterned in red, white, and blue. Her attention returned to Kitty. "Did Miss Busby tell you we're having a display of Japanese daylight fireworks this afternoon? You must observe them carefully and be sure to give them their due. They're quite spectacular, not at all flashy like the nighttime ones.

"Hotchkiss." She swung around to him. "See to it that Miss Meeks receives a copy of the guest list and the program. If you need further help, Miss Meeks, my secretary will be happy to assist you."

"It's 'Weeks,' actually," Kitty corrected, but Elizabeth Basshor had already stepped off the terrace and was busy making sure that the lanterns were being hung to her satisfaction.

"You mustn't take it personally." Hotchkiss tried to smooth things over as soon as his employer was out of earshot. "Names aren't her strong point—I'll leave you to imagine what she called me when I first started working for her." He shuddered at the ghastly memory and handed Kitty a page from his clipboard.

She glanced at the notes: *Guests to arrive at three. Japanese fireworks from four to five. Illumination of the clubhouse terrace and Italian gardens at six. Dinner and dancing to follow.*

"Have you been with Mrs. Basshor for long, Mr. Hotchkiss?"

"About five years, Miss Weeks." He took a deep breath. "I must point out that we've had some cancellations because of Saturday's incident on Long Island."

Kitty nodded. He was referring to the shooting of Mr. J. P. Morgan, the nation's foremost financier, who had been attacked by an intruder who barged his way into the Morgan mansion. The story had made front-page headlines and pushed aside news of the war in Europe.

"Fortunately, Mr. Morgan seems to be recovering well." Hotchkiss pulled a handkerchief from his pocket. "Otherwise— who knows—we might have had to call off the party." He wiped the perspiration from his forehead. "Do you know how much work it took to get to today, Miss Weeks? Months of agonizing. Menus changed and changed again. The guest list vetted, entertainment fixed—and we have the impossible task of ensuring that each year everything is the same, and, at the same time, *utterly* different."

"It sounds extremely demanding, Mr. Hotchkiss." Kitty looked around her. "But this is a beautiful location." The patio gave way to green lawns, which sloped toward formal gardens and the Hudson River, and backed up against the majestic brick-and-stone clubhouse, which had once been home to a Vanderbilt granddaughter.

"It is much more pleasant than trying to do something in Manhattan."

"Hotchkiss!" Mrs. Basshor trilled just as a long-haired Oriental beckoned to her secretary from the far side of the terrace.

"If you will excuse me"—he sounded flustered—"I should go take care of business."

Kitty left him to negotiate the competing demands for his attention and wandered off to explore the grounds before the party began. She made her way past trimmed topiaries, through a vine-covered pergola, and down neatly graveled paths that led to a fountain burbling at the center of a peaceful Italian garden.

In the distance, ships steamed up and down the broad expanse of the Hudson. Kitty watched the water surge in their wake for a few quiet moments. Just a year and a half ago, in the spring of 1914, she had been nothing more than a recent boarding-school graduate arriving by sea to set foot on home soil for the first time. She had been born abroad and, as a child, had followed her businessman father on his travels through the Indies and the Orient; then, for almost a decade, she boarded at the Misses Dancey's school in Switzerland until he sent for her to join him in New York.

She had applied for the position at the Ladies' Page after she had settled in and grown accustomed to her new town. Without any practical experience, she had been certain she wouldn't be selected. But somehow, Miss Busby had hired Kitty as her apprentice—and then set her to opening mail, reading proofs, judging cookery contests, and, every now and then, writing a piece about domestic matters.

The Morgan shooting, which reawakened Kitty's urge to write a real news story, seemed like just the latest instance of how the world could turn on a dime. Last summer, an assassin's bullet in far-off Sarajevo had launched the entire continent into war. This May, a torpedo from a German U-boat had struck the majestic ocean liner *Lusitania*, which sank in a mere eighteen minutes, killing nearly twelve hundred passengers—128 of them Americans—and it felt as though the United States might be sucked into Europe's madness.

Kitty turned away from the river to a shady path that wound its way toward the club's golf course.

"The example of America must be a special example," the president had said in his rousing speech in the aftermath of the *Lusitania* tragedy. "The example of America must be the example not merely of peace because it will not fight, but of peace because peace is the healing and elevating influence of the world and strife is not."

The clack of hedge cutters jolted Kitty from her reverie. A gardener trimming bushes with a ferocious pair of blades scowled as she walked by.

She came across a groundskeeper shoveling manure into a wheelbarrow outside a two-and-a-half-story yellow-brick building. With its tiled roof and arched windows reaching all the way to the roofline, it looked formal, but the layout didn't seem right for a residence. "What is this place?"

"It's the stables, miss."

"Is that so?" Kitty smiled to herself. Some horses had all the luck.

A couple strolled along arm in arm. He was big and burly in his formal attire; she was about half his size and wore a lavender gown with muttonchop sleeves that overwhelmed her petite form.

"I don't know what we're doing here," the woman said to her companion before her words were drowned out by the sound of touring cars crunching down the gravel drive.

Kitty hurried back to the party, where the band had begun to play, and chose an inconspicuous position beside a pillar on the terrace from which to observe the goings-on.

The lawns soon filled with gentlemen in dark suits and ladies in wispy organza gowns. Pearls glowed around necks; diamonds sparkled on languid wrists. Silver trays bobbed up and down as waiters made their way through the crowd, proffering bubbly drinks and savory appetizers. Children darted between the grown-ups' legs.

Bang! "You're dead, Willie!" A gunshot went off. Kitty searched for the source of the sound.

One of the boys had fired his toy pistol.

"I'm not Willie," his playmate cried indignantly.

"Are too."

"Why don't you play Cowboys and Indians?" Kitty suggested.

The boys stared at her in confusion. "Why would we want to play that?"

"Look at us," the first one demanded, "and tell me who looks like Kaiser Bill and who"—he stuck his hand in his pocket and assumed a debonair pose—"resembles King George."

Kitty laughed. No one seemed to care for the German kaiser these days. She wondered whether he was as bad as the press made out.

The boys ran off, continuing their battle, and she found herself drawn to another conversation. Two men, one with a chest full of medals, discussed the details of the Morgan shooting. How Mr. Morgan's attacker panicked and fired when he saw the 250-pound banker charge toward him—and then found himself pinned below the massive financier, who toppled forward when the bullets hit his groin and thigh. How the Morgans' butler had conked the fellow in the head with a lump of coal after Mrs. Morgan pried away his guns. The would-be assailant was in police custody.

"Wouldn't you know, he's German," the man with the medals said. "Thank goodness he's safely behind bars," the other replied.

"Doing a little eavesdropping, were we?" Hotchkiss startled Kitty by materializing noiselessly beside her.

"I'm just doing my job." She felt her cheeks flush.

"Aren't we all?" Tiny moon-shaped gold cuff links flashed from under his cuffs as he clasped his hands together. "Would you like me to help you put names to faces?"

"That would be wonderful." Although Kitty and her father went to parties from time to time, they didn't hobnob with New York's high society, and it would be important for her to identify the most important guests in her article as well as to say who was wearing what.

"The woman with the turban"—he nodded toward a striking figure in iridescent Turkish-style pantaloons—"is Mrs. Poppy Clements. She's the wife of Mr. Clement Clements, the theater producer, and is a playwright herself. The handsome buck to her left is Justice Stevens, a cad of the first order.

"He's with his grandmama," Mrs. Basshor's secretary continued with a smirk, as a good-looking fellow with an old lady on his arm made eyes at all the pretty girls going by. "She's richer than Croesus, and he has to keep on her good side." He turned to another cluster of guests. "Those over there are the Goelets in conversation with the Burrall-Hoffmans.

"Mrs. Wilson Alexander is behind them in red and blue. Mr. Wilson Alexander has the white beard. There's John Parson with the glasses. Miss Winnie Slade is wearing a wonderful bracelet—do you see those emeralds?"

Kitty nodded. She wished she could take notes, but Miss Busby had forbidden her from writing anything. "Notepads and pencils staunch the flow of conversation, so it all stays in here." She had tapped her temple.

"And... Oh no." Hotchkiss pretended to take cover. "Here comes Hunter Cole with his wife, Aimee."

Kitty spotted the couple she had seen wandering about the grounds stop to speak to the turbaned Mrs. Clements.

"What's wrong with them, Mr. Hotchkiss?" she said, surprised that he would be so indiscreet in front of a reporter.

"Have you seen her dress?" The secretary sneered. "He's a bully, and she's a nobody—but, of course, you didn't hear me say that."

Kitty watched the couple for a few moments; when she looked up once more, the secretary had vanished.

What a strange man, she thought to herself before she stepped out onto the lawns.

Kitty felt the urge to mingle. These were people whom a girl in her position might be expected to know, that is, if her father took more trouble to socialize. Realizing that she didn't have to wait to be introduced because she was there on business, Kitty approached the first lady she saw heading her way—Mrs. Goelet. The older woman seemed amused by the young reporter and was soon joined by the inquisitive Mrs. Burrall-Hoffman. Kitty had no illusions that the women were interested in her for her own sake. From their remarks she could tell that what they really wanted to know was how someone who dressed well and spoke well could be there to work, and that they wouldn't mind a mention in the Page's Social Scene column.

"Isn't she delightful?" Mrs. Basshor joined the group and took Kitty's arm as well as the credit for her being there. "I told dear Frieda Eichendorff that her husband's paper must send someone other than that beanpole, Helena Busby, who usually comes."

Kitty didn't care to hear Miss Busby described so disparagingly, but this was hardly the moment to leap to her boss's defense.

Mrs. Basshor beamed at her friends. "The fireworks will start in fifteen minutes or so." Her smile hardened as she turned to Kitty. "I look forward to your description, my dear. Don't let me down."

The women drifted away to find their husbands, and Kitty returned to the terrace, pleased with the results of her first foray into social reporting. She hadn't gone into journalism to become a society columnist, but she had to admit that the profession had its pluses: one could speak to whomever one wanted, for starters.

Given her lack of formal training, Kitty realized that she couldn't afford to be choosy. Moreover, the skills she required today—to observe, ask questions, come forward when necessary, and disappear into the scenery when not—were all skills required for any good reporter, even a newswoman.

A sudden flurry of movement caught her eye. A feminine voice, shrill enough to be heard above the din of the party, called, "I'm sorry!"

A figure in a lavender gown with muttonchop sleeves pushed her way through the guests.

"She bumped into me on purpose," Mrs. Cole hissed to her heavyset husband as they made their way toward the terrace.

CHAPTER TWO

D on't make a scene, Aimee. They're all watching us," Mr. Cole said.

"What do I care about them?" she retorted, her pale complexion blotched with anger. "I hate it here. Let's go back to Manhattan."

Mr. Cole held his wife by the wrist. "We're not going anywhere. Clean up your clothes, and let's pretend that none of this happened." He dropped her arm.

Kitty stepped forward. Mrs. Cole's dress had been soiled by a greasy spill that ran down the front of her bodice. "I beg your pardon. I couldn't help overhearing—"

"And who are you to be listening in to our conversation?" Mr. Cole demanded.

"I'm Capability Weeks, from the Ladies' Page of the *New York Sentinel*."

Husband and wife stared at her, aghast.

"I could help," Kitty offered. "I'm good with stains."

"You make them, or you clean them?" Mr. Cole said.

"Well, both, I suppose." Kitty couldn't tell if he meant to be funny. In any case, his tone wasn't very nice.

"That's very kind of you, Miss Weeks." Mrs. Cole smiled brightly. "I could use a hand." She couldn't have been much older than Kitty, twenty-one or twenty-two at most.

"I have no time for this nonsense," her husband muttered. "Do what you want, and come find me when you're done." He strode back toward the crowd on the lawns.

"Don't mind Hunter." Aimee Cole turned to Kitty. "His bark is worse than his bite. And he thinks he can get away with anything because the Coles go almost all the way back to the *Mayflower*... Shall we?"

Kitty followed her into the clubhouse.

"Have you heard of them?" Mrs. Cole opened the door to the powder room.

"The Coles? I'm afraid I haven't."

"Don't worry." Aimee Cole giggled. "Before I married Hunter, neither had I. My family goes back a whole two generations. All the way to Brooklyn!" She stared at her reflection in a gilt-framed mirror above a porcelain sink and said wistfully, "You wouldn't believe that I was rather pretty once."

Kitty felt sorry for the young woman. "Let's clean up this mess."

"You don't look like a reporter." Aimee Cole turned around.

Kitty smiled and asked the attendant for talcum powder and a towel.

"You seem pretty competent for someone your age."

"I'll take that as a compliment." In addition to a basic education, Kitty's boarding-school teachers, the Misses Dancey, had taught their charges how to speak, read, and write in French, German, and Italian; memorize poetry; sketch from life; play an instrument; and run a household. They hadn't taught the girls politics, algebra, or any of the sciences.

Mrs. Cole wiped the greasy residue from her dress, and Kitty dusted powder on the stain.

"That Lizzie Chilton bumped my arm and made me spill my canapé." Mrs. Cole frowned, then added, "Don't put that into your report."

"I won't be writing about any of this." Kitty waited for the powder to soak up the grease and then brushed off the remains. "Better?"

Mrs. Cole stood back and looked in the mirror. "Much better, thanks."

"I'm so clumsy, I rarely eat at parties," Kitty confessed to her.

"If I didn't eat at these things, I wouldn't have anything to do." Mrs. Cole laughed. She seemed in a more cheerful mood.

Kitty checked the time on her watch. It was almost four o'clock. "I think we should get back."

There was no sign of Mr. Cole when they came out on the terrace.

"Where could he be?" Mrs. Cole looked around. She said she would wait for her husband at the children's tables and thanked Kitty again for her help. "It means a lot to me."

"It was no trouble at all." Kitty returned to her position by the pillar.

From a stage on the lawns, Mrs. Basshor rang a bell. The crowd went quiet.

"Your attention please." The hostess addressed her guests. "Please join me in welcoming our visitors who've traveled here all the way from Yokohama to delight us with the daylight fireworks that are the specialty of Japan!"

Mrs. Basshor brought her hands together, and everyone joined her in an enthusiastic round of applause. Two kimonoed men in wooden sandals emerged from behind the trees and took a quick bow in military unison. They were joined by a third with a bandana wrapped around his head, who slowly and deliberately beat a round brass gong.

The sound faded into silence.

All Mrs. Basshor's guests waited under the blazing summer sun. A toddler in a sailor suit cried out and was hushed by his nursemaid. The air was still, and the waiters seemed frozen, trays suspended in midair. Groundskeepers looked on from behind the bushes, and even the stable lads had come up to watch the proceedings from a safe distance. When nothing happened, some of the ladies exchanged glances, smiling to hide their embarrassment.

Then a bomb blast went off, startling everyone, and jets of pink and blue smoke shot into the heavens. A collective gasp ran through the crowd as tiny packages of paper and wire unfurled below the clouds, and orange goldfish, golden carp, and green serpents floated downward. Another explosion rang out, and this time dwarfish goblins and gorgeous butterflies came to life. Bursts of smoke in different hues filled the atmosphere. The show went on and on, like a rainbow continuously changing its colors, shape, and form. One explosion followed another, and the patterns bloomed and dissipated as if by magic. Finally, the pièce de résistance: an ephemeral vision of red, white, and blue stripes pierced by a quick succession of exploding stars.

A shower of tiny tissue-paper figures rained on the guests. The children shrieked and scrambled to catch silhouettes of turkeys, George Washington, trumpets, and flags. Many of the adults couldn't resist either and held out their hands for a souvenir.

Kitty had never seen anything quite like it. The display ended almost an hour after it had begun, and she decided that she ought to head back home. The drive to Manhattan might take some time, and Miss Busby had told her she could leave once the fireworks were done.

She went to look for Mrs. Basshor but spotted Hotchkiss instead. The secretary stood at the edge of the lawns, his hands behind his back, surveying the delighted crowd with pride.

Kitty walked over and held out her hand. "Congratulations, Mr. Hotchkiss."

"Thank you, Miss Weeks. Are you leaving us already?"

"I think I have the best part for my story."

"Yes." He nodded. "Those daylight fireworks are quite a sight."

"Someone seems to need to speak to you," she said, looking over his shoulder at the groundskeeper running toward him.

"Mr. Hotchkiss!" the groundskeeper panted, out of breath, holding his cap in his hands.

Hotchkiss turned. "What's the matter, man? Don't you know better than to interrupt in the middle of a conversation?"

"I'm sorry, sir"—the fellow shot a glance at Kitty—"but it's one of the guests."

"Yes?"

"The lads found him in the stables."

"Go on." Hotchkiss sounded impatient.

The groundskeeper seemed to be struggling to find the right words. Then he came out and said it: "He's dead, sir. He's been shot."

CHAPTER THREE

Kitty didn't ask for permission to follow. She picked up her skirts and hurried after the men, thankful not to be wearing a gown or Louis heels that would sink into the soft grass.

Her thoughts were jumbled. *Someone murdered? In the stables? Who could it be? How did it happen?*

A crowd of lads had gathered by the entrance to the attractive brick building that Kitty had admired just a few hours before. Sunlight bathed the copper-domed monitors atop the tiled roof, and Kitty caught her breath. It didn't seem possible that there could be a dead body inside.

The men parted to make way for the secretary and his escort.

"I wouldn't go in there, if I were you, miss," a stable hand said, but Kitty didn't listen. One moment, she was out in the bright sunshine, surrounded by voices; the next, she was enveloped in darkness and silence broken only by the clatter of hooves and the occasional whinnying of a horse.

It took Kitty's eyes a second to adjust. Then she caught sight of a figure, stretched out like a beached whale along the wooden aisle between two rows of stalls. Her reluctant gaze traveled from the soles of polished shoes, up a pair of sharply creased black trousers, over the mound of a belly, to a slack jaw and glassy stare. A single bullet hole pierced the forehead.

Kitty felt her legs give way. She had never been to a funeral, let alone seen a corpse. She held on to the door of a stall and forced herself to look again.

The body was that of Hunter Cole, someone to whom she had spoken not more than an hour before.

She turned to Hotchkiss. The secretary's face was ashen.

So forceful in life, Mr. Cole was nothing now. "I should go." Kitty tottered from the barn. She sat on a nearby bench, lowered her head in her arms, and waited for the dizziness to pass.

Around her, the stable hands chattered. The man must have been killed while they were out watching the fireworks. They had been gone for forty minutes. Not one of them had stayed back. No one saw any stranger come or go. They had discovered the body only when they returned to check on the horses.

Kitty looked up to see one of the club's employees arrive on the scene and announce that the police had been called and that everyone must remain on the premises and nothing should be touched.

Hotchkiss said something to him about breaking the news to Mrs. Basshor.

Kitty made her way back to the party in a daze. She couldn't, and didn't want to, leave now.

The news had evidently filtered through the guests. They huddled together, whispering in uneasy clusters, as children were packed off with their nursemaids and chauffeurs. The band had fallen silent.

"How could this happen?" someone said.

"Where's the killer now?"

"I hope they don't think one of us is involved."

"Must we stay to talk to the police?" A lady's sharp voice signaled her disdain for lawmen.

"If horses could speak, then everything would be resolved," another remarked.

Kitty looked for Aimee Cole and found her sitting at one of the children's tables beside the pantalooned playwright, Mrs. Clements.

"Now, now, my dear," Poppy Clements said, patting the widow's shoulders gently. "Now, now." She snapped her fingers at a waiter, who jumped to attention, and ordered him to bring a cup of tea with rum.

Aimee Cole stared blankly into space. She appeared to be in shock.

"What in damnation was Hunter doing at the stables?" a man beside Kitty said.

Another replied, "Just like him to be lurking off."

A uniformed policeman approached Mrs. Cole a short while later. "I'm sorry to disturb you at a time like this, madam, but I'm afraid that I will have to ask you some questions." He flipped open his notepad.

Aimee Cole responded dully to his questions. "I don't know why my husband went to the stables."

"Did he have any enemies, Mrs. Cole? Anyone who might want to do him harm?"

"No one that I know of."

Kitty was amazed by the speed of it—a flesh-and-blood person had just been killed, and now it was straight down to the facts.

"When did you see him last?" the policeman inquired.

"Shortly before the fireworks began." She noticed Kitty and pointed. "This young lady was with me at the time."

"Wait for me, miss," the policeman said to Kitty just as one of his colleagues handed him a small bundle wrapped in a handkerchief. He placed the bundle on the table and then opened it.

Aimee Cole's hand flew to her mouth. "It's Hunter's," she said, staring at a small gray revolver. "Where did you find it?"

"On the floor of the stables, madam. Was Mr. Cole in the habit of carrying guns to garden parties?"

"No, he wasn't. And I begged him not to bring it here, but he wouldn't listen. He told me he had to be prepared." Her voice cracked. "He said—because of the Morgan shooting— that there were too many crazies running about."

The waiter brought over a cup of tea.

"Drink this," Mrs. Clements ordered.

Aimee Cole took a sip. "Did Hunter fire it?" Her eyes never left the pistol. "Was he able to defend himself?"

The policeman lowered his gaze. "We're not certain, but we believe that this is the weapon that killed him, madam."

Horror flooded the widow's face.

"Enough!" Mrs. Clements put an end to the conversation. "The poor girl has had plenty of suffering for one day." She held her hand out to Mrs. Cole. "Clement and I will drive you home. Officer, you can speak to her tomorrow."

The policeman raised an eyebrow but didn't argue. "A moment of your time, miss." He beckoned to Kitty after Mrs. Clements led Mrs. Cole away. "Have a seat." He nodded toward the chairs that the women had vacated and took down Kitty's name and occupation. "So, are you and Mrs. Cole friends?"

"We just met." Kitty explained how she'd bumped into the Coles on the terrace and helped Aimee Cole with the stain on her gown.

"And that was when exactly?"

"About a quarter to four."

"You're certain?"

"I didn't want to miss the fireworks so I checked my watch."

"And that's the last you saw of Mr. Cole?"

"Yes."

"There was no sign of him after you returned from the ladies' room?"

"No."

"Anything else you can tell us?"

"I don't believe so."

"Well, if anything comes to mind, please give us a call." He handed her a card.

Kitty rose from her seat as Hotchkiss hurried by, clipboard under his arm.

"Can I be of any use?" she asked.

"The police want names of all the guests. It's too ridiculous." He brushed a lock of hair from his forehead. "They were here watching the fireworks. What can they possibly have to say about what happened?"

It occurred to Kitty that she should put a call in to the *Sentinel*. There ought to be a telephone in the clubhouse. When she arrived at the reception area, a long line had formed outside a single booth. Kitty waited her turn, filled her name in the ledger, and under "Guest of" wrote "Mrs. Basshor."

She made her call as quick as possible—long distance rates could be astronomical—and since it was nearly seven o'clock and Miss Busby wasn't in, she told the operator at the paper to let the City Desk know what had happened.

She returned to the lawns, where the evening had taken on the character of a wake. Waiters brought out trays laden with food, and everyone ate and drank while the police made their rounds. By the end of it, Kitty noticed plates of pastries and meat being ferried out to the chauffeurs and staff. It was past nine o'clock when the guests were finally allowed to depart.

On the drive home, Kitty asked her chauffeur, Rao, whether he had seen or heard anything strange.

"No, Miss Kitty," he replied. "We were all watching the fireworks. We only found out what happened afterward."

As the car raced through the darkness, it occurred to Kitty that, save for his wife, no one seemed to have mourned Hunter Cole. Sure, she had heard a few whispered murmurs of sympathy here and there, but those had been what any stranger might have said upon hearing about the murder. For the most part, there seemed to have been a sense among the guests that Mr. Cole's fate was of his own making. It was almost as though someone who had wandered off to the deserted stables in the midst of the party was thumbing his nose at his hostess, and deserved whatever happened to him.

Since her own impression of the man hadn't exactly been favorable, Kitty could hardly find fault with the others who had known him longer and evidently never cared much for Mr. Cole while he'd been alive.

Still, she thought, pulling her jacket tightly around her. They should have pretended to be sorry, if not out of common decency, then at least for the sake of his wife.

CHAPTER FOUR

Sparrows chirped beneath the windows of the New Century Apartment House on the corner of West End Avenue and Seventy-Ninth Street, where Julian Weeks sat at the head of the breakfast table reading his newspaper. He lowered it when Kitty came in, dressed for work in a pale green skirt and white shirtwaist with a floppy bow at the neck. "Did you manage to sleep?"

"A little." Kitty took her seat beside him, shook out her napkin, and swallowed an Aspirin with her water. Try as she might, she hadn't been able to wipe away the image of Hunter Cole on the floor of the stables. His puffy face with the wound below the hairline. The scuffed soles of his shoes with the neatly tied shoelaces. "Is it in the papers yet?"

"Just a one-paragraph write-up." Mr. Weeks's usually stern face registered concern as he looked at his daughter. "I still can't believe that you witnessed a shooting."

Kitty tried to make light of it as she helped herself to toast from the caddy and their cook, Mrs. Codd's, homemade jam. "It's not so bad, Papa. I didn't actually see the deed take place, you know."

She had told him about what had happened when she returned from the party last night, but she didn't want to discuss it any further, partly because she needed time to come to terms with it herself and partly out of fear that he would insist that she stop working. A proud, self-made man, Mr. Weeks had been surprised when Kitty announced that she wanted to apprentice at the Ladies' Page but hadn't complained once he realized that her work wouldn't interfere with their domestic routine. Mrs. Weeks had died from complications due to childbirth, so now that she was an adult, it fell to Kitty to run the household. She had arranged her schedule so that she came home every day by lunchtime to take care of her responsibilities. Fortunately, both Mrs. Codd and Grace, the maid, didn't need much direction, and they made sure that Mr. Weeks's meals were served on time and that his linens were always ironed.

Kitty took a bite of toast and switched the conversation to her father's favorite subject. "What's the latest news on the *Lusitania*?"

"It's a stalemate, but it shouldn't be." Julian Weeks scratched his chin. His rugged features were weather-beaten from years spent outdoors in Malaya. Since May, he had been following the tense back-and-forth correspondence between Washington and Berlin regarding the sinking of the passenger liner.

He tucked his napkin into his collar as Grace brought in his steak and eggs. "The Germans should be responding to the president's second note any day now."

"What do you think they will say?"

"I can't tell for sure, but I understand why they're angry. Frankly, I'm amazed that the president continues to insist on our right to travel unmolested as passengers on merchant vessels, of any nationality, even in a war zone." The *Lusitania*, an

English ship, had been struck just a few miles away from the coast of Ireland.

"I find it all so confusing," Kitty said. "Is the president trying to say that we deserve to be unharmed because we're neutral?"

"That's correct." Julian Weeks looked Kitty in the eye. "But there's a war going on, Capability. And the simple fact of the matter is that even neutrals aren't innocent."

Rao drove Kitty to work in the Weekses' touring car, a Packard, and dropped her off at the corner of Forty-Ninth Street and Broadway. She pushed her way through heavy brass revolving doors into the *Sentinel's* towering office building. A three-faced clock in the center of the entry hall told the time in New York, London, and Tokyo, and a compass rose with the paper's motto, *Guarding the Truth*, had been inlaid in mosaic tile on the marble floor below.

The *Sentinel* had moved its offices uptown from Newspaper Row shortly after the *Times* had set up its headquarters at Broadway and Forty-Second Street, now known as Times Square, after its famous tenant. Before arriving in New York, Kitty had heard that the city was awash with crime, with dirt, foreigners, skyscrapers, and money, and all of which was true. But to her, more than anything else, New York was awash with news. Its citizens consumed staggering amounts of the stuff, and she had been amazed by the newsboys who stood at every street corner and shouted out headlines all morning, evening, and afternoon. New Yorkers devoured the *Sentinel* and the *Times*, the *Herald*, the *Tribune*, William Randolph Hearst's *Journal*, Pulitzer's *World*, the *Wall Street Journal*, the *Sun*, and the *Post*, not to mention dailies in Yiddish, Chinese, Croatian, French, German, Hungarian, Italian, and Russian.

Kitty came into work every day thrilled to be a part of such a vital enterprise. The paper's archivist, Mr. Musser, had told Kitty that the *Sentinel* printed nearly 337,000 miles of paper each year. As the custodian of every article ever published by the *Sentinel*, grizzled Mr. Musser knew something about everything. He worked from a room in the basement, otherwise known as the morgue, and supervised a team of boys who cut, pasted, and filed away each story, carefully arranged by subject matter.

Kitty thought she might visit him today as she waited in front of a bank of elevators, the only female among advertising men and mail clerks. When she stepped out on the third floor, she turned left, away from the smell of fried eggs and bacon wafting from the cafeteria and toward the cacophony of metallic clacks and clings resounding from the cavernous typists' hall. She skirted past the rows of women in starched shirtwaists tirelessly pecking away at their machines—which gave the hall its name, the "hen coop"—and hung her purse from a seat at a desk in the front of the room.

"We heard all about it, Miss Weeks!" From the table behind Kitty, Jeannie Williams's pale round face shone with excitement. She wore her flaxen hair twisted around her head in braids like an Alpine milkmaid and was built sturdily like one too. "You were at the party, and you called in the story. Do you think the City Desk will allow you to assist with the reporting?"

"I doubt it." Kitty couldn't permit herself to hope. Like other respectable papers, the *Sentinel* didn't allow women into the newsroom. Even her guidebook, *Careers for Girls*, stated in no uncertain terms that the problem with women reporters was that they couldn't be sent out at all hours and couldn't stand the strain of working under deadlines like men. "Don't look so disappointed, Jeannie. It will all change some day."

"You think so, Miss Weeks?"

"It has to, doesn't it?" Kitty said in order to buck her up. Usually it was the other way around—buoyant Jeannie, a shop-girl who had studied nights and weekends in order to land her job as a typist at the paper, encouraged Kitty while she labored with her assignments.

Kitty picked up her pad and pencil and made her way to Miss Busby's office, which was in an alcove connected to the hen coop via a narrow corridor.

Gray-haired Helena Busby stopped sifting through her papers when Kitty knocked at the entryway. "Come in and sit down, Miss Weeks," she squawked. "I have a bone to pick with you."

"Have I done something wrong, Miss Busby?" Kitty pulled up a chair.

Miss Busby wagged a scrawny finger at her. "I sent you out to cover a party, and you called in a murder?" The bracelets on the editor's wrist jingled, her dangling earrings swinging as she shook her head. From his portrait behind the editor's desk, even President Wilson seemed to disapprove. "The Ladies' Page has no connection to crime of any sort. It all belongs to News. And now, Mr. Hewitt wants to speak to both of us." She rummaged in a drawer for her medicine bottle.

"What for?" Kitty asked, taken off guard. Mr. Hewitt was Miss Busby's supervisor.

"I have no idea, Miss Weeks." Miss Busby gulped down a spoonful of Rowland's Remedy. "All I will say is that I will do the talking and you will remain silent. Is that clear?"

"Yes, Miss Busby."

"I hope I won't have to regret sending you to the party yesterday." Miss Busby rose from her seat, and Kitty followed the lanky figure down the hall toward Mr. Hewitt's office.

They knocked on the door and found a florid man with a full head of pomaded hair, picking his teeth with an ivory toothpick while Mr. Hewitt rocked back in his chair.

"Good morning, ladies." Mr. Hewitt sat up straight, and the stranger leisurely slipped the toothpick into his breast pocket.

"Miss Busby," Mr. Hewitt said. "Meet Mr. Flanagan from the newsroom."

Miss Busby nodded, while Kitty remained silent as directed.

"Should we sit?" Miss Busby said.

"Please do. I have a favor to ask of you," Mr. Hewitt began. He was the only rooster among hens on this side of the floor. A balding, unintimidating man, he wore spectacles and supervised the weekend section of the paper, which included the Ladies' Page, photography, cartoons, and theater, motion picture, and book reviews.

Kitty sensed Miss Busby's back stiffen—Mr. Flanagan's presence didn't bode well for the Ladies' Page editor. She wished she could sit on her hands; instead, she twined her fingers loosely in her lap and tried to appear unaffected by the conversation.

"The City Desk has its men camped outside Mr. Morgan's

hospital room," Mr. Hewitt said. "The rest are at the Morgan estate or down at police headquarters—it seems that a bomb went off there today, and the Anarchists are up to their old tricks."

"What does this have to do with me, Mr. Hewitt?" Miss Busby sounded as sweet as the syrup she drank by the bottle.

"We need to borrow your girl for a couple of days. Or rather, Mr. Flanagan does. He's out of reporters."

Kitty thought she had misheard him.

"Miss Weeks attended the party," Mr. Hewitt said. "She saw what went on. She can assist him."

"Impossible." The tendons on Miss Busby's stringy neck tightened. "I have one girl working for me. One. And City has how many men? Over a dozen? And still, they want to steal *my* one apprentice?"

"No one is stealing anyone, madam." Mild-mannered Mr. Hewitt wouldn't allow the situation to escalate. He polished his glasses and put them back on. "It's just for a few days. And since I don't get the chance very often, I'd like to be able to oblige my colleague in News."

Mr. Flanagan spoke up. "All I need is some assistance with background material. We wouldn't have asked if it weren't for the fact that your girl was present when the shooting took place."

Kitty observed the proceedings with the nervous tension of a spectator at a tennis match. The only difference was that it was her fate being smacked back and forth across the net.

"With all due respect, sir," Miss Busby addressed Mr. Hewitt, "when I agreed to take on help, we both agreed that my apprentice would work solely for me."

"And she does." Mr. Hewitt kept his voice low. "This won't be for long."

"We're busy, Mr. Hewitt."

"With what, may I ask? Articles about hats, hemlines, holidays?" Flanagan smirked.

"Laugh away, young man," Miss Busby retorted. "My stories bring in more advertising revenue than yours do."

"So you won't reconsider?" Mr. Hewitt pushed his glasses up the bridge of his nose.

"Have you thought that *I* might be stretched to my limits, Mr. Hewitt? Isn't that why you wanted me to hire an apprentice in the first place? So that I'd have help if things went"—Miss Busby hunted for the word—"south."

Kitty had no idea what her boss was referring to.

"All I need is a day or two at most," Mr. Flanagan said. "If you can't give me that"—he shrugged—"well, I'm sure I'll manage."

Kitty felt her chance slipping away. Miss Busby had outplayed the gents.

"Let's do this." Mr. Hewitt adjusted the notepad on his desk. "Since your girl only works until lunchtime at present, she can stay later and work for both of you until this case is closed." He turned to Kitty. "Does that suit you?"

Kitty hadn't realized he knew she worked there, let alone that she worked only in the mornings. "Me?" Three sets of eyes stared at her.

"Well?" Mr. Flanagan said.

Kitty turned to Miss Busby for guidance.

"I can't prevent you from taking on longer hours, Miss Weeks. Clearly what *I* want doesn't matter," her boss snapped.

"Then I'll do it," Kitty replied without missing a beat.

"Good, that's settled then." Mr. Hewitt pulled a pile of papers toward him.

"Just to check, Mr. Hewitt. You'd like me to report to Miss Busby in the morning and Mr. Flanagan in the afternoon?"

"Manage it however you like, Miss Weeks. You're free to go now."

"I'll speak to you in five minutes," Mr. Flanagan called to Kitty as Miss Busby closed the door behind them.

The editor's face twisted in disappointment once they were alone in the hallway. "I didn't think you would be so treacherous, Miss Weeks. City must be really desperate to have poached from me. And if you think this is going to end well, you are sadly mistaken."

Sorry it had come to this, Kitty watched Miss Busby head off to her alcove. But, rebuke or no, she could no longer contain her delight at finally being allowed to assist on a news story.

CHAPTER FIVE

K itty met Mr. Flanagan in the cafeteria, one of the few spots at the paper where employees from different divisions could mingle. Generally, staff from unrelated departments didn't cross paths: the Circulation and Administration departments were on the lowest floors, followed by the Weekend Supplement on third, and other, less time-sensitive—and therefore less prestigious— divisions on the fourth and fifth. The City Desk occupied the sixth floor, along with International News, while Business, Advertising, and Management were right at the top of the hierarchy.

"Do the police have any leads, Mr. Flanagan?" Kitty leaned across the metal table. She had spent hours the night before running through the events at the party, trying to come up with potential leads to the murder.

"They have some ideas, yes."

"Everyone was so excited to see the fireworks, and I've been wondering what prompted Mr. Cole to leave the lawn," Kitty went on. She hadn't been able to wipe away the grim memory of Hunter Cole's body between the rows of stalls. "Do you think he went to the stables to meet someone in secret?"

"That's not for you to worry about." Flanagan rubbed the fleshy pads of his fingers together. "What I need from you is *texture*. Details about the evening: who came, what was said, emotional reactions and such. How did the guests respond when they heard the news? How did the police handle matters? The feminine viewpoint on things."

"Ah, yes, I see. The woman's angle." Kitty swallowed her disappointment. "Well—"

"Don't tell me—write it down. Write it down," he repeated. "And then, I need you to speak to a few of the key players— let's say the widow, the hostess, and another guest at the party—and get some reactions. If you've already spoken to the first two, well, now's your chance to pay them a personal visit. Call on them, sit down, show some interest, and get them to talk. You'd be amazed at the things people say."

"Yes, Mr. Flanagan."

"Have you conducted an interview before?"

"Ah…" Kitty wasn't about to draw attention to the fact that the first time she actually spoke to anyone on official *Sentinel* business had been yesterday, at the party.

"Tell me, how does one go about it?" Flanagan didn't notice her hesitation.

"An interview," Kitty began, "is a journalistic form first attempted on this side of the Atlantic."

"I'm not asking *what*, Miss Weeks. I am asking *how*. Please, answer the question precisely."

"Yes, Mr. Flanagan." Kitty quoted from Shuman's *Practical Journalism*. "The reporter meets his man, has a talk with him on the subjects desired, and instead of taking a faithful record of every word, watches to catch the spirit of what is said and the manner in which it is uttered. He jots down the speaker's exact words only on vital or technical points."

"Exactly," Flanagan murmured.

"With his materials mostly in his head, he goes to his desk and writes the interview. Half of the words credited to the speaker may not in fact have been uttered by him, yet if the work is well done, it will be more just and infinitely more readable than any dialogue reproduced verbatim."

"That's correct." Flanagan ran a hand through his leonine mane.

"The most difficult part of the task is getting the subject to talk," Kitty continued. "You must remember what he has said while keeping up your side of the conversation and keeping in mind the questions that remain."

"All right, Miss Weeks, you know your stuff. Now all that remains is for us to see if you can do as you say."

"Yes, Mr. Flanagan." Kitty's heart raced. "You'd like me to speak to Mrs. Cole and Mrs. Basshor and one guest"—her thoughts immediately flew to the turbaned Mrs. Clements— "and have my report for you by—"

"This afternoon."

Her eyes opened wide.

Flanagan groaned. "This is real news, Miss Weeks. Not your Ladies' Page stuff. We have hard deadlines." He relented. "All right. Since you're new to it, you can give me the third report tomorrow. Hand in your notes on the other two by three o'clock today." He pushed back the bench. "You're familiar with the term 'Sob Sisters'?"

"Yes, Mr. Flanagan."

"They're the four lady reporters who covered the trial of Harry Thaw for murdering Stanford White back in '07."

"Yes, Mr. Flanagan." Kitty knew their names: Miss

Greeley-Smith, Miss Dix, Miss Patterson, and Miss Black. "Isn't Mr. Thaw to have another trial soon?"

"I believe so, but that isn't my point. What I want to bring to your attention is the type of writing that those females produced. They did your kind a great disservice by splashing their personal opinions on every line. They churned out page after page of purple prose that made me sick to my stomach. Not that you will be writing anything other than notes, but you cannot forget"—he slowed down—"the *Sentinel* does not tolerate that kind of… garbage. While you're working for me, you keep it simple, keep it dignified, and you keep to the facts. Can you manage that?"

Kitty had no intention of doing anything else. "Absolutely, Mr. Flanagan."

Kitty decided it might be easier to speak to the hostess first, since she felt uneasy about conducting an interview with Mrs. Cole at a time when what she really ought to be doing was paying a condolence visit. It seemed that the freedom from social niceties that came with being a reporter might also have its drawbacks. How did one bring oneself to question a widow the day after her husband had been murdered?

She took a cab to Mrs. Basshor's apartment house on Park Avenue.

"Lovely, ain't it?" the cab driver observed as they motored down the broad boulevard, which was flanked on either side by gracious apartment buildings and bisected down the middle by a tree-lined pedestrian path.

Kitty agreed. This avenue and nearby Fifth were the most desirable residential stretches in Manhattan.

"You wouldn't know that twenty years ago, trains belched smoke and soot right here," the driver said. "They chugged along tracks dug into the ground where the trees are planted now. And these apartment houses?" He gestured out the window. "They only came up once the rails were buried underground and the street was paved over. There used to be tenements here before."

"So we're driving over hidden railway tracks?" Kitty liked the idea.

"Oh yes, miss." He pointed to the imposing terminus behind them. "The trains going in and out of Grand Central Station are clattering along beneath us."

He pulled up at Mrs. Basshor's a few minutes later. Kitty hunted in her purse for the fare and added a tip. The very sidewalks seemed to radiate heat as she stepped out into the muggy summer air, and the cool interior of Mrs. Basshor's building provided welcome relief. A uniformed caretaker buffed the marble floors, while a liveried doorman ushered her to an elevator, which whisked her up to the hostess's fifth-floor triplex.

Kitty rang the doorbell. A maid answered the door and asked her to wait in the vestibule—an octagonal room papered in silver-leaf wallpaper painted with herons, lily pads, and bridges in an Oriental theme.

A tall vase of irises stood on a table in the center. The last home Kitty had visited in this part of town belonged to her friend Amanda Vanderwell's family. Their slender brownstone stood in the Seventies between Park and Madison Avenues. Mrs. Vanderwell liked to call apartments "tenements" and declared that they were only for Johnny-come-latelies. Looking around her, Kitty suspected her claim might be fueled by envy. The Vanderwells were among the last of the old guard to jump ship from points further south in Manhattan, which was why, when it came time to buy, they couldn't afford much. Kitty guessed that Mrs. Basshor's opulent apartment might have cost more than the Vanderwells' freestanding house.

Footsteps clicked down the hall, and a few moments later, Hotchkiss appeared with a poppy in his lapel. His youthful, handsome face looked haggard.

"Miss Weeks." If the secretary was surprised to see her, he didn't show it. He asked Kitty to follow him to an anteroom where he drew back heavy velvet curtains to let in the light.

"You will understand, of course," he said, adjusting his sleeves, "that Mrs. Basshor is quite overcome and as such is unavailable to members of the press. We are all shocked and dismayed by what took place yesterday and offer our sincerest condolences to the Cole family." His words sounded mechanical, and only a slight tremor of his long-fingered hands betrayed his agitation. "If there's anything you need, I will be happy to assist. My employer has asked me to make myself available for questions. Is there anything in particular that you'd like to inquire about, Miss Weeks?"

Kitty didn't know how to begin, how to get past the secretary and to Mrs. Basshor.

"I'm shocked too," she said, trying to buy some time. "That something so terrible should have happened…and it must be much worse for you. You knew Mr. Cole, and you had been preparing for the party for ages."

"I gave it everything I have, Miss Weeks," the secretary said. "Mrs. Basshor is a true patriot, and this event is the most important in her calendar. As you say, we prepare well in advance. Those fellows who did the fireworks—they didn't just trot up from Chinatown. No, *I* found the best in the business; we paid for their passage from Japan."

Hotchkiss removed a doily covering a jug. "Will you have some water?"

"No, thank you."

He poured himself a drink.

"The fireworks were wonderful," Kitty said to keep the conversation going. "Really spectacular. I hadn't seen anything quite like them."

"Mrs. Basshor wanted something that would be novelty for her guests, and given that crowd, I can tell you, it wasn't an easy order. I had hoped to take a short vacation afterward. Nothing elaborate, just a trip to the coast to recover from the strain. But I can't, not after what's happened. To be honest, Miss Weeks"—his lower lip trembled—"it's hit both Mrs. Basshor and myself very hard indeed."

"How could it not, Mr. Hotchkiss? And that's why you must let me speak to her." Now that Kitty had stumbled onto her ploy, the words came out in a rush. "All the other papers are going to print something about what happened last night. And they have no scruples. They'll say anything to sell an extra copy. But together, you and I can help her. With your assistance, she can share her perspective with our readers. I'm sure she will want her side of the story faithfully represented to the public."

"And why should I trust you over the others, Miss Weeks?" Hotchkiss replied. "They've been calling, you know, since eight this morning."

"You forget that Mrs. Eichendorff, our publisher's wife, is a friend of Mrs. Basshor's."

The secretary blinked. "That's right. Yes."

"And that's exactly why you must trust me, Mr. Hotchkiss. Our paper would never allow anything to be printed that might do Mrs. Basshor an injustice." Kitty hoped she wasn't telling a lie.

"Hunter Cole was the black sheep of a good family," Elizabeth Basshor said, sounding neither out of sorts nor devastated. She lay on a pale silk-covered chaise in her morning room with a shawl wrapped around her shoulders and a light throw draped across her legs. "He was a bit of a bore and a show-off, but I invited him for his parents' sake."

She held out her teacup, to which Hotchkiss added an extra squeeze of lemon. "Do take that poppy off," she commanded as he bent over her. "You know the smell makes me quite faint."

Her secretary turned to a wastebasket in the corner.

"No, not here! Outside." She returned her attention to Kitty. "So, yes, it's Hunter's marriage to that girl that was his undoing. Not that Dr. and Mrs. Cole ever complained about it. They're far too well-bred for that. But the wedding, in Connecticut, was much smaller than it ought to have been—no one but the closest family and friends were invited. I remember it as though it was yesterday. Had the circumstances been different, they'd have done things on a much grander scale."

"You were at the wedding?"

"Naturally. And then I had to telephone last night to break the news. Quite terrible to have to tell parents that their own son has been killed. But between you and me"—Mrs. Basshor leaned in conspiratorially—"I always thought Hunter would come to a bad end. Not like this, of course. It's just that his marriage was the last straw. He never settled, if you know what I mean. Never occupied himself with any one pursuit. Always skulked around on the fringes of things.

"I couldn't say that to Dr. Cole, of course. I just told him that it must have been a tragic mistake. Hunter must have gone off to take a look at the horses, and some deranged madman mistook him for someone else."

"That's what you believe?"

"I don't know what to believe."

"Did Mr. Cole have a special fondness for horses?"

"He loved them. It's the one thing one really knew about him. An avid horseman, and always at the races. But there was talk, you know." She paused.

"What kind of talk, Mrs. Basshor?" Kitty asked, pleased with the flow of the conversation. She hadn't anticipated that conducting an interview would be so straightforward.

"Hunter lived beyond his means," Elizabeth Basshor said. "Spent far too much money gambling. It's true, but it's sad that he should be killed for it. A gentleman makes mistakes, my dear, but if there's one thing he has, it's his word. If Hunter said he'd pay his debts, then he would. There was no need to come after him with pistols loaded."

"I'm sorry, Mrs. Basshor, are you suggesting—"

"It had to have been his bookmakers or someone else from the racetracks," the hostess declared with certainty. "Why else would he have been killed there? You agree with me, Hotchkiss?"

"I beg your pardon, madam?" The secretary came back, *sans* the offending bloom.

"Don't you agree that Hunter was killed because of his gambling?"

"It's possible, Mrs. Basshor." Hotchkiss stared at his feet.

"Either that or some Germans mistook him for someone else and did him in." She finished her tea and handed her man the empty cup. "One thing I know without a doubt is that none of *my* guests had anything to do with it. Please make sure you put that in your article, young lady. I want all my friends to be quite certain that they are completely above suspicion."

"I'll let Mr. Flanagan know," Kitty replied. "He will write the final story."

"That's a nice dress you have on." Elizabeth Basshor took a moment to rearrange her shawl. "I liked your frock yesterday too. What did you say your name is again?"

"Capability Weeks," Hotchkiss replied before Kitty could answer.

"Capability?" Mrs. Basshor's eyes widened. "As in Capability Brown?"

"You're familiar with his work?" Kitty hadn't expected the hostess to recognize her name's origins. Mr. Brown was England's most famous designer of landscapes, but an eighteenth-century gardener nonetheless.

"He's a man!"

"Yes, but the name isn't very common, so most people don't realize—"

"I've seen examples of Mr. Brown's brilliance in parks all over Britain," Mrs. Basshor cut in coldly, "particularly at the grounds of Blenheim Palace. The Duchess of Marlborough, whom I've known from when she was just little Consuelo Vanderbilt, is a great friend of mine. It's not done to give a girl a man's name. And your surname is 'Weeks'?" The hostess waved a dismissive hand. "Never heard of it."

Kitty's head spun with the speed at which Mrs. Basshor jumped between topics.

"Allow me to tell you something for your own sake, my dear," she went on. "Don't get ahead of yourself. You will never marry if you continue in this vein."

The pronouncement caught Kitty off guard. "I beg your pardon, Mrs. Basshor?"

"I have no quarrel with women who do what they need to in order to take care of themselves. But girls like you who don't need to work but do so anyway? That's intolerable. It's showing off. What does your mother have to say about it?"

"My mother has passed away, madam." Kitty had lost control of the conversation and didn't know what she had done to prompt the change.

"Well, that explains it. And your father hasn't remarried?"

Kitty's ears burned. "No, he has not. But perhaps we might return to the matter at hand?"

"In a moment, my dear. Given your situation, I feel it is my duty to warn you that your problem will be—if it isn't already—that you will never fit in. You're obviously much too well-off to have working friends, and you work too much for the rich ones. You can't be in two worlds at once. If you try, you end up in neither. I *know*. I learned that the hard way. Today's young men don't have the courage of their convictions. They may flirt with a girl who seems different, but they'll never marry her. Aren't I right, Hotchkiss?"

Kitty had heard enough. "Well, thank you, Mrs. Basshor. I'll try to keep your advice in mind." She stood.

"Are we finished then?" The hostess sounded disappointed.

"Yes, we are." Kitty kept her voice carefully neutral.

"I hope you haven't taken any offense, my dear. I may have my faults, but varnishing the truth is not one of them."

As she left the room, Kitty heard Mrs. Basshor call, "Mark my words, you will benefit more from scrutinizing your own life than from any amount of inquiry into Hunter Cole's murder."

CHAPTER SIX

By the time Kitty was seated at Tipton's tea shop on Madison Avenue, she had calmed down a bit. She pressed the glass of ice-cold water that the waitress served her against her forehead. She couldn't fathom Mrs. Basshor's behavior. *Mark my words* indeed. What was she, a punching bag for the older woman to beat about as she pleased?

"What will you have to eat, miss?" asked the young waitress in her starched cap and white apron. Kitty ordered a roast beef sandwich. At the tables around her, women in small groups laughed and chatted easily to one another.

It occurred to Kitty that there might be another reason Mrs. Basshor didn't want her poking around in the circumstances surrounding Hunter Cole's death. The hostess might be protecting someone. But whom? One of her guests? Hotchkiss?

She recalled the secretary's remark about Hunter Cole being a bully.

Perhaps, Kitty thought, Mrs. Basshor was worried that Kitty had seen or heard something incriminating during the party, and that's why she had deflected the attention away from Mr. Cole.

Kitty took a bite of the salad that came with her sandwich and looked around at the smiling, laughing faces. Young or old, not one of them sat alone. All the ladies had come out with company. *Perhaps Mrs. Basshor was correct.*

She reached into her purse for a pencil and pulled out a postcard advertising *The Romance of Elaine*, the new series featuring her favorite motion-picture actress Pearl White. "Fearless, Peerless Pearl" had been set loose in a hot-air balloon, kidnapped by bandits, and regularly faced all sorts of perils. She would never allow any setbacks to deter her—let alone one middle-aged woman's disparaging comments.

Kitty put away the postcard, taking solace in the fact that Pearl and the intrepid characters she played probably had occasion to eat alone in tea shops and hotels. That was the price they paid for their independence. She finished her sandwich and left a dollar bill on the table.

Mrs. Basshor's stinging attack could have been nothing more than the older woman's attempt to protect herself or someone close to her—but she, Capability Weeks, had seen through it.

The smell of frying onions wafted through the sixth-floor landing. Kitty hadn't expected the Coles to live in such a modest place. The building was on a noisy side street in the Fifties, just west of Broadway. The stairwell looked like it hadn't been painted in years, and the elevator creaked and shuddered all the way up. Kitty was quite relieved when the operator—who also doubled as the building's doorman—shut the metal grille behind her with a clang, and she stepped out to safety on the landing.

A small, hard-faced woman peered out from behind the Coles' door when Kitty knocked.

"From the *Sentinel*?" she asked after Kitty introduced herself.

"Let her in, Mama," a girlish voice called from within.

Kitty entered the flat with trepidation. It was small and compact: a simple foyer opened into a living room, which was connected by French doors to a dining room.

Aimee Cole sat in an overstuffed brown sofa beside an army of fragile porcelain shepherdesses. Her skin looked sallow, and her dull hair hung uncombed around her shoulders.

"It's so kind of you to come." She introduced Kitty to her mother, Mrs. Henderson, who mustered a grim smile. "It's so nice for me to have a friend here."

Kitty thought it odd that Aimee Cole thought of her as a friend when they had only met the day before and under such strange circumstances. Then she wondered whether the widow hadn't realized that Kitty had come as a representative of the paper.

"Have one." Mrs. Henderson held out a plate of brightly wrapped bonbons in a cut-glass serving bowl.

Kitty demurred. She found the atmosphere in the apartment oppressive and would have liked to open the windows to let in some fresh air. More Dresden shepherdesses filled the sideboard in the dining room. Aimee must have a real fondness for them.

"Go on, take one," Mrs. Henderson insisted.

Kitty unwrapped a chocolate and put it into her mouth. It tasted dusty and dry like some her father had once sent her from Russia. She swallowed quickly and offered both daughter and mother her condolences.

"I'm so sorry for your loss, but I'm afraid I'm here on business."

"I know all about business," Aimee Cole managed with a laugh. "How can I help you?"

"I'll leave you young ladies to yourselves." Mrs. Henderson withdrew to the adjacent dining room, where she busied herself dusting the porcelain figurines. Another girl peeked in, only to scurry away when Aimee's mother flashed her a warning glare.

Kitty asked Mrs. Cole whether she would mind talking about her husband so that the *Sentinel* could print an accurate, respectful report of the tragic occurrence.

"I'd be happy to." Aimee twisted the fringes of the throw draped over the sofa around her finger. "You know, we haven't had any visitors so far. The police were here earlier this morning, and other than that, it's just been me, Mama, and Alice, my sister."

"The Learys brought cake," her mother spoke up from the other room.

"That's right. The Learys are our downstairs neighbors. Hunter's parents called on the telephone but decided to remain in Connecticut."

"It must be dreadful for you." Kitty perched on the far edge of the sofa, leaving the cushion between her and Aimee vacant.

"I've been up all night, asking myself why we went to that party."

"Was it Mr. Cole's idea to attend?" Kitty felt like a vulture circling for a tidbit, but she reassured herself that the public ought to know more about the man who had been killed.

"We went every year for the three years we've been married. It's just something we did," Aimee replied. "Although Hunter never enjoyed it."

"He wasn't one for society?"

"My husband despised Mrs. Basshor and her friends. But he liked to get dressed up and appreciated good food and drink… Hunter had been jittery ever since he heard about the Morgan shooting on Sunday," she added in a quiet voice, "which is why he decided to bring his pistol with him. The police told me this morning that they're certain he was killed with it."

"That's terrible." Kitty paused for a moment. "And you arrived early to the party?" She phrased it as a question, but of course she'd seen them strolling about.

"Hunter hated to be late. But I didn't want to be a nuisance, so we walked around the grounds."

"Do you recall who Mr. Cole spoke to during the party and what kind of mood he was in?" Kitty asked.

"Well, let me see. Things weren't any different than usual. Hunter seemed content once we arrived. He said hello to Mrs. Basshor and some of the men, and we both spoke to Mrs. Clements. She's always been very kind to me. As you've probably gathered by now, Miss Weeks"—Aimee Cole's pale skin flushed red—"even though I married Hunter, the others have never let me forget that I'm not one of them."

Kitty sympathized with the widow. From her years abroad, she knew what it was like to feel like an outsider.

Mrs. Henderson stared in from the dining room, but Aimee turned away from her. "This morning, the detective asked why I didn't go looking for my husband when the fireworks began. I said that Hunter often went off on his own and that he liked his privacy. Was I wrong in remaining where I was, Miss Weeks? Would you have gone if you had been in my shoes?"

Kitty glanced at the frumpy blue slippers on Mrs. Cole's feet. They matched her dark blue housecoat. "No," she said. It made no sense to add regret to the widow's grief. "How could you have known what would happen?"

"Hunter had very little patience for society and no interest in fireworks. He must have decided to see the horses just to amuse himself." Aimee's voice cracked. "Sometimes, I think he loved them more than he loved people. You'll hear people say that Hunter went too often to the races, but I never faulted him for it, Miss Weeks."

In the background, Kitty could see Mrs. Henderson shaking her head.

"He grew up riding," Aimee Cole went on. "What else was he to do?"

"Aimee's too generous." Mrs. Henderson couldn't hold back any more and rejoined them in the living room. "I don't like to speak ill of the dead, but I'll tell you this: my son-in-law was no good either as a man or as a husband. He went to the racetracks, frittered away whatever little fortune he might have had, and even though we heard so much about the great Coles of Connecticut, his people never helped my daughter one bit. Whatever they have, Aimee brought to the marriage. People like to say that she connived to get him, but that's a lie. My girl didn't do anything underhanded to win his affections. He met her, he fell in love, and he asked her to marry him. She said yes, and that was the problem."

"Mother," Aimee protested, but Mrs. Henderson wouldn't be silenced.

"It's true, Aimee. He got the better half of the bargain. What were you ever but a good, decent wife to him, and what did he give you? Nothing!" Mrs. Henderson waved an arm across the room. "Even this apartment is rented. Now, if you'd accepted that nice Padrewski fellow like your father and I told you, you'd be lording it over everyone in a mansion, and he'd be smothering you in furs from head to toe."

"Paderewski, Mother." Aimee smiled unguardedly for a moment, her watery blue eyes lighting up, and Kitty thought she might have caught a glimpse of the spark that had attracted Hunter Cole when he met her. "And I never married in order to be smothered."

"He still wants to marry you, my dear."

"Mother." Aimee's tone turned sharper.

"I'm just saying, Aimee. I'm just saying."

A dwarfish maid brought tea on a tray, and Mrs. Henderson poured three cups.

"I hope I don't seem like I'm prying," Kitty said delicately, "but did Mr. Cole have an occupation?"

"Hunter didn't really work," Aimee replied. "But we got by. We always managed."

Mrs. Henderson pursed her lips. "It's nothing like what you'd have had if you'd married the furrier. And you'd be living just down the street from us in Brooklyn."

Kitty took a sip of her tea. It was probably time to leave mother and daughter to each other's company. "I should be on my way."

"Can I show you around the apartment?" Aimee said.

"Of course." Kitty put down her cup and rose.

The tour didn't take long, since all that remained for Kitty to see were the dining room, the bedroom (to which Mrs. Cole didn't open the door), and Mr. Cole's study.

To Kitty's surprise, she felt most at ease in the dead man's private room. It had been sparsely yet tastefully furnished with a rolltop chestnut desk, swiveling chair, rich Persian carpet, and curtains that reached the floor. An antique clock with a mother-of-pearl face sat on his desk. An eye-catching canvas of a muscular stallion posed against mountains hung on the wall above low walnut bookshelves.

"Is that a Stubbs?" Kitty stepped in to take a closer look.

"Hunter's grandmother left it to him in her will. I don't know much about art, but I do know that it's the one good piece we have from them."

The widow put her hand on Kitty's arm. "I hope I can trust you to be kind, Miss Weeks. The public will say cruel things about me. They may even point fingers in my direction."

"Mrs. Cole—" Kitty pulled away.

"Call me Aimee. After all we've been through, I think we might allow ourselves that."

"I just work for the *Sentinel*." Kitty hoped to avoid the invitation to be intimate. "I'm not in charge of what they print."

"I understand."

"I do hope the police will apprehend the culprit—"

"You have a lot to learn, Miss Weeks," Aimee Cole burst out in anger. "Where I'm from, we know what the police do and what they don't, how they pin the crime on whoever happens to be convenient. What I want is *justice* for my husband." She spoke with force. "I'm not interested in watching them haul away some poor sod just so that they can cross the case of their list."

Kitty took her leave of the widow shortly afterward.

Mrs. Henderson walked Kitty to the landing and waited with her for the elevator. "We're supposed to go to Connecticut on Friday for the funeral, but none of them will come here to see my daughter."

The rattling machine arrived, and the operator pulled open the fretwork grille. Kitty stepped inside.

"The Hendersons may not have come here on the *Mayflower*," the older woman continued as the gate shut between them with a clang, "but Aimee will be so much better off without Hunter."

With a jerk, the elevator lurched downward, slowly erasing Kitty's view of Mrs. Cole's bitter parent.

For once, the typists' incessant clacking didn't drive Kitty to distraction. She filled two sheets of paper with neat script and brought them upstairs to the sixth floor, where a glass wall partitioned the newsroom off from the rest of the hallway. Behind it, the real reporters, all men, went about their business. Some spoke on the telephone; others sat at their desks, writing or chewing on their pencils; still others smoked cigarettes or chatted with their colleagues.

Kitty knew she wasn't allowed to enter, so she tapped on the glass, caught the attention of one of the reporters, mouthed the words "Mr. Flanagan," and then, acutely aware of sidelong glances in her direction, waited until Flanagan emerged from within.

"Not bad," he murmured, glancing over her notes. "I can do something with this." He looked up. "You'll speak to a third party tomorrow?"

"Yes, Mr. Flanagan. First thing." Kitty planned to telephone Mrs. Clements to set up an appointment.

"All right then. You're free to report to Miss Busby."

But the Ladies' Page editor still seemed miffed by Kitty's disloyalty, and when Kitty went in, she said that all she needed was the result of this week's home cookery contest.

"Did Mr. Flanagan like your work?" Jeannie asked when Kitty returned to her desk.

"I think so." Kitty sifted through the entries and picked a recipe for breaded mutton cutlets with onion sauce. It didn't sound too appetizing, but she was in a rush. She dropped it off on Miss Busby's desk.

"I'll see you tomorrow, Jeannie." Kitty left the hen coop without looking back, so she didn't notice the typist staring after her.

CHAPTER SEVEN

Kitty hurried home and changed into her leather boots, a split skirt, and a linen shirt. Then she telephoned Mrs. Clements before calling for her Stutz Bearcat, the sporty yellow roadster that her father had given her for her birthday. Like riding a horse, Kitty drove for pleasure. She went downstairs, hopped into her car, and covered the distance to Durland's Academy on the west side of Central Park at top speed, only to find Amanda Vanderwell already mounted on Lucky Number 7, waiting for her.

"Sorry I'm late." Kitty parked the car. A lad brought Damsel forward, and she hoisted herself into the saddle. Kitty and Amanda had met the previous summer and struck up a conversation over the rose garden plantings at the Botanical Gardens. Kitty had been dazzled by Amanda's beauty and effortless confidence; what Amanda admired in her had been less obvious—perhaps it was Kitty's freedom to move about the city, which was so foreign to Amanda's rarified and tightly controlled experience of New York, although the Vanderwells and their set had been on the island for generations.

"I hope you have a good excuse." Amanda flicked Lucky with her crop, and the horse trotted along with Amanda poised elegantly sidesaddle.

"Work," Kitty said, following a few paces behind, acutely aware, as always, how awkward she appeared in comparison astride on Damsel. But Mr. Weeks insisted. It was safer to ride in the mannish style, he said, for both horse and equestrienne.

"I don't know why you carry on with that nonsense." Amanda turned and raised an eyebrow behind her veil, but her lips parted in a smile. Coppery hair glinted from below her hat.

"How was your weekend?" Kitty asked as they headed toward the bridle paths that crisscrossed the park.

"Lovely." Amanda shrugged. "As was to be expected. Did you know that this was the first big party the Astors have held since Colonel Astor drowned on the *Titanic*? And then we found out about what happened to Mr. Morgan, and I can tell you, it gave everyone quite a scare. But"—a roaring sound from one of the automobile mowers trimming the lawns in the distance distracted her—"I did have a fascinating time at Saturday's dinner."

"Did you meet someone?" Kitty grinned at her friend. Amanda had no shortage of beaus, all of whom she found some reason to reject sooner or later.

"Not in the way you're thinking, naughty girl." Amanda laughed. "I was seated next to the most intriguing little man though, one of those newfangled psychoanalyst fellows. He regaled us with one story after another, the best of which was that the kaiser started the war in order to win his mother's approval."

"Really?"

"Oh yes. Of course, the kaiser, King George, and Tsar Nicholas of Russia are all cousins, related through their grand-mama, Queen Victoria—"

"Yes, yes." Amanda sometimes treated Kitty like she didn't

know basic facts, as though attending boarding school in Europe had somehow stunted Kitty's intelligence.

"And Princess Victoria, Queen Victoria's daughter who was married off to the German emperor," Amanda went on, "had to have her son, the present kaiser, pulled out of her with forceps. He was born with a crippled arm as a result and had to undergo excruciating treatments to straighten it. They say he always felt like he was never good enough for his parents. When he was five years old, his mother decided he must learn how to ride. He had British royal blood, so it was unthinkable that he couldn't. But his mother was determined that her son learn to ride like a British king. Of course, it's hard when you have one arm that doesn't work. And although he kept falling off and begged her to stop, she wouldn't give up until he learned how to do it to her satisfaction."

"And that's why he declared war on Russia, France, and England?" It was Kitty's turn to be skeptical.

"He wants to prove that he can keep up with the rest," Amanda replied. "That neither he nor the German nation are to be trifled with. Don't look at me like that," she said to Kitty. "I'm just repeating what I heard."

"I thought you found your dinner companion fascinating."

"He was. You should have been there to hear him tell it in person."

"So no new beaus?" Amanda's parents had their hearts set on her making "a good match," which meant a wealthy match, since the Vanderwells, although they were descended from a distinguished line, had very little cash at present.

"It was the same old boring crowd: Jerry, Potty, and Neville, prattling on as usual. But I did make a decision that I want to tell you about. I said it in front of everyone at our table, including Mummy and Daddy, so I can't back down now."

"What is it?" Kitty turned to face her friend.

Amanda's cheeks were flushed, and her eyes sparkled. "I plan to enroll in a nurse's aide course at the YWCA, and when it's over, I'm going to go to Europe to tend to the wounded."

"You?" Kitty slowed down. The Amanda she knew barely deigned to tie her own shoelaces, let alone tend to others.

"Yes! And why not? I'll be twenty-four this year, Capability. I haven't met anyone who suits my tastes and Mummy and Daddy's requirements, and I won't have people calling me a spinster. Besides"—she resumed her breezy manner—"nursing is terribly glamorous. Who knows? I may even meet a wounded nobleman who dies in my arms, leaving me his fortune."

"You mean debt, don't you?"

Amanda grinned. "All the best girls are becoming nurses these days, which is why I want you to give up the paper and come join me."

"Excuse me?"

"That's right. Give up the paper. You've been complaining about that Miss Busby since you started."

"She's not so bad..." Kitty began to regret anything unkind she might have said about the Ladies' Page editor.

"You told me she doesn't give you any real work. Just makes you judge contests and open mail."

"Not any longer."

"Is that so?" Amanda flicked Lucky with her crop, and he broke into a canter.

After a moment's pause, Kitty urged Damsel forward and followed her friend down the empty path, free and fast on her mount with nothing but greenery around her and snippets of clear blue skies overhead.

They came to a turnoff in the trail, interrupted by a low wall. It was against the rules to ride there, but many of the young bucks did, to get in a jump. Amanda sped up her horse some more, and one-step, two-step, she was in the air, soaring across the barrier as Kitty watched, her heart in her mouth.

Her friend looked so precarious, perched there with both legs on one side of the horse—she could slide off or her skirt might get caught in the stirrups. A moment later, she was safely back on the ground.

"So what's changed for you at the paper?" Amanda called, exhilarated.

Kitty gathered her reins, took the jump herself, and rejoined her friend on the path.

"A man was killed at a party I covered."

"Hunter Cole at Bessie Basshor's do?"

"How did you know?"

"Mama is a great friend of Bessie's. The only reason we weren't there was because we had been invited to the Astors'."

"I've been asked to help out with the story. I spent this morning speaking to Mrs. Cole and Mrs. Basshor."

Amanda snickered.

"What's wrong with that?" Kitty couldn't fathom her friend's response.

"She was a dance-hall girl."

"Mrs. Basshor?"

"No, silly. Aimee Cole. I bet she didn't tell you that, did she? 'Rising star of burlesque stage marries Hunter Cole, American blue blood and ne'er-do-well.' It caused quite the scandal."

"I had no idea."

"She was called Fatima, or something of that sort, and performed exotic numbers with a serpent and veils. They say"—Amanda lowered her voice even though there was no one else around—"that she was half-naked when Hunter first set eyes on her."

Kitty couldn't picture timid Aimee dancing on a burlesque stage—or any other stage, for that matter. "You're teasing me."

"She was scantily clad."

"Oh my." The description didn't fit the drab woman Kitty had met. They had come to the end of the loop and paused near the turnoff to the stables.

"If you ask me," Amanda said, "she's the one who did it. Fatima Cole strangled Hunter with one of her scarves."

"He was shot," Kitty corrected.

"Shot, strangled, what's the difference? He's dead. She's not and is probably waiting to collect what remains of the Cole bounty. Anyway, don't forget: four o'clock next week at the YWCA on Fifteenth Street." Amanda blew Kitty a kiss before she trotted off.

Kitty watched her friend disappear around the curve. Then she gave a pull on her reins and began another round. She knew that Mrs. Vanderwell disapproved of their friendship. Amanda didn't say as much, but from the hints she dropped, Kitty guessed that Mrs. Vanderwell thought she was a nouveau-riche upstart from the wrong side of town, which was why Amanda never came to Kitty's place, and only rarely invited Kitty over. Mostly they met at Durland's or out shopping.

Kitty wondered whether Amanda wanted her company at the YWCA only to aggravate her family. Then she dismissed the thought as uncharitable. Stuck in her world of endless social commitments and obligations, Amanda needed a friend from outside her circle just as much as Kitty needed someone to talk to. She considered attending the introductory session to humor her, even though she had no intention of leaving the paper. Especially not at the moment.

Damsel clopped down the turf in the dappled shade, and Kitty urged her to go faster. The horse's speed matched Kitty's galloping thoughts: Aimee Cole might have been a burlesque dancer who married above her station, but that didn't make her a murderess. Still, the widow's past would explain why others dismissed her. It would also explain why Mrs. Cole had seemed so worked up when she told Kitty that the police would pin the murder on someone convenient—after all, who would be more convenient than a dance-hall girl?

CHAPTER EIGHT

Y our name, please, sir?" Prentiss, the photographer, said to Mr. Weeks.

"Julian Conrad Weeks," Kitty's father replied.

Kitty paced up and down the stifling front office on Broadway, staring at the sample portraits displayed on the walls. She had a nine thirty appointment to speak to Poppy Clements, the theater producer's wife who had been at Mrs. Basshor's party, and here she was, waiting for the punctilious Prentiss to fill out official passport application forms.

"Occupation?"

"Businessman."

"Your age, please, sir?"

"Forty-seven."

"And date of birth?" Prentiss's nib scratched against the cheap government-issue paper. He wrote carefully, blotting each entry so that the ink wouldn't smudge.

Kitty couldn't see what all the fuss was about. When she'd arrived in New York the previous year, all she'd carried by way of identification were two letters, one from school and one from her father's attorneys, and the nervous young customs official who boarded the ship had seemed embarrassed to check even those.

But this morning, Mr. Weeks explained that the State Department had issued new regulations. Since the war broke out, it had become mandatory for all Americans traveling abroad to carry a passport, and by the end of the previous year, the rules had become even more rigid, requiring a sworn application before a clerk of a court and the inclusion of two unmounted photographs.

"And will you be traveling with your wife, Mr. Weeks?" Prentiss said.

"My wife is deceased. I will be traveling with my daughter."

Julian Weeks provided Kitty's particulars: Capability Violet Weeks, nineteen years of age, born February 10, 1896, in Selangor, Malaya.

The scratching nib paused. "Selangor?" the photographer said. Then he added, "No matter, sir. Miss Weeks's citizenship follows yours. Your place of birth, Mr. Weeks?"

"Dover, Delaware."

"And you have a birth certificate to prove that?"

Kitty suspected that Prentiss enjoyed the liberty of asking the many questions that the form required of his customers, although he presented it as a courtesy that he offered gratis to those requiring a photograph.

"I don't have a birth certificate," Mr. Weeks said. "Do you, Mr. Prentiss?"

Prentiss coughed. "So many men of our generation don't possess one. Was your father native born or naturalized, Mr. Weeks?" Pen poised, he waited for a reply.

Julian Weeks said, "That's a bit much."

Kitty read from a news clipping, pinned beside a list of the photographer's services and prices:

Statement from Secretary of State Bryan, November 13, 1914: The President, upon the advice of the Secretary of State, has this day signed an order under which the rules governing the granting and issuing of passports in the United States are made much stricter than they have been in the past. The immediate cause of the amendment to the passport regulations was the fact that the Department of State had been recently informed of several cases in which aliens holding themselves as native American citizens have obtained, or attempted to obtain, American passports for purposes of espionage or otherwise in foreign countries.

"I don't believe this," she said and read out loud: "'Under the former rules it was not difficult to obtain passports fraudulently.' Anyone claiming citizenship through birth in the United States only had to make a sworn application before a notary. 'It was not required that either the applicant or witness be known to the notary.'"

She turned to her father. "Now you will need a witness, who must also be an American citizen, to make a sworn statement in support of your application. And that individual must be known to the clerk of the federal or state court."

"The new regulations have been instituted to keep us all safe," Prentiss observed.

"My father was native born, Mr. Prentiss." Mr. Weeks checked the time on his pocket watch. "Miss Weeks will fill out the rest of the form. Why don't we go ahead and take that photograph?"

"As you wish, sir." The photographer blotted the document

and slid it into an envelope. He pulled back a black curtain. "This way, please, sir and madam."

He instructed the Weekses to remove their hats, posed them in front of an off-white backdrop, and requested that they face the camera head-on.

Kitty joked, "Just like criminals."

"No smiling, please," Prentiss said.

Kitty tried to keep a straight face.

"Just keep your expression neutral, Miss Weeks." He ducked behind his camera and held up a flashbulb. The negative was exposed in a burst of light. For good measure, he repeated the process.

"Well, that's that." Mr. Weeks put his hat back on as they left the studio. "Thank you for being patient. It's something I've been meaning to take care of for a while."

They climbed into the waiting Packard, and Kitty gave Rao Mrs. Clements's address. The playwright lived on Central Park West, so she might not be too late after all.

"Where did your father originally come from?" Kitty didn't know much about her family's ancestry. Her mother didn't have any relatives, and Mr. Weeks preferred not to talk about his parents, who had died when he was young.

"I'm not sure." Julian Weeks picked up his paper. The headline had to do with Muenter, the man who had shot J. P. Morgan, committing suicide in his jail cell. "What do you make of this business?"

"It's horrid." Kitty had read the story this morning: Muenter had climbed the bars of his cell and jumped to the floor, cracking open his skull. "They say he had a history of mental problems and tried to kill himself earlier this week by digging into his wrist with a jagged blade he made from the metal eraser holder of a pencil." She winced at the gruesome image.

"And the police left him unsupervised long enough that he could try again?"

"The constable in charge walked away for a few minutes—"

"Why did the constable walk away, Capability? *That's* the real question." He shook his head and opened the paper, but not before adding, "I'm afraid the unfortunate Muenter was dead meat the moment he barged into Mr. Morgan's mansion with his guns drawn."

Kitty thought hard. Among the documents that had been found on Erich Muenter's person was a press clipping announcing the Morgan bank's recent flotation of a hundred-million-dollar war bond on behalf of the British government. When reporters had questioned him about it, Muenter said that he didn't support one side over another. All he wanted was to put an end to America's export of war materials to Europe and to "persuade" Mr. Morgan to use his "great influence" to put a stop to the United States's role in Europe's bloodshed. The result of his good intentions? Mr. Morgan lay in the hospital, recovering from his injuries, while Mr. Muenter had been found in his jail cell with his head smashed on the concrete floor.

"Welcome, my dear, welcome." Mrs. Clements greeted Kitty with open arms. She wore a brocaded caftan with Japanese lacquered chopsticks holding her hair in place. A couple of unruly locks fell onto her forehead. "I can't believe it's been almost two days since Hunter passed." She closed her eyes. "I can't bring myself to say 'killed'... Come this way."

She led Kitty down a hallway lined with books on every conceivable topic, from art to politics, science, and literature. Above the bookshelves hung framed posters of Mr. Clements's productions: *The Lost Girl*, *Beauty's Demise*, *Antigone by the Lake*, and others.

"I'm so glad that the *Sentinel* has put a girl on the case," Poppy Clements went on. "In my heart, I believe that this is a woman's story."

"What makes you say that, Mrs. Clements?" Kitty asked.

"I just sense it. My Clement tells me that I should follow my instincts, and so I do—even if they're contrary to popular opinion. My entire career as a playwright is based on that principle. For instance, my current project has to do with the sinking of the *Lusitania*—but from the U-boat captain's perspective."

Kitty must have looked surprised, because Mrs. Clements laughed.

"You see? I already have your attention."

Kitty followed Mrs. Clements past a souk-like living room. The floor was covered with Turkish rugs, and colorful throws had been flung across every piece of furniture.

"No one thinks about the men who live in those tin cans," Poppy Clements continued in her lazy drawl. "And I can tell you that it's awful—they're stuck inside for days on end, unable to stand straight, no sunlight, no fresh air, no fresh food. As a matter of fact, they have so little oxygen that they're ordered to sleep when they're not on duty in order to conserve it. And that's not all."

Kitty marveled at the Bohemian decor as they walked through the apartment. It all seemed slightly haphazard and yet of a piece, in keeping with Kitty's sense of Mrs. Clements's exotic tastes, and perhaps, her penchant to shock.

"The toilets blow back refuse into the user's face, which makes me thankful for our American plumbing," the playwright continued, "and the sailors are forced to wear a single leather uniform for the duration of the journey, which must stink like hell by the time they get home." She threw open a door. "Welcome to my den." The Oriental theme continued here too, with a low-slung divan in one corner and filigreed lamps hanging from ornate metal hooks.

"Excuse the mess." Mrs. Clements cleared away a pile of pillows with a sweep of her hand. "Come sit." She leaned against an embroidered bolster and patted a seat beside her. "Do the police have any leads on who killed poor Hunter?"

"Not as far as I'm aware," Kitty replied. All she knew was what she'd read that morning, and the story had been short. "Mr. Cole died of a single bullet to his head. And there were no signs of struggle on the body, so he must have been expecting whomever it was that assaulted him."

"How awful." The playwright frowned. "There weren't any fingerprints? That's normal police procedure, isn't it?"

"I believe so." Kitty was hardly an expert, but she answered, "Apparently, the pistol had been wiped clean."

"And he was killed with his own gun?"

"Yes." The woman certainly had a lot of questions.

"And it's certain that he was killed while the fireworks were in progress?"

"That's what is being said. Mrs. Clements?"

"Of course, you need to ask me things, not the other way around. Forgive me, my dear. It's my instinct as a writer. Ask, ask, ask. Never rest until I'm satisfied." She took out a cigarette from a silver case. "Do you mind?"

"Go ahead."

"Would you like one?"

"No, thanks."

"Too young? You'll get the hang of it soon enough." Mrs. Clements fitted the cigarette into an engraved silver holder and struck a safety match to light it. She inhaled deeply and blew out a long stream of smoke from between her lips.

"I've been asked to gather background information. Details about Mr. Cole and how he was regarded—"

"You mean the woman's angle."

"That's right." Kitty nodded.

"Well, let's see." Mrs. Clements picked a fleck of tobacco from her tongue and, with a flick of her elegant fingers, tossed it into the air. "Let's start with Mrs. Cole. You could say I always made it a point to speak to her."

"She did tell me you were very kind."

"And I spoke to Mr. Cole too."

"Did you talk to him the afternoon he died?"

"Oh yes."

"Do you recall what he said?"

"He'd had one too many to drink, you know. And he was rambling on. He seemed preoccupied with something, but—and

I've been thinking about this ever since it happened—for the life of me, I can't remember the specifics of our conversation. The thing is, I never paid much attention to what Hunter said. He was the kind who always went about something or other, and I pretended to listen, because nobody else would, but mostly I observed. How he held himself, how he moved. It's useful for my writing."

"And how did he seem to you that afternoon?"

"As I said, preoccupied. Excited about something or other. But then again, maybe I'm imagining that because of what happened afterward."

"Do you have any idea what he might have been excited about?"

"You're a persistent one, aren't you?" Mrs. Clements seemed amused. She shrugged. "Some people are just like that. They get into a tizzy over nothing. I'm sorry I can't give you anything particular to work with."

"Did Mrs. Cole mention anything?"

"No, she kept her mouth shut. And quite rightly, I'd say. Look, Miss Weeks, I meet all kinds of people in my line of work, and I don't hold anyone's past against them. So Aimee did what she did—"

"By that you mean she was a dance-hall girl?" This would be a good time to verify Amanda's information, since Mrs. Clements didn't seem the least bit prudish.

"She was indeed a dance-hall girl. One of the naughtier ones, possibly." Mrs. Clements seemed unbothered by the insinuation. "But what you must understand, Miss Weeks, is that it doesn't matter. People used her as an excuse to avoid *him*."

"I'm sorry—"

"If Hunter had more to offer, they'd still gossip, but in the end, they'd overlook Aimee's past. If he had real money or influence, do you think they would care what his wife did?"

"I see." Kitty considered the point. "And Mr. Cole had neither money nor influence?"

"Exactly."

"And not many friends."

"True again."

"But he was from a good family."

Mrs. Clements shrugged. "That only gets one so far these days."

"Have you heard that he liked to bet on horses?"

"That's what they say."

Mrs. Clements seemed frank and intelligent. She knew everyone and was held in high esteem. Kitty wanted to learn what the playwright really thought had happened. She knew she wasn't supposed to be investigating the murder, but Mr. Flanagan hadn't explicitly forbidden her from asking the witnesses about their suspicions.

"Would you have any idea who might want to see him dead, Mrs. Clements?"

"His wife?" Poppy Clements laughed a throaty laugh. "I'm only joking. But wouldn't you, if you were her? The thing that bothers me, Miss Weeks, is that Hunter really wasn't worth killing. Unless I'm missing something, and I don't believe I am, Hunter was a big, hearty, somewhat stupid but not evil man. Maybe he was short of cash and had some debts. But to shoot him at the stables at a party?" She shook her head. "It doesn't make sense."

She stubbed her cigarette into a chased copper bowl and pressed down on it until the final spark had been extinguished. "What's sad is that he was killed after he was feeling so much better—"

Kitty perked up. "Was he ill, Mrs. Clements?" Finally, something to "work with," as Poppy Clements said.

"Yes, he was. He must have been. He told me that he had been seeing a doctor when we met at an exhibition back in March or April. He told me that he had been seeing this man regularly and that he never felt better."

"Did he tell you what for?" Kitty leaned forward. If Mr. Cole had been cured of a serious illness, that would add a poignant twist to the tale.

"Someone pulled him away in the midst of our conversation. I remember clearly because Mr. Clements's physician had recently retired, and I was looking for a replacement. What's strange is that when I asked Hunter about it a few weeks later, he denied that he'd been seeing anyone."

"Do you think he had something to hide?"

"Possibly."

"You didn't happen to catch the doctor's name?"

"Yes, I did. It was Michael... Or Lawrence. No, that's not right. It was one of those names that could either be a Christian name or a surname." She struck a match to light another cigarette. "It was Albert. Dr. Albert." The match hovered in the air.

"Dr. Albert. You're certain?"

"Positive. But the oddest part is that I asked all my friends, and no one seems to have heard of him."

"Come now, that's not possible." Mr. Flanagan flipped through Kitty's notes. "This Dr. Albert must be in the telephone directory. Look him up and find out what kind of doctor he is. If Cole suffered from a serious illness, then our readers need to know."

"Have the police made any further progress, Mr. Flanagan?" Kitty said. The fact that her usefulness to him wasn't over, that he was treating her like one of the boys—straight to the point and no-nonsense—was more than she could have wished for.

"If they have, you will be the first to find out. Now run along. You have work to do." He turned back to the newsroom, and Kitty raced down the stairs, the cool metal banister gliding beneath her fingers.

She found her workplace confidante, Mr. Musser, eating a sandwich in his basement lair.

"May I borrow your telephone directory, Mr. Musser?" she asked the grizzled archivist.

"*Was?*" The old man brushed a crumb from his beard. "*Keinen 'Guten Tag' heute Morgen?*"

"*Guten Tag, Herr Musser,*" Kitty replied, unable to wipe the smile from her face. "Have you heard of a Dr. Albert?"

He put down his sandwich, shuffled out from behind the counter, and pulled a volume from one of the stacks. "Why do you ask?" He thumped a copy of the *Bell Telephone Book for Greater New York, Including All Five Boroughs* in front of her.

"Hunter Cole." Kitty flipped through the pages. "The man who was shot at the Sleepy Hollow Country Club—he may have been seeing a physician by that name."

"Albert." Musser stroked his droopy walrus mustache. "Sorry, it doesn't ring a bell."

Kitty took out her pencil and began to copy a list of subscriber numbers.

Musser looked over her shoulder while she wrote. "Did you know that the Bell system has ten times the number of telephones, proportionate to the population, of course, as in all of Europe? The company's cables, buried underground, carry as many as *eighteen hundred* wires?"

Kitty kept her finger on the page of tiny type to make sure she didn't lose track. The one drawback to coming to Mr. Musser for advice was that he was lonely and liked to chat about his current preoccupations. Usually, she didn't mind. In fact, for the most part, she enjoyed his little lectures.

"Their switchboard," he continued as she copied the information she needed, "used to require a roomful of boys to handle just a few calls and now needs only two or three girls to serve much larger numbers faster, and with far less confusion."

"That's progress." Kitty finished and returned the directory.

"And what is this?" He pointed at her notes.

"It's a list of every Dr. Albert in the city."

"What do you plan to do with it?"

"I'm going to call each one of them and find out who treated Mr. Cole."

"Miss Weeks." Musser's blue eyes twinkled. "You think they'll tell you?"

"I'll find out if you allow me to use your telephone."

"Help yourself. I have work to do." He shuffled off to the back.

Kitty sat in his chair and took a moment to formulate her plan. This was no different from being in drama class, she reminded herself. All she was doing was playing a part.

She picked up the receiver and asked the operator to connect her first call.

"May I speak to Dr. Albert?" she said when a male voice came on the end of the line. It turned out that there was no *Dr. Albert* at the residence, only a Mr. Albert, but Kitty decided to pursue the conversation regardless.

"I beg your pardon," she said into the instrument. "My brother passed away recently and left a note for his doctor, but he didn't leave an address. I thought I would try every Albert in the telephone directory to see whether I could track him down."

Silence.

"My brother's name was Cole. Hunter Cole. You don't happen to have known him?"

"I'm sorry, miss. I just own a dry-goods store."

Kitty thanked him and hung up the receiver.

"Mr. Cole's sister." Musser ambled out to the desk. "That's a nice touch."

Kitty grinned. The next Albert was a doctor, but he was out of town on vacation, and his nurse said he had never had any patients by that name. The third was an astronomy professor, who told her that the only Cole he knew was one of his students, and that young man had been fit as a fiddle when he came to class that morning.

Kitty kept going. There were only five names left, and her approach didn't seem to be setting off any alarms. She told herself that she was entitled to make such inquiries, and any doctor would surely want to know what had been written to him by a recently deceased patient.

She struck gold on her fourth attempt.

"Cole, but of course!" the male voice on the other end of the line exclaimed. "Have the note sent over. I'll give you my address."

"I'd like to verify a few details first, sir." Now it was Kitty's turn to be cautious. "Would you mind telling me my brother's Christian name?"

"Don't *you* know?"

"Of course I do. I'd just like to be sure that you do as well so that I don't send his letter to the wrong individual."

"Are you accusing me of lying?"

"No, sir. It's my duty to my brother's memory. I'm sure you understand."

There was no reply.

"Sir? His Christian name, please?"

The voice turned sullen. "I don't recall the Christian names of all my patients."

"Could you describe him for me?"

"Five foot ten, brown hair, brown eyes."

Hunter Cole was taller. "Where did you meet?"

"At my club."

Kitty heard someone speak in the background. The man giggled. A woman came on the line. "I beg your pardon. May I help you?"

Kitty explained.

"I'm sorry," the woman said. "Dr. Albert suffers from a weak mind. He isn't allowed to speak on the telephone. Please don't call again."

Disappointed, Kitty hung up the receiver. Before she could move on to the next name on her list, a mail boy popped his head in.

"Miss Weeks, Miss Busby wants you."

Kitty slipped the list into her pocket and hurried upstairs. She would finish later.

"Good to see you again, Miss Weeks." The Ladies' Page editor seemed in a chipper mood that afternoon. Her hair was up in curls, she wore dangly tourmaline earrings, and she appeared ready to forgive and forget Kitty's betrayal. "Have you had lunch?"

"Not yet."

"The longer day isn't proving too difficult?"

"Not so far, Miss Busby."

"Wonderful, wonderful. Well, with all this excitement, I hope you haven't forgotten about your meeting with Mrs. Stepan tomorrow."

Kitty's blank look must have suggested that she had, because Miss Busby said, "Mrs. Stepan, the chairwoman of the ladies division of the Early Risers Riding Club. You are to meet her and report on their plans for the upcoming season, as we had discussed."

"Of course."

"You have the address?"

"Mrs. Stepan lives on Madison Avenue."

"And you're prepared?"

Kitty hesitated to remind her boss that she had already undertaken three interviews for Mr. Flanagan in the past twenty-four hours. "I am. I'll meet her at eight, right after her ride."

"All right then, Miss Weeks." Miss Busby handed her a sheaf of notes on "What to Wear This Summer." "I'd like you to put this into article form for me by four o'clock. Twelve hundred words, no fluff."

"Yes, Miss Busby." Kitty paged through the disjointed ramblings of a prominent ladies' dressmaker: *wide skirts will stay with us until August...pleating is in high demand...knife pleats... three-quarter sleeves or double sleeves (opaque above, transparent below).* This would take all her ingenuity to convert into something coherent.

Her mind swimming with visions of chiffon and muslin, skirts and sleeves, Kitty returned to the hen coop. She would take care of Miss Busby's article, then finish her telephone calls from home.

CHAPTER NINE

Julian Weeks picked Kitty up from work. "You seem busy these days." He stared out of the window as Rao drove them to the west side. Kitty's father had never learned to operate a motor vehicle. He said it was too much trouble; she suspected that he preferred to be chauffeured.

"I've been asked to help out a bit on the Hunter Cole story," Kitty said. "It's nothing much, just a little background since I was at the party and met some of the people involved."

"That's good." He seemed distracted. "You know, I've been thinking that it might be time for us to travel again. Did you know that it's not too difficult to take a trip through Europe? I looked into the matter, and it seems that all we would require is a stamped *sauf conduit*—and then, with American passports, we can go wherever we like, even sightsee on the battlefields."

"I hope you're not serious." Kitty turned to him, but his face was impassive. "That sounds morbid."

He shrugged. "Some of the smaller countries over there still rely on tourist dollars."

"And how do you intend for us to get there? Swim?"

"Don't be silly. We'd sail on an American vessel. The Germans aren't about to blow those up."

"Their U-boat captains do make mistakes."

"That's true. It's possible there might be some danger."

"It's more than possible." Kitty knew he said these things just to get a rise out of her.

Rao slowed the Packard and let them off in front of the New Century's colonnaded entryway before driving around the corner to park in the garage at the rear. Not for the first time, Kitty reflected that Mr. Weeks had selected the perfect place for the two of them to live when he finally decided to settle down after a lifetime of doing business abroad.

New York was the business hub of the East Coast, and Manhattan its center. Within the island, the east side was too snooty and downtown too commercial, but the area west of Central Park consisted of the perfect blend of families and self-made men like Mr. Weeks: doctors, lawyers, politicians, and artists from all corners of the globe. He could have picked a gracious home on Riverside Drive, but they required too much maintenance for a no-frills individual like himself. The apartments on Central Park West would have been lovely, but the New Century on West End Avenue turned out to be perfect. Just a block to the west from the stores on Broadway and a block to the east from the park and the river, the New Century combined old-world comfort with new-world conveniences. Filtered water poured out of every tap, and the garage at the back offered facilities for charging one's batteries should one happen to drive an electric vehicle. The construction was solid and entirely fireproof. Each floor contained only two apartments, and in addition to the three main bedrooms, Kitty's home featured a comfortable foyer, a sizable dining room, living room, and study, as well as a pantry and kitchen, two servants' rooms, and a servants' bathroom.

Grace opened the front door, and Mr. Weeks handed her his hat and cane. He told Kitty that he had an appointment that evening and wouldn't be in for dinner.

Kitty looked in on Mrs. Codd and gave the order for a light supper. She didn't mind being on her own too much, and she wanted to finish telephoning in privacy and then write some long overdue letters to her friends in Europe.

Kitty had converted the two bedrooms at the back of the apartment, overlooking the garage, into a suite for herself. She went inside to change. Opening the bureau for a fresh blouse, she caught sight of a photograph in a tiny blue-and-green-enameled frame. A woman in a broad-brimmed hat that cast a shadow over her features smiled at Kitty. It was the only picture she possessed of her mother.

Julian Weeks had said the photograph was taken before he and Violet were married; it was an early one from when she arrived in Malaya as a penniless young governess. He met her a few years later out in a remote area where, friendless and alone, she hired him to help manage the modest rubber estate left to her by the late Mr. Hiram Smith, her first husband. They fell in love, married, and had planned to have another photograph taken with the baby, but since Mrs. Weeks died shortly afterward, that never happened. Julian Weeks had given the photograph to Kitty when she left for boarding school.

Kitty changed into a clean blouse, put on a pair of knicker-bockers, and did her exercises: jumping jacks, marching in place, neck and hip rolls, ankle stretches.

She heard footsteps in the hall. Her father must be on his way out. She called good-bye, washed the perspiration from her face, put her skirt back on, and, after making sure that Mrs. Codd and Grace were safely in the kitchen, walked across the foyer to his study, slipped inside, and shut the door behind her.

The apartment had been wired for two telephones: one in the foyer, right outside the pantry, and the second one in Mr. Weeks's study so that he could speak in private. He kept his room dark, with the heavy curtains drawn. It was the one room in the apartment that Kitty hadn't been allowed to decorate and wasn't supposed to be in on her own. She switched on the desk lamp.

Books interspersed with souvenirs that Mr. Weeks had gathered on his travels filled the wall behind his desk. Real estate guides gave way to an ivory Chinese coolie pulling a cart loaded high with fruit, cloisonné bowls stood on top of atlases and almanacs placed sideways, and an antique jade dagger leaned casually against Adam Smith's *An Inquiry into the Nature and Causes of the Wealth of Nations*.

Kitty particularly loathed one piece that her father had placed on a shelf so that when he sat at his table, it appeared to be looking over his shoulder: a jet-black human figure whose milky eyes seemed to follow one everywhere. She felt its gaze bore into her back as she pulled back his chair and reached for the telephone.

It rang, and she flinched, then laughed at herself for being foolish. He couldn't possibly know she was here—that's not who was calling. She lifted the instrument and felt inexpressibly glad to hear Amanda's voice.

"You didn't tell me whether you'd come to the YWCA training, Capability. It's just the introductory session, and I can't go by myself. Promise me that you will be there?"

"Remind me when it is again?"

"Next week." Amanda gave her the date and time. "I'll pick you up. And if you like what you hear, might you consider joining?"

"Amanda!"

"I'll quit while I'm ahead."

Kitty smiled. If Amanda ever chose to go into journalism, she would be a force to be reckoned with. She never gave up. On the other hand, she didn't listen—or she did, but only when it suited her.

Kitty removed the list of Alberts from her pocket and resumed making her calls. Dr. Albert number five turned out to be a dentist; Albert number six was a chemist; and number seven ran a clinic for the needy on the Bowery.

The final Albert, Dr. Beverly Albert, was a woman for whom the name Cole rang a bell. "Is this the Mr. Cole who was recently murdered?"

"Yes," Kitty replied, her excitement mounting. "Were you acquainted with him?"

"I'm afraid not. I just heard about the shooting from a friend who attended the party."

Kitty replaced the receiver and stared at the sheet of paper. Something was wrong. Either Mrs. Clements hadn't heard the doctor's name correctly, or one of these people had lied to her. Or perhaps, just perhaps, the Dr. Albert she was looking for wasn't on this list.

She pushed the chair back into its place, stuck her tongue out at the statue, and made sure her father's desk was exactly as she had found it before she switched off the light and left the study.

She wrote her letters to her friends from boarding school and, alone at dinner, mulled over the events of Monday, July 5. Why did Hunter Cole go down to the stables that evening? That seemed to be the central, unresolved question. Was it just to get away from the other guests, or had something or someone pulled him away while everyone else was busy enjoying the fireworks?

Kitty spent the next morning chatting with Mrs. Stepan in the back garden of the Stepans' home on Madison Avenue. The chairwoman of the Early Risers Riding Club was a young mother, pretty and active with three boys ages four, six, and eight who dashed into the garden and hugged her around the legs before going off to play under the supervision of their nurse. She glanced at them fondly and resumed her story about the glanders virus that killed her childhood pony. "It came as such a shock. One day little Zsa-Zsa was there, and the next day she was gone. I've never cared for any animal as much since, although I do ride every day."

"That sounds awful, Mrs. Stepan."

"It was tragic. A terrible disease, but tell me, what would you like to know about our group?"

"Can you describe the events you have planned, who the members are, and some of the benefits of early morning equestrian exercise?" Kitty said.

"With pleasure." Mrs. Stepan rattled off a list of fetes, charity breakfasts, and a gala. She mentioned names—some were prominent women who Kitty had heard about—and then the benefits of regular riding: improved circulation, better complexion, and a chance to begin one's day in communion with the natural world, away from the commotion of the city.

"Of course, we're in the city." Mrs. Stepan laughed as they finished, and she lead Kitty to the door. "We ride in Central Park, but that's an oasis, don't you think? Do you ride, by the way?"

Kitty nodded.

"Well, then you must join us sometime if you can be there by six. We're a friendly group, I promise."

Kitty walked back to the *Sentinel*. It wasn't that far, and the route wasn't complicated. Most of Manhattan's streets and avenues were organized along a rational, unswerving grid. Numbered streets ran from east to west, bisected at sharp right angles by avenues that ran north to south. There were those who said the plan was motivated by shameless commercial considerations (it resulted in nice rectangular plots for development) and had none of the grandeur of avenues radiating outward from the city center, like Haussmann's Paris.

But Paris was Paris, Kitty thought, picking her way down the sidewalk, dodging litter, peddlers, and a steady stream of businessmen and women. There were some people who didn't care for New York, who found it too crass, too brash, and visually unappealing. Kitty had to admit that she had felt the same way when she first arrived. She'd been alarmed by the throng of humanity in all colors, by the metal trains that rattled along overhead rails, and by the skyscrapers, some twenty, thirty, and even forty stories high, that pierced the heavens.

But she had become accustomed to it all; even the smell of rotting garbage on a hot summer day no longer repelled her. She smiled as she pushed through the heavy revolving doors at the *Sentinel*. This was home. She lived in a city that always looked toward the future.

Kitty was in one of the stalls in the women's restroom when she heard a couple of the typists enter and start chattering away at the basins.

"Who does she think she is?" The sound of running water threatened to drown out the words, but Kitty could still hear them.

"All hoity-toity and never in like the rest of us. Where is that pricey miss this morning?"

Kitty's face flushed.

"Give her a chance." The voice belonged to Jeannie Williams.

"What chance? She's already been here six months."

The taps shut off; there was a shuffle, and then the door closed behind them.

Kitty emerged from her cubicle and washed her hands. Her cheeks burned. It was one thing to suspect that the others didn't care for her, another to have one's guess confirmed.

Jeannie was the only decent one of the lot, the only one who bothered to speak to her or show any interest in what she was doing. Because Kitty worked for a shorter day, she didn't take the eleven o'clock break with the typists, and even if she did, she wouldn't have known what to say because their lives were so different.

She walked through the hen coop without looking left or right and knocked at the entryway to Miss Busby's alcove.

"I just got off the telephone with Mrs. Stepan," the Ladies' Page editor trilled, looking up at Kitty. "She was most pleased with you. 'So pleasant, so personable, such a good listener.' Her words, not mine."

"I'm glad I made a good impression."

Miss Busby's coral earrings swung back and forth as she nodded. "Good impression? She thought you were just right! And so it seems that my plans are coming to fruition sooner than I expected."

"Just right for what, Miss Busby?" Kitty pulled up a chair. "What plans are you referring to?"

"Just right to interview Miss Anne Morgan about her new book."

"I beg your pardon—*the* Miss Anne Morgan?" Kitty dropped into the chair.

"That is correct." Miss Busby looked like a girl who had won the first-prize ribbon at a school contest.

"Why me, Miss Busby?" Anne Morgan was the philanthropist daughter of the first J. P. Morgan, the sister of the current, wounded J. P. "Jack" Morgan. She was known around the world for her personal fortune and charitable endeavors. "Why would Miss Morgan want a girl like me to interview her about her book?"

This was all happening too fast—in less than a week, Kitty had gone from spending all morning behind her desk to covering a party, interviewing a bereaved widow, a hostess, a playwright, a horsewoman—and now an heiress? And not just any heiress but quite possibly the wealthiest unmarried woman in the world.

Miss Busby thrust a slim volume in front of Kitty. "Because her book has been written for and about girls." She ran a finger beneath the title: "*The American Girl: Her Education, Her Responsibility, Her Recreation, Her Future*. And Miss Morgan would like an American girl to discuss it with her."

"I don't know what to say. I'm overwhelmed. And honored."

"As you should be."

Kitty panicked. "And I'm not very American. I wasn't raised here."

"Really?" Miss Busby paused, but just for a moment. "Well, no one can tell."

"Do you think I'm up to it, Miss Busby?"

"Well, you better be up to it, Miss Weeks, because I'm not about to refuse Miss Morgan, and I hardly qualify as a girl myself."

"Yes, I see."

"Take a deep breath, Miss Weeks."

Kitty did as she was told.

"There's just one rub."

"Yes, Miss Busby?"

"Miss Morgan maintains a busy schedule. The only time she has available to speak to you is Monday morning."

"This Monday?" The words came out in a squeak.

"That is correct."

"But that's four days away."

"I am aware, so you will not come in to work tomorrow. As soon as we're finished, you are to go home and start preparing.

Don't think of doing anything else. You must study the book from cover to cover and formulate a list of questions. I'll do the same, and we will discuss it first thing on Monday morning. The interview is scheduled for ten thirty, and I'll expect you here at eight o'clock sharp. That should give us enough time. Or if you prefer, I can come in on Sunday to help you."

Kitty flipped through the book. It was short, just about sixty-five pages. She could read it in an afternoon. "That won't be necessary, Miss Busby. I can manage."

"Music to my ears. And you never know—you might find some advice in it that could be of value to you personally. Lord knows, if I were your age, I'd jump at the opportunity." She twirled a strand of gray hair around her finger. "Sadly, *my* best years are almost over."

"I hope I can be worthy of your confidence, Miss Busby."

The editor's eyes moistened. She blinked. "Go on. You better finish up."

Kitty returned to the hen coop in a daze, the volume clutched to her chest. *Responsibility... Education... Future.* These were momentous topics. And she would have the chance to discuss them with no less a personage than Miss Anne Morgan.

"There's someone here to see you." Jeannie Williams looked up from her work when Kitty came in. She stared at the book in Kitty's hands. "Is that *The American Girl*? Is it for the Ladies' Page?"

Kitty nodded. "I'll be doing the interview." The words didn't seem real.

"Oh my!" Jeannie's hand flew to her mouth. "I admire Miss Morgan so much. She's such a fine lady."

Kitty put down the book. "Did you say that someone wants to see me?"

"Silly me." Jeannie glanced at a chit beside her typewriter. "A Mr. Lucian Hotchkiss. He said to tell you it's urgent."

Chapter Ten

It never rains but it pours. Kitty ran down the stairs. She had been stuck behind a desk and bored for months, and now it seemed as though everyone clamored to speak to her. What could Hotchkiss possibly want? She pictured the handsome, fretful secretary before she saw him adjusting his tie beside the three-faced clock in the *Sentinel*'s lobby. He looked nervous. A young man, likely a reporter, sauntered over and murmured something to him.

In response, Hotchkiss reached into his breast pocket and pulled out a lighter. The young man put a cigarette in his mouth and bent over the secretary's cupped hands.

"Mr. Hotchkiss." Kitty approached them.

Mrs. Basshor's secretary fumbled and dropped his lighter.

"Thanks." The young man strolled off, puffing away.

Hotchkiss picked up his lighter and put it back into his pocket. "Good morning, Miss Weeks." He sounded more than a little flustered.

"What brings you here, Mr. Hotchkiss?" Kitty said. "May I help you with something?"

The secretary wiped his forehead with a handkerchief. "Can we speak in private?"

"This way." Kitty led him to a marble bench in a quiet corner of the atrium.

"Mrs. Basshor doesn't know I'm here." The secretary remained on his feet. "She'll worry if I'm not back soon. You might think it odd of me to be so concerned, but I owe her everything. I'd be nowhere and nothing without my employer."

"I understand, Mr. Hotchkiss."

"Yes, well." He coughed into his hand. "Let me start by saying that I came to you, Miss Weeks, instead of anyone else because I thought I might be able to count on your discretion. You seem to me like a young lady of tact and understanding."

"I appreciate the compliment, Mr. Hotchkiss, but I haven't got all day."

"Of course." His smile was apologetic. "I believe you are aware that when Mrs. Cole was questioned by the police detectives, she said that she'd been waiting for her husband at the children's tables for the duration of the fireworks?"

"Yes." As far as Kitty was aware, no one had been able to confirm Mrs. Cole's claim. On the other hand, no one had disputed it either.

"I have reason to believe that that may not be entirely accurate."

"Go on," Kitty urged.

"When I was at the club yesterday, wrapping up some housekeeping matters, one of the waiters approached me and said that he had something troubling to report. Apparently, one of the ladies had lost her bracelet and asked him to search for it. He hunted around the children's tables for at least five or six minutes while the fireworks were in progress. During that time, the tables were empty. He said there was no one sitting there at all."

"Why didn't he tell the police?" Kitty's mind raced through the implications of this new information.

"He didn't think it mattered at the time."

"I see. Well, perhaps you should report it now."

The secretary smiled nervously. "Mrs. Basshor would fire me on the spot if she knew that I was talking to you out of turn, let alone bringing one of her guest's movements to the authorities' attention. The waiter won't say anything for the same reason— the club frowns on it. I could have kept quiet," he added, "but instead, I decided to come to *you*."

"What can I do about it, Mr. Hotchkiss?"

"You could speak to Mrs. Cole and find out what happened. She won't mind if it comes from another young lady. And in the end, it might be nothing. She may have needed to powder her nose, or something like that. Something she wouldn't have wanted to tell the detectives."

"And suppose she doesn't have a convincing answer?"

"Then perhaps you could inform the authorities?"

"Really, Mr. Hotchkiss." He wanted her to do his dirty work. He wanted her to question Mrs. Cole and then point fingers if necessary.

"I leave it in your hands," the secretary replied. "But I would appreciate it if you didn't mention to anyone that you heard this information through me."

Kitty sighed. He looked so anxious, and Mrs. Basshor probably would be furious if she found out. "I won't tell anyone about our conversation, but what I do with what I learn is my decision."

"That's all I can ask." He seemed relieved to have transferred the burden and shook Kitty's hand. "Thank you, Miss Weeks."

Kitty watched him leave. So devoted to Mrs. Basshor, and yet he wasn't without his own scruples and, perhaps, grudges.

She waited for the elevator to the sixth floor. If Hotchkiss was correct and Mrs. Cole had indeed been absent for some time during the fireworks, Mr. Flanagan ought to be informed. The tidbit might offset her news that the Dr. Albert lead hadn't amounted to much.

She tapped on the glass partition and mouthed Flanagan's name, but a tall, scholarly man emerged in response to her summons.

"Miss Weeks?" He looked down at her from his rimless, President-Wilson-style pince-nez. "I'm Rathbone, Mr. Flanagan's colleague. He's asked me to give you a message."

"Is he out?"

"He's up in Connecticut with the police. It seems that the Cole case is about wrapped up. He says to tell you that they're hot on the killer's trail and should have him in custody by this evening."

CHAPTER ELEVEN

I beg your pardon?" The revelation transported Kitty to a moment in the misty past, when her native *ayah* had taken her to prayer hall in the mountains. Kitty had been absorbed in the rich orange of the monks' robes, their strange droning chants, the golden statues draped with silky white scarves. She hadn't noticed her father barge in until he'd grabbed her wrist.

"You have to remember who you are," he'd said through gritted teeth. Seven-year-old Kitty had been terrified; she'd never seen him look so grim. It wasn't long after that that he packed her off to Switzerland, and Kitty never saw the *ayah* again. She had promised herself that she would never make the same mistake: she would never believe that she was part of something, or that she belonged somewhere, when she didn't.

The problem was, her hopes got the best of her sometimes, and judging from the stab of pain she felt in response to Mr. Rathbone's abrupt announcement, she realized that she had forgotten her childhood vow and had imagined herself to be more central than she really was to Mr. Flanagan's investigations.

"One of the stable hands did it." Rathbone twirled a pencil between his fingers.

"A stable hand? Why? Why would a stable hand want to shoot Mr. Cole?"

Mr. Flanagan's associate shrugged his shoulders. "Calm down, Miss Weeks. I'm not conversant with the details, but I believe it has something to do with the fellow being Cole's acquaintance from the racetrack. He was dismissed from his job there because of some wrongdoing and only found employment at the country club by providing a false name. Mr. Cole recognized him... Really, it's best you wait until tomorrow. There will be a full account in the papers, and you can read all about it."

Kitty shook with anger. *How dare he?* How dare he treat her like another member of the news-hungry public?

"It's all I can tell you." His tone was dry as he returned to the newsroom.

But she wasn't a little girl anymore, Kitty thought as she made her way downstairs. And she no longer had to accept others' valuation of her place in the world and what she should or shouldn't do as a result of it.

Kitty collected her things and hailed a cab to take her home. She had gone less than half a block before she changed her mind and redirected the driver to Aimee Cole's address.

She had a role in this story too. She had met the dead man. She had met his wife. No one had been charged with the crime yet. She still had opportunities to have her questions answered.

A striking woman with sparkling eyes and red hair arranged in ringlets opened the door to the apartment. "Can I help you?"

Kitty tried to contain her disappointment. Mrs. Cole probably wasn't in.

"It's me—Aimee!" the woman squealed once it became clear that Kitty hadn't recognized her. She pulled off the wig and transformed back into her unremarkable self. "I know you must think I'm awful, playing around so soon after what's happened, but I'm all alone, and I've nothing to do except look through my old things."

She flung the door wide open, and Kitty followed her inside. Open boxes and cartons littered the living room. Flouncy garments spilled out of one; another overflowed with shimmery bits. Aimee tossed her wig into a box of hairpieces.

"It started with my not being able to find my black gown," she explained. "The funeral is tomorrow, and I need something decent to wear. Mama's gone to the shops to buy me proper mourning."

She cleared a pile of scarves from the couch. "Souvenirs from my former life. Will you have some tea?"

"I don't want to trouble you."

"It's no trouble at all. Here, take a look at this while I put on the kettle." She handed Kitty a linen-bound album.

Kitty opened it, expecting to find photographs from Aimee and Hunter Cole's marriage. Instead, the album was filled with page after page of clippings, photographs, and postcards of Mary Pickford, the motion-picture actress famed for her long, red curls—no doubt the inspiration for Aimee's wig.

Kitty leafed through the pages: here was thoughtful Mary in an advertisement for *Mender of Nets*; there she was looking saucy in *Female of the Species*. She was on alert in *Tess of the Storm Country*, forlorn in *Cinderella*, and ready for romance in *Hearts Adrift*. Reviews from *Photoplay* and *Motion Picture Weekly* had been interspersed with the pictures. Some had been starred with a thick red pencil, while portions of the others had been circled or underlined for extra emphasis.

"*The Eagles Mate* is a lively feature without a real kick," Kitty read a marked review to herself, "but it has Mary Pickford, the best kick or punch that could be put in."

"Isn't she wonderful?" Mrs. Cole returned to the parlor. "She looks like she's not much more than a child, but she's America's highest-paid motion-picture heroine."

"I'm partial to Pearl White myself." Kitty put the album on the coffee table. She loved Pearl's films, but she hadn't created a shrine to her like Aimee Cole had for Miss Pickford.

"Pearl doesn't hold a candle to Mary," Aimee replied. "We're the same age, you know. Both twenty-three this April. But Mary's been working forever. She started onstage when she was five years old. Her mother brought her down from Toronto, and little Gladys Smith, as she was called then, has been supporting her family ever since."

"Have you seen all her pictures?"

"All her features. The one- and two-reelers are too numerous to count. But take a guess—tell me how much you think Mary makes."

"How much she earns, you mean?"

"That's right." Mrs. Cole's eyes blazed.

"I have no idea." Kitty hadn't encountered such devotion to an actress even among her school friends. And for a married lady of twenty-three, the passion certainly seemed, well, unexpected.

"Give it a try," Aimee cajoled.

"A hundred dollars a week?" It was a wild guess. Kitty knew

that society reporters made fifty, and they were the highest paid in the business, so she took that number and doubled it.

"Try two thousand." Aimee sounded giddy, as though she'd just been handed that sum in cash.

"That's astounding," Kitty replied. "Every week?"

"Yes."

"But that's more than a hundred thousand dollars a year!" Kitty couldn't believe any woman could command such a salary. It was a heady figure.

"And the best part is that Mary started just like everyone else," Aimee said. "Five dollars a day, which doubled to ten, and then, when the public began to recognize her, she signed with IMP for $175 a week. She switched to Majestic for $225, then signed with Zukor for $500"—she rattled off the numbers—"and last year, Mr. Zukor raised her to a thousand a week, and this year, she got him to raise it again. In addition to her salary, she earns a percentage of all her pictures' profits, and he even pays her mother a stipend."

"That's quite something." Kitty was fascinated.

"I don't bring this up lightly," Aimee said as the kettle in the kitchen began to whistle. "I would have liked to try for a career in pictures. Even a quarter of what Mary earns would have been enough to support us, but Hunter wouldn't allow it."

The whistle grew louder and more insistent. "I know I look plain in person, but that changes in front of the camera." Aimee Cole stood. "I've been photographed plenty of times. But the Coles would rather have us be poor than for me to act in the 'movies.'" She hurried off to the kitchen.

Kitty wasn't surprised that a man from a family like Mr.

Cole's would stand in his wife's way. Like the Vanderwell family, honor was probably all that was left to them. But poor Aimee Cole. Marriage and work didn't sit well together. Kitty had been to a symposium at Barnard College some months ago where, barring the motion-picture producer Madame Alice Guy-Blaché, all the career women who spoke had been unmarried. Dr. Katharine Bement Davis, the city's commissioner of corrections; Dean Virginia Gildersleeve of Barnard; the journalist, Miss Ida Tarbell. All spinsters.

Mrs. Cole returned with tea on a tray, and Kitty took advantage of the break to change the subject. "Mrs. Cole?" she began.

"Aimee."

"Aimee," Kitty said, relenting. "Would you mind if I asked you a delicate question about the evening Mr. Cole died?"

"So that's why you're here." Aimee gave a small laugh as she stirred a spoonful of sugar into Kitty's cup. "Of course. Ask away."

"There is one small matter." Kitty picked up her cup and took a sip. "It seems that a member of the staff noticed you were missing from the children's tables for a short while."

Aimee stiffened. "Was I?"

"That's what he said."

"You spoke to him yourself?"

"No, I didn't. But a reliable source"—she was about to say "Hotchkiss" but checked herself in time—"told me."

"Thank you for your concern, Miss Weeks." Aimee Cole stared at her Dresden figurines. "It was, as you say, just a trivial matter." She paused, and then said, "I'm a vain thing, and despite your kind efforts, the stain on my dress continued to trouble me. I slipped away for a few moments to give it another rinse. You can check with the attendant, if you like." She smiled. "I'm sure she'll vouch for me."

"I'm glad to hear that." As if in sympathy for what had happened to Mrs. Cole that day, Kitty's hand shook, and tea spilled on her blouse. "Silly me." Her laugh sounded unsteady.

She looked down to see the splash spread like ink in water on the white fabric.

"Don't worry." Aimee led her to the bathroom.

Kitty locked the door behind her. She held on to the sides of the porcelain sink and lowered her head. What was happening to her? Was it guilt over questioning the widow, or the strong tea on an empty stomach? Whatever the case, she felt wretched.

Kitty stared into the mirror. A hollow-eyed stranger stared back.

She opened the door to the medicine cabinet. Her reflection gave way to rows of bottles and jars, tooth powder, body powder, and various hair and body lotions. Nothing to soothe her nausea.

Hunter Cole's things lined the shelf above: shaving soap, a razor, witch hazel, a jar of hair pomade, and a black toiletries case.

"Are you all right, Miss Weeks?" Aimee called through the closed door. "Is there anything I can do for you?"

"I'll just be a minute." Kitty stood on tiptoe and pulled down the case of toiletries. She undid the clasps and peered inside: gauze, cotton balls, and a bottle of bitters. She reached for it and felt a hard bundle wrapped in chamois beneath her fingers.

Kitty pulled out the bundle and found herself staring at six glass vials filled with clear liquid, and a hypodermic syringe. There was no needle.

"Miss Weeks?" It was Aimee again.

Kitty's heart beat wildly. She had a moment in which to decide her next step. She dropped one of the vials into her skirt pocket, wrapped the rest away, took a swig of the bitters, and replaced the case in the cabinet. She rinsed the stain from her shirt, then dried her face and hands and joined Mrs. Cole outside, her heart still pounding.

"I'm sorry to keep calling," Aimee apologized, "but you looked pale, and I was worried."

Kitty couldn't bear her own duplicity any longer and took leave of the widow.

"So soon?" Aimee seemed disappointed. She walked Kitty to the elevator.

"May I ask whether Mr. Cole had been ill recently?" Kitty broached the question while they waited for the machine.

"No. Did you hear that somewhere?"

"I probably misunderstood." Kitty's hand rested against the tube in her skirt pocket. Could this be why Dr. Albert wasn't listed in the telephone book?

Chapter Twelve

The Misses Dancey, Kitty's teachers from her Swiss boarding school, were a pair of British sisters with strict ideas about decency and decorum. Kitty knew that becoming a reporter would strain what she'd been taught and how she'd learned to conduct herself, but it wasn't until that moment in the Coles' apartment that the rules she followed unthinkingly for the most part were put to the test.

It was rude to snoop through other people's belongings. Then she stole Hunter Cole's vial. There was no other way to put it. She had taken the tube without asking his widow's permission.

The question was what to do now that she had it.

The liquid in Kitty's pocket seemed to get hotter with every step she took, as though it might burn a hole through the fabric. She could throw it away and pretend none of this ever happened, or she could take it to the chemist and find out what it contained.

Kitty felt awful. How would she feel if someone poked around in her medicine cabinet and took one of her potions to be analyzed? However, the truth of the matter was that she didn't have any secrets, she assured herself.

If she heeded the dictates of her conscience, she would never amount to much as a journalist. If she didn't, she might learn something worthwhile, but at what price?

Recently, the yellow papers—the ones that ran shocking headlines in order to sell the news—had been full of stories about Harry Thaw being a dope fiend. It was part of their bid to whet the public's appetite for his upcoming trial, which would take place shortly, almost a decade after the initial trial that had been covered so colorfully by the Sob Sisters: A poor, pretty girl comes to New York. A powerful architect takes advantage of her. Later, she marries the millionaire Thaw who, in a fit of jealousy, shoots the architect on the rooftop of his own creation, Madison Square Garden.

There were some clear similarities between the Thaw case and the Hunter Cole shooting but also obvious differences. For one, Hunter wasn't rich like Thaw, and it was he who had been murdered. And for another, Kitty hadn't heard anything about Aimee Cole having been taken advantage of. Then again, with Mrs. Cole's past, anything was possible.

Kitty walked up Broadway, one of the few avenues that didn't follow the right-angled grid and instead cut across Manhattan on a diagonal. On the way home, she would pass Murray & Son pharmacy on Broadway and Seventieth.

Thaw's addiction to morphine and opium and who knew what other drugs fueled his violent and unpredictable behavior. Even though Kitty had no other evidence to support such a theory, given Hunter Cole's vials and syringe, dope addiction was a possibility worth considering. It might shed a completely different light on his murder.

Kitty passed the greengrocer and the stationery shop and paused in front of the pharmacist's. A bell tinkled as she opened the door.

"Good morning, Miss Weeks." Mr. Murray Sr. poured a quantity of fine white powder onto a set of scales. "I'll be with you in a moment." He adjusted the counterweights, tipped the powder onto a sheet of wax paper, deftly divided it into seven equal portions with his scraper, and wrapped each portion into individual sachets.

"One a day after breakfast, dissolved in a glass of milk or water." He scooped the sachets into a brown paper bag, which he handed to his customer, a portly, middle-aged woman.

"Thank you, Mr. Murray. My heartburn has been giving me no end of trouble."

"That's what I'm here for, madam." The pharmacist turned to Kitty. "How can I help you today, Miss Weeks?"

In addition to medicinal preparations, his shop carried a variety of household supplies, soaps, and beauty remedies, and Kitty often stopped by to pick up one thing or another.

Kitty made up a list as quickly as she could. "I'll take phenyl, Albi-Denta tooth soap, cough syrup, and some Aspirin."

"Good, good. Anything else?" He repeated the names of the items one by one, and from the storeroom at the back, unseen hands tossed them out to him.

"Do you have something for freckles? Not for me—it's Grace again."

"You tell that girl of yours that preparations with arsenic won't do her any good."

"I've tried, Mr. Murray. I've tried."

"This just came in." He scanned the shelves and pulled down a small bottle. "White Lily Face Wash." The pharmacist put on his glasses and read from the label: "'Guaranteed to brighten the skin and smooth out wrinkles, roughness, freckles, and imperfections. Free of lead, arsenic, and mercury.' It'll run you ninety-five cents for four ounces."

"That's fine. What's this?" She glanced at her purchases and picked up a tiny sealed package marked with a cross and the word *Bayer* in bold letters.

He laughed. "The company doesn't want us dispensing the Aspirin powder anymore, so now they make their own pills. It comes directly from their factory so that you can be sure you're purchasing the real thing."

"I trust you, Mr. Murray. Oh, there is one other matter." Kitty reached into her pocket. "I found this in my medicine chest, and the label seems to have fallen off." She placed the vial on the counter. "For the life of me, I can't remember what it is. I was hoping that you might be able to tell me."

The druggist held the container up to the light. "This is good quality," he said, tapping the glass. "Top quality, as a matter of fact. Very sturdy. Did you happen to purchase it in Europe?"

"I'm not sure. Why?"

"Oh, it's nothing," the old man replied. "I was just curious. We really don't see this type of thing here."

He tugged at the stopper, and a shining globule of the liquid fell on the back of his hand as the cork came free with a jerk. Kitty watched as he brought the drop to his nose and inhaled deeply. Then he put out his tongue and licked his hand.

Kitty gasped.

"Don't you worry about me, Miss Weeks." The pharmacist seemed amused. "Belladonna, arsenic, sulfur, lead—you name it, I've tasted it, and nothing has gone wrong with me yet."

He patted his belly with satisfaction. "I think I know what you have here. The scientific name for it is dihydrogen monoxide."

"What is that?" It sounded fearsome.

"Di-hy-dro-gen mon-ox-ide," the pharmacist repeated, clearly enunciating each syllable. "Water, Miss Weeks," he chortled, pleased with his little joke. "It's just water. H_2O. Whoever sold it seems to have cheated you." He was about to tip out the contents when Kitty stopped him.

"Please don't!"

Puzzled, he returned the vial, and she tucked it away inside her purse. "I'd like to hold on to this as a reminder not to be so foolish."

She picked up her packages and left the shop disappointed by Mr. Murray's verdict.

Hunter Cole could have had no reason to store test tubes of *water* in his toiletries case. Either he had been misled about what the vials contained, or—and she thought this highly unlikely— the pharmacist didn't know his business.

CHAPTER THIRTEEN

"Capability!" Julian Weeks yelled for Kitty as she emerged from her bedroom the next morning, still in her night-gown and robe since she didn't have to go to work. She had hidden the dratted vial in her bureau drawer (out of sight, out of mind, she thought) and woken up early, eager to find out what the *Sentinel* had printed about the stable hand who allegedly murdered Hunter Cole; she then planned to begin her study of *The American Girl*.

But Mr. Weeks had other ideas. "Are you awake? Come to my study."

She padded in to find him sitting at his desk, scowling and tossing his paperweight from one hand to the other.

"Have I done something wrong, Papa?" Kitty felt a frisson of anxiety. Perhaps he'd guessed that she had been in his study the other day.

"I'm not pleased," he said finally.

"Why, Papa?"

"Take a look at this." He pushed an envelope across the desk.

Kitty picked it up and removed two, two-by-two-inch square photographs. A hatless, expressionless man and young woman stared blankly into the camera. "That's you and me?" she said after a moment. "I almost didn't recognize us."

"Exactly." Mr. Weeks slammed the paperweight on his desk. "What's the point of it, then?"

Kitty sighed.

"And in addition to that infernal photograph, which is no identification as far as I'm concerned, they want me to complete this." He handed her a document. "The other side."

She flipped it over. It was the passport form that Prentiss had partially completed. The second half required a written description of the applicant's physical features.

"Who's going to vouch for you?" Kitty glanced at the Proof of Identity section; the witness had to be an American citizen known to the applicant for several years. "One of your lawyers?"

"I'll find someone." Mr. Weeks handed her a pen. "All right, let's begin."

"You want to do this now?" Kitty hadn't even had a sip of tea.

"Let's get it over with. What's the first one, stature? That's easy. Six feet." He picked up the paperweight again and rolled it between his hands as he waited for her to fill in the blank. "Next."

"Forehead."

"Forehead?"

"That's right."

"What do they care about my forehead?"

"What do you want me to fill in?" Kitty said. "Broad? High? Noble?"

"That's not funny. Just keep it simple."

"All right, broad. Now, eyes."

"Brown."

"Nose."

"Ha! Broken."

"Really? I would have said crooked."

"Broken," he repeated. "In a brawl."

"I had no idea."

"Well, yes. What's next?" He leaned forward. "Mouth? Let's put medium."

"Chin?" Kitty said.

"Square."

"All right. And I'll put hair—black. Complexion—olive. And face—square again? I'm afraid I'm not very good at this."

"You're better than I am."

Kitty finished writing and blotted the sheet.

"Thanks for your help." He sounded grudging.

"You're welcome." She returned the paper and stood.

"It's all a meaningless charade," he muttered under his breath and then asked, "By the way, did I tell you a business acquaintance will be joining us for dinner tonight?"

"No, you didn't." They rarely had guests.

"Sorry about that. Will you see to the menu?"

Kitty went to speak to Mrs. Codd and then to breakfast. The morning's copy of the *Sentinel* lay folded beside her place with a prominent headline: BERLIN SHUNS LIABILITY FOR *LUSITANIA* SINKING, OFFERS ALTERNATE PROPOSALS FOR THE SAFETY OF AMERICANS.

How much longer would the president and German officials go back and forth on the subject, Kitty wondered before turning to the inside of the paper. The story she was looking for,

"Country Club Shooter Arrested," appeared below the fold on page seven.

Marcus Lupone, a twenty-one-year-old stable hand and recent arrival to New York City from Sicily, was found in a shed by the banks of the Connecticut River where he had been hiding since early Tuesday morning, following the shooting death of Mr. Hunter Cole at the Sleepy Hollow Country Club.

Prior to his employment at the country club, Mr. Lupone had worked at the Aqueduct Racetrack, which was where, police say, he first became acquainted with the victim. It is believed that he was fired from the racetrack for colluding with book-makers and that he managed to secure his position at the coun-try club by providing the management with forged letters of reference as well as a false name—Lipton. He also shaved off his mustache in order to avoid being identified, but while walk-ing about the grounds, Mr. Cole recognized him nonetheless and this, in turn, led to their fatal encounter during the July Fourth fireworks.

Kitty recollected spotting the Coles strolling near the stables before the party began; she read on to learn that the police had questioned Lupone when they arrived at the club after the shooting and that he fled the scene only afterward. Because of the recent mishap at the jail in Mineola—where Mr. Morgan's attacker had committed suicide—Lupone would be held in custody at the infamous Tombs prison in Manhattan.

Mr. Weeks joined Kitty at breakfast. "Aren't you going to work?" He took his seat at the head of the table.

"Not today. I'm interviewing Miss Anne Morgan on Monday, so I have the day off to prepare."

He shook out his napkin. "*The* Miss Anne Morgan?"

Kitty nodded.

"My, my." His grin had a touch of amusement to it. "You are moving up in the world."

She reached for the caddy and spread a pat of butter on her toast. Something about the police's case against the stable hand troubled her.

On the surface, it all sounded reasonable enough—false identity, discovery, altercation—but Flanagan seemed to be pushing the Sicilian angle as though the facts alone weren't sufficient. He concluded his article with a quote from the commissioner of corrections, Dr. Katharine Bement Davis, who said that over half of those confined in the murder cells at the Tombs had Italian names. "'I have been in Italy,' Dr. Davis said, 'and especially, I have been in Sicily. Sicilians bring with them their own primitive ideas of vengeance when they migrate to this country.'"

Marcus Lupone probably didn't have very many friends here, Kitty thought, taking a bite of toast. More than likely, his English wasn't good. Perhaps, once he realized that Mr. Cole had been murdered and the police would be questioning everyone, he panicked and fled. He understood that he would be an obvious suspect. But to the police, his act of self-preservation would only make him seem that much more suspicious.

Grace came in with a message for Mr. Weeks. "Rao says the Packard has to be taken to the mechanic this morning, sir."

"What's the matter?"

"He didn't tell me, sir. At least, he said something about the oil, but I didn't understand."

"I see." Julian Weeks let out a deep breath and turned to Kitty. "I hate to ask, but would you drive me downtown?"

"What time do you need to be there?" she said.

"By ten."

That meant she wouldn't be able to start reading until eleven at the earliest.

"You don't have to wait," Mr. Weeks said. "You can drop me off and come straight back."

Normally, she would have been happy to oblige him, but still she hesitated.

"This isn't a request, Capability." His tone was sharp. "I have a meeting to attend."

"Of course." Kitty pushed back her chair. His needs came first.

CHAPTER FOURTEEN

The Bearcat wouldn't start. It sputtered to life when Kitty turned on the electric ignition and then went dead in a couple of seconds.

"What's the matter now?" Mr. Weeks drummed his fingers impatiently against the leather seat.

Kitty stepped out of the car, removed her gloves, and lifted the hood. "Just some leaves." She pulled them out and dusted off her hands.

This time, the engine roared. Kitty made sure her hat was securely fastened with her silk scarf and stepped on the gas. With a lurch, the vehicle surged forward.

Wind on her cheeks, she sped past other automobiles on West End Avenue. Ladies used to be relegated to electric motors since they were slower, cleaner, and safer, but no longer. These days, almost everyone drove gasoline-fueled cars. The Bearcat had no sides or doors and no top, just two leather chairs, the driver's controls, and a jaunty round monocle windscreen behind the hood. Kitty loved the sensation of being in control of such a powerful machine and the thrill of being completely exposed to the elements.

Julian Weeks held his hat in his lap and his cigar clamped between his white teeth. Stronger, braver men might have quaked at some of his daughter's maneuvers. She swerved around a horse-drawn cart and raced past a tram coming around the bend, its bells clanging. Through it all, she maintained good form, sitting confidently upright in her seat, neither looking stiff nor slouching behind the wheel, as her instructor, Mr. Berriman, had informed her that "certain classes of motorists" were wont to do.

While motor-vehicle owners didn't have to pass a test to operate their vehicle, Kitty knew the rules: She must not drive while intoxicated. She should stop after an accident. She must signal with her hand before making a turn and should remain within the speed limit or else face a penalty of up to one hundred dollars.

"Who are you meeting today?" she asked her father after several blocks.

"Someone from out of town."

Julian Weeks didn't seem in a particularly talkative mood. Kitty didn't mind since she enjoyed just being in his company, and besides, she needed to have her wits about her to negotiate the chaos that came with driving through Manhattan on a weekday morning. Mr. Weeks's destination, the Edelweiss Café on the southern tip of Manhattan, obliged them to drive through some of the most congested parts of the city and negotiate shoppers with packages, rushing businessmen, and peddlers pushing carts, not to mention other motorcars and autobuses.

The right-angled grid gave way to the city's original winding paths, now paved over and flanked by commercial buildings like the Morgan Bank and the U.S. Sub-Treasury as the Bearcat neared Mr. Weeks's destination. Wall Street, so called because it had once been the site of a wall built by early settlers to defend themselves from the natives, was now the nation's—if not the world's—financial hub. The sun barely penetrated the valleys where pedestrians and motorcars inched along on narrow roads, hardly suited to their present heavy use.

Kitty pulled up at the corner of the block where the café was located and let her father out.

"Thanks, Capability." He patted her shoulder and stepped out of the vehicle. She watched him disappear into the sea of businessmen on the sidewalk.

It was all men, Kitty realized as she retied her head scarf. Men in suits, men with sleeves rolled up, men hurrying along as though civilization depended on their efforts, and men loitering—like those two fellows in dark suits with newspapers under their arms who hurriedly looked away when she noticed them staring at her.

There wasn't another woman in sight. All at once, Kitty felt vulnerable and ill at ease in her bright yellow motorcar. She switched on the engine and drove past the café, then turned right at the end of the street and right again, thinking she would be headed home. Instead, within a few blocks, it became clear that she had no idea where she was going.

A sense of panic threatened to overwhelm her, and she slammed her palm against the steering wheel. That was what came from doing a favor. Kitty hated losing her bearings and had no internal compass. It appeared that she only managed as well as she did because of the city's grid. Take away her usual markers, and she was lost.

She didn't slow down to read the signs on the lampposts. She turned right, then left, then right again. Nothing looked familiar. The eerie sounds of an Oriental violin led her to believe she might be close to Chinatown and the police headquarters.

She drove past a group of men gathered on the sidewalk. One grabbed his crotch and called out something crude. Kitty stepped on the gas, made a sharp turn, and escaped down a quiet street. She allowed the motor to coast while she caught her breath. New York had never seemed so ominous.

Something at the end of the road caught her eye. Of its own accord, the Bearcat rolled forward.

A covered stone bridge floated above the street. It spanned the distance between a redbrick building and a forbidding structure with turrets on top and slit-like windows. Kitty had seen this view depicted in postcards: this must be the infamous Bridge of Sighs connecting the criminal courts to the Tombs prison.

Kitty's hands clenched around the wheel. These thick walls right in the middle of Manhattan held thousands of prisoners, condemned men and women packed into cold, damp cells without adequate sunlight or ventilation. She'd heard horrible stories about the place. That it had been built on the site of the old Collect Pond, which was once Manhattan's source of fresh water and later became so polluted from the waste of nearby abattoirs and tanneries that it had to be filled in. That the prison's foundations started to sink into the sludge from the moment construction began, and that vestiges of the old waterways still trickled beneath it, leading inmates to claim that the entire building swayed in sympathy with the East River.

A whistle's sudden blast nearly deafened Kitty.

"Didn't you hear me, madam?" an irate policeman barked. "Move on. There's no sightseeing permitted here."

"I'm sorry." Kitty hadn't realized she'd been gawking. "Am I correct that this is the Tombs?"

"That's right." He folded his arms across his chest. "Murderers, thieves, the worst of the worst. They're all holed up in there." He nodded with satisfaction. "It's no place for a young lady like yourself."

It was no place, Kitty thought, for the stable hand Marcus Lupone either. "Do they bring inmates over in the mornings?"

"At all hours."

"I think I may have a friend inside."

"You may?" The policeman seemed skeptical.

"I do." Kitty had read stories of wives going into the prison to see their husbands, mothers delivering food to their sons. "Are visitors allowed inside?"

"Ye-es," the policeman said hesitantly.

"Could I go to see him?"

The policeman looked at her with incredulity. "You're sure you'd want to go in there?"

"Should I be afraid?"

"No, no. It's perfectly safe for the rest of us. Who is it that's inside anyway?"

"His name is Lupone."

The officer shook his head. "Never heard of him, but park your vehicle over there"—he pointed to a vacant area—"and follow me."

"Ah—" Kitty had asked about visiting out of curiosity. She hadn't expected to succeed.

"You want to come back tomorrow? The place is packed on Saturdays."

"I see."

"Just leave your car right there." He chuckled. "I promise no one will steal it."

Kitty turned off the engine and followed him to the prison like a sleepwalker. She gave the guard at the front desk her name, stated the purpose of her visit—to see Mr. Lupone—and signed her name and time and date of entry in a thick ledger.

The policeman left her, and she waited on a wooden bench, beginning to regret her impulsive decision. What would she say to Hunter Cole's alleged killer? Since he didn't know her from Adam, how would he react? Would they bring her to his cell?

Two guards led a shuffling prisoner by, his shackles clanking on the floor. His face was bruised and battered.

Kitty stood. This was too much. Had she lost her mind? She should leave this minute.

"This way, please." A bored-looking guard with a circle of keys hanging from his belt beckoned.

"Oh dear," Kitty said.

"Scared?"

She nodded.

He laughed. "They're just criminals."

She followed the man down a gloomy, mildewy hall. She heard footsteps, prisoners' voices. She could be killed in here—or worse. And no one would know.

They turned the corner and came to a row of doors. The guard unlocked one and motioned for Kitty to step over the threshold.

"I should go inside?"

"I'll be with you."

She didn't like the look on his face. "Where is Mr. Lupone?"

"He's on his way."

"I prefer to wait outside until he arrives."

"Suit yourself."

Kitty drew herself up straight. "I'm a reporter with the *New York Sentinel*."

The guard smirked. "And they let you in?"

"Yes, they did." Kitty hoped she sounded firm.

Lupone soon arrived, escorted by another guard, his hands cuffed behind him. "Who is this?" he asked in thickly accented English. A mop of dark curly hair fell over his forehead.

"Why don't you both wait outside?" Kitty told his guard. "I'd like to speak to Mr. Lupone on my own."

The guard snickered. "Very pretty for your first visitor, Marcus. Don't pretend you don't know her."

Bruises darkened the stable hand's neck and one side of his face. The guard pushed the door open. A single lightbulb hung from an electric wire above two chairs and a table.

Lupone lowered himself into one. The door closed behind them. "Who are you?" he said.

"I'm here from the newspapers," Kitty replied. "I'd like to help you."

"I no do anything, lady," Lupone said. "I no shoot anyone. You help get me free."

"Can you tell me what happened the evening Mr. Cole was shot, Mr. Lupone?" Kitty couldn't believe how composed she sounded. Just like a professional.

"I take everyone out of stables like Mr. Cole say."

"He *asked* you to take the other lads out?"

"*Si.*"

"When? That afternoon?"

"No, no. A few days before. I meet him outside, and he say, 'Marcus, on Monday, at the party, take all the lads to see the fireworks.'"

"Did he tell you why he wanted everyone out?" Kitty had conjectured correctly. Hunter Cole hadn't just strolled down there; he'd had a plan. A plan to meet someone. His killer, no doubt. He may have been concerned about the meeting, which was why he'd brought the pistol to Mrs. Basshor's do.

Lupone shook his head. "Mr. Cole tell me nothing."

"But you weren't surprised to see him at the club on the day of Mrs. Basshor's party?" If Lupone was telling the truth, the police's case against him no longer made sense.

"Of course, no. I know he was coming."

"Did you tell the police?"

"They no believe me! But why I kill Mr. Cole? He a very nice man."

It was the first time Kitty heard anyone say that. "Do you have proof that Mr. Cole met you before the party? Did anyone see you talking to him?"

"I no think so."

Kitty believed him. "But you were working at the club under false pretenses."

Lupone looked confused.

"You made up a false name when you worked at the club."

"Sure. I try to be English, but I no kill anyone." He leaned toward her. "Signorina, you find me a lawyer."

"I'll try," Kitty said. "I'm just a reporter." She knew it was a weak excuse when a man's life was on the line.

"I understand." Lupone's handsome face turned fierce. "You only want to speak to me for story."

Embarrassed and ashamed, Kitty had no reply.

"Guard," he called. "Guard!"

The door swung open.

"I finished." He rose to his feet.

"So fast?" The jailer winked.

Kitty felt dirty from the way he leered at her. Lupone's guard led him one way, and the other man led Kitty toward the entry hall. Before they reached it, he turned and held out his hand.

He expected a tip. Kitty gave him a dollar. Anything to get out. The hand didn't budge. She put in another.

Minutes later, Kitty was back on the street. She felt inexpressibly relieved to have made it out of the prison in one piece and didn't blame the stable hand for feeling used.

She asked a passerby for directions and started the Bearcat. She would make it up to Lupone. She wouldn't be able to hire him a lawyer, but she could find the evidence to prove his innocence.

CHAPTER FIFTEEN

Back at the apartment, Mrs. Codd was busy preparing dinner, and Grace had set the table for their guest. Kitty said she'd take a sandwich in her rooms for lunch and hurried off to shower. She scrubbed her body and washed her hair and then soaked in the tub until she felt she had released every last bit of grime from the prison. She cleaned inside her ears and brushed her teeth. Then she changed into a comfortable robe and ate her sandwich while Grace brushed her hair. It was nearly three o'clock. Kitty had a few hours left before their visitor arrived. Her father hadn't yet returned.

She sat at the desk in the bedroom that she had converted into a private workroom for herself and began to read. Anne Morgan opened her first chapter, titled "Her Education," with a question:

How can the girl of America be prepared and prepare herself for all that life will bring to her? How can her secret garden best be planted and watered, so that its soil may bring forth an ever-growing beauty of blossom and fulfillment, and its shady walks and running brooks bring rest and inspiration to the weary traveler along the road of life?

By way of an answer, Miss Morgan turned to her own

experience of the American girl abroad—a type she'd had
ample opportunity to witness in action, she said, pointing out
that it was sometimes possible to make accurate deductions
about a whole class based upon the careful observation of a few
"isolated specimens."

It has interested me exceedingly to observe the American girl
who lives abroad, insignificant numerically though she is, and
to note that notwithstanding her marvelous adaptability to her
surroundings she is still the American Girl, unlike any other
girl in the world.

Kitty liked the "notwithstanding her marvelous adaptability"
point—it reminded her of herself, both in New York and in
Switzerland. She read on, ready to be bowled over by Miss
Morgan's insight and candor.

No intelligent person can fail to remark how the qualities, both
desirable and unfortunate, which make her unique, are, after
all, American qualities.

Yes! But what were those qualities? Kitty hoped Miss Morgan
would enlighten her readers.

For generations, now, current literature has been filled with
descriptions of the American girl. We find her in English novels
as a wild, undisciplined creature, with a desire for every luxury and
a corresponding objection to any personal restraint. Germany
and France present her to the world as an unsexed primitive

force with an appendage of dollars, which should unquestion-
ably be used to reinstate financially some old and historic name.

Kitty smiled. No doubt the author spoke from personal
experience. On his death, her father, the first J. P. Morgan,
had left her three million dollars. It was a staggering amount
to bequeath to an unmarried daughter, especially when his
married daughters had received so much less. (The current J. P.
Morgan, Miss Morgan's brother, had received the lion's share
of his father's fortune.)

Kitty continued reading:

The internationalism of the American girl is far in excess of
that of any other nationality. Intermarriages always have existed,
and always will exist, but never, since the days of the barbarian
invasions, has one country supplied so many instances.

A good point—Consuelo Vanderbilt, Jennie Jerome, there were
so many examples—but it still wasn't the answer Kitty needed.

America is a country where, to its own undoing, individual-
ism has reigned supreme. The time has come when forces of
group conscience and group consciousness must be drawn up
in hostile array against the doctrine of individual egotism.
The American girl who seeks to avoid the inevitable conflict by
looking to European sanctuary is indeed deceived. She longs
for the finish and the beauty of the old order... She fails to
realize that it lies in her own hands to bring that same beauty
into her own surroundings.

Kitty shifted in her chair. When would Miss Morgan answer her own excellent question? What were the qualities, good and bad, that constituted the hallmark of an American girl?

Kitty flipped through the pages. Modern educators allow children to follow their own whims, they insist that the child must have complete freedom, so the girl "will rush with spasmodic enthusiasm into the mood of the moment."

Miss Morgan went on to discuss immigration and the need to teach foreigners to understand the responsibilities of American freedom.

Kitty heard her father enter the apartment.

"Capability," he called, "are you ready for this evening?"

She scanned through to the end of the chapter. While she agreed with many of Miss Morgan's shrewd observations, Kitty couldn't find a central thesis. And she couldn't see an answer to what made the American girl unique.

Kitty changed into a red gown and matched it with garnet-and-gold drop earrings and a garnet bracelet. She checked Grace's table setting and then joined her father in the living room.

"You look lovely." Mr. Weeks nodded his approval.

"Thanks." She smoothed her hair.

"I think you will like Mr. Maitland. He's Canadian. The smartest fellow I've met in a long time."

Coming from Julian Weeks, who was particular about the company he kept, that was quite a compliment.

Their visitor arrived soon enough. He had buttery skin like

a baby and must have weighed over two hundred fifty pounds. He could have been as old as forty or fifty, or perhaps as young as his midthirties. It was hard for Kitty to tell. His size and his flair—he tied his cravat with the élan of a Frenchman—made him seem ageless.

His twinkling blue eyes followed Kitty as she served drinks. He was quite the conversationalist and described—of all things—how the bubonic plague spread through China.

"A Chinese trapper contracted the disease through contact with the tarbagan, a furry creature native to Mongolia," he said. "Once infected and back in Harbin, he transmitted it to anyone who happened to be near him during his coughing fits. What amazes me is that that's all it took. All one needs is a single spark to start a fire—and one sick man can contaminate an entire nation."

Kitty poured herself a glass of sherry and listened intently as her father and his guest spoke about a variety of topics, from the Panama-Pacific International Exposition in San Francisco, to Viennese art and architecture, to last July's murder of the Austrian archduke that precipitated the war in Europe.

"It was only because of a series of errors and unlikely coincidences that the Serbian gang's ringleader, Gavrilo Princip, managed to do in Franz Ferdinand," Mr. Maitland declared, his deep voice rumbling.

Julian Weeks held his drink loosely in one hand, legs crossed at the knee.

"The archduke and duchess rode in their motorcade alongside the Appel Quay."

Kitty pictured the scene—the duke in his military garb with

medals at his chest, his adoring wife in her white dress and ornate hat, both waving to the crowds they passed.

"The first plotter threw a bomb, which landed on a car behind his target," Mr. Maitland continued. "The fool panicked and threw himself into the river, but the summer's sun had reduced it to a trickle, and so it was no trouble for the police to catch him.

"At that point, all should have been settled, everyone should have been safe, but in the confusion that ensued, the leader, Princip, ducked into a nearby coffeehouse. The motorcade changed its route, but somehow the archduke's driver hadn't been informed of the decision. He drove up a side street, following the original itinerary, when a general who was accompanying the royal couple ordered him to stop and turn the car around. But the street was too narrow, so all the chauffeur could do was to drive in reverse. Can you believe it? The heir to the Austrian Empire being driven backward down a narrow street after an attempt on his life had been botched just minutes ago!"

Kitty knew the outcome of the shooting—who didn't?—but hadn't heard this version of how it unfolded.

"In the coffeehouse nearby, Princip heard noises and stepped out to see what was happening. He couldn't believe his eyes. His targets were just feet away, crawling along like tortoises in their open car. He didn't hesitate. He raised his pistol, took aim, and fired. The archduke and duchess fell. At such close range, there was no chance of their survival."

"Do you think the war might have been avoided if the archduke hadn't been killed?" Kitty asked.

"He was a fool to visit on one of the holiest days in Serbia, a fool to visit while tensions in their empire ran so high, but no. I think anything could have set Europe off last summer. German, Russia, England, and France, all had been building up their weapons and armies and jumped on the opportunity to discharge them. If not the archduke's murder, they would have found some other pretext. And now each side has lost too much to call the whole thing off and admit that the war has been an unmitigated disaster."

Grace knocked on the door to the living room and looked in. Someone had telephoned for Mr. Weeks.

"At this hour?" He didn't seem pleased.

"He said it was urgent, sir."

Julian Weeks excused himself to take the call, leaving her alone with his guest.

"Your father tells me you plan to become a journalist, Miss Weeks." The big man took a sip of his drink and stared at her so intently that Kitty didn't know where to look.

"I hope so." She smoothed the folds of her gown. "Right now, I work for the Ladies' Page of the *New York Sentinel*."

"I own shares in a paper in Canada, the *Star-Journal*—it's a daily. The editors there tell me that female reporters, thanks to their tact and intuition, catch stories that the men miss."

"You should tell that to our publisher." Kitty kept her tone light. "He doesn't allow women to step foot inside the newsroom."

"Well, I'll leave that for him to discover, but I'm sure both he and you are aware that your sex are the most powerful force behind any newspaper."

"How is that the case?"

"It's quite simple. Advertising brings in more revenue than subscriptions or direct sales. The most frequent advertisers are the department stores and other merchants whose clientele is primarily female. I assume that the situation is only more pronounced here in the United States."

"Why are women's stories confined to a single page then?"

"Because most newspapers are still obliged to report the news, by which I mean politics and foreign affairs," Maitland replied. "And I don't believe female readers care for that kind of information… May I be forward with you, Miss Weeks?" The big man set down his glass.

Kitty nodded.

"I'd like to invite you to accompany me to the Cloisters Museum before I return to Toronto. It opened last year, and I haven't yet had a chance to visit."

Kitty opened her mouth and shut it again.

"What's that you say, Maitland?" Julian Weeks returned to the room.

"I just invited Miss Weeks to join me on a trip to the Cloisters Museum—that is if you don't object. You're welcome to join us," the big man said.

"I don't care for that sort of thing, but I don't mind if Capability goes." He turned to Kitty. "It's getting late. Would you check on dinner, my dear?"

Relieved not to have to reply at once to Mr. Maitland's offer, Kitty excused herself. She wondered about his intentions. Given the difference in their ages, he couldn't possibly think—

She fiddled with her bracelet, then looked in on Mrs. Codd. All burners were on, and dinner would be ready soon.

She and Grace made a final examination of the dining table. The corners of the starched damask tablecloth hovered a few inches above the floor, each cover had been set with geometric precision, the starched napkins seemed to float on the plates, and the polished silver reflected the light from the candles placed on either side of the centerpiece.

Mr. Maitland and Mr. Weeks joined Kitty in a few minutes, and then Grace brought out course after course in leisurely succession. Mr. Maitland ate heartily and maintained a steady stream of conversation throughout the meal. If he had any particular interest in Kitty, he hid it well.

She left the two men to their cigars and brandy after dessert and had a cup of coffee in the pantry while Grace washed and dried the dishes and put them away in the cabinet.

"I've never seen anyone eat so much," the maid exclaimed.

"He has quite an appetite," Kitty agreed.

Grace giggled. "I pity his wife."

"I don't think he's married," Kitty said, surprised by the sharpness in her own tone.

It was close to midnight when Mr. Maitland left. Kitty had already said her good-byes and was in bed when she heard the front door close.

She lay under the covers, mulling over the day: Mr. Maitland, Miss Morgan's book, her visit to the prison. As she drifted to sleep, one question nagged at her: What to do about Lupone's revelation that he had known that Mr. Cole would be at the stables.

"Maitland seems to have taken a shine to you," Mr. Weeks said when Kitty joined him at breakfast the following morning. "I didn't expect him to invite you to the museum. Not that I'm worried, of course." He sipped his coffee. "I don't expect you to have any interest in a man like him."

"What kind of man is he?"

"You know. Older. And so large. I'm sure it causes health problems."

"He's a fascinating speaker."

"That he is, that he is."

Kitty helped herself to a slice of toast and changed the subject. "So what do the papers have to say about Germany's latest response to President Wilson's proposals on the *Lusitania*?"

Mr. Weeks picked up his copy of the *Times*. "They've printed the reply in its entirety. Would you like me to read it to you?"

"Just the gist," Kitty said.

Julian Weeks began:

"Berlin, July 9, 9 p.m. via London, July 10, 2:37 a.m. The text of the German reply to the American Note is as follows: On November 3, 1914, England declared the North Sea a war area, and by planting poorly anchored mines and by the stoppage and capture of vessels, made passage extremely dangerous and difficult... Long before the beginning of submarine war England practically intercepted neutral shipping to Germany. On November 14, the English Premier declared it was one of England's primary tasks to prevent food for the German population from reaching Germany through neutral ports. Since March 1—"

"I get the gist." Kitty laughed. "Not the full text."

"The gist is that Germany won't back down. They insist that Britain's actions have left them no other choice than to retaliate with submarines in order to be able to feed their people. Do you need Rao today?"

Kitty had decided to visit the country club and ask some questions on Lupone's behalf. "I thought I might go shopping at Altman's. But I can drive myself."

"All right." He returned to the paper. "This is really quite amazing," he murmured to himself.

"I should be back by three."

"Don't forget we have the concert this evening."

"Which concert?"

"At Carnegie Hall." Mr. Weeks enjoyed music and often bought tickets for performances without checking with Kitty first.

"Oh." That would cut into her time with *The American Girl*, but the longer it took to find any exonerating evidence, the less inclined the police would be to believe her. And while she was at the club, Kitty thought she may as well look into Mrs. Cole's whereabouts during the fireworks.

"Leaving so soon?" Julian Weeks asked as Kitty stood.

"I'd like to get an early start."

Her father frowned, puzzled. "What time does Altman's open on Saturday?"

"I'm not sure." To distract him, she added, "By the way, is Mr. Maitland a friend or business acquaintance?"

"A bit of both, I suppose. We might embark on a venture together."

"That's nice." She pushed in her chair. "What kind of venture?"

"Ah." He nodded. "If it turns out right, it could be very good."

Kitty studied the map and wrote out directions. She dressed for the day, called for her car, and drove to northern Manhattan, then on to the Bronx, past the Botanical Gardens, Fordham University, and Van Cortlandt Park. Fortunately, there were fewer streets here so fewer choices and fewer opportunities to lose her way.

She stopped once to have the car filled with gasoline, and then pulled up outside the Sleepy Hollow Country Club where a sign that she hadn't noticed previously informed visitors that the club was *Private Property* and *Trespassers Will Be Prosecuted*.

As if that would dissuade a criminal, Kitty thought, parking her car outside. She pushed in the gate and entered on foot.

With her parasol open, she roamed across the lawns as nonchalantly as though her father were a member. No one stopped her.

Kitty wandered over to the rear patio where a few elderly sorts with nothing else to do on a Saturday morning sipped tea or leafed through magazines and newspapers. Some of them may have looked up as she went inside, but no one asked any questions. She made her way to the ladies' room, only to discover that the woman on duty that morning wasn't the one who had been there on the evening of the murder.

Kitty washed her hands. "You weren't here for Mrs. Basshor's party on Monday, were you?" she said to the attendant who waited for her with a towel.

"No, ma'am. I'm only here on the weekends. Is there something that I can help you with?"

"Would you happen to know the name of the attendant who worked here that day? I think I may have lost my comb and was wondering if she found it."

The woman opened a cupboard and brought out a wicker basket for Kitty to inspect. "We keep all lost and found items here."

Kitty rummaged through the contents. "I'm afraid I don't see it. When will—what did you say her name is again?"

The attendant blinked. "It's O'Malley."

"That's right—O'Malley. And when will she be back?"

"On Monday. She works during the week."

"Of course, yes."

"If you give me your name, madam, I can ask her to keep an eye out for it."

Kitty had the feeling that the attendant sensed that something wasn't right, that she was neither a member nor a member's guest. She picked up her purse and dropped a few coins into the bowl. "That's quite all right. I'll be back again soon and ask her myself."

She hurried through the clubhouse and back out onto the patio. The sun was out, the trees rustled in the breeze, and the majestic Hudson River shimmered in the distance. Kitty recalled the scene at Mrs. Basshor's party. There must have been at least a hundred people out on this patio and on the lawns. A hundred guests, plus waitstaff and grounds staff, and kitchen staff and chauffeurs at the entrance. Any one of them could have murdered Hunter Cole.

When he was shot was clear: during the fireworks. Where was at the stables, how was with his own gun. The only questions that remained were why and by whom.

As far as Kitty was concerned, those questions hadn't been properly answered.

A horse-drawn cart clopped briskly down the driveway toward the front gate. A driver holding the reins urged the animal on; beside him, a gentleman clutched his hat and doctor's bag while the cart bounced up and down over the gravel. From where she stood, Kitty couldn't make out what was in the back, except that a large tarpaulin covered the mound.

Kitty walked on. A girl's voice called, "Thirty love," as she passed the tennis courts. The speaker wore a long white skirt, her shirtsleeves rolled to her elbows. She tossed a white ball into the air and smacked it across the net with her wooden racquet.

A young man in sharply creased white trousers lunged to return the ball. He hit it back, but it shot over the fence, and Kitty, who had it firmly in her sights, caught it in midair. The ball slipped from her hands, and she ran to pick it up again and tossed it back.

"Thanks," the man called.

"Thirty fifteen," the girl said, and play resumed.

She could have been that carefree girl. Kitty's chest tightened as she neared the stone stables. The yellow-brick building looked lovely with the summer sun hitting its tiled roof, and colorful pansies in planters hung from wrought iron hooks.

The police had their man, Kitty reminded herself. No one had asked her to come here—not even Lupone, trapped in prison.

Whatever the outcome of her visit, it would be on her own head. There would be no going back. She had already done much more than she ought to, with her trip to the Tombs.

She took a deep breath, put her hand against one of the heavy wooden doors, and pushed it open.

Chapter Sixteen

A dusty shaft of light filtered through a single window at the back of the barn and formed a puddle of brightness along the aisle between the two rows of stalls.

"*I'm on my way-way-way, To Mandalay-lay-lay…*" A young boy with knobby knees and a reedy voice sang and swayed in the circle of light, dancing with his broom.

"*Oh, let me live and love for aye, on that island far away.*" His eyes were closed, so he didn't notice Kitty watching. "*I'm sen-ti-mental—for my Ori-ent-al love, so sweet and gentle—*"

"Excuse me," Kitty interrupted, hating to break the moment.

The little lad swung around to face her just as a burly fellow in overalls emerged from the darkness of a stall, grooming brush in hand.

"G'morning, miss." He touched his cap. "Back to work, Turnip," he said to the boy. "And quit the warbling."

Kitty stepped forward gingerly, not wanting to tread on the spot where Hunter's body had lain. She had thought she remembered the area exactly, but now she wasn't sure, since all traces of the tragedy had been cleaned away. The place looked just like an ordinary stable ready for business.

"I was passing and thought I'd check in on the horses," she said.

"Are you an owner, ma'am?" The groom wiped his brow with the back of his sleeve. "Beg your pardon for asking, but only owners are allowed inside these days."

"New rule?" She tried to seem unconcerned.

"Don't know if you heard, but there was a murder on the premises."

"Ah, yes." Kitty nodded. "I was there. I'm a friend of Mrs. Basshor's."

Groom and boy exchanged nervous looks.

"Is something wrong?" Kitty asked.

The boy opened his mouth to speak, but the man silenced him with a glare. "I told you to get back to work, Turnip." His calloused hand reached out to stroke a velvety nose that poked out from a stall. "One of our animals fell ill and had to be seen to by the vet."

"Was that him in his cart I just saw?"

"That's right," he replied. "You're fine, girl. Just fine," he murmured to the horse he was petting and fed her a carrot.

"That must be hard after all that's happened. I heard that they caught the fellow who did it. He worked here?"

The stable hand stiffened. "He did."

"Was he a foreigner?" If the stable hands held any grudges against Lupone or thought he was guilty, her question might prompt them to talk.

"We guessed that, didn't we, Turnip?" the older man replied. "From his accent. Still, he wasn't a bad sort. Kept to himself."

"You must have noticed something." Kitty tried to probe. "Didn't you hear or see anything suspicious?"

"Well…" The groom took off his cap, scratched his head,

and put it back on. "Actually, no. He was a hard worker. Went away on his days off but always came back on time. We never had any trouble." Behind him, Turnip's head bobbed up and down in agreement.

"There wasn't anything suspicious about him at all? Did he know Mr. Cole from his previous employment?"

"That's what they're telling us. That Mr. Cole recognized him, and he would have lost his job—"

"Madam!" The door burst open, and a man in a blue pin-striped suit rushed in. "Madam," he said again, out of breath. For a while, it seemed to be the only word he could manage. "I'm Phillips, the club secretary," he added finally. "And you are?"

Kitty froze. "Miss Lodge." The only name she could think of on the spur of the moment was Elaine *Dodge*, the character played by Pearl White.

"She's a friend of Mrs. Basshor's," the groom offered.

"Well, Miss Lodge," said the club secretary, "I must inform you that only owners are allowed into the stables at this time and that all guests must be properly signed in at the front desk and be in a member's company for the duration of their visit. Is Mrs. Basshor expecting you? I don't believe I've seen her this morning."

"I'm afraid she isn't." Kitty didn't think it wise to lie any more than necessary.

The boy started to whistle.

"Stop that," Phillips said. He turned to Kitty. "I regret to tell you then—"

"That I must leave the premises." She finished his sentence.

"I know. I was in the vicinity and thought I'd stop in to see how things are going."

He bowed and held the door open for her. She passed through. "In the future, madam, please feel free to drive right up to the front. One of our porters will park your vehicle, and you are welcome to wait in the reception area until Mrs. Basshor is able to meet you."

Kitty felt three pairs of eyes following her as she made her way to her car. She walked a good fifty yards before she turned back to the stables.

"I'm sorry," she said to the secretary, who didn't seem too pleased to see her again. "May I take your boy to help me? Something got caught under my chassis and made the most terrible racket all the way over here. I thought he might be able to slide underneath and take a look."

"That's fine." He nudged Turnip. "Go on."

The boy hurried behind Kitty, and as soon as they were out of earshot of his superiors, he slid his hands into his pockets and started singing again: "*Sister Susie's sewing shirts for soldiers…*" It was another hit tune but faster and catchier than his previous choice.

"Such skill at sewing shirts our shy young sister Susie shows,
Some soldiers send epistles, say they'd sooner sleep in thistles
Than the saucy, soft, short shirts for soldiers sister Susie sews."

"That's excellent, Turnip." Kitty laughed at the tongue twister. "I wouldn't be able to manage it myself."

"I know you," the boy said. "You're not Miss Lodge. You're that lady from the papers, aren't ya?"

Kitty had the grace to blush.

"I was there the night Mr. Cole was killed. I saw you. You went all woozy, and Lewis brought you a stool."

"That's right."

"So what brings you back to our neck of the woods?" He seemed terribly confident for such a little fellow.

"I have some questions," Kitty said.

"It's gonna cost you, y'know. Five dollars, if you want to know what I know." He walked half a step behind her.

"Five dollars?" That was a lot of money. "What *do* you know?" she asked.

They approached the Bearcat.

"I know," the boy replied, "that if this is your car, you can afford it."

Kitty stifled a smile and pointed to the vehicle. "Slide under— they're watching us. Don't worry though. I'll pay you."

She stood beside the car with her back to the stables. "What can you tell me about Lupone?"

"Well, he was the one who said we should all go out to see the fireworks. Joe—the man you saw inside—wasn't feeling too good, but he dragged him out as well. Said it was a chance none of us should miss."

"I see." That matched what Lupone had told her. "And he was with you the entire time?"

The boy paused, and then said, "I can't be sure, but I think so. That's what we all said to the police anyhow."

"What's that—that he was with you, or that he wasn't?"

"That we thought he was but couldn't be sure. The coppers told us we were just sticking up for him. But that's not true. Lipton—I mean Lupone"—he corrected himself—"was one of us, but none of us would lie if we really thought he killed someone."

"And he disappeared later that evening?"

"That's right. After talking to the cops like the rest of us."

Kitty put five single dollar bills on the running board, and a second later, they disappeared. "Tell me, have you heard anything about Lupone speaking to Mr. Cole a few days before he was murdered?"

Turnip peered out from under the car. "No." Noticing her disappointment, he added, "You want to know something for free?"

"I wouldn't call it free. I just paid you!"

"Do you want to know or not?"

"I'm all ears."

"It's about Breedlove, Mrs. Basshor's pony. That's the one that took ill this morning. They put him down and carted him off before you could say Jack's your brother."

"What's wrong with that?" Kitty tied on her hat. The boy was just talking for the sake of talking now.

"It's just that they told us he stepped on a nail and was starting with tetanus, but I know that's not true." He looked aggrieved. "I sweep the stalls myself. There aren't any nails lying about."

Kitty agreed. The place seemed spotless for a barn. But Mrs. Basshor's pony's sickness had nothing to do with her.

"I think we're all set." She climbed into the car and waved at the club secretary who still watched her from the door to the stables. "They'll wonder what's taking you so long."

Turnip slid out from under the chassis. "Did you see the look on Mr. Phillips's face? He must be terrified that if word spreads about Breedlove, all the owners will take away their animals. Two deaths in one week."

"Two?" Kitty looked down at the boy.

"Mr. Cole and the pony."

"That's right." Kitty turned on the engine and drove away. Two deaths in one week. A man and a horse.

She shook her head. There couldn't be a connection.

CHAPTER SEVENTEEN

W hat do you think?" An hour and a half later, Kitty told Amanda what she had learned.

Amanda examined her reflection in the mirror and wrinkled her nose. "Too feminine." She returned the swatch of Liberty's fabric to the Altman's salesgirl. Then she said to Kitty, "How can Hunter's death have anything to do with a horse being put down?"

"I know."

"You're confused and clutching at straws." They strolled toward a bank of elevators.

Kitty hadn't told her friend about her trip to the Tombs. Amanda had been shocked enough that she drove up to the country club by herself. "You'll get a reputation," she had warned.

"Where to, miss?" The elevator operator held open the door.

"World bazaar," Kitty replied. At Altman's department store, she was on home turf. She knew the giant emporium, which occupied an entire city block, like the back of her hand. The trick was in understanding the logic to how the store displayed its merchandise: impulse purchases, like cosmetics, gloves, notions, small wares, and also men's apparel, were placed on the street level; ladies' ready-to-wear, millinery, lingerie, mourning, and other specialty items occupied the middle floors;

the topmost levels sold items that warranted a special trip, like home goods or the world bazaar; and groceries and discounted wares were buried in the basement.

"I'm glad we're here." Amanda linked her arm through Kitty's as they stepped out into a pavilion of colorful stalls. "And I'm glad Mama said I could join you."

"I am too." Kitty had wanted to run her thoughts by someone, and besides, she had to buy at least a couple of items, or else her father would never believe that she had spent her entire day shopping.

Kitty returned home by three as promised. She planned to bathe and then study for a couple of hours before the concert. The telephone rang as soon as Kitty put down her parcels.

Grace picked up the line. "It's for you, Miss Kitty," she said after a moment.

Kitty pressed the instrument against her ear.

"Miss Weeks?" It was Mrs. Basshor's secretary. "I must speak to you. This is urgent."

"How did you find my number, Mr. Hotchkiss?"

"I asked the operator. You're the only Weeks on the west side of Manhattan, so I thought it must be you."

Kitty checked her watch. "I don't have much time, Mr. Hotchkiss."

"Please, Miss Weeks."

She could sense the anxiety in his voice. "Go ahead."

"Did you talk to Mrs. Cole?"

"I did, and she told me that she went to the powder room for a few moments during the fireworks."

"I see. And you didn't happen to say anything about me? That it was I who told you that she went missing?"

"No, I did not." Time was ticking away. Kitty wished the secretary would stop beating about the bush.

"I think she found out somehow." He sounded distressed. "She suggested as much when I saw her at Mr. Cole's funeral. I accompanied Mrs. Basshor to Connecticut."

"Well, I can assure you that I never said anything."

"I appreciate it, Miss Weeks."

Kitty heard Mrs. Basshor calling in the background. "Hotchkiss," she trilled in an insistent tone. "Hotchkiss."

"I'm finished," Hotchkiss whispered. "Finished."

"I don't understand, Mr. Hotchkiss. Did Mrs. Basshor find out that you came to see me? Will you lose your job?"

"It's much worse than that." The line went dead.

The secretary's woes weren't her problem, Kitty told herself as she hurried back to her rooms. She asked Grace to bring in a cup of tea and raced through chapter 2, "Her Responsibilities."

"The girl must be a link in the chain of life… A woman's appeal…is supposed to be an emotional appeal. Let us accept the fact and glory in it. Let us train our girl's quick instincts and emotional reaction to be the biggest and best force in the community…"

Kitty scribbled notes furiously. There was much to discuss here.

"The eighteenth century brought to the world a deeper and better understanding of the rights of man; the nineteenth century has carried the message on; but it remains for the twentieth century to develop a new interpretation of the *duties*"—Kitty paid special attention to the phrase—"*rather than the rights of woman.*"

She began the third chapter, "Her Recreation," in which Miss Morgan described "developing the limited, class-conscious, or group-conscious girl into the socially conscious woman" and discussed the work of the National Vacation Committee, one of the branches of the Woman's Department of the National Civic Federation, in meeting the recreational needs of self-supporting women and girls. Kitty was halfway through the passage detailing how a fund had been created to help city girls rest from the stresses and strains of their everyday life when Grace knocked on the door.

"Mr. Weeks wants to know when you will be ready, Miss Kitty."

Kitty left her pencil in the book to mark her page. She would have liked to finish the section today. She washed her face, did her hair, and changed into a pearl-gray dress with lace around the neck and at the cuffs. Then she joined her father for a light supper before Rao drove them to the concert.

Carnegie Hall thronged with New York's finest. In a recent bit of busywork for Miss Busby, Kitty had counted the number of families who provided foreign addresses to the Summer Social Register, and compared the figure to the same time last year. In 1914, nine hundred families had left for Europe by May; this year, only two hundred had gone away by the beginning of June, and by the looks of it, the rest were here this evening.

On her way up to her seat, Kitty caught a glimpse of Mrs. Basshor in conversation with her friends, Poppy Clements with a man Kitty assumed was her husband, and other faces that looked familiar but she couldn't name—she must have seen them in the papers.

Kitty and Mr. Weeks took their places; she unfolded her mother-of-pearl opera glasses and scanned the crowd. Unlike her father, Kitty didn't care too much for classical performances and would much rather spend the concert watching people.

She spotted Amanda in a box diagonally opposite. Amanda wore a pretty sea-foam-blue gown, Mrs. Vanderwell was dressed in dark brown with a string of pearls around her neck, and Mr. Vanderwell sat beside them staring vacantly off into space and fanning himself with a program.

Kitty watched Amanda laugh and flirt with the two young men in the row behind her. She envied and admired the expert way in which her friend seemed to deflect their comments and managed being the center of attention. Kitty found that she became tongue-tied on the rare occasions when she was introduced to an eligible bachelor. The supreme self-confidence of the New York City man unnerved her, as well as his assumption that the world revolved around Manhattan, with a few forays to Harvard or Yale, Groton or Andover. She never knew what to say, and the harder she tried, the more stilted she sounded.

The orchestra started to tune up, and the lights dimmed. Kitty put away her glasses and glanced at the program: Mozart's Symphony No. 40 in G Minor, followed by Haydn's Concerto in D Major for Violoncello and Orchestra, then an intermission.

She wished she could have brought along Miss Morgan's book and read while they played, but even if the light had been sufficient, that wasn't the proper thing to do. She would have to sit through it all. She closed her eyes and dozed off. It had been a long day.

Mr. Weeks nudged her awake when the pieces ended. "Tired?" he said.

She smiled. "Who knew that shopping could be so exhausting?" She followed her father out, glad to stretch her legs.

"I say." A business associate approached Mr. Weeks.

"I didn't expect to see you here, Schweitzer," Julian Weeks replied and introduced the man to Kitty. "Are we settled, then?"

"Good to go, Mr. Weeks."

Kitty felt someone jolt her arm.

"I beg your pardon."

She found herself staring into friendly brown eyes framed by a pleasant face.

For a moment, Kitty thought she might have seen the man before, but she couldn't put her finger on the occasion.

"I hope you're all right," he said.

It had been just the slightest of bumps. "I'm fine, thank you."

He smiled, nodded, and moved on. Kitty wouldn't have minded prolonging their conversation, but she didn't know how, and clearly, he wasn't good at small talk either, or he had no interest in her.

She turned to watch him from the corner of her eye—he spoke to a friend, a stocky older man, then he seemed to glance her way. She instinctively avoided his gaze and pretended to be absorbed in a flyer from the previous night's show.

"What Miss Addams Learned about Peace in the War-Torn Nations—Hear It from the Eminent Emissary First-Hand!" the flyer said.

A woman behind Kitty spoke a few words in German. Kitty glanced over her shoulder. The speaker was a buxom, raven-haired beauty with sapphires cascading from her ears. When Kitty searched for him again, the personable young man had disappeared.

"*Er müsste längst da sein.*" He must be late, the woman said to her companion.

Kitty couldn't help listening in to the conversation. The woman had a piercing voice, and hearing German spoken aloud brought back a rush of nostalgia for her days in Switzerland.

"*Es ist eine lange Reise aus Washington,*" the woman's companion replied. "*Vielleicht hat Herr Doktor Albert seine Plan geändert.*"

Kitty caught her breath. Did the man just say that Herr Doctor Albert might have changed his mind because it was a long trip from Washington?

The woman asked him to check at the ticket booth downstairs.

"*Ja gerne,*" he replied.

"I'll be right back," Kitty said to her startled father and his business associate, who were deep in conversation. She followed the German-speaking gentleman.

She kept her eyes trained on the back of his head, determined not to lose him. He wore black tails just like every other man in the place, and she hadn't seen his face.

He made his way to the central staircase; Kitty noticed the pleasant-looking young man heading downstairs as well, a few paces behind him.

"Capability!" Amanda emerged out of nowhere with a girl-friend on either arm. "I've been looking for you."

"I'll be right back—I left something at the front door." Kitty couldn't afford to stop, but Amanda and her friends barred the way.

"Not so fast." Amanda smiled. "Not before I've introduced you to Miss Hibben and Miss Nicholls."

Kitty had no choice except to curtsy.

"Miss Hibben and Miss Nicholls will be joining me at the YWCA training." Amanda turned to her friends. "I'm trying to convince Miss Weeks to join us too."

"Please excuse me." The foreign gentleman had disappeared from Kitty's sights. She edged past the ladies and raced down the staircase, not caring what they or anyone else might think of her.

She reached the bottom of the stairwell, out of breath, but the foyer was empty. There was no one near the ticket booth, and even the pleasant-faced young man had vanished.

CHAPTER EIGHTEEN

Sunday morning brought extras with the news: cartoons, fashions, reviews, and queries. Kitty set aside "Doings and Sayings in the Real Estate World" and "Riverside Regatta Well-Patronized" and smiled at an advertisement in Apartments and Automobiles: "The Tires That Fell Off Looked like Goodyear Tires—at First." She browsed through the photograph pages, which featured the lavish interiors of the New Bankers Club of America at 120 Broadway that had completed its renovations to the tune of six hundred thousand dollars, an amazing sum of money.

"Where did you run off to during the intermission last night?" Mr. Weeks asked, neatly cracking the top from his soft-boiled egg.

"I lost my handkerchief."

"Must have been a pretty important handkerchief."

"Grace embroidered it for me." Kitty quickly finished her cereal. "I'd better get back to work."

"Preparing for the Morgan interview?"

"Yes." She took the napkin from her lap and dropped it onto the table. "By the way, is it true that Mr. Morgan loaned the British government one hundred million dollars to support its war efforts?"

"His bank did. Why do you ask?"

"I'd like to understand why he supports England."

"The family has connections there. Morgan spent years running the bank's London branch while his father dominated the American business scene."

Kitty returned to her rooms and finished "Her Recreation" before continuing on to "Her Future," Anne Morgan's final chapter.

Miss Morgan began feistily, observing that "the problem now facing the American girl is her utter inability to realize that her future can only be a logical development of her present."

A few pages later, she declared that the average girl has "the tools of reading, writing, and arithmetic…placed in her hands with such blunted edges that they are of little value, and the basic qualities of accuracy, concentration, thoroughness, and ambition are conspicuous by their absence."

Industry could only be improved when employer and employee worked side by side to reach a common end, "thus bringing about an additional financial return as well as a larger opportunity for development of the individual."

Kitty wondered what Miss Morgan's brother would make of that proposition.

Although eight million American women had entered industry, Miss Morgan claimed that girls still believed that "woman's duty is not to work, but simply to exist until such time as she can find someone who will work for her and support her parasitic existence. The harder her struggle the more she considers marriage as an ultimate goal where she can rest from her labors."

Too true, Kitty thought. Then again, not everyone had the

freedom and courage to buck expectations and remain unmarried like Miss Morgan and her cohort.

Grace looked in. "Mr. Weeks asks if you'll join him in the study."

"In a little while," Kitty replied. She reached the end of the chapter and then jotted down questions based on her notes. She would review and memorize them, but first, she took a break and went to see her father.

"Are you done?" he said. "How was it?"

"Stranger than I expected."

"In what way?"

"I agree with much of what Miss Morgan says, and then I find some of her points strange. For instance, she says that girls should have the courage to remold the circumstances in which we find ourselves, rather than seeking different problems elsewhere. And that we should have self-control and self-discipline so that we can take our place in the general scheme of the universe."

"A little self-control and self-discipline never hurt anyone," Julian Weeks said with a smile.

"She's forty-one and unmarried, Papa. She's traveled all over the world and does whatever she wants, and yet she advises girls to embrace the domestic feeling."

"And that's what you object to?"

"I don't see how she can make such a strong case for domestic life when she hasn't followed that path."

"There are some women," he replied, choosing his words with care, "who prefer to fulfill their domestic obligations in the company of other women."

"Do you mean the Versailles Triumvirate?"

"That's right." It was the term the press used to refer to Miss Morgan's living arrangement in France, where she had kept home with the theatrical agent Miss Elisabeth Marbury and Miss Elsie de Wolfe, now a well-known interior decorator.

"If she can live a carefree life, why do the rest of us have to settle down and marry?"

"You don't want to marry?"

"That's not the point."

"The point is that she has millions at her disposal in the bank, and most women don't."

"That's not fair," Kitty said.

"To whom?"

Kitty sprang to Anne Morgan's defense. "To her, as a matter of fact. She didn't have to write this book, and she didn't have to dedicate herself to public service."

"You could be right." Julian Weeks picked up his papers.

The telephone rang, and Mr. Weeks picked it up. "It's for you, Capability," he said. "Amanda Vanderwell."

"Really?" Mrs. Vanderwell never allowed Amanda to chat on the phone on Sundays. She thought it went against the spirit of the Sabbath.

"Is everything all right, Amanda?" Kitty said, speaking into the mouthpiece.

"You'd better sit down. You're not going to believe this."

"What is it? Are you engaged?"

"Hardly." Her friend's voice was dry. "Remember Hotchkiss, Mrs. Basshor's secretary?"

"Of course, I spoke to him yesterday."

"Well, one of Mama's friends called this morning. It seems that Hotchkiss has gone and killed himself."

CHAPTER NINETEEN

E xcuse me, Amanda." Kitty turned to her father. "Do you mind if I take this outside?"

He noticed her stunned expression. "What's wrong, Capability?"

"I'll tell you in a minute." She went to the foyer, picked up the receiver, and heard him hang up his line. "Are you sure?" she said to her friend.

"Certain as the day I was born. He didn't come to work this morning. So of course Bessie Basshor was distressed."

"He works seven days a week?"

"It seems so. Anyhow, she sent her chauffeur to his place in the Bronx. He had to break down the door and found Hotchkiss lying in the bathtub. The poor fellow was in his dress clothes, his shoes on and everything. He had slit his wrists. Apparently"— Amanda's voice shook—"the water was red with his blood."

"Oh my goodness." Kitty pulled up a chair and sat down. "Have the police been called? Do they know why he did it?"

"I think they have. I wanted to telephone you earlier, but I didn't get a chance. Bessie's fallen to pieces, so Mama has gone over, which is why I've been able to reach you. Do you think there could have been foul play?"

"Foul play?" Kitty struggled to make sense of things. What had Hotchkiss been so upset about when they spoke yesterday?

Amanda asked, "Maybe he knew who killed Hunter?"

"They're saying the stable hand shot Mr. Cole."

"Well, that can't be it then."

"Thank you for telling me, Amanda." Kitty hung up the line.

Throughout the day, she recalled snippets of her interactions with the secretary: how flustered he had seemed at the party, the gossipy manner in which he filled her in on all the guests. Meeting him in the silver-papered foyer to Mrs. Basshor's apartment. His conversation with her at the *Sentinel*. And finally, their telephone conversation yesterday.

Why hadn't she paid more attention? She had been so preoccupied about preparing for her interview that she couldn't recall exactly what he'd said.

He had told her that he was finished. What did that mean? Was it significant that he whispered it just as Mrs. Basshor called his name?

She pictured him fully clothed and floating in the bathtub in his own blood and screwed her eyes shut to drive away the image.

Had he left a note? Did he suspect that Mrs. Basshor might fire him? What could be worse than that?

The first thing that popped into Kitty's mind was that Mrs. Basshor had killed Hunter Cole and that the secretary was trying to protect his mistress. But she dismissed the thought at once. Someone would have noticed if the hostess had gone missing.

Kitty stared distractedly into her closet and finally chose a white pleated dress paired with a bolero-style velvet jacket to wear the next morning. She wrote down her questions and memorized key paragraphs and phrases from Anne Morgan's book.

Tomorrow's interview had lost some of its luster.

She arrived at the *Sentinel* the following day less rested and more agitated than she ought to have been, but Miss Busby didn't seem notice.

"Turn around. One more time." She put Kitty through her paces, scrutinizing her apprentice like a *maître de ballet* examining his prima ballerina.

"I like it." She nodded in approval at Kitty's choice of outfit. "Attractive yet no-nonsense. Just the right balance." She unscrewed her bottle and downed a spoonful of Rowland's.

They went over Kitty's notes, with Miss Busby muttering under her breath and making corrections. "I don't know about suffrage," she said, pausing at one of Kitty's notes. "It's controversial." Then she changed her mind. "Feel her out. If she's willing to reply, you can try asking."

They spent half an hour practicing Kitty's entrance and delivery. How she must talk and present herself. What to do if she forgot a question—ask for a glass of water. "Don't panic. It will come back to you," Miss Busby said. "And in the meantime, you will be surprised how much people talk to fill in the silence."

The clock on the editor's desk showed it was half past nine. "Are you ready?"

"I am now." Kitty felt like she was on the way to the gallows.

"Remember that you're from the *Sentinel*." Miss Busby clapped her on the back. "Hold your head high."

She accompanied Kitty downstairs and hailed her a cab. Just as Kitty was about to climb in, the editor reached into her purse and handed her a dollar for the fare.

"Thank you, Miss Busby," Kitty said.

The cab merged into the traffic.

Fifteen minutes later, it pulled up at the corner of Park Avenue and Sixty-Second Street beside a five-story marble-and-brick building with a mansard roof and pillared facade still partially covered by scaffolding. The Colony Club was a ladies-only establishment, of which Miss Morgan was a founding member. Kitty had heard that in order to join, one had to be either fabulously wealthy or fabulously accomplished.

"Are you Miss Weeks?" A businesslike woman hurried down the stairs. "I'm Daisy Rogers, Miss Morgan's secretary. Unfortunately, Miss Morgan has been detained, but I can give you a tour of our new premises while you wait."

Kitty eagerly accepted the offer.

"Mind your step," Miss Rogers said as they entered a vast circular entrance hall. She gestured to a door to the right and smiled. "A kennel purpose-built for our members' dogs. They will be cared for here while their mistresses are within."

Four arches opened onto different sections of the facility. One was a members-only sitting room paneled with wood flown in from London.

"We're a bit of an experiment," Miss Rogers said. "This is the first clubhouse in America—in the world perhaps—built especially for ladies. There are those who wonder why we need so much more space, but we had no choice, really. The old location on Madison just wasn't large enough to accommodate everyone. All thirteen floors here—"

Kitty couldn't hide her surprise. From the outside, it seemed there were just five or six.

"I know." The secretary seemed pleased. "Appearances can

be deceiving. We have thirteen levels inside—each catering to our members' needs and desires."

Wide-eyed, Kitty followed the secretary into a one-and-a-half-story ballroom, complete with a retractable stage on one end and a balcony for the orchestra on the other. Above it was a seventy-foot lounge, a suite of card rooms, public and private dining rooms, and private dressing rooms for members who didn't wish to stay overnight.

"Do you happen to know how the club was founded?"

"No." Kitty shook her head, overwhelmed not solely by the opulence—that was commonplace—but by the fact that all this had been built as a female-only enclave.

"About ten years ago," Miss Rogers told her, taking the stairs up, "Mrs. J. Borden Harriman wanted to come to the city for a few days to run errands. The problem was that she had nowhere to stay. The Harrimans were renting in Newport while their town house was being renovated, and Mr. Harriman didn't approve of ladies taking a room at a hotel by themselves. Mrs. Harriman realized then and there that what was required was a woman's club, a place where ladies could spend the night, have parcels delivered, make telephone calls, and receive guests. She applied to Miss Morgan, and Mr. Pierpont Morgan put up the first ten thousand dollars on the condition that they find nine others to contribute equal sums. That bought the place on Madison Avenue. And now, ten years later, we've grown to need a million-dollar building."

They passed two floors of sleeping and sitting rooms en route to a gymnasium equipped with the latest equipment. Members could book private rooms for manicures, hairdressing, or individual sessions with fitness instructors; they could play a game of squash at the squash courts, then step into the express elevator—which Kitty and Miss Rogers did—and drop down six floors to arrive at the edge of a sparkling underground marble swimming pool. It was the deepest indoor pool in the city, Miss Rogers said, at sixty feet long and twenty feet wide. Another section was devoted to special treatments usually found only in the best health spas in Europe.

The door to the elevator opened, and a messenger looked in to tell them that Miss Morgan had arrived. Kitty and Miss Rogers went back upstairs to wait for her on the third floor loggia, where a flock of pink flamingos, painted by the muralist Robert Chanler, soared across a vaulted ceiling. Live macaws and a marble fountain designed by Mrs. Harry Payne Whitney would complete the scenery closer to opening day, Miss Rogers whispered.

"Do you know what one of the members said to me the other day?" The secretary stood at attention. Sensing her anticipation, Kitty began to feel nervous once again.

"She told me," Miss Rogers went on, "that it wasn't the facilities that mattered to her. What she liked best about the club was being able to telephone her husband at the eleventh hour and tell him that *she* wouldn't be coming home for dinner."

A set of double doors swung open, and a crisp voice called, "I'll see you later, Elsie." Moments later, a surprisingly tall, broad-shouldered woman strode forward to greet Kitty.

"Nice to meet you, Miss Weeks." Anne Morgan shook Kitty's hand with a firm grip.

She wore her short hair swept away from her forehead. Dark eyebrows framed a no-nonsense gaze. She wore four strings of pearls around her neck. Only the wide Peter Pan collar of her blouse softened her appearance.

"So, Miss Weeks." She spoke in clipped, patrician tones. "What do you think of our little place?"

"It's wonderful," Kitty replied breathlessly.

Miss Morgan pulled up a chair around one of the pretty white-painted, wrought iron tables. "And my book, what do you think of that?"

"I enjoyed it, but I do have questions."

"As it should be." Miss Morgan laughed. "Fire away!"

"Well." Kitty wasn't prepared to begin with such little pre-amble. "May I have a glass of water?"

"Of course. Daisy." She shot a glance at her secretary. Miss Rogers slipped away. Contrary to Miss Busby's advice, Miss Morgan said nothing to fill in the silence and instead waited for Kitty to begin.

Kitty forced herself to breathe. She smiled and dove in with one of the first questions on her list. "May I ask what prompted you to write this book?"

"You may ask me anything. That's why we're here." Miss Morgan launched into an answer about her interest in bettering working women's lives.

Miss Rogers arrived with two glasses of water on a tray. Kitty gulped hers down and moved on to a different question that she and Miss Busby had prepared. Miss Morgan's reply sounded practiced, as though she had given a similar response many times before.

This didn't feel like the easy give-and-take of a conversation. Kitty found it difficult to focus; even Miss Morgan seemed slightly bored.

She decided to shake things up a bit. "What are your views on suffrage, Miss Morgan?"

The philanthropist's eyes narrowed. "I'm not against suffrage," she said after a moment. "I am simply not interested in the topic. I believe many things are more immediately necessary, such as the economic welfare of women. And once suffrage comes—and I believe it will—we must regard it not as a right but as a duty. With greater freedom comes greater responsibility—that I believe to my core."

Kitty nodded. Finally, they might be getting somewhere. "I think our readers would like to know," she said, "why, when men are encouraged to do and see so much, you suggest that girls focus more narrowly on their domestic and local responsibilities?" Her question wasn't one from the list that Miss Busby had vetted.

Miss Morgan paused to think, and Kitty worried she might have spoken too boldly.

"Excellent question," Anne Morgan replied finally as she adjusted her pearls. "Men and women are fundamentally different creatures, with different abilities and different temperaments. To me, equality of the sexes in no sense means similarity. For women to move forward, we must embrace our difference from men. For most girls—working women who come from families struggling to make ends meet—the best way to improve their lot is by improving the condition of their communities."

"But what if a girl isn't interested in public service?" Kitty persisted. "Must she give up her own ambitions in order to serve the greater good?"

"Let's make this more concrete," Miss Morgan proposed. "I take it that you plan to be a journalist?"

Kitty nodded.

"My great friend Ida Tarbell writes for magazines and newspapers."

"I know of Miss Tarbell," Kitty said.

"Of course you do. Her investigation into the monopolistic activities of Mr. John D. Rockefeller and the Standard Oil Company opened the public's eyes and resulted in the government taking decisive action. I bring up this example not to point fingers but to illustrate my conviction: any vocation, if pursued courageously and with a pure heart and honest motives, will bring about a betterment of one's community. It's just that it's more realistic for most women to limit their scope of activities, whereas a smaller group benefits from having a freer rein."

Kitty liked Miss Morgan's turn of phrase and hoped she'd be able to remember it.

"My book has been written for girls who must work to make ends meet," Miss Morgan continued, taking a sip of water. "They don't have the luxury of choosing between professions. I have long been an advocate for a living wage for both men and women. Only when she can support her family can a woman realize her true potential."

She looked Kitty in the eye. "I have the same attitude toward suffrage. I want to prepare women so that they may be able to make proper use of suffrage when it comes."

Kitty took the bit between her teeth. Neither her questions

nor Miss Busby's questions would do. She had to treat Miss Morgan as a person in order to breathe some life into this interview and get behind the public persona.

"May I ask how Mr. Morgan is faring?"

"He has been released from his sickbed, thank you. He will spend the next month or so recuperating on the *Corsair*. That's my father's yacht." Miss Morgan smiled to herself. "My father and I used to sail all over Europe together. We even hosted the kaiser on board once, if you can believe it."

That was exactly the kind of thing that would fascinate their readers.

"You met the kaiser in person, Miss Morgan?"

"Only for a short while, but yes, I did."

"May I ask what he was like?"

Kitty had wondered about the man behind the pointy, upturned mustaches. The man who everyone said had single-handedly started the war.

Anne Morgan thought for a moment, and Daisy Rogers stepped forward as though to intervene.

"That's all right, Daisy," Miss Morgan told her secretary. "She means well, and after all, I have met Germany's emperor."

Kitty realized that with Jack Morgan so firmly on Britain's side, any comment, positive or negative, made by his sister might be misconstrued.

"You see," Miss Morgan said, "his Prussian stiffness might seem comical to us, but like anyone born into a position of great power, the kaiser has a difficult part to play. Men jump to his command. He must choose his words with care. But he is an impulsive individual."

Miss Rogers coughed discreetly in the background.

"Daisy is worried that I might say something foolish"—Miss Morgan laughed—"so don't quote me on this. I don't believe that fellow who took a shot at Jack had anything to do with the kaiser or the German government. If Berlin had wanted to finish my brother off, they would have sent someone far more competent than that half-cracked professor."

Daisy Rogers tapped her watch.

"I suppose it's time for us to finish," Miss Morgan said.

"May I ask just one more question?" Kitty couldn't leave without getting her answer. "In the first chapter of your book, you say that the qualities that make the American girl abroad unique are truly American qualities, but unless I missed it, you don't specify what they are. Can you tell our readers now?"

Miss Morgan threw her head back and laughed. "Very good."

"I beg your pardon?"

"You see, Miss Weeks." She leaned forward in her chair, dark eyes flashing. "If you don't find it in my writings, then your readers must look in the mirror and discover the truth for themselves."

On the taxicab ride back to the office, Kitty scribbled a quick outline of her conversation so she wouldn't forget. She walked into the *Sentinel* surprised to see it looking so much the same when she felt so altered. She couldn't have said in what way; she just felt that spending three quarters of an hour in the company of a woman of Miss Morgan's stature had somehow left its mark. She felt elevated, special, ready to leave her own mark perhaps.

Jeannie Williams pounced on Kitty when she entered the hen coop. "How did it go, Miss Weeks? I wish I could have been there."

Miss Busby materialized beside Jeannie's desk before Kitty could reply. "What are you girls chattering on about? You should know better, Jeannie. You were supposed to send Miss Weeks in to me right away."

She caught Kitty by the elbow and steered her to her alcove, but not before Jeannie pointed furiously to a half-typed sheet in her machine and mouthed *sotto voce*, "You have to see this."

"Start at the beginning," Miss Busby told Kitty, sitting her down. "Don't leave out a single detail."

Kitty opened her mouth to speak and realized she wasn't yet ready to describe the meeting. She needed a few moments of peace and quiet first. A few moments to digest it. "Would you mind if I get a bite to eat before we start, Miss Busby?" she asked.

"Of course, of course." The editor could afford to be magnanimous. "Interviews can make you ravenous. Go on to the cafeteria. I'll be waiting."

Kitty thought she might take a moment in the basement but had to walk back through the hen coop to get there.

"Miss Weeks." Jeannie beckoned her over.

"I'll be back soon," Kitty said. "We can talk after I finish with Miss Busby."

"I think you'll want to see this." Jeannie turned the wheel on the carriage and pulled out a typewritten page, which she handed to Kitty.

Kitty took a look. "In a letter written before he killed himself," it began, "Mr. Lucian Hotchkiss, secretary to Mrs. Elizabeth Basshor of Park Avenue, confessed to murdering Mr. Hunter Cole, a guest at his employer's annual Fourth of July gala."

CHAPTER TWENTY

Kitty tore up the stairs to the City Desk. As usual, the men were huddled behind their glass barricade. She tapped on the glass and mouthed Mr. Flanagan's name. The door wasn't locked. What, she wondered, would they do if she barged in? Call for help? Scream and jump on their chairs as though they'd seen a rat? The thought of the reporters panicking like ladies diverted her as she waited for Mr. Flanagan to make an appearance.

"Back again, Miss Weeks?" His thick black mane gleamed under the overhead light bulbs.

"I read about Mr. Hotchkiss's confession."

"Ah, did Miss Williams show it to you? Last I heard, her job consisted of typing up stories, not broadcasting them to whomever she chooses."

Kitty ignored his comment; she had no interest in arguing over Jeannie's actions. "The story said that not only had Mr. Hotchkiss confessed to *killing* Mr. Cole, but that he also had been *stealing* from Mrs. Basshor at the party and Mr. Cole caught him in the act."

"That sounds about correct."

"It just *sounds* correct, Mr. Flanagan?"

The reporter took a step toward her. "I think you're forgetting who you are, Miss Weeks."

"Hotchkiss wouldn't have stolen from her," Kitty said. "He was devoted to Mrs. Basshor."

"Stranger things have happened."

"But did they, in this case?"

"Look here, Miss Weeks. The secretary told his employer that she would be paying one sum for the fireworks, and then he paid those Chinamen quite a bit less so that he could pocket the difference."

Kitty recalled those gold cuff links. She wouldn't have expected Hotchkiss's salary to pay for them. "The men were Japanese," she said. "From Yokohama."

"That hardly changes the fact that the secretary would have gotten away with his trickery if Mr. Cole hadn't overheard their conversation."

"Is that what he wrote in his suicide letter?"

"That's what the police gathered from it."

"Do they know what happened?"

"Mr. Cole arranged to meet the secretary in the stables, and there's no doubt about what happened after that."

"But Mr. Lupone told me—" Kitty stopped herself.

"Yes. What did Mr. Lupone tell you?" Flanagan flipped open his penknife. "I was wondering when you would get to that."

Kitty stood stock-still; she had no reply.

"You think I didn't know you went to the prison?" He leisurely cleaned under his nails with the blade. "You signed your name in the ledger, Miss Weeks."

Kitty's cheeks flamed. "Mr. Lupone told me that Mr. Cole arranged with him a few days beforehand to make sure the stables were clear."

"Does he have any witnesses, any evidence to prove it?"

She shook her head.

"And still, you believed him." The penknife closed with a click. "The good or bad news, depending on how you view it, is that Mr. Lupone will be released this afternoon. And Mr. Hotchkiss, who went on in his letter to beg Mrs. Basshor's forgiveness for who he was and what he had done, will officially be listed as Mr. Cole's killer. Since he's dead, he can't be prosecuted for the crime, but at least justice will have been done."

"Did Mr. Hotchkiss explicitly confess to shooting Hunter Cole?" Kitty couldn't picture him pulling the trigger.

"Men," Flanagan said, his voice rising, "do not commit suicide because they've stolen a few hundred dollars, but they might kill themselves over a more serious crime, even if it happened by accident."

"I see," Kitty said. "Well, thank you for explaining it to me." She turned to leave.

"One question, Miss Weeks. How did you manage to get into the Tombs?"

"I asked," Kitty said.

"That's it?"

"Just about."

He made a rumbling sound in his throat. "Why is it that, preposterous as it sounds, I believe you?"

Kitty passed Jeannie's desk on her way back to Miss Busby.

"What did he say, Miss Weeks? Was he angry that I showed you the article?"

"You probably shouldn't do that again, but it's all right, I think."

"So the secretary did it?"

"That's how it appears."

Kitty returned to the alcove and began reviewing her notes with Miss Busby. The editor didn't seem too concerned that the interview had veered away from the prewritten questions. About twenty minutes into their discussion, she told Kitty to go down to the morgue and bring the file on Miss Morgan so that they could add some background information to the write-up.

"Where were you on Friday?" Mr. Musser asked Kitty when she requested the file.

"I took the day off to prepare for my interview with Miss Morgan. That's why we need the extra material."

"Finally, a subject worthy of your talents. Did you know that she received an award this year from the National Institute of Social Sciences for making public service her private vocation?"

"I did not."

"See, you should come to me first." He smiled beneath his mustache. "Besides, I was looking for you."

"Anything in particular?"

He called to one of his boys, who went off to the back to unearth the file. "I think I know your Dr. Albert."

She took a step back. "You do?"

He stroked his chin, clearly enjoying the effect he had produced. "Well, it's as though you had asked me about a Mr. Wilson, and I say, sure, I know someone by that name: he lives in a big white house in Washington on Pennsylvania Avenue."

"Go on, Mr. Musser. Please don't keep me in suspense."

"He's a diplomat," Musser said.

"Really?"

"He's Germany's commercial attaché to the United States, as a matter of fact. His full name is Dr. Heinrich Friedrich Albert."

"That's a nice coincidence, Mr. Musser." The old man's filing-cabinet brain produced little marvels. "But I'm not looking for a diplomat. Dr. Albert is a physician. Mrs. Clements told me so."

"Ach." The archivist shrugged his shoulders. "I tried."

"You did. Thank you." She took the file on Miss Morgan and walked toward the elevators, sifting through the stories, many of which had to do with Miss Morgan's years in France and the well-known guests that she, Miss Marbury, and Miss de Wolfe entertained.

She pressed the button and waited for the elevator, but when the door opened, she realized that she was missing something.

"Go ahead without me," she told the operator. She dashed back to Mr. Musser's counter. "People keep jumping to conclusions based on incomplete information," Kitty said to the baffled archivist. "The police think Hotchkiss shot Mr. Cole because he begged Mrs. Basshor's forgiveness and then killed himself; Mrs. Clements assumed Dr. Albert must be a physician because of the word *doctor* and Mr. Cole's remark that he had been seeing him regularly and never felt better."

"That is generally how it works with physicians," Mr. Musser said.

"On the other hand," Kitty went on, "he didn't tell Mrs. Clements what illness he suffered from, and when she questioned him later, he denied being sick. His wife also told me he was fit as a fiddle…" Kitty's thoughts began to race. "The Coles needed money. What does a commercial attaché do?"

"Dr. Albert, you mean? Well, during peacetime, his responsibilities would include promoting trade between Germany and
America. But now that his country is at war, his main duty must
be to purchase all necessary war materials and ship them home."

"Does Germany need horses?"

"I'm sure they do. They need everything."

"Well, could Mr. Cole have been buying them for him?"
That might shed light on his visit to the stables.

"He could have been." Mr. Musser considered the idea. "Yes,
Britain has contracted with the Morgan bank to handle all their
American purchases. As far as I know, Germany has no such
counterpart here. Maybe they rely on individual contractors."

From the little she knew of Hunter Cole, Kitty could imag-
ine that he might have liked to hobnob with diplomats and
have a hand in wartime business, whether for the Allies or the
Germans. It might have fed his sense of self-importance, and
Berlin no doubt paid well for any assistance. Could that be why
Hunter Cole told Mrs. Clements that he "never felt better"?

"There is just one problem," Musser said.

"What is that?"

"Jimmy, get me the Albert file," Musser called. "Albert
comma Dr. Heinrich Friedrich."

The file appeared a few minutes later.

"Look at this." Mr. Musser opened it and handed Kitty the
two articles it contained.

Both stories dated from the start of the year, and both had
to do with the *Wilhelmina*, a shipping vessel that Dr. Albert
had chartered and that the English navy seized and detained
in port.

"I don't understand," Kitty said.

"Read it carefully."

Kitty did. The *Wilhelmina* had American registry and had been transporting grains to Hamburg. After capturing the ship, Britain had quarantined the cargo on the grounds that the English courts had ruled foodstuffs bound for enemy nations to be contraband.

American shippers protested, but the British government stood behind the decision. They paid the shipper's invoice price for the grains and issued a warning that henceforth any such cargo bound for Germany was liable to be seized without compensation.

"Don't you see?" Musser said. "If they can't get food across, do you think England will allow them to transport horses?"

"There's only one way to find out." Kitty recalled her wild-goose chase at the concert. "And I think Dr. Albert might be in New York."

"Quite possible. He keeps an office at the Hamburg-American Line downtown. On Broadway, you know." He frowned. "You're not thinking of going, are you?"

"Why not?"

"He's a diplomat," Musser sputtered. "Second only to Ambassador von Bernstorff. What do you think you're going to say him?"

"I'll ask whether he knew Mr. Hunter Cole."

"And if he did, what of it?"

"If Mr. Cole was working for the Germans, that might explain why he was shot. It would make more sense than some ridiculous story about a secretary stealing from Mrs. Basshor and being found out, and so on and so forth."

Kitty stared at the Anne Morgan file during the ride back upstairs. Impressive though Miss Morgan might be, Kitty knew which story meant more to her.

One could go into journalism to educate and inform, or to uncover the truth. This was Kitty's chance to do the latter. It would come at a high price—abandoning the Anne Morgan piece and disappointing Miss Busby—but the interview wasn't timely, and one day here or there wouldn't make a difference. In a murder case, however, things moved fast. Who knew where Dr. Albert might be tomorrow?

Kitty hurried into the hen coop and handed Jeannie the file from the morgue. "Would you please see that Miss Busby gets this?"

She went out to the street to hail a cab. She had given the Ladies' Page editor everything she needed to write the article that her heart desired.

Kitty jumped into the taxi that screeched to a halt by the curb. Now it was her turn.

CHAPTER TWENTY-ONE

Colorful posters advertising travel to exotic destinations filled the plate-glass windows at the Hamburg-American Line's street-level ticket office, just south of Rector Street at 45 Broadway. *Around the World—110 Days—SS* Victoria Luise— *Departures from New York and San Francisco—$650 and Up. Cruise to Panama with onboard dance instructors trained by Vernon and Irene Castle.*

Kitty caught a glimpse of her reflection in the glass—and that of two men watching her. She swung around. There was no one there except the usual pedestrians hurrying along. She blinked. Had she imagined it? No matter. She took a deep breath and pushed her way inside via a brass revolving door.

Inside, the single attendant behind a row of black-marble-topped counters stifled a yawn. A plaster cherub gazed down from its perch on a ceiling, surveying the luxurious but empty ticket office. An intricate model of an ocean liner stood in a glass case in the center of the spacious waiting area. Kitty recalled hearing somewhere that most of the Line's sailings had been suspended since the previous autumn.

"*Guten Tag,*" she said. "*Ich bin hier, um Herrn Doktor Albert zu treffen.*" She could easily be mistaken for a native speaker.

The attendant looked up, startled by the newcomer. "*Herr Doktor Albert?*"

"*Ja.*"

The woman shook her head and said that there was no one by that name there.

"*Ich heiße Fräulein Wochs,*" Kitty made up a name for herself on the spur of the moment. She asked whether the attendant was certain that Dr. Albert didn't have an office in the building.

The Hamburg-American employee eyed her up and down, taking in the white dress with the bolero jacket, the silk purse, and the expensive hat. "*Hat Frau Held Sie geschickt?*"

Kitty had no idea who Frau Held might be, but she answered yes, that was indeed who had sent her.

The woman picked up her telephone, waited for a moment, then hung up the line.

No one was answering on the other end, she said, but Fraulein Wochs could go upstairs. She would find Dr. Albert in Room 74, on the seventh floor. She apologized for her caution earlier. One could never be too careful these days.

Kitty took the elevator upstairs, and the operator pointed her in the right direction. The hall was eerily quiet for a commercial building on a weekday afternoon.

She knocked on the door to Room 74. No one replied.

She heard voices within and knocked again. Still, no answer.

Kitty twisted the handle and eased the door open.

Someone was being reprimanded in an inside room. "*I* take the train, Hiliken, and you *take a cab?* Do you want Ambassador von Bernstorff to hear about this? You know a full accounting of all expenses will be sent to Washington and then on to Berlin."

"*Guten Tag,*" Kitty said loudly. The room before her was

evidently a front office and contained nothing more than a desk with a chair and a telephone.

A flustered man in a pince-nez peered out from behind a connecting door. "*Kann ich ihnen behilflich sein?*" Could he help her?

Kitty replied that she had come to see Dr. Albert. Like the attendant downstairs, she allowed him to think she was a fellow countrywoman.

The man inquired whether she had made an appointment.

"*Nein.*" Kitty smiled and dropped a curtsy. Like a coquette, she looked at him from below her lashes.

"*Warten Sie, Bitte.*" He took her name and disappeared inside.

While Kitty waited, she peered at a framed map hanging from the wall. Colored in pink, the tiny island of Großbritannien and its dominions—Canada, Australia, New Zealand, and India, parts of East Asia and Africa—covered most of the habitable world. Giant *Russland* and its territories loomed large over the rest of Europe, while *Deutsches Reich*—the proud state of Imperial Germany—only exerted its influence over a tiny sliver of Asia, a small patch of western Africa, and the island of Madagascar.

With a few simple blocks of color, the map summed up yet another cause for Europe's conflict. Germany hungered for more territory to feel on par with its powerful neighbors.

An aristocratic gentleman emerged from the adjoining chamber, bowed, and introduced himself. "*Ich bin Doktor Heinrich Friedrich Albert.*"

He must have been in his midfifties, Kitty thought. His watchful eyes had a slightly downward cast, and his neatly trimmed gray mustache ended at the sides of his lips. "You wanted to see me?" He radiated quiet confidence.

Kitty forced a smile. "*Ja, gerne.*" Now that she had succeeded in meeting him, it was time to come clean and tell him exactly who she was and why she had come to see him. She sensed that he'd be able to detect a liar.

He invited her into his office and took his seat behind a fine mahogany desk. "*Sie heißen Wochs?*" He sounded skeptical.

Behind him, in a stiff, high-collared military uniform, Kaiser Wilhelm II gazed toward the heavens, his waxed mustaches also pointing upward.

"I'm Miss Weeks, actually," Kitty replied, switching to English. "I work for the *New York Sentinel.*"

"You are American?"

"Yes."

"You speak my language without any accent." His face betrayed no emotion.

"I studied in Switzerland for ten years," Kitty said. "Afterward, I traveled through Europe for several months in the company of a chaperone from Karlsruhe."

"I see." He sat back in his chair. "And is Weeks a common name?"

The question puzzled Kitty, but she replied, "It's not an uncommon name, but I wouldn't say that it is too common either."

He nodded, apparently satisfied. "So how can I help you? And why the subterfuge?"

Kitty blushed. "I wasn't sure whether they'd let me in… I have a bit of an odd question." He didn't flinch, so she continued. "I wonder—may I ask whether by any chance the name Hunter Cole means something to you?"

The diplomat sniffed. He removed his hands from the desk,

his actions unhurried and measured. He opened his mouth to speak when his secretary knocked on the door and looked in to say that they should leave for his next appointment.

Dr. Albert rose to his feet. "You will excuse me, please."

"This is very important," Kitty said. "Could you please give me just one more moment?"

The diplomat checked his pocket watch. "Very well, you can walk with me." He reassured his secretary: "*Das geht in Ordnung, Hiliken.*"

The secretary glared at Kitty as they rode downstairs in the elevator. They walked out on the street, crossed Broadway, and continued westward on foot.

Kitty struggled to keep pace with Dr. Albert's long strides; other pedestrians swerved to make way for him since the diplomat didn't deviate from his course.

"Who is this Mr. Cole?" he asked once they'd reached a quieter corner and waited for a break in the traffic to cross. "And why do you think he has anything to do with me?"

"Hunter Cole was shot last week at the Sleepy Hollow Country Club, sir," Kitty replied. "One of his friends said that he spoke about knowing a Dr. Albert, which is why we're making inquiries."

"There must be plenty of Dr. Alberts in this great city," the German remarked and stepped into the street. Kitty and Hiliken followed.

"I've called every Dr. Albert in the telephone book," Kitty said, "but none of them knew Mr. Cole. Then my colleague mentioned you, and I thought I would come and check in person. We don't want to print anything inaccurate."

"That is commendable. Much better than most of the other newspapers. I must assure you though: I have nothing to do with this Hunter Cole. I've never heard of him."

Kitty told herself she had done her best and she wouldn't learn anything else from a man whose profession it was to manage relationships and keep secrets. She ought to get back to the office and try to patch things up with Miss Busby.

"Allow me to show you something," the diplomat said. Seagulls circled the blue skies overhead; a flea-bitten dog strolled past them. They had reached the docks.

"Herr Doktor." A well-built Negro ran over to the diplomat.

"Not now." Hiliken steered him away.

With almost a thousand miles of waterfront as measured around the piers, New York's ports surpassed those of London, Hamburg, and Liverpool in foreign trade. Kitty had read in *King's Views of New York*, a popular photographic guide to the city, that almost six thousand crafts traversed these waters each day, and three thousand immigrants daily landed at the barge office.

She followed the attaché past sailors and stevedores. Foremen barked orders in all languages and accents that made it hard to detect whether they were speaking English. Men of every color—white, black, and the shades in between—loaded and unloaded massive pallets, hauled carts, or lounged in the shade smoking cigarettes.

Kitty ignored a couple of low whistles. She sensed the eyes staring at her. Even in the diplomat's company and the bright light of a Monday afternoon in summer, she began to feel afraid.

Dr. Albert came to a halt. He stood in the shadow of a vessel taller than a four-story building. "What you should know as a reporter is that there are sixty-six ships of German and Austrian registry valued at over thirty-three million dollars currently being held in American ports. All these craft have been forbidden from sailing since the war broke out last August. My country has a problem: if the United States enters the war on the side of the Allies, not only do all sixty-six vessels automatically become American property, but they can be converted into warships and used against us."

"But that won't happen, will it?" Kitty said, wondering what grounded ships had to do with Hunter Cole. "We're neutral."

"For the moment, yes. But pressure to enter the war is mounting." The diplomat gave a short laugh. "Your press has incited the feelings of the public against Germany. Especially in the wake of the *Lusitania* sinking, they don't shy away from hurling the most foul insults. They call us beasts, baby killers, barbarians."

He tapped his cane on the ground for emphasis. "None of this is true. Germany has given the world Bach and Beethoven, Kant and Goethe. We are the most civilized nation on earth. Right now, however, we are simply fighting for our survival."

Kitty looked up at the gigantic black hull looming over them. When she first heard the news about the *Lusitania* sinking, she had tried to imagine the experience of the passengers as their ship went under, but her mind hadn't been able to comprehend it. For her, boarding a boat to cross the Atlantic was an act of faith in itself. Once she took that step and believed that such a huge hunk of metal could cross the ocean, then it seemed perfectly normal to be one of two or three thousand people dining and dancing above water a mile or two deep.

To have that security ripped from you in a mere eighteen minutes, to have the world under your feet tilt by a full ninety degrees, to have the china fall from your hands and chandeliers crash and slide down the floor, to have water fill your lungs—if that didn't constitute terror, she didn't know what did.

"Were you aware that my embassy printed a warning in the papers right before the *Lusitania* sailed?" Dr. Albert asked. "We reminded travelers that a state of war exists between Germany and her allies and Great Britain and her allies, and that the zone of war includes the water around the British Isles. We clearly stated that anyone sailing in a British vessel through the war zone does so at his own risk. The *Lusitania* was secretly loaded with ammunition for the British, which is why she sank so quickly after a single torpedo hit."

"Why are you telling me all this?" Kitty said. "I came to you to inquire about Mr. Cole."

"A third of Americans, a good thirty-two million citizens, are in fact born in other nations," Dr. Albert went on. "Nearly ten million of those come from Germany and the countries of the Central Powers. Millions more Irish support us because of their grievances against England. The president is correct to espouse neutrality: the United States will be ripped apart along ethnic lines if it takes sides. Your streets will erupt in riots. But your country's desire to remain neutral is matched neither by its trade practices nor its domestic actions."

"Dr. Albert," Kitty interrupted. She didn't want to hear any more. All she wanted was to return to the *Sentinel.*

"Still," he continued, "they're shutting down German papers, closing our churches, harassing our leader, and it is not wise to speak my language in public. A certain politician has even gone so far as to suggest that German reservists will hang from every lamppost in America if we attempt to bring them home to fight on behalf of the Fatherland." He thought for a moment.

"To return to your question: Have I met this man Hunter Cole? Upon further consideration, I realize that I have. Mr. Cole came to me with a business proposition—as do many others—and I turned it down. I don't believe we met again. If you like, you may check the date book at the office in which Hiliken records each and every meeting I attend, no matter how insignificant."

"Thank you, Dr. Albert," Kitty said, astounded by his candor.

"But would I wish you to report even that single encounter in your paper?" he continued. "Never. Because I know that what will happen next is that some scoundrel—not you, I can tell that you mean well—who catches hold of the story will find a way to insinuate that my government had a hand in Mr. Cole's murder. Everything that goes wrong these days"—he fixed Kitty with a steady gaze—"seems to be our fault, laid at our doorstep."

His color was high, and Kitty thanked him for his frankness. "It was not my intention to cause you any distress," she added in German.

"That's quite all right." He gave a short bow. "I'm happy to explain and to have found a sympathetic listener."

"May I ask one final question? Do you recall what sort of business proposal Mr. Cole made to you?"

Dr. Albert seemed distracted. "It might have been about bandages. You can go back to the office with Hiliken and check. I really don't remember."

"That won't be necessary. Thank you for your time."

"Very well, Fraulein." He bowed again. "Good luck to you." He went to attend to his business, while Hiliken, who had reappeared toward the end of their conversation, escorted Kitty to the gate.

"Would you like me to find you a taxi?" he asked when they reached the street.

"No, thank you." Something about the man made Kitty's skin crawl. "I'm sure I'll find one on Broadway." She took her leave of him and hurried off down the lonely side street back toward the bustle near the Hamburg-American Line offices.

How strange of the diplomat to confide in her, she thought. He did have a point though—even if he had met innocently with Mr. Cole, that meeting was liable to be misconstrued. Had they only met once? That seemed to be the key question. Didn't Hunter Cole tell Poppy Clements that he met Dr. Albert regularly? Could he have been exaggerating? Kitty could imagine Mr. Cole overstating his connection to the German diplomat to make himself seem important. He had seemed like a man full of bluff and bluster.

A tap on her shoulder made her heart jump from her skin. She swung around to face a stocky fellow.

"Are you Capability Weeks?"

"I beg your pardon?" She assumed her most haughty demeanor.

"I'm Agent Booth from the United States Secret Service." He flashed a badge. "This is my colleague, Agent Soames." He nodded toward the young man at his shoulder.

What a coincidence, Kitty thought. He was the same young man who bumped into her at Carnegie Hall.

"What is this about?" she asked.

"You will come with us, please." It wasn't a request.

"Is something the matter?"

The stocky agent replied, "We have to ask you some questions about Mr. Julian Weeks, your father."

Chapter Twenty-Two

I'm expected back at the *New York Sentinel* in fifteen minutes," Kitty said, fear gripping her. "They'll be waiting for me."

The agents didn't respond and instead led Kitty to a nearby dive, a greasy joint that reeked of boiled mutton and beer. They headed for a table behind a group of sailors telling bawdy jokes to a couple of women.

The older, stocky agent, Booth, ordered three glasses of water from a passing waitress.

"That's all?" the waitress said with annoyance.

"We won't be long." He showed her his badge.

"Oh, I'm sorry. Yes, sir." She disappeared.

"All right then." The agent turned to Kitty. "Let's start with first things first. What were you doing at the Hamburg-American?"

Kitty gasped. "How did you know I was there?" The laughter from the next table made it hard to concentrate. "Have you been following me?"

"We ask the questions, Miss Weeks," Booth replied.

Kitty's mind raced. How could they know where she'd been? Had they seen her with Dr. Albert? Surely it wasn't a crime to converse with a diplomat from a foreign country. Could

Hiliken have telephoned to report her? But no—it was her father they were interested in.

Kitty explained about Mrs. Basshor's party, the shooting, and Hunter Cole's mention of a Dr. Albert. Throughout, Agent Booth listened impassively, his arms folded across his barrel chest, while Agent Soames didn't look at her once. He had his pad open and took notes as she spoke.

"I don't know where I'm going with this," Kitty finished sheepishly. "Mrs. Basshor's secretary confessed to the crime, so that's that. I suppose there were just a few loose ends nagging at me."

"And what did Dr. Albert have to say to your question about whether or not he knew Mr. Cole?" Booth and Soames exchanged glances.

Kitty felt she had implicitly given the diplomat her word not to repeat what he had told her, but she couldn't lie to the representatives of the Treasury Department.

"He said he might have, but if he did, it didn't lead to any-thing," she replied. "He said I could check his daybook at the office to confirm, but I believe him."

Agent Soames kept scribbling. If their positions had been reversed, she would have had to memorize all this information rather than writing it down, Kitty thought.

"Why," Booth went on, "did you drop off Mr. Julian Weeks at the Edelweiss Café? Who was he meeting and for what purpose?"

Kitty's hands flew to her mouth. "You've been spying on us! How long has this been going on?"

Silence. Or, at least, silence from the agents. The diner resounded with joke-telling and raucous laughter. The disgruntled waitress thumped three glasses of water onto the table so hard that some of it spilled.

"This makes no sense." Kitty's eyes filled with angry tears. She wiped them away with the back of her hand. "You must have the wrong person."

"Did you or did you not drop off Mr. Weeks at around ten a.m. on Friday, July 9?" Booth said.

"Yes, I did."

"Why?"

"Our chauffeur had to bring the other car to the mechanic's for an inspection. My father doesn't drive and didn't want to ride in a taxi." She took some satisfaction from her answer.

Booth continued, unperturbed. "Who was Mr. Weeks meeting there and for what purpose?"

"I have no idea."

"I see." The big man didn't sound convinced. "You're sure?"

She shrugged. "He said it was someone from out of town."

"And that's it?"

"That's it." The disbelief showed on his face, so she added, "If you met my father, you would know. He doesn't tell me anything." She waited a moment. "May I ask you something?"

Booth gave a grudging nod.

"Has he broken the law?"

Soames finally spoke. "You can help us prove that he hasn't."

Kitty wanted to ask whether Soames had bumped into her on purpose. "How can I do that?"

Booth said, "Tell us whom Mr. Weeks met at the café and why."

"I just told you I don't know."

"You're his daughter," Booth replied, unmoved. "I'm sure you can cajole it out of him."

"You'd be helping your father and us, Miss Weeks," Soames added. "Your actions would count in his favor."

Kitty began to feel cornered.

"We're from the Secret Service." Booth leaned in, his beefy face just inches from hers. "We'll get what we need whether or not you help, but unlike you, we won't have a light touch." Pockmarks scarred his cheeks. "The stain of being under government investigation doesn't wash away easily. Once we start asking questions, everyone will find out."

"I see—"

"So give us what we need, and we'll leave you in peace. Just remember, you can't breathe a word to anyone. This is strictly government business."

It was too late to go back to work at this point, and Kitty was in no mood to face Miss Busby. All she wanted was to speak to her father. She would find out the information somehow, and then the two Secret Service men would leave them alone. There was something about the agents that frightened Kitty: the older one seemed like a bully; the younger one—he spoke well and he was nice-looking, she had to give him that. But he was too reserved: his smile didn't reach his eyes.

She found it odd that they didn't want anyone to know about their conversation, but for the moment, at least, she had to trust them. She wished she had someone to whom she could turn for advice, but she had no one, and even if she did, what could she say when she had been forbidden to breathe a word about it to anyone?

She returned home shaken from the encounter, hoping to find her father in his study sipping a whiskey so she could engage him in a nice little chat. Instead, he had left her a note saying he would be out to dinner with Maitland.

Kitty handed Grace her hat and purse.

"I have to check something," she said to the maid before opening the door to the study.

A pair of milky white eyes stared at her from the darkness. Kitty took a deep breath and turned on the lamp. How she hated that infernal sculpture.

She wasn't betraying her father, she told herself. She was helping him. If she found any information that was even the slightest bit incriminating, she wouldn't hesitate to warn him.

She found his leather-bound notebook in the second drawer of his desk and leafed through the thick cotton pages, smiling fondly at the sight of his spidery handwriting. In contrast to Julian Weeks's imposing physical presence—the sculpted head, the strong arms, which caught her when she jumped off trees in her childhood—his script resembled that of an elderly man's.

Kitty traced the shaky letters with her finger. From the authors on his shelves—Adam Smith, Rousseau, Gibbons—one would never guess that he had taught himself to read and write. He'd mastered the former with no apparent difficulty. The writing, well... As the Misses Danceys said, that required practice, practice, and more practice. Julian Weeks came from humble beginnings and, unlike Kitty, hadn't had years of leisure to perfect his penmanship.

What he didn't have himself, he had given her: a good education and every conceivable luxury.

Kitty began to read, ignoring her twinges of guilt. She would tell the men from the Treasury Department what they needed to know, and then they would vanish without her father or any of their acquaintances being the wiser.

Most of the diary was blank. On weekdays, he simply wrote *club*, *home*, or sometimes *mtg* followed by a brief note.

He recorded details about his Sunday outings with Kitty, however. Kitty was touched to see the entries, which ranged from *Botanic Gdns* to *F.T. Park* to *Chinatown* with an exclamation mark. He'd even noted the items that they'd ordered from the restaurant on Mott Street: *Duck soup; fried squid in cracker dust, 79¢; Chinese noodles, 50¢.*

He had jotted down the ferry timings for the day they drove to Jersey City. Kitty recalled how surprised she had been to discover that they could cross the Hudson by train or take their car across on a boat, but that no bridge connected New Jersey to Manhattan.

Here and there, Kitty saw his lawyer mentioned, and in late June, Mr. Maitland's name popped up. For Friday, July 9, the morning Mr. Weeks went to the Edelweiss Café, he had written the address and *H.S. + 1.*

Kitty replaced the diary in his drawer, switched off the lamp, and closed the door to the study behind her. *H.S.*

She didn't know of anyone by those initials. In fact, save for his lawyer, doctor, and a handful of other business colleagues, she didn't know the names of any of her father's friends. He so rarely mentioned them. And who was the plus one?

CHAPTER TWENTY-THREE

Kitty arrived at the hen coop the next morning steeled for the worst. An uneasy night's sleep only intensified her sense of dread at facing her boss.

"How is Miss Busby?" she asked Jeannie as she passed by the typist's desk.

"Not pleased," Jeannie replied, her round face pinched with concern. "She sent me out three times to look for you. Why didn't you tell anyone you were leaving?"

"I hardly know myself." Kitty put down her things and began the long march to the editor's office. She found Miss Busby buried behind ominous headlines:

PRESIDENT MAY DELAY REPLY TO BERLIN BY A WEEK. PRESENT ATTITUDE IS ONE OF DELIBERATION.

"I'm so sorry about yesterday." Kitty came in and sat down.

Helena Busby lowered her paper. She didn't respond for a moment. Then a single tear trickled down her withered cheek and splashed onto the news. Her hand trembled as she unscrewed her bottle of Rowland's.

Miss Busby looked worn out. The older woman had no

personal photographs on her desk, no family or friends that
Kitty had heard her speak of. Beneath the president's portrait
hung a faded clipping from the '90s, which Kitty had once read.
It described the new type of "bachelorette girl." "She paddles
her own canoe, works for a living, and *chooses* to make her own
way in the world."

Kitty had assumed that the piece referred to the kind of life
Miss Busby lead or, at least, to the life that she dreamed of.

She tried to imagine her editor young and carefree, with stars
in her eyes. Had Miss Busby wanted to write breaking news or
travel the world like Nellie Bly? Then twenty, thirty, maybe
even forty years later, the once-fresh girl reporter finds herself
chained to her desk, stuck in an airless alcove, and all for what?

Miss Busby tilted the bottle over her spoon, but only a drop
came out. She rummaged in her drawer for another but found
it was empty too.

"Hundreds of girls would kill to be in your shoes." She tossed
both bottles into the waste bin.

"I'm so sorry, Miss Busby," Kitty repeated. She meant every
word. She would give anything for a second chance.

"Do you know what Mr. Bennett says about female journalists?" Miss Busby asked.

Mr. Bennett wasn't a colleague—he was the English author
Arnold Bennett, and Miss Busby considered his *Journalism for
Women* her bible.

"He says we are unreliable as a class. He says that it is
not surprising that the young woman who is accustomed to
remark gaily, 'Only five minutes late this morning, Father,'
confident that a frown or a hard word will end the affair,

should carry into business the laxities so long permitted to her around the hearth," the editor went on. "I've coddled you. That's the problem. You don't know what it's like to have to start from nothing. To have to scratch and fight for every inch of opportunity."

Kitty stared at the papers on the editor's desk, contrite.

"I've met all kinds of girls in the course of my work." Helena Busby rose to her feet and continued, like an orator addressing crowds. "There's the sprightly type who martyrs herself because she must work with other women whose dullness and primness jar on her vivacities; the girl who feels insulted because men don't accord her the deference to which she is accustomed; the woman who says, 'I forgot to do so and so, I'm so sorry,' and stands like a spoiled child expectant of forgiveness…"

The beanpole frame thrummed with emotion. "In men destined for business or a profession, carelessness is harshly discouraged at an early age. In women, who usually are not destined for *anything whatever*, it enjoys a merry life."

Kitty wondered whether she should call for help, but what would she say was the matter? That Miss Busby was quoting Mr. Bennett almost word for word?

"In journalism, as perhaps in no other profession, success depends wholly upon the loyal cooperation, the perfect reliability of a number of people," the editor said. "Some are great, and some are small, but none are *irresponsible*."

"Won't you sit down, Miss Busby?" Kitty suggested. "Let me get you something to drink."

"A vast number of women engaged in journalism secretly

regard it as a delightful game." Spittle collected at the corner of the thin lips. "On no other assumption can the attitude of many women journalists toward their work be explained. My final words as I leave you on the threshold of an office are these"— she gasped—"journalism is not a game, and in journalism there are no excuses."

And like a tree hacked at exactly the right angle, Miss Busby toppled forward.

Mr. Hewitt addressed the stunned typists an hour after the doctor came to take the Ladies' Page editor away, summarizing the medical diagnosis. "The female constitution cannot withstand the pressure of working at a newspaper year after year for eight- to ten-hour days. I hope for your own sakes that you will all someday marry."

He nodded at Kitty. "Come with me, Miss Weeks."

Kitty followed him down the hall to his office. She couldn't bring herself to look Miss Busby's superior in the eye.

"This is why we insisted that she take on an apprentice," he said, settling into his seat behind his desk. "Still, she didn't exactly keep you busy, did she? No. She held on to the reins too tightly."

He rummaged through his papers. "You needn't worry though. Mr. Eichendorff will make sure that she's sent to a sanitarium. She went to one upstate a couple of years ago. Came back in fine fettle. But enough talk; we have a Ladies' Page to publish."

He cleaned his glasses with his kerchief. "Did you bring me her proofs?"

Kitty handed them over. She had overheard whispers between Mr. Hewitt and the doctor. The physician had said something about displaced ovaries and a collapsed uterus, the effects of working too hard and not having borne children. The strain on Miss Busby's system had also been exacerbated by neurasthenia, a complete depletion of the nerves, the doctor had added.

Mr. Hewitt wrinkled his nose while he scanned the pages that Kitty had given him. "In the words of the late, great Horace Greeley, the only way to succeed in this business is to eat ink and sleep on newsprint. Miss Busby certainly did that. No one could accuse her of shirking. Yes, it seems we have a head start on this week, and there are more than enough advertisements and announcements to fill in any blank spaces. What matters most"—he glanced at Kitty over his glasses—"is that the Morgan interview be top-notch. It's to be the centerpiece of Saturday's edition. Get a draft done by this afternoon, and we'll review it."

"Yes, Mr. Hewitt."

"Call the compositor," Mr. Hewitt continued, "and let him know that I'll speak to him at five. I expect you to be present to take notes. Now that Miss Busby is gone, you will take over some of her responsibilities. Who knows? This might even lead to a promotion for you... That will be all."

Kitty turned to leave. She couldn't believe that she hadn't been reprimanded, and that moreover, she might benefit from Miss Busby's collapse. "Yes, Mr. Hewitt."

She returned to her desk. All the typists were back at work as though nothing had happened. Kitty retrieved her notes from the Anne Morgan interview. Somehow, the sight of her scribbles reminded her of Agent Soames and his note-taking. She pushed away the attendant anxiety that the thought brought up and focused on the task at hand.

In no time at all, Kitty found herself immersed in the world of the Colony Club. She could see the ballroom, the underground swimming pool, and the loggia with its mural of pink flamingos. She recalled Miss Morgan's flashing dark eyes, her clipped speech, and the string of pearls—and Kitty's writing flowed, as though Miss Busby herself guided her hand.

She reviewed the draft when she finished, corrected the grammar, and removed any trace of unnecessary gush or shrillness—Mr. Arnold Bennett disapproved of superlatives, overpunctuation, trite expressions, and wordiness. She prepared a fresh copy and brought it to the Weekend Supplement editor in his office.

"You called the compositor?"

"Yes, Mr. Hewitt."

"All right, come back and see me at five. I'll have read this by then."

And then Kitty remembered—she had to meet the agents first thing tomorrow and so couldn't stay late today. "I'm afraid I can't, Mr. Hewitt."

"Can't what, Miss Weeks?"

"Stay past five." She needed time to speak to her father.

"I beg your pardon?"

"I have to be home for dinner this evening."

The editor held up his hand. "Don't give me any excuses.

I have no interest in your domestic affairs. As far as I'm concerned, the choice is simple: either you give your work one hundred percent, or you don't."

Kitty remained silent.

"All right, send that girl"—he snapped his fingers—"Janie Williams to see me."

"You mean Jeannie Williams, Mr. Hewitt?"

"That's correct."

"Will that be all, Mr. Hewitt?"

He nodded. "You're free to leave."

Kitty told herself she couldn't expect anything else under the circumstances. Hopefully, he would feel better once he had read her interview.

CHAPTER TWENTY-FOUR

Rao drove Kitty home and let her out in front of the New Century. She half expected to find the Secret Service agents staring from across West End Avenue, but all she noticed was a crumpled ball of newsprint blowing down the scorching sidewalk like tumbleweed.

The doorman greeted her at the front of the apartment house. "There's a letter for you, Miss Weeks." He tipped his hat. "Two men dropped it off." He reached into his pocket.

Kitty took the unmarked envelope and made her way past the display of cut gladioli in the vestibule. She didn't open the letter while she rode upstairs in the elevator.

"You're back at last," Mr. Weeks called from his study when Kitty came in through the foyer. "You've been having some late evenings."

She slipped the letter into her purse and handed her gloves and scarf to Grace. "I was only late yesterday, sir."

"I'm sorry Maitland and I couldn't join you for dinner."

"That's quite all right." Kitty peeked into his room. "Do you mind if I freshen up? I'll be back in a minute."

"Of course." He resumed reading his papers.

Once in the safety of her bedroom, Kitty removed the envelope from her purse and extracted a small sheet of notepaper.

"Riverside Park tomorrow, 8:30 a.m. sharp," it said. It was signed "R. Booth. U.S. Treasury Dept."

Kitty tore the note into tiny strips and tossed them into her wastebasket, then changed into an evening dress and joined Mr. Weeks in his study.

"Will you have a drink?" he asked. She nodded, and he poured her two fingers of black-currant cordial, which he diluted with a spray of fizzy water and a cube of ice.

He served himself a tumbler of bourbon, pulled back the curtains, and opened the windows. "Much better, don't you think?" He loosened his collar and dropped into his favorite armchair, crossing one leg over the other. "I read in the papers that Mrs. Basshor's secretary confessed to shooting Mr. Cole, and that the stable hand was set free. You must be pretty happy."

"Ah." Kitty didn't want to get into that.

"What's the matter?" He swirled the amber drink in his glass. "Aren't you pleased? I thought you believed that that fellow, Lupone, was innocent."

"I don't think it matters what I believe."

"Come now, don't go feeling sorry for yourself. What has always baffled me," he went on cheerily, "is why people with a lot of money put those with less of it in charge of paying their bills."

"I beg your pardon?"

"Wasn't the secretary cheating Mrs. Basshor?"

"That's what the papers said." Kitty took a sip of her drink.

"It seems as though he would have gotten away with it since those Japanese were on their way back to Yokohama and had no idea what they were missing. It's just his bad luck that Cole found him out."

"And Mr. Cole's bad luck too. He was killed for his efforts."

Julian Weeks shrugged. "He shouldn't have gone around meddling in other people's business."

"You think that's a fair outcome?"

"Not exactly—"

"Hotchkiss told me he owed everything to Mrs. Basshor, but I didn't think he was talking about money."

"It's always about money, my dear." Mr. Weeks laughed.

Kitty gathered her courage. "May I ask you a question?"

"Go ahead."

"Why don't you tell me anything about your business?"

"Which business?" He seemed legitimately confused. "I have my hand in several pots."

She tried to sound casual. "Well, for instance, why did you go to the Edelweiss Café on Friday? You told me you had to meet someone from out of town. Who was it?"

"Why the sudden curiosity, Capability? I had to meet the colleague of a colleague, that's all."

"Can you give me a name?"

"A name means nothing. You don't know him. I hardly know him myself."

"Why won't you tell me anything about yourself?" The words came out much more forcefully than Kitty had intended. Her questions, she realized, were as much to satisfy her own curiosity as to provide the agents with answers.

"Whom I met at the café has nothing to do with you. But you're right, I have kept you in the dark, so allow me to tell you this: my lawyers have a copy of my will and my life insurance policies, and when I'm gone, everything I have will be yours."

Kitty could have screamed, but she forced herself to keep calm. "That's not why I asked."

He checked the time on his pocket watch. "You know, I should have dinner at the club this evening. Forgive me, Capability." He put down his glass and stood, his expression maddeningly opaque. "I'll see you at breakfast."

CHAPTER TWENTY-FIVE

How can I be sure that you're with the Secret Service?" Kitty said to the two agents. They stood near the entrance to Riverside Park with the wind rustling through the trees and the skies a bright summery blue.

"Our badges should be proof enough, Miss Weeks," Soames replied, "but if you'd like additional assurance, you might telephone the Treasury Department's office at the Customs House downtown." He dropped his formal manner. "But I promise, we're not lying to you."

"What do you have for us, Miss Weeks?" Booth stepped forward.

Kitty had so little information to report that she didn't think she could hurt anyone by answering. "My father told me nothing, but I did check in his daybook, and all it says for the day he went to the café is 'H.S. + 1.'"

Kitty noticed Soames watching her. "Am I free to go now?"

"Not so fast." Booth held up his hand. "We can guess who 'H.S.' is—Hugo Schweitzer, a German chemist with whom Mr. Weeks has been doing some business."

Schweitzer. Kitty wondered why that name sounded familiar. "Well, I'm glad I could be of use." She turned as though to leave, but Booth wasn't finished.

"Have you heard Mr. Weeks mention the word 'phenol,'" he said, "or seen it in any of his documents?"

Kitty stopped in her tracks. "Household cleaners don't really concern my father, Agent Booth."

"I'm not talking about *phenyl*, Miss Weeks, although you are correct that phenol is used in its manufacture. In fact, phenol is used to make a variety of domestic products, everything from phonograph records to disinfectants. It is also used in the manufacture of trinitrophenol, a powerful explosive that both sides are using to deadly effect in the war."

Soames stared at the ground.

"Maybe you've heard it called TNP or picric acid," Booth said.

"I've not heard of it by any name, Mr. Booth," Kitty replied angrily.

"Well," he went on, "in the past, we imported all the phenol we needed from England at 10 cents a pound. Now, a year later, it costs $1.25 for the same amount, and even if you're willing to pay, it's almost impossible to get ahold of."

Kitty's chest started to feel tight.

"There aren't many players in the phenol business these days." Boats drifted along the Hudson behind Booth. "We know all the key names, where they buy their phenol and who they sell to. Only one newcomer remains a mystery. Mr. Julian Weeks. We don't know where he gets it, and we'd like to know what he's doing with it."

"My father has no use for phenol," Kitty said. But her denial was reflexive and not heartfelt.

"He's been buying significant quantities of the stuff."

"How do you know?"

"I'm afraid we can't tell you."

"Where does he store it?"

"Again, that's confidential."

"Well, if the price has gone up more than ten times over the past year, I'm sure it's a good investment," Kitty said.

"You can invest in gold or stocks, but you don't invest in phenol, Miss Weeks. At least not at the present moment."

"You think this has to do with whomever he met at the café."

The agents didn't reply.

"He's not some anarchist!" she said. Although he could perhaps be a war profiteer. "Look." She faced both men. "This is beyond me. You must speak directly to my father."

Booth pulled a paper from his jacket. "Does this look familiar?" He handed it to Kitty.

The words danced in front of Kitty's eyes. "This is my father's passport application. Where did you get it?"

Booth flipped the paper over. "Do you recognize this signature?"

Kitty shook her head.

"It belongs to the man who Mr. Weeks chose to vouch for his identity. We know him well because he signs on behalf of Krauts trying to return home with falsified documents."

"What are you saying, Agent Booth?" Kitty was furious.

"Julian Weeks has no birth certificate, no proof for what he's written here. The Bureau of Citizenship will scrutinize his claim. And I don't have to tell you, an unmarried daughter's nationality follows that of her father's."

"All right. Enough, Booth." Soames stepped in.

Kitty blinked away tears.

"Help us, and we'll make all of this go away." Booth folded the form and replaced it in his pocket.

"I'm sure there's a reasonable explanation for Mr. Weeks's lack of documentation," Soames added.

"You mean, he's not a German spy." Kitty stood still. This was ridiculous. Just because her father didn't have proof of his birth didn't mean he was lying. He may have lived abroad most of his life, but that didn't make him any less American than the two men standing in front of her. And just because they had badges and worked for the government didn't mean that they could threaten her, a wealthy, well-brought-up young woman.

Then it hit her. Something else must be going on.

"Why me?" Kitty said finally. "I've been wondering why you need to go through me to get to him. Why you followed *me* to the Hamburg-American building when it's my father you're interested in."

Both agents stiffened.

"But I'm beginning to suspect that you're not interested in either one of us."

Their faces went blank.

"The only way you could have known that I went to the Hamburg-American," she continued, testing her theory as she spoke, "is if you'd been waiting for me outside the *Sentinel* all morning. But why would you do that? No, you knew I went downtown because you were there already. It's not me or my father you've been following... It's Dr. Albert."

"That's not true," Booth said. But his voice and manner lacked conviction.

"You followed Dr. Albert and me to the docks," Kitty

continued. "Two out of the three times that you've seen either my father or me—at the Edelweiss Café, at Carnegie Hall, and at the docks—there has been another man present. *Dr. Albert* was expected at the concert, Dr. Albert was certainly at the docks, and now I think"—she worked it out as she went along—"that Dr. Albert was the '+ 1' at the meeting with my father and the German chemist, Schweitzer."

Soames tapped his foot. Booth exhaled deeply. "That's ridiculous."

"You've been suggesting that my father is selling phenol to the Germans," Kitty said. "But since we're neutral, that can't be against the law. So what is against the law then—and what are you both trying so hard to hide by approaching me and not him?"

No reply.

"You don't really think my father is doing something criminal or you wouldn't be talking to me. After all, you can hardly expect me to incriminate him." Kitty hoped to get a response—any response—so she could see the situation with more clarity.

"You're right, Miss Weeks. Our approach has been unorthodox," Soames replied. "These are unusual times. We're faced with unusual threats," he continued, ignoring Booth glaring at him. "And we're responding as best we can. I will tell you this—if word got out that we were shadowing Dr. Albert—"

"Which we are not," Booth butted in.

"—it would be considered a gross violation of protocol and cause an international incident," Soames finished. "Dr. Albert is the official representative of a nation with which the United States has no quarrel. He's a respected guest on our soil. And the Secret Service only acts in accordance with the president's orders."

"Fine," Kitty said. "If you were indeed shadowing me and not Dr. Albert, tell me where I was before I arrived at the Hamburg-American on Monday."

"We caught up with you late," Booth said.

"Where?"

"At the *Sentinel*."

"And how did you know you'd find me there?"

"We took a chance."

"You don't take a chance on anything. That's codswallop."

"Enough." Booth looked furious. "Mr. Julian Weeks has made false claims to the federal government. He could face jail time if the matter was brought to the right individual's attention. So you will do as we say, Miss Weeks." He patted the form in his pocket.

"I work for a newspaper, and I will tell everyone about this." Kitty's boldness amazed her.

"And who would believe you? A Ladies' Page reporter's word against that of two agents from the Treasury Department? We're in charge here," Booth continued as a girl with a pink ribbon in her hair rolled a hoop past them. "You tell us what your father is doing with all that phenol, and we'll do our best to help him with his troubles."

Kitty watched the hoop spin as the girl maneuvered it with her stick. That was her life, Kitty thought—she would have to keep moving if she didn't want to fall.

To distract herself, Kitty browsed through the papers on the
drive to the *Sentinel*. But the headlines, which she once would
have skimmed over, now took on a new significance:

**WILSON SAYS HE WILL ACT PROMPTLY AFTER
DECIDING REPLY TO GERMANY; AMERICAN
COMMENT DISTURBS BERLIN.**

Echoing the theme, a newsboy on the corner shouted:
"President Plans to Return to Capital. Talks of New Warning
to Germans!"

Kitty wanted to scream with frustration. Had the president
ordered the Secret Service to spy on a German diplomat? Was
the country, much as it might not want to, sliding into war,
as Dr. Albert himself predicted? How was her father mixed up
in it? Kitty thumped her fist against her thigh. And why was
he *lying* on official documents? It wasn't a crime to supply the
Germans with phenol, but thinking of him as someone who
profited from death and destruction was scarce consolation.

Never before had she been so glad to step inside the *Sentinel*.
Never had she been more relieved to see that clock or the
mosaic decorating the floor. At least here, for the most part, life
remained predictable.

She rode up in the elevator, eager to resume her duties. She
neared her desk and noticed that Jeannie's place was empty; the
typist was sitting in Kitty's seat.

Jeannie didn't hear Kitty approach over the din of the machines.

"I hope you approve," Kitty said.

Startled, the other girl dropped her pencil. "Oh, Miss

Weeks!" A crimson stain spread across Jeannie's cheeks. "You took me by surprise. Mr. Hewitt said I should check the Anne Morgan interview."

"And how does it stack up? Are there very many errors?" Kitty couldn't control the bite in her tone, but Jeannie didn't seem to notice.

"You write so clearly, Miss Weeks," she said. "What a treat it must have been to visit the Colony Club and speak to Miss Morgan."

"May I?" Kitty moved to hang her purse on the back of her chair.

"Mr. Hewitt said you should speak to him," Jeannie replied.

Could Jeannie have moved because she, Kitty, was being promoted to Miss Busby's position? That didn't seem likely.

She knocked on the Weekend Supplement editor's door.

"I suppose you're wondering why Miss Williams is in your place," he said when Kitty came in. "She's a surprise, that girl." The editor removed his glasses, fogged them with his breath, and gave them a quick polish with his handkerchief before returning them to his nose. "Much more competent than I expected. Stayed until eight last night without my having to ask and was back at seven thirty this morning."

"Miss Williams is a hard worker," Kitty agreed. She couldn't compete with that kind of dedication, but still, she had other skills to offer.

"You will be happy to know that I spoke to Miss Busby's physician, and he told me that she would need plenty of rest, as well as complete peace and quiet for the next four to six weeks in order to recover. In the meantime, I will take over as Ladies' Page editor."

"Yes, Mr. Hewitt."

"As such," he went on, "I require an assistant who is able to work long hours on short notice."

"I understand, Mr. Hewitt." Kitty noticed that he hadn't invited her to pull up a chair.

"You see, I warned Miss Busby when she hired her apprentice to pick a workhorse and not a thoroughbred, but she wouldn't listen. And she's paid the price. Thoroughbreds look pretty, and they do a few things well, but they're fussy. They don't stand up to everyday use. You may as well know that Miss Williams applied for your position when it was announced."

"I see," Kitty said. No one had told her that. Not Miss Busby, not Jeannie, nor any of the other girls.

"She was my first choice, but Miss Busby rejected her. She said that you had something none of the other applicants possessed."

"May I ask what?" Kitty hoped to hear something complimentary, like intelligence or eloquence, but right now, she'd settle for good penmanship or a mastery of grammar.

"Miss Busby told me that she wanted someone with class, someone who dressed well and spoke well. It didn't trouble her that you had never worked before, either at a newspaper or anywhere else."

Kitty staggered as though she'd been punched. How could she have flattered herself that Miss Busby had seen some latent merit in her, some untapped potential?

"It's not my fault," she protested. "Miss Busby didn't allow me to do any heavy lifting. It's only recently that she gave me any freedom—"

"That's exactly my point." The editor sounded firm. "This

isn't about you or your talents—such as they may be. It's about work. Hard work, day-to-day work. The ability to churn out paragraphs day after day on any subject, for any reason.

"I'm afraid I don't have much patience for thoroughbreds. I have enough on my plate as it is, and what I need is a work-horse. Miss Busby is free to hire you back once she returns."

"Please, Mr. Hewitt," Kitty begged. "Give me one more chance." She didn't offer any excuses since she didn't think he would care to hear them.

The editor pulled a stack of files toward him. "I suggest, Miss Weeks, that you think long and hard about whether you are suited to our profession. I think you're unhappy because humble Miss Williams has displaced you. After some time, you will real-ize that today was a blessing in disguise. And if you don't"—he opened one of the folders—"well, that's not my problem."

Kitty returned to her desk—or, rather, Jeannie's desk. "Did you know about this?" she demanded.

"I'm sorry, Miss Weeks." Jeannie stood to allow Kitty to col-lect her things. "If I thought that it would end like this, I would never have agreed to help yesterday." She sounded contrite, but her wisp of a smile revealed the pride she felt in her promotion.

Kitty swept her few personal items into her purse: a pen, a rabbit's foot good-luck charm from a school friend, and a pocket dictionary.

"I hope you can forgive me," Jeannie said. Kitty's Anne Morgan interview sat on the desk, neatly corrected in red ink.

"Good luck, Miss Williams." Kitty hurried away before she said something she might regret.

She had been ousted by Jeannie Williams, a girl she hadn't

even perceived to be a threat. She had been found lacking, not because she had disobeyed Miss Busby and gone off on her own, but because she didn't work hard enough or—and perhaps this was the same thing—for enough hours in the day. Miss Busby had hired her not because of what she could do, but because of her breeding.

None of the typists batted an eyelid as Kitty left the hen coop. As she made her way through the cavernous hall for the last time, it seemed that the music from their machines swelled to a crescendo.

It was her send-off, Kitty thought, trying to stifle any feeling of self-pity: a screeching symphony of metal against metal that produced nothing but line after line of black type against white paper, each and every day.

CHAPTER TWENTY-SIX

Kitty couldn't believe that all her efforts had been for nothing: her meeting with Mrs. Stepan, the interview with Anne Morgan, the months of drudgery leading up to it. None of it mattered, and worse still, Mr. Hewitt believed that she wasn't cut out to be a journalist.

A newspaper boy shouted, "Harry Thaw to Know His Fate Tonight!" Streetcars clanged noisily. Elevated trains clattered in the distance. Whoever said that New York was a great city had blundered. It was mayhem, a place where a million and a half souls feverishly pursued their business without regard for any niceties.

Kitty walked back home. There was no need to take a cab, because she wasn't in a hurry. She recalled the questions Miss Busby had posed to her when she came in to apply for the position as her assistant. They had been lifted straight from *Journalism for Women*, although Kitty hadn't realized that at the time.

"Are you seriously addicted to reading the newspapers?" Miss Busby had said. "Does the thought frequently occur to you, apropos of incidents witnessed, that this would make fine copy for a story? Do you have the reputation among your friends for being an excellent letter writer?"

Kitty had replied yes to each question. She read the

newspapers—not necessarily the political stories, but those with human interest.

"Quite right." Miss Busby had nodded.

"And I do see things I would like to know more about." Kitty had several questions about the city and how society functioned. "And I think my friends enjoy my letters."

In retrospect, her answers hadn't been terribly compelling, but Miss Busby hired her nonetheless. Of course she had—she didn't require an apprentice reporter. She had wanted someone with the social graces to enter any living room in town, and Kitty fit the bill exactly.

She had been a fool, Kitty thought. Naive and vain. So self-centered that she couldn't see that Jeannie's goodwill toward her might not have been entirely disinterested.

Kitty stopped herself. The past was the past. She would do better next time—and there *would* be a next time. If not at the *Sentinel*, then elsewhere.

The doorman at the New Century tipped his hat as Kitty entered, dusty and perspiring.

"Good morning, Miss Weeks."

"I hope you don't have anything for me, George." She managed a smile.

"No, ma'am, nothing today."

The cool foyer, which usually felt like a sanctuary from the busy streets now felt like a hotel—some luxurious but temporary accommodation from which her trunks would be shipped off to the next destination.

She rode up in the brass-trimmed elevator. Grace opened the front door when she rang the bell.

"You're back early, Miss Kitty." The maid took Kitty's purse and gloves.

The telephone rang in the foyer, and Kitty picked it up.

"I'm coming to get you," the voice on the other end of the line said.

"What?" Kitty's grip on the receiver tightened.

"Say 'I beg your pardon,' silly girl."

"Oh, Amanda. It's you." Kitty relaxed.

"Of course it's me. Who else could it be? I hope you haven't forgotten today."

"What is today, Bastille Day?"

"It is that." Amanda paused. "It's also the first day of the YWCA training. You promised me you'd come, Capability. I told all my friends that you would be there."

"What time is it at?"

"Four o'clock. I'll pick you up. By the way, Mama wants me to ask you a favor."

"I don't think I'm in a position to do anyone a favor at the moment." Normally, Kitty would have jumped at the chance to oblige snooty Mrs. Vanderwell.

"You can pay a visit to Mrs. Basshor," Amanda said. "Poor Bessie has been reduced to a puddle of jelly over the business with Hotchkiss, and Mama thought it might help to have someone from the outside hear her out. You can tell the old dear that you will write a story about it. You don't have to actually do anything—just tell her you might. I think Bessie would like to feel that someone cares. That someone is willing to listen to her side of things."

The words echoed Kitty's remark to Hotchkiss just eight

days before. That she would help Mrs. Basshor tell her side of the story. It didn't feel like eight days; too much had happened since then.

"I don't work for the paper anymore," Kitty said.

"You don't? No wonder you're home." A pause. "Well, just pretend that you do for one more day. And, Capability—"

"Yes?"

"You do realize that this gives you one less reason for turning me down."

"If I hadn't realized before, I do now, Amanda."

"See you at three thirty?"

"I'll be ready." Kitty hung up the telephone.

She went to her rooms and opened a black-lacquered Russian keepsake box, decorated with a painting of a young man on a horse jumping over the shining sun. It contained letters and cards from friends as well as the last letter her father had sent her. In the winter of '13, while Kitty was still on her European tour, Julian Weeks had written to tell her that as soon as he found a suitable place for them to stay in Manhattan, she would be joining him for good.

The remaining month of her trip had passed in a haze, overshadowed by visions of their future together. The last week of her Atlantic crossing aboard the *Aquitania* had seemed interminable. She had flirted with a handsome young man from Virginia, but her heart hadn't been in it. All she'd really wanted was to set foot on native soil and enjoy living with her one remaining parent. Their arrangement—him at his club, her at the *Sentinel*—might have continued until the day she married or the day one of them died if she remained a spinster.

Kitty put her father's letter back in the box. Instead, it would all come to an end because of the Secret Service men and their talk of phenol and falsified passport applications.

"More than three million soldiers have perished," the representative from the Red Cross told the audience of young women who were gathered on wooden benches, watching images flash across a cloth screen.

"I will enumerate the death toll for you: France has lost three hundred thousand men; Germany, a quarter of a million. Thirty thousand British troops have perished. Austria-Hungary has lost a million and a quarter, and Russia one and a half million."

On the screen, helmeted soldiers, their rifles at the ready, stood in twisting gullies of narrow trenches. At some unheard signal, they scrambled to the surface, fountains of dust erupting around them, and they fell like dominoes.

The image shifted to a scene of infantrymen, cavalry, and teams of horses pulling carts loaded with cannons marching down a country road as though to take the place of their fallen comrades.

"All told, that's five times the number who were killed during the entire Civil War," the woman from the Red Cross continued. "In the span of less than a year."

Kitty turned to look at Amanda, who seemed rapt in concentration. To kill more than three million men in a little under a year must require a tremendous amount of weaponry. If her father sold phenol to either side, he had a hand in the horrific death toll. She had always assumed that, like any decent man,

Mr. Weeks must be against war-profiteering. On the other hand—she hated to even think this—she could imagine him saying matter-of-factly that someone would make money from the war, so why shouldn't it be him?

The Red Cross representative, a no-nonsense woman with her hair pulled into a tight bun, had moved on to the subject of the injured and wounded.

Kitty couldn't bear to watch a nurse unwrap bandages from charred and oozing limbs. The images became worse: a soldier screamed in agony as a doctor sawed off his leg; another moved his hand away from the side of his head, revealing a hole in the place where his ear should have been. To Kitty's surprise, Amanda didn't flinch.

"Chlorine gas has been used to devastating effect," the Red Cross representative continued, "and has killed scores of soldiers as well as civilians."

The newsreel concluded with images of injured and crippled men recovering in a convalescent home, tended to by uniformed women in white caps.

"We need your help," the speaker said. "This is woman's work, and there is no one more suited to the task, but those planning to go abroad must be ready to remain calm and resourceful even under the most taxing conditions. You must be prepared to set aside all sentimental feelings and obey without question the orders of your superiors. If you are able to do all of this, then I can think of no better reward than the effect you will have on your patients."

A round of enthusiastic applause broke out. Amanda took Kitty's arm. "What do you think?"

The lights came back on, sparing Kitty from having to answer.

The representative from the Red Cross began to describe the training course. It would last five weeks, and graduates of the program would receive an official certificate signed by the president. They wouldn't become registered nurses, just nurse's aides, so they should give up all hopes of wearing the cap.

Laughter rippled through the room.

She went on to outline the course of study in further detail: mornings would be spent in lectures and demonstration, afternoons at hospitals. Fridays would be devoted to practicing invalid cookery and working on first-aid techniques using dummies.

"Registration forms can be found at the back of the room," the speaker said. "Feel free to check with me if you have any questions."

A trio of well-heeled girls came up to Amanda. Kitty recalled Miss Nicholls and Miss Hibben from the concert at Carnegie Hall, and Amanda introduced her to the third, Miss Amour.

"If the course is good enough for Miss Cleveland, it's good enough for me," Miss Amour said with a giggle, referring to the former president's daughter, who had become a nurse's aide.

"Mama says we can be placed with her friends, the Haywards, who have given over their country home entirely to the convalescing men," Miss Hibben added.

Miss Nicholls turned to Kitty. "So, will you be joining us, Miss Weeks?"

Four pairs of eyes stared at Kitty. Four young women, all about her age, all the cream of society, waited for her answer.

Kitty knew that, once made, the offer would not be repeated.

"Miss Weeks?" Miss Nicholls prompted.

Kitty's future flashed before her eyes: Arm in arm with

Amanda. Working hard. Traveling to Europe. Accomplishing something worthwhile. Accepted as part of a set. And not just any set, the best one.

"I'm sorry. I can't." Not while so much was up in the air.

"You can't or you won't, Capability?" Amanda said, dismayed.

"I don't know."

Miss Hibben linked her arm through Amanda's. Miss Amour and Miss Nicholls curtsied. Four backs turned on Kitty. Only Amanda looked over her shoulder, and that was just for an instant.

ren't you going to work this morning?" Julian Weeks looked out from behind his paper. Kitty had joined him at breakfast later than usual.

She filled a glass with water and swallowed an Aspirin for her headache. "I am." If he could hide the truth, then so could she. After all, wasn't she his daughter?

"This is amusing." He sniffed and read, "'Austria-Hungary Protests Our Export of Arms to Britain and Her Allies; Says We Have Means of Exporting to All Alike.'"

"I don't see what's funny about that." She buttered her toast with such force that the slice broke in two.

"It's the Austrian foreign minister's language. You can tell he's terrified of upsetting us. Listen to how he dances around his complaint—on the one hand, he observes that the United States has been exporting war materials on a great scale to Britain and her allies, and that Austria and Germany have been almost entirely cut off from the American market. Then he says"—Mr. Weeks quoted from the article—"'the question arises whether conditions as they have developed during the course of the war, certainly independently of the wish of the American government, are not of such a kind as in their effect to turn the Washington cabinet in a contrary direction from neutrality.'"

He turned to Kitty. "Can you decipher that?"

"I'm not sure that I care to." She brushed crumbs from her hands.

"What's the matter?"

"Nothing." Nothing, she thought, except that his actions had compromised them both. If she believed she might get a direct answer, Kitty would have spoken to him directly, but from experience, she knew she needed to be better informed, or else he would deflect her questions.

As if to underscore the point, his newspaper went back up, creating a wall of words between them.

Kitty finished her breakfast in silence, dressed for the day, and told her father she would take a cab to work. Instead, she walked toward Broadway.

"Miss Weeks!" She was halfway down the block when a voiced called her name. She turned around to see one of the Secret Service men running after her.

"Mr. Soames."

"I have a message for you from Agent Booth. He'd like to meet tomorrow at nine o'clock."

"And what if I don't have any additional information?"

"Look, Miss Weeks." He took off his hat and ran a hand through his hair. "I'd have preferred to have done this some other way—but now that we're at this point, please, do both of us a favor. Give Agent Booth what he needs, and let us move on." His brown eyes looked sincere.

"I have no guarantee that you won't use what I tell you to hurt my father."

"How should I put this?" He looked away for a second,

thinking. "What we're interested in is the phenol, Miss Weeks. Tell us about that, and I promise—unless Mr. Weeks has committed some monstrous crime, which I'm sure he hasn't—I will personally make sure that any irregularities in his actions are treated with the utmost leniency."

Kitty hesitated.

"I've already told you more than I should," Agent Soames said, "so please believe me."

Kitty continued on to the public library. Unless there was some other highly profitable use for the compound, her father could only be selling phenol to the Germans. There was only one hitch to that guess—one that Mr. Musser had pointed out when he and Kitty had discussed Hunter Cole and horses. Germany was finding it almost impossible to ship supplies across the Atlantic, so even if they bought the phenol, what would they do with it?

Kitty spoke to the librarian, Miss Evers, and asked for a book on the uses of various chemicals.

"Any chemical in particular that you're interested in, Miss Weeks?" The librarian seemed curious.

Kitty cleared her throat. "Phenol."

The woman's eyes widened. "I see. Just a moment."

She returned with a heavy volume. Kitty carried it away to a table. She opened *Common Chemical Compounds and Their Applications* and flipped through densely printed columns of text. The long strings of C's and H's and O's with tiny numbers dangling below, as if from a laundry line, looked like symbols from a foreign language. The Misses Dancey saw no reason to teach their charges chemistry or physics. When one of Kitty's classmates had pointed out Marie Curie's accomplishments, the older Miss Dancey had replied, "That's fine for her. She's Polish."

Kitty consulted the index at the back to find the chemical name for phenol—"C_6H_5OH, hydroxybenzene." There was a page number listed beside it.

Kitty read the full entry to herself. "Also known as carbolic acid...derived from coal tar...crystalline compound at room temperature." A list of uses followed. "Key ingredient in the manufacture of disinfectants and germicides. Also used in the manufacture of dyes, perfumes, carbolic soap, household cleaners, photographic chemicals, phonograph records, and in the production of salicylic acid..."

Although none of the uses seemed promising, Kitty copied down the list and returned the book to Miss Evers.

Who could she turn to for advice—Amanda? Mr. Musser? Kitty groaned. She must telephone the old man and let him know that, for the present, she no longer worked at the *Sentinel*. She had left in such a hurry that she forgot to say good-bye.

She headed down Broadway and passed the Majestic, which was playing Pearl White's latest picture. Kitty wondered what Pearl would do in her shoes. How did the feisty heroines she portrayed respond to seemingly impossible situations?

She paid ten cents and bought herself a ticket. Since each episode of Miss White's serials lasted only about twenty minutes, she might as well take a look. If nothing else, a short break would do her good.

She settled into a seat between two schoolgirls playing hooky and a mother with young children. Usually, Kitty took Grace with her to the movies, but the audience at matinee shows, especially for Pearl's pictures, was mostly female. She need not worry about being molested in the darkness.

A colored slide advertising a new book appeared on the screen: "A Chicago Girl's Harrowing Adventure…Drugged in a Restaurant, She Barely Escapes! *THE GIRL WHO DISAPPEARED* by Clifford G. Roe. Published by the Uplift Press. $1.00 only." The Junior League House was next: "Absolutely fireproof hotel for unmarried women. Prices include three meals per day."

The Romance of Elaine began a few minutes later, following the production company Pathé's emblem, the proud French cockerel. Like all of Pearl's wildly successful serials, it was an adventure. Kitty had missed prior episodes, but it didn't take her too long to find her bearings. A title card introduced the audience to Elaine's nemesis, German secret agent and saboteur Marcus del Mar.

It hit too close to home, Kitty thought, and she watched with growing unease as del Mar and his female accomplice drugged the unsuspecting Elaine and spirited her away to a secluded cabin in the woods. When Elaine regained consciousness, she found herself bound and gagged in an empty room. She struggled free from her bonds and snuck out, but del Mar discovered that she had escaped and chased her through the forest.

Fortunately, Elaine found an abandoned canoe, jumped in, and paddled away, but one of del Mar's well-aimed bullets shattered her only paddle.

A steep waterfall thundered in the distance, the current pulling Elaine toward it.

What would the desperate girl do?

Kitty sat on the edge of her seat.

In the nick of time, Elaine's admirer, Walter Jameson, who had been searching for her, tossed her a rope. Elaine caught hold of it and leaped to safety seconds before the canoe plunged into the abyss.

"To Be Continued…" A title card flashed on the screen while the audience, stunned for a moment, clapped and cheered.

Kitty rose and squeezed her way out of the theater; others remained to see the picture that followed.

She stepped out onto the street, blinking in the bright daylight. Unlike Elaine, she had no Walter Jameson to come to her rescue. She was on her own.

Chapter Twenty-Eight

Kitty knew she was killing time. She didn't have a plan, and yet, she couldn't stand idle. One of the Misses Dancey favorite mottoes was "When in doubt, do something. Activity pays dividends."

With Amanda's request in mind, she took a taxi to Mrs. Basshor's apartment.

"Delphy Vanderwell told me you'd come if her daughter asked." The hostess's lips twisted into a smile. She lay bundled in a shawl on her chaise longue, the windows to her pale-yellow morning room tightly closed. "My world is smaller without Hotchkiss. I relied on him completely, but I didn't realize how much he meant to me until he was gone."

"May I be of assistance?" Kitty fanned herself with a magazine. She hoped Amanda would return the favor one day if it became necessary.

"You can tell those damned police fellows to believe me for a start," the hostess said. "Hotchkiss would never shoot anyone, let alone kill himself. He begged my forgiveness in his letter, but he knew I would have forgiven him for anything. What I can't stand is his absence."

"So Mr. Hotchkiss wasn't stealing from you?"

"Of course he was. I knew it. And he knew that I knew."

Elizabeth Basshor pulled herself up from her recumbent position. "I told the police that we never discussed what he did
with my money. I looked the other way. Did you read the
letter he wrote to me before he took his life?"

"Only the parts that were printed in the paper."

"That was garbage. And the police took away the original
for evidence. But I remember it clearly, and nowhere did he
confess to shooting Hunter. Nowhere."

"Why commit suicide then? I mean, if you knew he
was stealing—"

"Exactly!" Life flooded back into Mrs. Basshor's face. "He
begged my forgiveness, but as I say, there was nothing to
forgive. So I have to conclude that he was trying to tell me
something that all of us have missed."

Kitty began to feel light-headed. It was either the heat or
Mrs. Basshor's wild guesses. She asked for some water.

The hostess tinkled a bell. "Do you keep a cook, Miss Weeks?"

"Yes."

"Does she do the marketing or someone else?"

"She does." Kitty wondered where Mrs. Basshor was going
with this.

"Then you must know what I'm talking about."

"I'm afraid I don't, Mrs. Basshor."

"What do they teach you girls these days?"

The maid brought in water on a tray, and Kitty gratefully
took a sip.

"In my day," the hostess said, "we had to draw, paint, play
an instrument, sing, and dance, as well as run a house. Do you
pay your cook well?"

"The going rate." Kitty wondered whether Mrs. Basshor would come up with another of her personal ambushes. If so, this time she would be ready for it.

"There's a going rate for cooks who do the marketing, and a higher rate for ones who don't," Elizabeth Basshor said. "You are familiar with that arrangement?" She looked at Kitty in dismay. "No, I can see that you aren't. A cook who does the marketing charges less, because she takes a cut of whatever she buys for her mistress." She explained it as though to an imbecile.

Fairly certain that Mrs. Codd did no such thing, Kitty replied with a touch of asperity, "I keep a running tab at the grocer's and pay in full at the end of each month."

"That's what you think." Mrs. Basshor laughed. "Speak to your grocer, my dear. Ask him whether he's slipping your cook a couple of dollars each month. Not that he'll tell you anything. But that's the way things are done.

"I knew Hotchkiss was pocketing a portion of my expenses. That's par for the course. And when it came to the party, of course he would expect a bonus. So you see, if Mr. Cole had threatened him about it, he wouldn't have been concerned. And certainly not concerned enough to murder Hunter and then take his own life. If your cook was pinching a bit from you when she did the groceries and I accused her, would she shoot me and then kill herself? Really."

"Put that way, it does make sense." Kitty's head spun. She had been lectured about phenol by Secret Service agents and now about how to pay one's cook by a society hostess.

"Can you do something about it then?" Mrs. Basshor leaned forward eagerly. "I know what I said when you first came here, about your wanting to be a reporter and all. But you should ignore that. I was angry that you were doing what I had wanted to do and were getting away with it."

"You wanted to be a journalist?"

"Not exactly. But I did want to do something daring and provocative. I still do." Mrs. Basshor fluffed her hair. "Anyhow, that's not the point. I'd like you to tell your readers my story."

"I no longer work for the paper, Mrs. Basshor. They let me go," Kitty said.

"Who did—the beanpole?"

"Miss Busby has been taken ill. It was her supervisor."

"Well, that's ridiculous. You're very good. I'll have a word with Frieda Eichendorff, shall I?"

"Please, Mrs. Basshor, don't say anything to anyone."

"Well, who will help me with what I want to say about Hotchkiss?"

"I'm afraid I can't help you there."

Mrs. Basshor sighed. "The police, my lawyer, and even my friends think I'm a fool... What will you do now?"

"I haven't formed a plan yet."

Mrs. Basshor leaned back and placed an eye pillow over her face. "You shouldn't let one individual's actions stop you."

"What about everything you said about my not being able to get married?"

"Didn't I just tell you to forget it? When you're ready to settle down, come see me. And in the meantime, please help me clear my secretary's name."

Kitty reached a decision on the taxi ride back home: if she couldn't glean the information she needed from her father, she must try to extract it from one of his associates.

"Back so soon?" Mr. Weeks called from his study.

Kitty handed Grace her purse and gloves. "It's one o'clock," she said as she went in.

"I suppose I've grown accustomed to the longer hours you've been keeping recently."

She drummed her fingers on the back of his sofa. "Would you mind telephoning Mr. Maitland? I think it's a good day for an outing to the Cloisters. If he's free, I'd like to go."

"Wouldn't it be better if you went with a friend your own age?" Julian Weeks sounded baffled. "Maitland is entertaining but hardly a spring chicken."

"It's only a trip to a museum, Papa." The comparison amused Kitty, but she couldn't help resenting him for putting her in this position. If she knew more about his life, she wouldn't have to resort to such tricks.

"Should I accompany you?" Julian Weeks said. He seemed unsure about how to proceed.

"Please don't," Kitty replied at once, then added, "You've told me time and time again that you don't care for religious art."

Mr. Maitland arrived in a chauffeur-driven limousine at three. Kitty and her father exchanged a glance before she climbed in.

"Are you sure you won't join us, Julian?" Mr. Maitland asked.

To Kitty's relief, Mr. Weeks waved them off.

The buildings on West End Avenue flashed past Kitty's window as the motorcar raced uptown. Kitty began to have misgivings. The Misses Dancey had warned their charges not to drive in automobiles with strange men after a discussion on how chauffeurs not only ignited motors, but also passions. The word *chauffeur*, after all, came from the French *chauffer*—to heat.

"Apparently, George Gray Barnard, the man behind the Cloisters' collection, bought many of his pieces from French peasants," Maitland said. "He paid as little as thirty francs for some."

"I had no idea. And this was recently?"

"Oh yes, within the last decade. He found farmers allowing their chickens to lay eggs on medieval platforms and supporting their vines on ancient columns. To my mind, that makes him not just a great collector but one of the best."

"Because he bought things cheaply?"

"Because"—Maitland turned to face her—"he saw beauty where others didn't."

Kitty shifted uncomfortably in her seat.

"He also acquired an arcade from the Abbey of Saint-Michel-de-Cuxa." Maitland resumed speaking like a lecturer. "No one thought much of it at first, but then the French government made quite a fuss about the arcade leaving the country. In hindsight, it's fortunate that it didn't remain on-site. If it had, it's quite likely that it might have been blown to smithereens by now. France isn't just losing thousands of men each day; she's also bleeding away her history."

Kitty struggled to find a way to broach the subject on her

mind. Should she start with general questions? And if that weren't enough, Mr. Maitland's talkativeness made it hard to get a word in edgewise.

"I'd like to create a museum in Canada someday," he told her. "One that will have my name on it." He chuckled. "I'm afraid I'm not self-effacing like Mr. Barnard."

They arrived at a barnlike building overlooking the Harlem River at 699 Fort Washington Avenue. Maitland's chauffeur opened the door, and Kitty stepped out onto the street and, a few paces later, into a world of pious saints, demure Virgins, and gargoyles sticking out their tongues from cornices and capitals.

She followed Mr. Maitland beneath ancient arches, between fluted stone pillars, and past entire walls that had been transplanted from their original faraway sites to create a magical experience that resembled neither wandering through a museum nor a church, but something altogether different.

Mythical beasts leaped out from friezes, tenacious flora curled up columns, fantastical creatures—some human and some animal, some a combination of both—mocked Kitty's astonishment.

Maitland paused to examine a six-hundred-year-old Madonna and Child. Kitty stared at a frieze in which the devil, burning with glee, prodded a row of protesting sinners into the flames of hell.

They walked on to the main attraction—the cloisters, a tranquil courtyard bordered on all four sides by a covered walkway with a fountain at its center.

"Mr. Maitland?"

"Yes?" His voice was hushed. "Did you know that hundreds of years ago, this is where monks prayed?"

"May I ask what kind of business you're doing with my father?"

Maitland turned away, but not before she noticed his look of distaste. "This is hardly an appropriate moment."

Kitty could have kicked herself. How could she have waited so long only to put the question so baldly?

He headed back inside. "I'm no fool," he said under his breath. "I had an inkling that you might not be interested in me personally, but I thought you might enjoy my company. I can see that I'm mistaken."

"I beg your pardon, Mr. Maitland." She would love to start again. "I only asked—"

He raised a hand to silence her. "Because you think I'm leading your father astray? Julian warned me that might be the case and he said not to say anything to you for that very reason. But I'm not a Rasputin—I'm a businessman—and whatever decision Julian has made, he's made of his own free will. I don't *lead* anyone anywhere. He came to *me* with the proposal."

"What proposal, Mr. Maitland?"

"Don't you know?"

"No."

"I see. You must speak to Julian then."

He gestured toward a section of the museum they hadn't visited. "I'm going to take a look over there. I'll meet you in a quarter of an hour."

Kitty took a seat on a bench beside a mother and daughter pair. All roads led to her father. She would have to find a way to broach the question with him.

The child tugged at her mother's skirt. "I want to go home! I don't like it here!"

"None of this is real. There's no need to be afraid," the mother said.

If only that were true, Kitty thought. The clock was ticking, and she hadn't made any progress.

Maitland returned, and he and Kitty climbed into the car in silence.

"Your father and I are going into the pharmaceutical business," he said after a while. "But it's complicated. That's the part that Julian doesn't like."

Kitty had no idea what he was talking about.

"I think you ought to understand that, unlike Canada, the United States upholds Bayer's patent."

"I'm sorry, Mr. Maitland—who is Mr. Bayer, and what does he have to do with my father?"

"Bayer is the company that manufactures Aspirin, Miss Weeks. But Aspirin is just an invented name for a chemical compound. Anyone can make it, and in other parts of the world, they do. However, Bayer currently has a monopoly on the American market.

"In two years, their patent will expire, and then we'll be able to sell our product here. We won't be able to call it Aspirin, of course—Bayer has trademarked that and spends a fortune on advertisements in the hopes that customers won't buy anything else."

"You and my father are making Aspirin?" Kitty said incredulously.

"ASA," Maitland replied, "short for acetylsalicylic acid, which is the same thing as Aspirin, but not the same name. And we're not making ASA in the United States, only in Canada— where it's legal."

"So why won't my father discuss it?"

"That's Julian for you. He gets nervous about details."

Kitty thought for a moment. "What did you say ASA stands for again?"

"Acetylsalicylic acid."

"That wouldn't happen to have anything to do with salicylic acid, would it?" Kitty vaguely remembered the word, or something like it, from her list.

"As a matter of fact, it does."

"And does my father supply you with the phenol to make it?"

Maitland's jaw dropped. "What do they teach you girls?"

"I read an article." Kitty waited for him to answer.

"Well, you're correct. Without Julian's supply, I'd have to close down my factory. In the short term, you see, it's much more lucrative to use phenol to make explosives."

A wide smile split across Kitty's cheeks. "Well, that's tremendous." And here she had been thinking her father sold the stuff to take lives, not save them.

"We stand to make a killing by '17," Maitland continued. "Everyone needs ASA, especially all those injured men coming out of the battlefront. Not to mention anyone with a garden-variety fever or headache."

"And your operation requires a large quantity of phenol?" All that remained was to check that her father sold his full supply to the Canadian.

"Yes, it does." Maitland stared at her in amazement. "I'm sorry. That word sounds strange coming from your lips."

It felt strange too, Kitty thought, and after tomorrow, she hoped never again to have to repeat it.

Chapter Twenty-Nine

Nothing could dampen Kitty's ebullient mood when she entered the apartment.

"How was the outing?" Julian Weeks called. He sat in his study, chewing on the end of a Cuban cigar and tapping his foot in time to the lively rhythm of the Clef Club playing on the gramophone.

"It was lovely, just lovely." She perched on the arm of his settee.

"And Maitland didn't talk your ear off?"

Kitty took a deep breath. "He told me that you're working with him to manufacture ASA in Canada."

Julian Weeks's foot stilled. He put down his cigar, rose, and lifted the needle from the phonograph record. The room went quiet.

"I hope you're not angry with him," Kitty said. "It was I who asked."

Julian Weeks poured himself a drink. "The world has become too complicated." He took a large swig. "It's all right for Maitland—he's Canadian—but I'm participating in the production of a drug that's still under patent in the United States."

"As far as I understand," Kitty said carefully, "he's neither producing nor selling it here. So your participation shouldn't be a problem."

"That's what my lawyer tells me." He sat back down, his mouth twisted in a grimace. "I'm an old-fashioned man, and I like to do business the old-fashioned way. Buy something cheap in one place, sell it for more elsewhere. I hate"—he almost spat out the word—"to depend on legal niceties that I must have interpreted for me by specialists."

One small matter troubled Kitty. "Why did you go to the Edelweiss Café?"

He looked puzzled. "Why do you keep going back to that?"

"I'm just curious. Does it have any connection to the phenol?"

"Who said anything about phenol?"

"Mr. Maitland did." Kitty spoke quickly to cover up her slip.

"That man talks too much."

"Are you buying the phenol from Dr. Albert?"

"Doctor who?"

"Ah." Kitty panicked. "Dr. Albert," she repeated, as though the name was common knowledge.

Her father glared at her. "I've never heard of him. Who is he?"

"He…" Kitty scrambled for an answer. "He's in the papers. I wanted to check something with you, so I peeked into the restaurant and saw him there. I recognized his face from a photograph. I thought you knew."

"No, I don't know." He seemed honestly surprised.

"He's Dr. Heinrich Friedrich Albert," Kitty said as noncha-lantly as she could manage. "The German commercial attaché."

Julian Weeks's brow darkened. "Out," he thundered. "Right now. And close the door."

Kitty did as she was told but waited outside in the foyer. She heard him pick up the telephone and speak to the operator.

As quietly as she could, Kitty picked up the earpiece in the hall.

"Schweitzer," she heard him say.

"Good evening, Mr. Weeks." The man at the other end of the line spoke with a thick accent. "What can I do for you today?"

"You can tell me the truth for starters—"

"I beg your pardon?"

"Who is this Dr. Albert who can be recognized from his photograph in the papers? You told me that we would be meeting a colleague of yours from out of town. Now I find out he's Germany's commercial attaché?"

After a pause, the voice replied, "I apologize, Mr. Weeks. It was not my intention to deceive you."

"But you did."

"You see, the problem is"—Schweitzer sounded nervous— "Dr. Albert—"

"So I did meet this Dr. Albert."

"Dr. Albert," the other continued, "is very particular. He wanted to make sure that you could be trusted."

"That *I* could be trusted?" Kitty would have heard her father's bellow without the telephone. "Who is this man? What right does he have to vet me?"

"He's the one who is paying for the phenol, sir."

"Come again?"

"I can't afford to advance the money for the purchase of surplus phenol from Mr. Edison's factories. As you know, they are one of the few firms in the United States capable of producing it—and they do so in order to be able to continue to manufacture their own gramophone records."

"Yes, yes. Go on."

"Dr. Albert put up the money for the purchase and used me as an intermediary, since Mr. Edison never would have sold to him. But since it has become almost impossible to send anything safely back to Germany, he, in turn, wanted me to find a buyer who could be guaranteed not to use it for the production of munitions that might fall into the enemy's hands. You see, I don't have much to do with it. I'm just the middle man."

"I gave you my word, Schweitzer. Pharmaceutical production in Canada, nothing else."

"And I told Herr Doktor that. But he insisted on meeting you in person. It was his idea that you should not know his identity."

"If I had," Kitty heard her father say, "I might have backed away."

"Now you know everything, sir. I promise there will be no further surprises."

"I hope not."

"Mr. Weeks?"

"Yes."

"I'm sorry, may I ask you a question?"

"Make it quick, Schweitzer. I must say I'm not in the best of moods. I'm still tempted to call this entire business off."

"May I ask how you recognized the commercial attaché from his likeness in the papers? I inquire because Dr. Albert goes to great lengths to avoid any kind of publicity. To the best of my knowledge, he has never been photographed."

Kitty helped herself to a handful of salted cashew nuts from the glass bowl in the living room. A few seconds later, she helped herself to some more. A pile of the latest issues of *Photoplay*, *Good Housekeeping*, and *Vogue* littered the sofa. It had been an hour since her father finished his telephone conversation, and she'd heard the front door slam behind him as he'd left the apartment.

She told herself that he would be back soon. Just a short while ago, she had doubted him, and now, what must he think of her?

Grace came in to ask whether Mr. Weeks would be home in time for dinner.

"Of course he will," Kitty snapped, "and please make sure that Mrs. Codd prepares his favorite chicken dish—the one with the apricots."

The telephone rang, and Kitty rushed to answer it. It was only Amanda, calling to thank her for visiting Mrs. Basshor.

"I don't think I accomplished much," Kitty said. "But I appreciate your taking the trouble to telephone."

"That you went so soon after I asked is enough. Bessie Basshor called Mama and told her you were the first person who really listened to what she had to say and that you understood her." Amanda's voice cracked. "It seems you have a talent for newspaper work, Capability, and if that's what you want to do, then you should do it. Don't worry about what the rest of us might say. But you ought not to have made a fool of me at the YWCA. It only makes matters worse when you pretend that you haven't made up your mind."

Kitty didn't think it would help to explain that at one point, she hadn't been certain she would refuse and that her choices, at the moment, were far from clear-cut.

"I put myself out for you," Amanda said, "and you let me down in front of my friends. I can allow bygones to be bygones once, but if it happens again, people will ask why I keep giving a girl from the wrong side of town another chance. You know that kind of thing isn't important to me—"

"But it is important in your circle." Kitty didn't have the strength to argue. "I appreciate the warning, Amanda."

"I don't mean it that way. Just make up your mind, and everything will be all right."

Coming from a long line of Vanderwells, it was easy for Amanda to say everything would be fine. She didn't need to worry about proving herself or her family's lineage. Kitty excused herself and hung up the receiver. She couldn't bear to be cooped up any longer, so she asked Grace to call downstairs for the Bearcat.

It was past seven, and Kitty had never driven alone at this hour. She headed toward Forty-Sixth and Madison. She thought her father might be at the Ritz-Carlton with Mr. Maitland, and she could bring him home. Or, if not (and Kitty didn't want to admit this to herself), she hoped that Mr. Maitland would make her troubles go away, as he had done this afternoon.

Kitty's hands trembled on the wheel. Her father used to call her his little Violet and tossed her in the air when he came home to their shady bungalow with the garden of palm trees and bougainvillea. When she made a mistake or did something reckless, he would correct her with a few well-chosen words or a smack on the hand, but he never walked out in disgust. He only started to call her by her first name, Capability, when she stepped off the gangplank in New York. Everyone else called her Kitty while she was growing up.

What had happened? Did she really know anything about him? They must clear the air between them. It had been far too long since they'd had an honest and open conversation.

"You will find Mr. Maitland in the Palm Court." The concierge replied to her query in hushed tones. If he thought it was unusual for a young lady to come in on her own, he didn't give it away in his manner or in his voice. "Would you like one of the bellboys to accompany you, madam?" he asked.

"That's quite all right." Kitty followed his directions and spotted Mr. Maitland at the far end of the glass-covered court. He was deep in conversation with a lady in an ostrich-feather hat.

He said something, and his companion threw her head back and laughed. There was no sign of Mr. Weeks, and Kitty turned to leave, but Maitland noticed her across the room and beckoned her over.

There was something about Mr. Maitland, perhaps his size combined with his intelligence, that exerted its own gravitational force over Kitty. She found herself drawn toward him, weaving her way through a field of circular tables.

There were couples in conversation to the right and left of her and, all around, the clinking of crystal glasses and silver knives and forks.

Mr. Maitland introduced her to Mrs. Cordell, recently arrived from Biarritz. His friend said something pleasant and then excused herself; she had to make sure that her packages had arrived.

"So how can I help you?" He pulled a chair back for Kitty. "Don't tell me you have more questions about acetylsalicylic acid, or phenol, or some other chemical compound?" He smiled.

"I thought I might find my father here." Kitty glanced at the two glasses of wine, the half-eaten plate of mushrooms on toast bread, and Mrs. Cordell's napkin tossed on the table.

"He wasn't home when you arrived?"

"He was."

"I see." Mr. Maitland folded his arms across his chest. "Then I'm sure he will be back."

Mrs. Cordell reappeared. "John," she called, "Lester's forgotten to deliver my music box."

Kitty stood. "I'm sorry to have disturbed your tête-à-tête." She felt stupid for not having recognized at once what she had interrupted. A man of the world, Mr. Maitland evidently had an eye for women, and they for him. "I should be on my way."

She left the hotel and climbed into the Bearcat. She was better off by herself.

CHAPTER THIRTY

W**here have you been?" Mr. Weeks demanded from his study. "I might ask you the same question." Kitty handed Grace her purse and gloves.

He had his back turned to her when she came in and then sat, having poured himself a tumbler of bourbon.

"Perhaps I made a mistake," he said. "Perhaps it was wrong of me to put you in a position where you had to ask my business colleague what I was doing. I still think of you as an eight-year-old, but I'm willing to change. Go on, ask me whatever you like, and I'll do my best to answer."

"Anything?" Kitty had expected a fight, not this laying down of arms.

"Within reason, yes." Mr. Weeks allowed himself a smile. "I won't pretend that I've changed overnight. But I do see that we can't allow this state of affairs to continue indefinitely, or it could easily spin out of control."

"Can we turn on some music?"

"No, let's talk. That's what you want, isn't it?"

The clock in the corner struck the quarter hour and kept ticking, its pendulum swinging back and forth.

Kitty laughed guiltily. "I don't know where to begin." She smoothed her skirts. "Do you have any questions for me?"

"Ladies first."

"All right, who vouched for you on your passport?"

She could tell that the question surprised him. But to his credit, he didn't flinch and replied at once, "I paid a stranger ten dollars for the favor, which he's probably already drunk through."

"Why do you need someone you don't know to lie for you?"

Mr. Weeks breathed in sharply. "I could tell you that it was the most expedient solution, but the truth is that I've spent years putting miles between myself and my past. I see no reason to undo that in order to satisfy some nitpicking requirement."

"What do you mean?" Kitty pressed him, eager for an answer. She had always suspected he was running away from something and that was why he never remained in one place for too long. She used to imagine him having committed some noble crime—killing a sailor in a barroom brawl, for instance, in order to protect a woman's honor.

"Did you do something wrong?" she said. His confession would explain his tight-lipped silence on certain subjects and his lack of childhood stories or mementos.

"No. Unless you consider it a misdemeanor to be orphaned." He cleared his throat. "Or perhaps my parents are still alive. I don't know who they are, so I can't be certain."

"But I thought—"

"I know what you thought, or rather, what I allowed you to think. But you should know what really happened. There were no parents who died when I was a boy and left me to be raised by uncaring relatives."

The image that Kitty had held in her mind for all these years dropped and shattered into a million pieces.

"I was abandoned on the doorstep of a crumbling convent when I was an infant and was raised by unforgiving nuns. My name was Peter then."

Peter? Kitty looked at him. *Peter?* She couldn't believe it. The words kept coming.

"We had three Peters, three Pauls, and five Gabriels, their favorite. Whenever they called a name, whichever ones of us had it had to come running. If you didn't run fast enough…" He shook his head at the memory. "Let's just say that their reed switch would help remind you to run faster. As far as I'm concerned, my story begins when I escaped and stowed away on a vessel sailing out of Baltimore."

At least she had heard this part before.

"Before then, I was no one. I became who I am on the ocean."

Kitty's wrenching relocation to Switzerland when she was eight hardly compared to his plight.

"I was about thirteen at the time. I'm not sure of my exact age, because no one knows it. When the ship's cook found me hiding behind a sack of potatoes and asked my name, I told him 'Julian,' after Caesar."

"Why?"

"I decided it was time for a change. Then I stole a look at the onion crate beside me and chose my surname in honor of Weeks & Co. Fresh Produce. Don't worry," he said, amused. "We may be named after root vegetables, but I don't feel sorry for myself, and you shouldn't either.

"The other boys weren't allowed to leave the confines of that cold, bleak place," he continued while Kitty hoped he had no more surprises. "I escaped, and I traveled the world. I don't know if you can understand what that means after the child-hood I've given you, Capability, but for a boy like me—with nothing to look forward to—it was heaven on earth.

"And somehow, after starting without two pennies to rub together, I've managed to amass a tidy fortune. I've done business in Russia, China, Mongolia, and Malaya. I've crossed paths with Cossacks and petty potentates and Burmese traders, and I don't owe my success to anyone. So now you know why I don't have a birth certificate or some document showing whether my father is 'native' or 'naturalized.' I don't know if he was ever married to my mother—from the way the nuns treated me, I suspect not."

"You're a bastard," Kitty said.

"What does that word mean?" He shrugged. "In the end, it's his inner compass that gives a man his bearings. And for the first time in ages, I haven't followed mine—"

"By making that fellow sign for you on your application?"

"No." He seemed surprised by the question. "I'd do that again in a heartbeat. My past is no one's business except mine—and now yours. It's my venture with Maitland that bothers me. I swore that I'd never undertake a dealing that I didn't fully comprehend, and this business of transporting phenol across the border turns out to be much more complicated than I thought.

"It's not just the difference in laws between the United States and Canada—which I will admit troubled me. But also that I appear to be buying phenol from someone who took pains to conceal his identity from me."

He put down his tumbler and leaned forward in his seat. "How," he said to Kitty, "did you recognize Dr. Albert?"

The world went still. Kitty could hear her own heartbeat. Two forks in the road in one day: the first, whether to join Amanda and her friends; the second, whether she should tell her father that *she'd* been concealing things from him for a while.

The clock struck the half hour, giving her a few seconds respite. In those seconds, Kitty realized, she would be making the most important decision of her adult life.

"The Secret Service," she said when the last chime died down.

"What?"

She started at the beginning—how the agents confronted her outside the docks and what they'd asked her to do. Mr. Weeks frowned when she mentioned looking through his diary, but she didn't let that stop her and plunged ahead.

When she finished, she closed her eyes, ready for the ax to fall. But instead, he laughed.

"What's so funny?"

"You outsmarted them." He thumped his palm against his knee. "You discovered what they wanted to keep secret— American Secret Service men tailing a German diplomat. If it was printed in the paper tomorrow, no one would believe it."

Kitty recalled Soames's words. "They told me it would cause an international incident."

He nodded. "That sounds about correct."

"Why take the risk?" Kitty said. "If the result of being exposed for tailing Dr. Albert could be so serious, why do it at all?"

Mr. Weeks stared at her blankly.

The answer dawned on Kitty. "They must think he's up to something dangerous—the question is what?"

CHAPTER THIRTY-ONE

W ake up, Miss Kitty." Grace drew back the curtains in
Kitty's bedroom.

Kitty opened her eyes a crack. She had stayed up late the previous night, discussing Dr. Albert with her father. Mr. Weeks
hadn't wanted to talk about his childhood any further—some
things never changed—but was eager to speculate on the diplomat's relationship with Hunter Cole and whether that had
played a part in Mr. Cole's murder. Then, Kitty pointed out
that—unless she had been completely mistaken, and she didn't
think she was—until she mentioned Mr. Cole's name, neither
agent seemed to have heard of him. So if Dr. Albert did have
something to do with Hunter Cole's death, the connection
must be obscure.

"It's almost eight o'clock," the maid said, offering Kitty her
dressing gown.

Kitty groaned and jumped out of bed. Now that she had
good news to share, she didn't want to be late to meet her new
friends from the Treasury Department. To his great credit,
throughout their conversation the previous evening, Mr.
Weeks hadn't once turned on Kitty. He never expressed dismay
that she hadn't taken him into her confidence.

Grace fluffed the pillows and straightened the sheets while

chattering on about the latest developments in the Harry Thaw case. "They let Mr. Thaw go, Miss Kitty. They said he had spent enough time at the lunatic asylum and that he didn't need to be punished any more for shooting the man who stole his wife's honor."

Kitty wondered whether the result would have been different if women were allowed to serve on juries. Judging from Grace's fervent support of the millionaire playboy, probably not. But, in every photograph that Kitty had seen, Harry Thaw looked like a demented leprechaun. If she had any say in the matter, millionaire or not, Mr. Thaw would remain behind bars.

Kitty sat at her dressing table while Grace combed her hair and pinned it into a chignon. "What do you think, Miss Kitty?"

Kitty glanced at her reflection. "Very nice, thank you, Grace." She looked older and wiser and felt stronger as well. It wasn't just the new hairstyle that made the difference. It felt liberating to be the daughter of a man without antecedents. It meant she could do as she pleased and that she too could be who she wanted.

Kitty stepped into her pale green skirt and slipped on the matching jacket with military-inspired cording on the edges. She fastened her earrings and joined her father in the dining room.

"You look lovely." Mr. Weeks smiled. "My Athena. Ready to do battle."

"I hope that won't be necessary." Kitty laughed.

"Have you seen this morning's news? The pressure seems to be mounting." He pointed to the paper.

GERMAN AMBASSADOR ANXIOUS TO SHOW THAT
BERLIN IS OPEN TO FURTHER COMMUNICATION
WITH PRESIDENT.

"I wonder how it will end." She took her place at his side.

Julian Weeks turned serious. "I could go with you to speak
to those men."

"You're not supposed to know about them, remember?"
She reached across her plate and squeezed his hand. "Besides,
I can manage."

"Aspirin in Canada." Booth whistled when Kitty finished her
story. "Well, I never." They met under clear skies in Riverside Park.

"ASA," Kitty corrected. "'Aspirin' would be illegal, and my
father and Mr. Maitland aren't breaking the law."

"At this point," Soames said, "I think we'd look the other
way even if they were."

"So, can I have the passport, please?"

"We'll verify your claims, Miss Weeks." Booth tucked his
newspaper under his arm. "If you're telling the truth, we'll see
that Mr. Weeks receives his papers."

"Then I'll expect them soon. Do you require any additional
information from me, or are we all done?"

"Just one question," Booth replied. "How did you find out
about the ASA?"

"I was keen to discover the truth for my own peace of mind,"
Kitty said, "so I persevered. It took a few tries."

Booth tipped his hat. "Thank you, Miss Weeks. By the way, you never met us, and none of this ever happened. Come along, Soames." He headed for their car, but the younger agent lingered behind.

"I'm sorry we had to put you through so much trouble," he said. "It's not our usual way, Miss Weeks. The Secret Service doesn't usually strong-arm civilians. It's just that we're in a bit of a struggle—"

"With the Germans?"

He looked sheepish. "Actually, with the Justice Department."

Now it was Kitty's turn to be astonished. "I don't see—"

"Justice runs the Bureau of Investigation. Since the war broke out, we've been facing new threats, and there's a bit of a battle going on between the Bureau and the Service about who will be in charge."

"So you're battling Justice?" Kitty said.

"When you put it that way, it sounds awful." Soames laughed.

"What are you two lovebirds going on about?" Booth yelled from up ahead.

"Tying up some loose ends," Soames called.

"May I ask *you* a question?" Kitty said. "Had you heard of Mr. Cole before I mentioned him?"

"We hadn't, but I went over your story." Soames dusted his hat and put it back on. "While I couldn't find any evidence that Mr. Cole had a connection to Dr. Albert, I did learn that, before they married, Mrs. Cole worked for one of Dr. Albert's associates, a Mrs. Martha Held. Mrs. Held was at the concert where we first met. She was standing right beside you, in fact."

"The beautiful woman wearing sapphires?" It had to have been the same woman she'd heard speaking in German to her companion.

"I didn't notice what she was wearing," the Secret Service man said. "At that moment, it wasn't her I was looking at."

"Are you coming or not?" Booth yelled, honking the horn from inside the car.

"Just a minute," Soames called back. "Can we drive you to the *Sentinel*, Miss Weeks?"

"I don't work there anymore. I lost my job." Kitty hoped Soames hadn't noticed her blush.

"Any particular reason?" They made their way out onto the street.

"I was busy. I couldn't stay late like they wanted."

He turned to face her. "Did that have anything to do with us?"

"Your partner is waiting, Mr. Soames."

"If there's anything you need"—Soames climbed into the driver's seat of the agents' parked vehicle—"please don't hesitate to telephone me at the Customs House."

Kitty watched the car drive away and walked home. As hellish as the worst moments of her encounter with the agents had been, life would seem empty now that they were gone.

Julian Weeks opened the front door. "All done?"

"All done," Kitty replied.

He enveloped her in a hug. "Thank you. I'm so proud."

She enjoyed his closeness, the familiar scent of his birch hair tonic, and then pulled away, smiling. She hadn't realized that something between them had broken when she went away to school, and now, a decade later, they were moving forward again, not just in tandem this time but in trust.

"So what's next?" he said. "Now that you don't have the *Sentinel* to go to, should I expect to have a daughter who spends every morning at Altman's?"

"I doubt it." Kitty laughed.

"Take the day off at any rate. Do something nice for yourself."

"I think I will."

Kitty decided to go riding at Durland's to work off some steam. At this time of the day, the trails would be quiet. Afterward, she could come home and take a shower, and then she would see if Amanda would join her for lunch.

Kitty telephoned the Vanderwells, but Mrs. Vanderwell informed her that Amanda had left for the YWCA and wouldn't be back until three.

That was quite the reversal, Kitty thought. Amanda working while she prepared to while away time.

"Thank you for your help, Miss Weeks," the usually grudging Mrs. Vanderwell went on. "I do appreciate your listening to my friend, Mrs. Basshor."

"How is she faring?"

"No better and no worse, I'm afraid. Still mourning her secretary."

"Did you know him well, Mrs. Vanderwell?" Kitty said.

"Not really," Mrs. Vanderwell replied. "He seemed a bit outspoken and overly familiar, but I will admit I would never have pegged him for the murdering type."

Kitty changed into her riding ensemble and drove herself to the stables. A groom saddled Damsel, and with a leg up, Kitty hoisted herself onto the animal's back. She cantered around the park for about half an hour but found she couldn't relax. Too many thoughts crowded her mind. At first, it was Soames, then from Soames, she drifted to the concert. Then to Martha Held, the buxom beauty with the sapphires cascading from her ears. Soames had said that Aimee Cole worked for Mrs. Held, who was an associate of Dr. Albert's. How did it all add up?

Kitty felt certain that Hunter Cole had met Dr. Albert more than once. He had told Poppy Clements so, and Dr. Albert wouldn't have recalled him or launched into the lengthy diatribe justifying his desire to keep their meeting quiet if Mr. Cole had only been a casual acquaintance. The murdered man had kept a syringe and vials, filled with some substance, in his toiletries case. He had been shot in a stable where, less than a week later, one of Mrs. Basshor's ponies had to be put down. Kitty recalled the singing stable hand, Turnip, and his indignation at the thought that Breedlove could have stepped on a rusty nail. *Sister Susie's sewing shirts for soldiers*—she heard the song as though he were humming it right beside her.

She screwed up her face in concentration: *syringes— vials—a sick horse—Hunter Cole—stables—Dr. Albert.* Could they all be connected?

She came to the end of her ride and waited for one of the grooms to take Damsel's reins.

"Frank," Kitty said, sliding to the ground. "Do you know of a disease that would make it necessary to put a horse down quickly, without any questions asked?"

"I don't understand, Miss Weeks."

"Is there something that could go wrong with a horse that the stable wouldn't want even the lads to know about?"

The groom stroked Damsel's sleek, dark neck. "Something that would scare the boys, you mean."

"Perhaps."

He bit his lip. "It would have to be something that they thought would make them sick too or infect the other horses fast."

"Exactly." Kitty nodded.

"Glanders," he said finally. "If one of our animals had glanders, we'd put it to sleep and wouldn't want anyone to find out."

Glanders. Kitty's pulse raced. Where had she heard about it before? Oh yes, that's what had killed Mrs. Stepan's pony, Zsa-Zsa.

"It spreads like wildfire," Frank continued. "You get fever and chills, sores all over your body, and then, in a few days"—he snapped his fingers—"you're gone. If the boys thought we had glanders at this place? Forget it, they'd disappear in a minute." He looked at Kitty. "But not to worry, miss. There's nothing like that here."

"I know," Kitty said. "I was just curious."

She stopped off at the library on her way back home to look it up. "Glanders," she read to herself, "one of the most loathsome diseases known to mankind… Almost always fatal to humans. Death may come rapidly or gradually. Victims undergo terrible sufferings… Disease common to horses… Transmitted through cuts in skin. Not harmful if swallowed with food or water." Kitty thought of the pharmacist, Mr. Murray, and felt thankful. "Germ known for twenty-five years but still no cure has been found."

"What kind of stories are you writing these days, Miss Weeks?" the librarian asked as Kitty returned her book.

"I hardly know myself," Kitty replied.

It didn't make sense. Even if it were possible to bottle glanders germs in a vial, why would Hunter Cole—of all people—want to harm a horse? And if Dr. Albert was behind it, why would he want to cause an outbreak at the Sleepy Hollow Country Club?

Just in case, as soon as she arrived home, she put a telephone call through to the Customs House. Soames would think she was crazy to call him just hours after they parted, but Kitty didn't care; she needed to be certain. The man on the other end of the line, one Agent Burke, told Kitty that Soames wasn't in, so she left a message for him to call her when he returned.

She rummaged through the bureau drawer in her bedroom, but she couldn't find Hunter Cole's vial. She ran into the pantry.

"Grace." The maid stopped folding linens. "Did you see a small glass tube that I kept in my bureau drawer? I had it beside my camisoles."

"Oh yes, Miss Kitty. The one with the cork stopper? I thought it might leak and soil your delicates—"

"What did you do with it?" Kitty said, panicked.

"It's right here." Grace opened the cabinet below the kitchen sink. She had wedged the vial upright between bars of soap and a lamb's-wool duster. "It looks like one of those chemical tubes they show in the movies, doesn't it?" She handed the vial over. "I even thought it might be dangerous." The maid laughed.

Sunlight streaming through the kitchen window hit the tube at just the right angle. The liquid inside seemed as clear and unclouded as before.

"Do you have a handkerchief, Grace?" Kitty said.

Grace handed her one from the linen pile, and Kitty wrapped the glass vial before sliding it into her pocket.

"Tell Mrs. Codd I may be late for lunch." Still in her riding gear, she ran downstairs and hopped back into the Bearcat.

CHAPTER THIRTY-TWO

C an I help you?" Aimee Cole's dwarfish maid peered out from behind the door.

"Is Mrs. Cole in?"

"She's gone for the day."

"When will she be back?" Kitty peered past the woman and noticed sheets draped over the living room furniture.

"Later this evening. I'm not sure." The maid didn't budge an inch.

"Is she traveling somewhere?"

The servant shrugged and started to close the door.

Kitty put her foot in the way. "May I come in for a moment?" She smiled apologetically. "I'm a bit far from home, and I need to...well, I need to powder my nose."

The maid stepped aside.

Kitty entered and was struck at once by the state of the apartment: sheets had been draped over every surface, even the lamps had been wrapped, and two large trunks stood in one corner.

This wasn't some temporary move; Aimee Cole would be gone for a long time.

"So, Mrs. Cole plans to move back to Brooklyn?" Kitty asked.

"This way please." Without answering the question, the

servant escorted Kitty directly to the bathroom and closed the door with a click.

"I'll just be a minute," Kitty called. She opened the medicine cabinet. Half of it was empty, but Hunter Cole's toiletries case remained, and Kitty pulled it down.

She undid the clasp and peered inside. Almost everything in the case was as it had been previously—but the vials were gone. Kitty replaced the case, pulled the chain to the toilet, and washed her hands.

She opened the door to the bathroom to find the maid waiting outside.

Passing through the dining room, she caught sight of a large envelope propped on the mantelpiece. She recognized the name of the rail company.

"Travel tickets?"

"Mrs. Cole is going to be Pequeñita Mary."

"I beg your pardon?"

"She will be Mexico's Mary Pickford. She's leaving tomorrow."

"You're going with her?"

"No." The maid looked sullen.

"Well, please congratulate her on my behalf. I'd love to say good-bye before she leaves town."

"You won't find her here. She wouldn't want me to tell you, but I suppose it doesn't matter anymore." A look of disgust spread across the maid's face. "She's gone off to spend the day in Van Cortlandt Park with some foreigner."

"A man?"

She nodded.

"Could you describe him to me?"

"I only saw him for a minute. He was a small, dark fellow. Not a gentleman."

That didn't sound like Dr. Albert.

"It's shameful." The maid pursed her lips. "And it's been barely a week since Mr. Cole passed."

Kitty called the Customs House again, this time from a telephone at a candy store around the corner.

"May I speak to Agent Soames?" she whispered into the instrument, trying not to be overheard by the shopkeeper. "This is Capability Weeks."

"Ah, it's you again. Well, you're in luck, Miss Weeks. Soames just walked in. I'll put him on."

Kitty flashed a smile at the shopkeeper while she waited. She'd already purchased a full bag of peppermints and paid him an extra quarter to use his line.

"Is something the matter, Miss Weeks?" Kitty could hear the worry in Soames's voice.

"I'm fine, but I'd like your help."

"Can we speak later today? I'm a bit rushed at the moment."

"I'm afraid it can't wait. I'm sorry, but it's difficult to explain on the telephone. I can come meet you—I won't take much of your time, I promise."

There was a pause. "I'll take a break for lunch." He gave Kitty directions to an eatery downtown.

She hung up the telephone, thanked the shopkeeper, and ran outside to her car.

Soames would help her. Soames would be able to make sense of all this. And then, if she needed to, Kitty could speak to Aimee Cole before she left town.

Kitty wove her way through the traffic, one hand on the horn like a taxi driver.

Who was Aimee with, and why, the day before her departure, would she be going to a park all the way up in the Bronx?

Some fool with a golfing cap on his head and a cigarette clamped between his teeth thought it amusing that Kitty was in a hurry and drove alongside in his roadster, winking and trying to get her attention.

When she didn't respond, he retaliated by attempting to cut her off at an intersection, but she stepped on the gas, and the Bearcat leaped forward.

Take that. Kitty arrived at her destination faster than she thought.

She hopped out of the car, passed a tobacconist's scowling wooden Indian, and pushed open the door to the luncheonette.

Soames waited for her at a table right in front. Kitty took the seat beside him and pulled out the vial from her pocket.

"What this?" he asked.

"Don't laugh, but I think it might contain the germ that causes glanders, and I found it in Hunter Cole's medicine cabinet."

Soames folded his arms across his chest. "This is all very far-fetched."

"I know, I know," Kitty said. "But Mrs. Cole leaves tomorrow, and this may be my last chance to find out whether I'm correct. And if I am, don't you want to know where those other vials are?"

"It could be something else that affects horses."

"It could be nothing," Kitty said. "Just water. Whatever it is, I want to know for sure."

"We'd need to bring it to a lab for analysis. But that would take days, not hours."

"Can we do it though?" Kitty persisted. "If you give me an address, I'll take it across myself. You have work, but I have time."

A newsboy came through the restaurant, waving a copy of the afternoon paper and calling in a singsong voice, "'Ambassador von Bernstorff to Explain German Note Today! May Offer *Lusitania* Disavowal.'"

"They won't open the door to you."

"Come with me then."

He checked his watch and placed a couple of coins on the table. "Let's make it fast."

"Do you always drive like this?" Soames held on to his hat with one hand while the Bearcat careened along. He glanced at the road flying beneath their wheels. "There's nothing to hold you in place. You could fall right out of this thing."

"That's what I like about it," Kitty said, enjoying his look of alarm.

He motioned her to stop in front of a row of ramshackle garages on Eleventh Avenue, jumped out of the Bearcat, and rapped on one of the metal shutters that stretched from the roof to the ground. "It's Soames," he called.

Moments later, the shutter slid up a couple of feet, and a freckled fellow with curly hair ducked out. He let out a long, low whistle. "Nice wheels, Soamsie. And who might this be…a girlfriend?"

"Miss Weeks is a reporter," Soames replied dryly and introduced Kitty to Evan Monroe. "We'd both be most obliged if you could look into something that she's brought along."

"Any friend of yours, Soames, is a friend of mine." Monroe lifted the shutter all the way and led Kitty inside with exaggerated gallantry. "This way please, miss."

The garage was outfitted with rows of burners on stone counters, mazes of interlocking glass tubes, and a profusion of tongs and flasks and water baths. A fan at the rear rattled feebly as it blew away some of the noxious odors.

Soames turned to Kitty. "Would you like to explain?"

Kitty showed Monroe the vial. "I think," she said, "but I'm not sure, that this might contain some sort of virus or bacteria—the one that causes glanders, perhaps?" She suddenly felt foolish speculating in the presence of a professional. "Is it even possible to bottle a disease?"

"Glanders." Monroe tilted his head. "I'm afraid I can't help you. I'm a chemist, and what you need is a pathology lab."

"Oh dear." Kitty tried to control her disappointment.

Monroe returned the tube. "But I can tell you that the vial is top quality. I'll bet you five dollars that it's made by the Krauts."

"How can you tell?" Soames asked.

"They have the best scientists, the best equipment, and the

best labs. If you speak to any chemist worth his salt, you'll find that he studied in Deutschland or trained under someone who has."

"Do you know any pathologists, Mr. Monroe?" Kitty looked around at all the scientific paraphernalia. Surely all he needed to do was examine the liquid under a microscope or something like that.

The shutter opened with a rumble.

"Bloody furnace out there." One of Monroe's associates entered, wiping his forehead with a rag. "Beg your pardon, ma'am. I didn't know we had ladies about."

"That's all right, Tuttle," Monroe told him. "I'm sure Miss Weeks has heard worse—she's a reporter."

"Doing a chemistry story? I could tell you about the time that Mr. Monroe spilled sulfuric acid on me and nearly melted my shoes off—say, what's this?" He picked up the vial from the stone-slab counter and turned to his boss. "Have the post office inspectors been back?"

"Post office inspectors?" Soames perked up.

"They brought in two tubes exactly like this a month ago."

Soames turned to Monroe. "And you didn't think to tell us?"

"I didn't know myself, Soamsie."

Soames seemed rattled. "How are we supposed to get anything done if one hand doesn't talk to the other? You know you're supposed to keep me informed about any inquiries that come your way—I don't care whether they're from the post office, the Bureau, or even Naval Intelligence. Whatever it is, we need to know *immediately*. Those are Treasury Secretary McAdoo's orders."

"It won't happen again." Monroe shot his employee a baleful glance.

"Damned right it won't, or you won't see any more of our business."

"Pardon me," Kitty interrupted, turning to Tuttle. "Did you happen to find out what was in the post office inspector's vials?"

Tuttle beamed with pride. "It took a few days, but I did, at last."

"And you didn't say anything?" His boss looked furious. "Did you even write it in the ledger?"

"I may have forgotten," he admitted. "We were busy, and I didn't think we were interested in bacteria."

CHAPTER THIRTY-THREE

"Are you sure you will be able to recognize Mrs. Cole?" Soames asked as the Bearcat sped toward the Bronx.

Kitty kept her hands firmly on the wheel. "And here I was thinking you wanted me along for my excellent investigative abilities, or even my chauffeuring skills."

"This is no time for humor, Miss Weeks."

Kitty looked over at him. "I can see that."

The Secret Service man had telephoned his headquarters and spoken to Booth. They had left Kitty's sample for Tuttle to examine and gone to look for Mrs. Cole, who, they hoped, would know about the missing vials.

"Van Cortlandt Park is huge, you know," Kitty said to Soames. "Maybe it would be better to wait until she comes home."

"By then it might be too late."

"Too late for what?"

Soames stared at the road ahead. "I'd just rather not take any chances."

"And one question still troubles me," Kitty went on. "If it is glanders, why would Mr. Cole or Dr. Albert want to spread the disease at a country club?"

"There's a time for questions and a time for answers," Soames replied. "But this isn't the time for either one."

"I should drop you off on the street," Kitty said. She was tired and hungry and hadn't even eaten lunch. "You go find Mrs. Cole and tell me all about it."

"I'm sorry." He cracked his knuckles. "I really can't talk."

They drove along in silence.

Kitty crossed Mosholu Parkway. Van Cortlandt Park stretched out into the distance, acres of green against a cloudless blue sky. She brought the car to a halt and brushed off her sense of foreboding. "Where do we begin?"

"Let's walk and see." Soames stepped out of the car and offered his arm, but Kitty felt too shy to accept and pretended she hadn't noticed.

On one side of the path, boys played football; on the other, families picnicked on the grass. A couple of children ran along, their kites soaring in the air.

"Are you watching for Mrs. Cole?" Soames said.

"I'm doing my best." Kitty thought she saw Aimee everywhere: in the woman strolling arm in arm with her companion, walking her dog, riding her bicycle, or pushing her baby along in a baby carriage.

"She's here with a friend," Soames reminded Kitty.

"As if I could forget," she replied with a touch of annoyance. Some of the ladies had their parasols open to shield their faces from the sun, while others took refuge under broad-brimmed hats. What if Aimee Cole was wearing one of her many wigs— how would Kitty recognize her then?

"You should be looking too," Kitty told Soames and tried to describe the widow. "She's about my height. Not too fat, not too thin. Medium-brown hair and medium-brown eyes."

"Middle of the road?" he said.

"Exactly. Then again, there's something about her." Kitty pictured Aimee in the brilliant red wig. "She can change. When she wants, she looks terribly attractive. I suppose that's what one should expect from an actress."

The sun beat down on them, and Soames bought Kitty a bottle of Coca-Cola to cool her off. She drank it quickly and returned the empty bottle to the vendor.

"We're never going to find her," she said.

"Never is a strong word."

"How can you be so confident?" Kitty heard the tinny sound of fairground music in the distance. The music grew louder as they walked on. Children bobbed up and down, spinning around and around, faster and faster on a carousel of gaily painted horses.

A couple trotted by on horseback. Kitty sidestepped a pile of manure. The children shrieked with joy as they clung to their wooden mounts.

Horses. It always came back to horses.

She stopped in her tracks. Why was Mrs. Cole here? Why had she come to a park in the Bronx, of all places, on her last day in New York?

What was here? A golf course, a parade ground, the former Van Cortlandt residence.

She stopped a passing stranger. "Excuse me, sir. Would you know whether there are stables or riding facilities nearby?"

"I don't know about stables, miss. Are you looking for a ride?"

"I'm looking for horses," Kitty said. "Any place here that might have horses."

"Ah." He threw Soames a sympathetic glance, as if to say one never could tell with the ladies, and pointed to a corner of the park. "There's a herd corralled in the meadows back there. If it's horses that you want, there must be at least two hundred."

Kitty quickened her pace. Soames followed. She picked up her skirts and broke into a run. The horses wouldn't disappear, but if Mrs. Cole wasn't with the animals, then Kitty would tell Soames that she had no idea where to find her, that they may as well sit in one spot and hope Aimee strolled by or wait until this evening and try to catch her at her apartment.

A good two hundred animals milled behind the pen. "Excuse me." Kitty approached a wiry lad hefting two buckets of water. "Why are all these horses here?"

"They're resting for a couple of days before they're shipped off," he replied.

Soames and Kitty exchanged a glance.

"Don't you know?" He put down his pails. "Our breeders send horses by the dozen to Europe. They come by rail from out west, then we put them on boats for the long journey. These beauties will be charging into battle next month."

"On whose side?" Kitty said.

"Oh." He grinned. "They're going to fight the Huns."

"It's absurd," Mr. Weeks responded when Kitty returned home and told him what she had discovered. "Desperate though they may be, I cannot believe that the German government has a *plan* to inject glanders into horses bound for France."

"Don't you see?" Kitty said. "It follows the same principle as what they're doing with the phenol. They can't get it for themselves, so they want to make sure that the enemy can't have it."

"But spreading disease among horses?" His face screwed up with distaste. "That's fiendish."

"It's brilliant," Kitty said. "It kills the animals and spreads the sickness to the troops at the same time."

"I won't hear any more of this." Julian Weeks stood behind his desk. "And I will not allow you to spend the night with two men in Van Cortlandt Park."

"They're Secret Service agents," Kitty said. "And I won't be sleeping there."

"Oh yes." His tone was acerbic. "You will be hiding, waiting for this Aimee Cole woman. And what will you do when she arrives?"

"I won't do anything, Papa. The agents will handle it. I'll just be watching."

"And these are the same agents who, until this morning, were investigating my business affairs?" He came out from behind his desk and sat in his armchair. "You know, I think I've given you too much freedom."

Kitty couldn't take it. She had thought asking his permission would be a formality. "So it's fine for me to go out on my own for your sake but not for mine?"

"Have you lost your marbles, Capability?" her father said. "When you met them today, it was daytime, and you were gone for twenty minutes a block away from our home."

"And now I'm meeting them farther away and for longer."

"That's exactly what bothers me. I may be lax, Capability, but I'm not stupid. I know how to take care of my own child."

Kitty put her hands to her head. "This is my life. The agents wouldn't have known about Mrs. Cole or the vials if I hadn't alerted them."

Mr. Weeks went to pour himself a drink but remained standing, his empty glass in his hands. "It could be dangerous."

"Agent Booth and Agent Soames both agree, which is why they didn't want me to stay on in the first place, but I insisted." Booth had arrived at the park shortly before Kitty had left for home. "They've selected a spot where I am to wait. I won't move until they tell me that it's all right."

He twirled the glass between his fingers. "You remind me of myself when I was a young man."

"So you'll let me go?" Kitty brightened.

"Against my better judgment."

She stood and kissed him on the cheek. "Don't worry about me. I'll be back."

Kitty changed into her darkest riding skirt and a dark shirt. She put on a pair of sturdy walking boots and asked Mrs. Codd to pack three sandwiches.

"You're certain you want to do this?" Mr. Weeks asked when Kitty looked in to say good-bye. "Let Rao drive you."

"What, and arrive at the scene of the potential crime in my Packard with my chauffeur?"

He gripped her hand tightly. "Then tell one of those men to

come back with you. I don't want you in the car on your own at night."

Much as she wanted to do this alone, Kitty didn't look forward to driving back from the Bronx unaccompanied. "That's a good idea." And before he could give her any further instructions or change his mind, she hurried out.

Once at the park, Kitty handed Soames and Booth each a sandwich. She'd been worried that Aimee Cole might arrive while she was away, but fortunately that hadn't happened.

"This is excellent." Booth wiped his mouth with the back of his hand.

"Do you think Mrs. Cole will come?" Kitty said.

"Did you telephone her apartment from home, like I asked?" he replied.

"I did, and she wasn't there."

Soames had been leaning against a tree, eating his sandwich. Now he finished it and tossed away the newspaper wrapper. He stood up straight, brushing the crumbs from his jacket. "We don't know anything about this Mrs. Cole or what she might do. I know I had said it was all right, but I'd really prefer it if you went home, Miss Weeks."

A chill stole over Kitty. She wouldn't have expected Soames, of all people, to forsake her.

"Let her be, Soames." To Kitty's surprise, it was Booth who came to her defense. "It's her doing that has brought us this far, and she understands that she can't write about or even talk about anything that happens tonight. Don't you, Miss Weeks?"

Kitty nodded.

"So far, all we've got to go on is guesswork," the big man went on. "A warning to you, Miss Weeks, before you go off and hide. You're on your own until we call for you."

"Yes."

"I have a family at home." His thuggish features softened for a moment. "I should be spending this evening with them, but instead, I'm here. And while Soames may be gallant, I don't throw myself in front of a bus for anyone."

"I understand."

The sun would set after eight. The park began to clear. Picnickers folded their blankets, sportsmen gathered their equipment, and children cried tears of exhaustion as their parents pulled them away from their games. The lads looking after the horses left shortly before closing time.

Kitty took up her position in a copse of trees and watched as the sky went dark. This wasn't Manhattan, with its blur of electric lights creating an eternal day. Here in the Bronx, in the midst of the park, she could see the stars clearly. She had forgotten how much she missed them since coming to the city, but even the glories of the night sky couldn't distract her for long.

Kitty's legs ached from crouching, and she was being bitten by mosquitoes. There was nothing remotely exciting or romantic about waiting for something to happen. She must remember that for the future. Kitty stood up slowly to stretch her legs.

It must be past ten by now. It looked like Pequeñita Mary wouldn't be arriving with a syringe loaded with glanders to finish the work that her husband had started. Mrs. Cole wanted to be an actress. Perhaps there was a mundane explanation for all of this—that, like many actresses, she was having an affair and had come to the park, a remote place where no one would recognize her, to spend one last day and night with her paramour.

Kitty wished Aimee luck. She felt guilty about suspecting her and speculating on her private life. Whatever Hunter Cole's involvement with Dr. Albert had been would remain a secret. The dead man couldn't tell Kitty, the diplomat wouldn't tell her, and the widow would be on her way to Mexico tomorrow.

Kitty caught a glimpse of light from the direction of the carousel. She blinked, and it disappeared. A few moments later, she saw it again: a yellow halo bobbing around at the far end of the meadow.

Slowly, it made its way toward the pen. At first, it was so far off that Kitty couldn't be sure of the direction. But it soon grew brighter, and the person carrying it became clearer until she could make out a hooded figure approaching the enclosure.

The lantern lowered, and the figure extracted something from a satchel and whistled softly. One of the horses ambled over to the fence.

Kitty's hand flew to her mouth as Booth and Soames rushed from their hiding places. "Don't move. Arms up," Booth bellowed.

The figure swung around, and the hood fell back. Soames raised the lantern. Even from a distance, Kitty could tell that whomever they had caught wasn't a woman, and it certainly wasn't Mrs. Hunter Cole. It was the small, slight stable hand she had met at the Tombs—Marcus Lupone.

Booth slapped a pair of handcuffs on the Sicilian's wrists. Soames grabbed the satchel from his shoulders and bent to reach for something that had fallen from his hands.

Kitty remained glued in place. A featherweight mosquito landed on the side of her neck, and she brought up her hand to swat it away—but instead of delicate flesh crumpling beneath her fingers, she felt a steel needle's cold, hard resistance.

"Don't move," a girlish voice whispered in her ear.

"Aimee," Kitty breathed.

"Did you think I wouldn't notice that nice yellow car?" She tugged at Kitty's arms. "On your feet." She slid one arm behind Kitty's elbows, pinning them behind her back. "Come along." She pushed her captive forward.

"Don't do this, Aimee," Kitty whispered.

"Don't do what?" The needle hovered inches away from Kitty's throat. "Take you away from your friends? Infect you with a deadly disease? I'll try my best not to. But you will have to cooperate. So tell me, who are those men you've brought along?"

"They're Secret Service." Kitty swallowed. She could feel Aimee's warm breath in her ear.

"My, my. To think that when I first met you, you were a scared little apprentice," Aimee whispered. "And now here you are, consorting with government agents. You *were* scared, weren't you? Or was that just an act? If so, you should try your hand at the movies. Who knows? You might be better than the rest of us."

"Where are we going?" Kitty asked.

"To your car."

"And then?"

"You're going to drive me to freedom."

Kitty couldn't see more than a few feet ahead of her. She stumbled on the uneven ground and righted herself just in time. "They'll notice I'm missing," she whispered. "They'll come looking for me."

"And what will they do when they find us? Risk that I might hurt you? I doubt that. No, Miss Weeks, you are my ticket to safety, my life insurance."

"You haven't done anything wrong yet, Aimee," Kitty said, feeling the ground with her feet to make sure she didn't trip in the darkness. "Don't make this worse by bringing me into it." They were moving farther away from the enclosure, farther from any chance of assistance. "Talk to the agents. Tell them who put you up to it. Tell them that you had to finish what Mr. Cole started—"

"What Mr. Cole started?" Aimee scoffed. "That's a joke."

"Then why did he go to the stables at the club?" Kitty slowed down.

"Hunter thought it would be amusing to test the serum on one of Mrs. Basshor's ponies, and at a July Fourth party, no less," Aimee said.

"And he was working for Dr. Albert?"

Aimee was silent for a moment. "Well, aren't you clever."

"And then what happened? Did someone catch him in the act?"

Aimee didn't reply at once.

"I'm pretty sure that Mr. Hotchkiss didn't shoot your

husband, because Mrs. Basshor told me that she was aware of his stealing. So that can't have been a factor. Who did it then?" Kitty asked.

Aimee's giggle made her shiver.

"What my husband knew about the secretary wasn't the same as what the secretary thought Hunter had discovered."

"I don't understand," Kitty said.

"The secretary had, let's say, a *fondness* for men. Hunter told him that he had found out his little secret. Of course, Hunter meant that he had overheard Hotchkiss talking to the fireworks fellows and that he had put two and two together once Mrs. Basshor told us what she was paying for the entertainments. But the secretary panicked. He assumed 'little secret' meant that Hunter had found out about his secret activities—"

"What kind of activities?" Kitty said.

"You don't know anything, do you?" Aimee snapped. "The secretary was a faggot. You don't mess around with that type, but Hunter had no idea, and he never could resist the chance to make an extra buck."

"So Hotchkiss shot him?" Kitty had never heard anyone use the word "faggot" in conversation but had a vague idea of what it meant.

"That's right. Men of his kind live in terror of being discovered. I only realized the truth later and confronted him at the funeral. He folded at once. The shame of it must have been too much for him to bear, which is why he killed himself."

Poor Hotchkiss. That would explain his frantic call the day before he died.

A twig cracked beneath Kitty's foot. Aimee stopped. For

a few moments, all Kitty heard was the sound of the other woman's breath. Then Aimee pushed her ahead. "You have to be more careful."

"Why didn't you tell anyone about Mr. Hotchkiss, Aimee?"

"I was going to. But then he went and slit his wrists before I had a chance to speak to the police. And after that—well, they pinned the murder on him in any case, didn't they? So what would be the point?"

Kitty saw the Bearcat parked on the street. And finally, she heard Soames calling her name.

"Hurry," Aimee said.

"Miss Weeks." Soames was about twenty feet away.

Kitty's moment of relief was short-lived. Aimee Cole brusquely swung her around, and she became a shield between the widow and the agent. The needle at her neck kept her in check. She couldn't move or Aimee would puncture her skin.

"Are you all right, Miss Weeks?" Soames came closer.

"Stop right there," Aimee shouted. "I have a syringe, and I'm not afraid to use it."

"I'm putting down the lantern." He bent his knees and placed the light on the ground. He stood, slowly. "Let's not panic. We can sort this out." He introduced himself. "Why don't you release Miss Weeks, and we can discuss this in private, Mrs. Cole? You are Mrs. Cole, aren't you?"

"Who else could I be?" Aimee spat.

Soames sounded calm and steady. Reasonable. If she were in Aimee's shoes, she would trust him, Kitty thought.

"I won't hurt you, Mrs. Cole," the Secret Service man continued. "Once we're done talking, I can help you. Miss Weeks tells me you're planning to go to Mexico to become an actress. I can make sure you get there safely."

"Likely story," Aimee scoffed. "Once you get what you want, you'll leave me in the lurch. I know men."

"What in God's name is going on?" Booth arrived, dragging a scowling, handcuffed Lupone beside him.

"What is happening is that I'm going to take Miss Weeks to her car, and she will drive me away," Aimee replied.

"Over my dead body." Booth raised his arm. There was a pistol at the end of it. He cocked the hammer.

Kitty gasped and closed her eyes. She would never get out of this.

"Calm down, Booth." Soames stepped into the line of fire. "Let's think things through."

"I'm done thinking," Booth said.

Kitty opened her eyes again. Were the two men playing some kind of charade to bluff Aimee into believing that Booth would shoot if she didn't do as Soames asked?

"Get out of my way, Soames. Now," Booth thundered. "Unless you want me to report you when we get back."

Soames stepped aside.

There was no one between the barrel and Kitty. If Booth fired, she would be hit. Kitty stared at his outstretched arm, mesmerized.

"My colleague has more patience than I do," Booth told Aimee. "I suggest you don't push your luck any further. Put down that syringe, and tell us who put you up to this filthy business, and why."

"Never!" Aimee inched backward, pulling Kitty along with her.

Booth took aim and fired, the shot deafening.

Kitty's heart stopped. The bullet had whistled right past her.

"Bullying won't work with me," Aimee yelled. "You could ask my husband, only he's dead."

Kitty felt completely out of her depth. She saw no way out unless Aimee spoke to the men.

"Let me handle this," Soames said to Booth.

"What? And stand here all night? I'm tired and ready to go home, and I won't have my hand forced by some hysterical cow. If she wants to act like a child, I'll treat her like one. I'm going to count down from five," he said loudly, "and if she doesn't start talking, I'll shoot again. And this time, I won't miss."

He looked fierce in the light of the lantern. "FIVE," he yelled.

"Say something please, Aimee," Kitty begged. Booth didn't seem to be bluffing.

"Put the gun down," Aimee called.

The pistol didn't waver.

"FOUR," Booth shouted.

"This is getting out of hand, Booth," Soames said.

Kitty smelled Aimee's fear.

"We're running out of time," Booth boomed. "I'm at THREE."

"Please reconsider, Mrs. Cole," Soames urged. "We can help you."

"Please, Aimee." A tear trickled down Kitty's cheek. "Just explain to them. Tell them you didn't understand what your husband was doing."

"I didn't understand? It's he who didn't understand, and he didn't do anything," Aimee whispered through gritted teeth. "He talked big, but he was a coward. He couldn't bring himself to hurt a horse. Not for all the money in the world, so I had to go down to the stables and do it for him."

"You injected Breedlove?" Of course, that made sense.

"It's why I left the children's tables for a few minutes. I found Hunter near the stalls with his pistol and the syringe. He was sniveling like a baby."

"And then you killed him?"

"Stop your chattering," Booth shouted.

"No one noticed." Aimee's voice was low. "Everyone looked right past me. No one—not even you—guessed that I had done it."

"TWO." The black barrel bore down on the women.

Kitty screwed her eyes shut. She was going to die.

"This is your last chance," Booth called.

Lupone slammed his head into his captor, and a shot sounded as Booth's arm jerked, Soames dove forward, and then the world went quiet.

Kitty yanked herself free from Aimee's grip. The widow stood still for a moment, her eyes bright, then she sighed, and her body tumbled backward. She fell so slowly, her feet coming off the ground for an instant, that Kitty felt as though she were watching a picture run by an overzealous projectionist who sped up the action once more when Soames rushed over to check Aimee's pulse.

"She's breathing." He turned to his partner. "You idiot."

"It's his fault." Still handcuffed together, Booth smacked Lupone on the head. "And besides, we needed an answer."

"*You* needed an answer." Soames applied pressure to the wound on the widow's shoulder. "You're not hurt?" he asked Kitty.

Kitty touched her neck. "I think I'm all right."

With shaking fingers, she picked up the syringe that Aimee had dropped, wrapped it in a handkerchief, and placed it on the ground beside the younger agent.

Soames took off his jacket and tied it tightly around Mrs. Cole's shoulder. A hint of color returned to the widow's cheeks. "We're going to take you to a hospital."

He picked her up and carried her in his arms to the agents' car. He told Kitty to follow them. They drove to the nearest police station, where she waited in the Bearcat while Booth, Soames, and Lupone went inside, leaving Mrs. Cole behind.

There were so many different Aimees, Kitty thought with a shiver. Wife Aimee, daughter Aimee, showgirl Aimee, captor Aimee. Even aspiring actress Aimee, and friendless Aimee. The only image that she had difficulty conjuring was Aimee as murderess shooting her husband through the skull. But that's exactly what Mrs. Cole had done.

A police matron and two policemen arrived, and Kitty watched them lift the widow onto a stretcher.

"What happens now?" she asked Soames, who came out to join her.

"Lupone goes back to prison, Mrs. Cole goes to the hospital, and you go home and forget everything that's happened."

"What about you and Agent Booth?"

"This won't look good on either of our records."

"You prevented a crime!"

"We injured someone and involved a civilian."

Kitty realized he was talking about her. "I won't tell."

"I know you won't, but Mrs. Cole or Lupone will." They stood alone under the stars for a few moments.

"What did she tell you before Booth fired?"

"She admitted that she had murdered her husband and that the vials came from Dr. Albert."

"Oh." Soames exhaled loudly.

"I think she must have hated Mr. Cole. Or hated him in that moment. It's hard to tell. She's a good actress."

The agent reached out and held Kitty's hand in his. "Well, Miss Weeks, I wish we had met under different circumstances."

"So do I." Kitty pulled away. "Good-bye, Mr. Soames."

"Would you like me to follow you home?"

"I'll be fine." She climbed into the Bearcat, turned on the engine and headlamps, and drove back to the New Century Apartments.

CHAPTER THIRTY-FOUR

Kitty's interview appeared on the Ladies' Page the next day, just as Miss Busby had envisioned it:

FOR AMERICAN GIRLS, BY AN AMERICAN GIRL:
AN INTERVIEW WITH PHILANTHROPIST AND
AUTHOR, MISS ANNE TRACY MORGAN

Kitty scanned the text, which had remained more or less faithful to her account. "Duties rather than the rights of women... with greater freedom comes greater responsibility...the girl must look into the mirror to discover who she is and what she might become." While Miss Morgan emerged from the piece a living, breathing woman with a will of her own, Kitty felt that the interviewer, referred to only as "the American girl," remained faceless and receded into the background.

"How are you this morning?" Mr. Weeks walked into the dining room. He had waited for her to come home the previous night and, after she told him everything, meticulously checked her neck under the glare of his desk lamp. "You feel all right? No headaches or fever?"

"Every time I sneeze now, you're going to think I might die."

"Do you blame me?" He tucked his napkin in his collar. "I want you to stay home this weekend."

"You won't get any argument from me." Kitty finished her breakfast and returned to bed. She slept through the morning, woke up for lunch, and—since she was exhausted, and nothing to do with horses would ever be the same for her—declined Amanda's offer to go out for a ride.

The Weekses boarded a train at Pennsylvania Station and set off for the Panama-Pacific International Exposition in California five days later. Julian Weeks had spent Monday and Tuesday at meetings, and then came home and announced that he needed a change and that they ought to leave town for a while.

Kitty hadn't heard from Soames or read anything about the incident in the park in the newspapers. Without her job to give her days a rhythm, she found herself drifting around the apartment, and new scenery sounded appealing. She had packed her bags without any argument and read old *Photoplay* magazines while the train rumbled through a tunnel beneath the Hudson.

They emerged on the other side into the warm, bright sunshine of the mainland. Clapboard houses replaced brick buildings. Lines of cable wire bordered farmland and woods, and here and there, a child on a bicycle waved to the train as it passed.

Kitty left the first-class compartment and took tea in the dining car with a group of young ladies. Later that evening, she chatted with their brothers and parents. She tried not to think about what had happened to Aimee or whether she would see Soames again. She hoped he wouldn't be punished for Booth's actions.

A few days into their trip, Mr. Weeks patted the seat beside him and gestured for Kitty. "The president has sent off his third note to Germany. Listen to what he says regarding submarine warfare: 'Illegal and inhuman acts, however justifiable they may be…are manifestly indefensible when they deprive neutrals of their acknowledged rights, particularly when they violate the right to life itself. If a belligerent cannot retaliate against an enemy without injuring the lives of neutrals…a due regard for the dignity of neutral powers should dictate that the practice be discontinued.'

"And then the president goes on to say that 'the Government of the United States is not unmindful of the extraordinary conditions created by this war…nor of the method of attack produced by the use of instrumentalities of naval warfare which the nations of the world cannot have had in view when the existing rules of international law were formulated, but'"— Julian Weeks emphasized each word as he read—"'*it cannot consent to abate any essential or fundamental right of its people because of a mere alteration in circumstance.*'

"Mere?" He turned to his daughter, shaking his head. "As you and I both know, there's nothing 'mere' about the changes that this war has brought about."

The train hurtled through the heartland, and the Weekses switched to the new Scenic Limited in Missouri. It was a fast all-steel train with a glass-walled observation car, and it took its passengers on a breathtaking journey along the Meramec and Missouri Rivers, the Royal Gorge, and the Feather River Canyon.

Kitty had never seen such vistas, natural beauty on such a grand scale. She felt as though she had tumbled out of the hurly-burly of Manhattan and into a universe where diplomats and Secret Service men had no place.

She and her father disembarked in San Francisco. They set off the next morning for the Exposition, which commemorated the opening of the Panama Canal, "a historic undertaking that connects two continents and the Atlantic and Pacific Oceans," as the pamphlets said. In size and scope, the fair was the third of its class in the United States and the twelfth of its kind held anywhere on the planet.

Kitty visited the Palace of Horticulture and was entranced by the Gettysburg display. She watched the dance performances at the replica Samoan and Chinese villages, while Mr. Weeks spent most of his time at the Palaces of Manufactures and Varied Industries, Machinery, and Mines and Metallurgy. Together, they attended concerts at the Festival Hall and marveled at the display of colored lights that gave the place an *Arabian Nights* air.

They posed for a photograph in front of the Liberty Bell (on loan from Philadelphia). They kept their hats on this time and appeared as they wished to be perceived: a prosperous father with his daughter on vacation. They watched craftsmen from all over the world ply their trades at souvenir stalls.

"Here you may observe up close the handicrafts of alien races," a tour guide informed them.

Julian and Kitty Weeks took a detour to Yellowstone on their journey back home. And when Old Faithful erupted, Kitty found that all the pent-up tension that she had accumulated over the past month shot into the air along with the cloud of vapor and gasses that hurtled to a height of over one hundred feet and rained back down on her like the tissue-paper nothings that fell from the skies during that fateful daylight fireworks display.

She realized that what Aimee Cole wanted more than anything was to make something of herself, and Hunter Cole had denied her that opportunity. He hadn't given her the place in the world that she craved and wouldn't allow her to try to achieve it on her own.

Thwarted women did strange things. They imploded, like Miss Busby, or exploded, like Aimee. Others were forced to channel their energies into acceptable pursuits, like Anne Morgan, and a lucky few—Pearl and Mary Pickford, for instance—found fame and fortune in the movies. But who knew what sacrifices each had to make and what injustices and indignities they put up with on the way?

She and Aimee were similar in many respects, Kitty thought. Both outsiders, both wanting to prove themselves. But what, Kitty wondered, would she do if she felt trapped? Would she be able to look another person in the face and pull the trigger?

Julian Weeks felt her shudder. "What's the matter, Capability?"

"It's nothing." Kitty took his arm, and they walked through the park in companionable silence.

Every day since she left New York, Kitty had scanned the papers, hoping for some tidbit of information on either

Soames, Aimee, Lupone, or Dr. Albert—anything, however
trivial, that might give her some clue to the aftermath of what
happened in the park. She found nothing and came to believe
that the affair would remain buried, but on August 15, when
she was just hours away from the city, the *New York World*
broke a major story, exposing Germany's "secret undertak-
ings" in the United States.

Kitty's arms felt weak as she held the paper and learned that
"no less a personage than Herr von Bethmann-Hollweg, chan-
cellor of the German Empire," had participated in the intrigues
from Berlin and that "his emissaries in America included the
German ambassador to the United States; his military attaché
in Washington; and his chief financial agent, Dr. Heinrich
Friedrich Albert."

Her eyes traveled across the page.

"The *World* today begins the publication of a series of articles
raising for the first time the curtain that has hitherto concealed
the activities and purposes of the official German propaganda in
the United States," the story began.

She glanced through the litany of charges: Dr. Albert had
secretly purchased a sham munitions plant in Connecticut,
which took orders from the British and French governments
that it never intended to fulfill. He participated in plans to
foment strikes in other munitions plants across the country and
plotted to buy the Press Association and so control the dissemi-
nation of war news in America.

She kept reading: there was no mention of glanders, no
mention of the Coles nor of Kitty and her father, but one Mr.
Hugo Schweitzer was named as a participant in the nefarious

proceedings. Kitty didn't find any mention of the Secret Service agents either.

Her father put down his copy of the paper. "I got out just in time."

"What do you mean?"

"Before we left town, I canceled the deal with Maitland and terminated my arrangement with Schweitzer."

"Mr. Maitland can't be pleased."

"No, he wasn't, but he'll survive."

The train chugged back to New York. Kitty marveled at a facsimile reproduction of a letter between Dr. Albert and one George Viereck, editor of a magazine called *The Fatherland*. "In thinking the matter over," the letter said, "I do not think that Mrs. R. would be the proper intermediary, inasmuch as she doesn't attend to her financial matters herself. If it must be a woman, Mrs. G., the mother of our friend, Mrs. L., would be far better..." and so on and so forth.

The commercial attaché had been busy. To Kitty, the letter begged the question of how the *World* had acquired this correspondence. Had someone given it to them? Had one of their reporters stolen it? She couldn't imagine just anyone walking into the Hamburg-American building and taking private papers from Dr. Albert's office.

Rao picked up Kitty and her father from the station. The traffic was terrible.

"This is nothing, sir," the chauffeur said. "Last week, twenty trucks from American Express blocked the avenue for hours. We were told that they were filled with gold all the way from England on its way to the Morgan bank."

The news at home wasn't as dramatic. Grace and Mrs. Codd had managed without arguing during their absence. Grace hadn't stepped out with any young men, but Mrs. Codd had taken Sundays off to visit her daughter on Staten Island.

Grace unpacked the trunks while Kitty sorted through her letters. She had received one postmarked from Washington, along with others from her boarding-school friends.

She opened the Washington letter once the maid left the room. Soames had written to say that he had been transferred away from New York and that Booth had been placed on indefinite suspension.

"You may want to know about Mrs. C," he added. "She recovered and told us what we needed. Although I think she should be in prison, she is on her way to Mexico.

"The strangest thing," he continued, "has to do with Dr. A. He fell asleep on the subway, woke up with a start at his station, and rushed off, leaving behind his briefcase. When he realized what had happened, he ran back to the train, but the briefcase was gone."

Kitty began to laugh. The Secret Service had "happened upon" Dr. Albert's briefcase—and they, for some reason, made the findings public?

"Capability." Mr. Weeks knocked at the door, an envelope in his hands. He sounded uncharacteristically pleased as he held up a single sheet of stamped paper. "Our passport has arrived."

Miss Busby rang bright and early the next morning. "Your maid told me you'd be back."

Kitty never expected to be so happy to hear that familiar squawking voice.

"I hope you're well rested, because we have heaps of work ahead of us."

"Are *you* well, Miss Busby?" Kitty said. It was as though Kitty was back in the alcove with her editor firing off orders.

"Fine. Fit as a fiddle. Never felt better, in fact."

"You do know that Mr. Hewitt let me go, Miss Busby?"

"Bah. Mr. Hewitt has no say in who goes or stays at the Ladies' Page. I will tell you one thing though. I plan to keep Miss Williams. She's wonderful, that girl. A real worker. And I've realized my limits, so she will take care of the day-to-day tasks while you handle special assignments.

"That interview with Miss Morgan struck a deep chord with our readers. They loved you as a questioner. The Page was flooded with letters praising your innocence and naïveté, and it got me thinking: Why not conduct a series of interviews with other prominent women? We'll start with Dr. Davis, the commissioner of corrections, and move on to Mrs. Isabella Goodwin, the only top-grade female policewoman in the city's detective bureau. And I'd like to throw in a few artists and writers."

"May I have a few days to think about it?" Kitty asked, overwhelmed by the barrage of information. "I'll need to discuss the offer with my father."

"Well, take all the time you need, but make it fast. Of course, it goes without saying that I will expect you not to engage in any more of your shenanigans."

"Of course, Miss Busby. And thank you. I'm flattered." Kitty hung up the receiver.

"What a voice. I'll bet the entire avenue heard that conversa-tion," Mr. Weeks remarked. "So what will you do? Do you think you will go back?"

"Do you have a preference?"

"It's not my decision to make. However, I will say that I don't envision you spending the rest of your days planning dinner for me and bossing about Grace and Mrs. Codd."

"I had considered working somewhere else."

"Where? A different Ladies' Page?"

"When you put it that way, it doesn't seem right." Kitty smiled.

Grace looked in on them, and Kitty gave her the lunch order. She began to think: Dr. Davis and Mrs. Goodwin, then artists and writers. Maybe she could add Miss Tarbell, the journalist; Dean Gildersleeve of Barnard; Alva Belmont, the socialite and suffragist; and perhaps even an actress like Mary Pickford or Pearl White.

"What's on your mind, Capability?" Mr. Weeks said.

Kitty pictured him busy in his study, Amanda headed to Europe to become a nurse, Soames posted in Washington. She saw her future unfold with Miss Busby at the helm, Mr. Musser in his underground lair, and Jeannie Williams scribbling away alongside her. "I think I will return to the *Sentinel*. Who knows? There might even be a story in it for me this time."

Author's Note

Much of what seems most unlikely in this novel actually happened. For instance, Dr. Heinrich Friedrich Albert did fall asleep on a New York City subway in the summer of 1915 and left his briefcase behind when he woke up at his stop. Agent Burke of the Secret Service, who was tailing him, picked up the case and turned it over to his superiors. Decisions were made at the highest levels of government to leak the contents to the *New York World*.

FURTHER READING

During the course of the novel, Kitty reads or refers to Anne Morgan's *The American Girl: Her Education, Her Responsibility, Her Recreation, Her Future*, 1915; Arnold Bennett's *Journalism for Women*, 1898; and *Practical Journalism: A Complete Manual of the Best Newspaper Methods* by Edwin Shuman, 1905. All are available online.

Kitty also has the following guidebooks on her bookshelf: *Peeps at Great Cities: New York* by Hildegarde Hawthorne, 1911; *Vocations for Girls* by E. W. Weaver, 1913; and *The Etiquette of Today* by Edith B. Ordway, 1913.

When Kitty visits Prentiss's photography studio, she sees a clipping taken from "Bryan Admits Spies Get Our Passports," from the November 14, 1914, edition of the *New York Times*.

The news about the Morgan shooting is captured in breathless detail in "J.P. Morgan Shot by Man Who Set the Capitol Bomb; Hit by Two Bullets Before Wife Disarms Assailant" from the July 4, 1915, edition of the *New York Times*.

Highlights of the tense back-and-forth between the German and American governments include "Germany Delivers Note Tomorrow, Shuns Liability for *Lusitania*, Proposals for Safety of Americans" (*New York Times*, July 9, 1915); "Wilson Says He Will Act Promptly After Deciding Reply to Germany;

American Comment Disturbs Berlin" (*New York Times*, July 14, 1915); and "Bernstorff to Explain Note Today; May Offer *Lusitania* Disavowal" (*New York Times*, July 16, 1915).

Austria's protests are recorded in "Austria-Hungary Protests Our Export of Arms; Says We Have Means of Exporting to All Alike" (*New York Times*, July 15, 1915).

Dr. Albert's activities (not all, however) were exposed in "How Germany Has Worked in U.S. to Shape Opinion, Block the Allies and Get Munitions for Herself, Told in Secret Agents' Letters" (*New York World*, August 15, 1915).

You can find full-text versions of President Wilson's speeches and responses to Germany online.

For an account of the challenges women journalists faced during the 1910s, as well as more about the Sob Sisters and the Thaw trial, see *Front-Page Girls: Women Journalists in American Culture and Fiction, 1880–1930* by Jean Marie Lutes and *Out on Assignment: Newspaper Women and the Making of Modern Public Space* by Alice Fahs.

Gail Collins offers an entertaining and informative overview of American women's history in *America's Women: 400 Years of Dolls, Drudges, Helpmates, and Heroines.*

Ron Chernow's *The House of Morgan: An American Banking Dynasty and the Rise of Modern Finance* explores the legacy of the Morgan family in detail.

Sabotage at Black Tom: Imperial Germany's Secret War in America, 1914–1917 by Jules Witcover contains fascinating accounts of some of the events narrated here and features Dr. Albert, German Ambassador Bernstorff, and other historical figures of the period.

The United States Passport: Past, Present, Future by the Department of State's Passport Office provides an overview of the development and use of the U.S. passport.

There is no shortage of good books on New York City's architecture. *New York 1900: Metropolitan Architecture and Urbanism 1890–1915* by Stern, Gilmartin, and Massengale combines beautiful photographs with detailed descriptions of the development of notable buildings, streets, and neighborhoods in the city.

Photographs of New York Interiors at the Turn of the Century and *Fifth Avenue, 1911, from Start to Finish in Historic Block-by-Block Photographs* offer a glimpse of everyday life in the city.

Philipp Blom's *The Vertigo Years: Europe, 1900–1914* spotlights social events that illustrate the hopes, fears, and contradictions of pre-war Europe.

And finally, something to watch—*37 Days: The Countdown to World War I*, a gripping BBC miniseries set in the foreign offices of England, Germany, and Austria, chronicles the political maneuvering that led to the declaration of war in August 1914.

Harder to find but comprehensive in scope, the many "bonus material" documentaries that accompany Lucasfilm's "Young Indiana Jones" series shouldn't be missed.

For more on *A Front Page Affair* and the Kitty Weeks mystery series, visit www.radhavatsal.com.

READING GROUP GUIDE

1. Do you think Kitty is the kind of person who fits in wherever she is? Why or why not? What is it about her that allows her to fit in (or not)?

2. In what ways does Kitty's financial status enable her to move about society?

3. How does Kitty's father's background influence his behavior and affect his and Kitty's relationship? How does their relationship influence how Kitty investigates?

4. What drives Kitty's friendship with Amanda Vanderwell? What do you think Kitty gets out of her relationship with Amanda, and vice versa?

5. What are the characteristics of some of the powerful, independent women we meet and hear about in the novel? Think of Mrs. Basshor, Anne Morgan, Miss Busby, Mary Pickford, and Pearl White. How are they similar? How are they different?

6. Why do you think Miss Busby suffered a nervous break-down? How might this be related to her hopes, expectations, and possible disappointment in Kitty?

7. How does Jeannie Williams feel about Kitty?

8. Do you think Aimee Cole genuinely likes Kitty, or does she try to turn her into a sympathetic ally for her own purposes?

9. Do you find the revelation about Hotchkiss's sexuality surprising? Do you think his contemporaries would have made similar assumptions about him as modern readers might?

10. Do you see Soames as a viable romantic interest for Kitty? What about him makes him a good match for her? What aspects of his life and career might prove problematic for a future relationship between them?

11. In her films, Pearl White plays an active heroine who never gives up but often has to be rescued from perilous situations. Are you surprised that those types of heroines existed a hundred years ago? How are they different (and similar) to action heroines today?

12. Jeannie, Kitty, and Amanda inhabit different but overlapping worlds. If you could live in one of their shoes for a day, which one would you chose, and why?

13. How did Dr. Albert's plan to infect the horses meet or defy your expectations of German warfare, especially compared to the torpedoing of the *Lusitania*?

14. In what ways does Kitty's world seem not dissimilar to our own? In what ways does it seem old-fashioned?

A Conversation
with the Author

What was your inspiration for *A Front Page Affair*?

There are too many to name here, but in terms of books, I'd say E. L. Doctorow's *The Waterworks* and Alexander McCall Smith's No. 1 Ladies' Detective Agency series. I wanted to write a novel that was entertaining and very readable, yet transported readers to a different time and place.

I also wanted to create a memorable heroine—one who was determined and tenacious, but also naive about the world around her—and watch her develop as her eyes are opened to complexities of the time in which she lives.

What drew you to the 1910s as the setting for the story?

I first became interested in the 1910s when I was a graduate student at Duke University researching early women filmmakers. It came as a shock to me that so many women were directing, producing, and writing films at that time. I was also amazed to learn about action-film heroines like Pearl White, who were the stars of highly popular action/adventure/mystery series. I soon discovered that this phenomenon wasn't just limited to film: women held prominent positions in many professional fields during the 1910s and then—remarkably—starting in the 1920s, their numbers began to decline and didn't go back up again until the second wave of feminism in 1970s.

But the 1910s weren't just an exciting time for women; they were an incredibly exciting time for the country. This was the period when the United States stepped out from the shadows and moved from being a regional power to taking its place on the world stage. It was a time when much that we take for granted today—things like car culture, movies, telephones, nation states (instead of kingdoms and empires)—was taking its modern form. And the transition wasn't an easy one.

I thought it would be exciting to combine the coming-of-age story for the country with the coming-of-age story for women and to tell it through the perspective of an unlikely protagonist: a young, well-off, pretty journalist who enjoys a privileged lifestyle.

How did you do your research?

I like to use primary sources, and when I started doing my research, a lot of materials hadn't been digitized, so I had to go to the New York Public Library, which fortunately has an amazing reference collection. I spent a lot of time looking at books published during the early 1910s—decorating guides and exercise manuals, for example. I also studied floor plans of different apartment buildings and the amenities they offered to pin down where Kitty would live and what type of home she has, and so on.

When historical characters speak in the novel, I like to remain as close as possible to their own words. So, I try to read books or articles written by them or about them from the

1910s. I go to secondary sources to get a general overview, but as far as specifics are concerned, I much prefer to go back to original material because that's where you find little unexpected bits of information that add something special to a character.

I also decided that each book in the series would be set at a specific moment in time. I had read about the Morgan shooting and the whole business with Dr. Albert, which culminated in his losing his briefcase. I then went back to the *New York Times* and read each day's paper in the days leading up to the shooting, through the period of my story, and right up to the date when Dr. Albert lost his briefcase and a bit after. Since these little-known historical events are entwined in the plot of the mystery and aren't just a backdrop to it, I wanted to give the experience of living that history.

What do you find to be most challenging about writing a historical novel?

What's most challenging about writing a historical novel is also what makes it so enjoyable: finding the right balance between fact and fiction. I enjoy keeping dates, places, and people accurate and not altering facts to suit the convenience of the story. If Kitty lives on the Upper West Side of Manhattan and she has to drive her father to a meeting downtown, it will take her a while to get there. If J. P. Morgan was shot on the third of July and the news appeared in the paper on the fourth, then that's not going to change.

The trick is to maintain a good balance and to digest all the facts and then forget about them and allow them to flow naturally through the story. I keep a 1915 calendar beside me as I write in which I track factual events and fictional events.

What is the most surprising thing you found in the course of writing and researching the book?

How far-fetched, almost implausible, many historical events seem from our present vantage point—Dr. Albert forgetting his briefcase on the subway; J. P. Morgan falling on top of the man who tried to shoot him, trapping the fellow beneath him. Accidents, sometimes absurd accidents, can have serious consequences. I like to find these seemingly trivial moments and try to understand their significance.

Real-life people, such as Anne Morgan, Nellie Bly, and Pearl White, as well as locations, such as the Colony Club and the Sleepy Hollow Country Club, appear in the book. How are/were they significant to their time? How have they changed since?

Anne Morgan, Nellie Bly, and Pearl White were all very different women. One was a philanthropist; another, a journalist; the third, an actress. But all three were very well-known in their day and provided different examples of what it meant to be a successful woman.

The Colony Club and Sleepy Hollow Country Club were both exclusive clubs, and both still exist today. I like to use real locations as much as possible because I think it creates a real geography and allows readers an opportunity to feel like they live in the world of the novel, which is something I enjoy when I read. I'm a sucker for maps in books and that type of detail.

How did you come up with the name Capability Weeks?

I wanted to find a name that would evoke something about the heroine's character—or the kind of person she aspires to be—and a name that could also be shortened into a milder-sounding diminutive. Names like Hope, Virtue, Patience, etc., seemed too soft. I don't recall exactly when I first heard about Lancelot "Capability" Brown, the famous landscape designer, but I loved that name because it sounds so competent. And I love the contrast between it and "Kitty," which sounds stereotypically feminine.

Which character do you feel most closely connected to?

All of them, really. I see the world through Kitty's eyes, but I can't help but sympathize with Miss Busby's frustration with her or enjoy her father's secretiveness and his desire to needle her a bit. I like the way Amanda condescends to her and Jeannie manages to "steal" her position. The fun thing about Kitty is that she isn't perfect, nor is she always smarter than the other characters. She's just willing to go the distance.

Writing is not your first career. How did you come to it?

At the back of my mind, I always wanted to write fiction. It was a way I could explore ideas that are interesting to me and bring together different strands that otherwise might not coexist. Fiction allows me much more freedom than academic writing, but I wouldn't have the subject matter that I do without my academic training. I chose mystery as a genre because I love to read it. It has a beginning, middle, and end—and it's all about discovery That's something I really enjoy—if a book can open my eyes to something new, for me, that's a huge bonus.

How does your background, both in film and as a woman who came from India as a teenager to study in the United States, shape the book you've written?

Without studying silent cinema, I doubt I would have discovered the 1910s as this fascinating and rewarding period in which to set a mystery. I also discovered the wonderful action-heroines and the actresses who played them, who were the inspiration for a character like Kitty.

Coming from India to attend boarding school in Connecticut on a scholarship as a teenager was a pivotal moment in my life. I was old enough to be able to look critically at the world I was entering, but also young enough to assimilate very quickly. I remember a friend telling me, "I keep forgetting you're not American." I used to keep forgetting that I wasn't American too! But it's this divided identity that gives Kitty her unique viewpoint—she can be in a certain milieu and seem like she's part of it, but she also has the perspective of an outsider looking in. This doesn't exempt her from the consequences of her actions, of course, but it does make her an effective, although unlikely, detective.

Funnily enough, I think my childhood in Mumbai helps me to imagine New York in the 1910s. I grew up among a very colorful cast of characters from all walks of life. And my family was, and is, filled with strong, outspoken women. My grandmother ran a large, rambling house in the style of a bygone era. Watching her converse with the tradesmen—everyone from the upholsterer to the fruit seller to the man who fixed broken necklaces—and hearing them talk about their families and lives gave me some insight, I think, into a more personal time. A time when you knew the person who brought your milk and sewed your clothes—although, by the 1910s in New York, that was slowly changing.

She also belonged to a country club where "everybody knew everybody." I think that's the way New York was in the 1910s (and perhaps still is now). If you were a part of a certain milieu, you knew everyone you had to know or, at worst, were just a step away from knowing everyone.

Who are some of your favorite authors?

The authors I turn to time and again are Agatha Christie and Dick Francis in mystery. Authors who create immersive worlds like Frank Herbert in *Dune* or Tolkien in the Lord of the Rings trilogy. I think I must know Jane Austen by heart. I love Gabriel García Márquez, Jorge Luis Borges, Elizabeth Gaskell, and Charles Dickens. When I was in my teens, I read everything from Isaac Asimov to *Gone with the Wind*.

What advice would you give to aspiring writers?

There's no magic to it. You have to start writing and then finish. For me, finishing and letting go is the hardest part. I never feel like I'm done, but when I start spinning in circles, I realize I must be done. I wish I had the ability to look at something I've written and feel content with it, but I'm not that lucky.

Selected References and Resources

"Austria-Hungary Protests Our Export of Arms; Says We Have Means of Exporting to All Alike," *New York Times*, July 15, 1915. http://timesmachine.nytimes.com/timesmachine/1915/07/15/issue.html.

Bennett, E. A. *Journalism for Women: A Practical Guide.* New York: John Lane, 1898. https://archive.org/stream/journalismforwo00benngoog#page/n8/mode/2up.

"Bryan Admits Spies Get Our Passports," *New York Times*, November 14, 1914. http://timesmachine.nytimes.com/timesmachine/1914/11/14/issue.html.

"Full Text of Germany's Reply to the United States," *New York Times*, July 10, 1915. http://timesmachine.nytimes.com/timesmachine/1915/07/10/issue.html.

"Full Text of the President's Note to Germany," *New York Times*, July 24, 1915. http://timesmachine.nytimes.com/timesmachine/1915/07/24/issue.html.

"How Germany Has Worked in U.S. to Shape Opinion, Block the Allies and Get Munitions for Herself, Told in Secret Agents' Letters," *New York World*, August 15, 1915. https://en.wikipedia.org/wiki/Great_Phenol_Plot.

Morgan, Anne. *The American Girl: Her Education, Her Responsibility, Her Recreation, Her Future.* New York and London:

Harper & Brothers, 1915. https://archive.org/details/
americangirlhere00morg.

Shuman, Edwin L. *Practical Journalism: A Complete Manual of the
Best Newspaper Methods*. New York: D. Appleton Company,
1910. http://catalog.hathitrust.org/Record/006507340.

ACKNOWLEDGMENTS

This book wouldn't be in its present form without the efforts of my talented and clearheaded agent, Christina Hogrebe at the Jane Rotrosen Agency, who took a chance on a first-time author.

The fabulous editorial team of Shana Drehs and Anna Michels at Sourcebooks patiently answered all my questions and shaped this into the novel that I hoped it could be. I look forward to working on many more together.

Thanks also to Heather Hall and the production and design departments at Sourcebooks.

And to Christina Prestia and Eric S. Brown on the business end.

Along the way, friends and family have come to the rescue. Mariah Fredericks, Denise Fulbrook, Julie Barer, Nicki and Henry Welt, Kelly Adams, Rebecca Gopoian and David Heatley, Marcia Lovas, Erin Toomey, Maria and Mitch Hoffman, Rebecca Gowers, Kevin Baker, Melissa Rathbone, Anandi Hattiangadi, Kiran Nagarkar, and Svetlana Mintcheva provided advice and support at critical moments.

My mother, Tulsi Vatsal, has read more drafts than I can count.

My husband, Daniel Welt, and our daughters have been there through all the ups and downs of this project. It's been a long journey, and their enthusiasm and support have made it all worthwhile.

About the Author

Radha Vatsal grew up in Mumbai, India, and came to the United States to attend boarding school when she was sixteen. Her fascination with the 1910s began when she studied women filmmakers and action-film heroines of silent cinema at Duke University, where she earned her PhD from the English Department. *A Front Page Affair* is her first novel. Radha lives with her husband and two daughters in New York City.

It's a Mall
World After All

Books by Janette Rallison

Playing the Field

All's Fair in Love, War, and High School

Life, Love, and the Pursuit of Free Throws

Fame, Glory, and Other Things on My To Do List

It's a Mall World After All

Revenge of the Cheerleaders

My Fair Godmother

It's a Mall World After All

JANETTE RALLISON

Walker & Company
New York

First published in the United States of America in 2006 by
Walker Publishing Company, Inc.
Paperback edition published in 2008

For information about permission to reproduce selections from this book, write to
Permissions, Walker & Company, 175 Fifth Avenue, New York, New York 10010

The Library of Congress has cataloged the hardcover edition as follows:
Rallison, Janette
It's a mall world after all / Janette Rallison.
p.   cm.
Summary: While working at the mall, organizing a school fundraiser, and trying to prove that her
best friend's boyfriend is seeing another girl, high-school student Charlotte's best intentions
always seem to backfire.
ISBN-13: 978-0-8027-8853-5 • ISBN-10: 0-8027-8853-X (hardcover)
[1. Interpersonal relations—Fiction. 2. Shopping malls—Fiction. 3. High schools—Fiction.
4. Schools—Fiction.] I. Title: It's a mall world after all. II. Title.
PZ7.R13455lts 2006   [Fic]—dc22   2006001971

ISBN-13: 978-0-8027-9797-1 • ISBN-10: 0-8027-9797-0 (paperback)

Visit Walker & Company's Web site at www.walkeryoungreaders.com

Book design by Nicole Gastonguay
Typeset by Westchester Book Composition
Printed in the U.S.A. by Quebecor World Fairfield
2 4 6 8 10 9 7 5 3 1

All papers used by Walker & Company are natural, recyclable products
made from wood grown in well-managed forests. The manufacturing processes
conform to the environmental regulations of the country of origin.

To all the people who've ever
come to a book signing,
written me a letter,
or e-mailed me that you liked my books.
I have the coolest fans.
Thanks for your support!

❧ *one* ❧

I've heard stories about supermodels that were discovered while shopping at the mall. That's sort of what happened to me. Only instead of being discovered by a high-powered talent agent, the perfume lady at Bloomingdale's discovered me. Two weeks ago while I walked through the store with my best friend, Brianna, the cosmetics manager came up to us and asked if either one of us would be willing to offer samples to shoppers through the holiday season. Brianna didn't need the job, but I did. So now I stand in front of the department store entrance like some sort of human air freshener and spritz the latest fragrance on unsuspecting strangers who pass by. This is the ultimate weird after-school job because if you did this anywhere else but a high-end department store, you'd probably be arrested.

It's not like I'm even good at this job. To tell you the truth, I'm not that impressed with designer fragrances.

I mean, what exactly do they put in the bottle that makes it cost so much? Ground diamonds? Nearly extinct flora? Every time some woman stops, sniffs her wrist, and murmurs, "Well, that's a delightful scent," I nearly say, "Yeah, but so is spring-fresh Tide, and they don't charge a hundred dollars a bottle for it."

Never once have I told a woman, "Yes, it's expensive, but you're worth it," or "It will drive men crazy." The only man this perfume will drive crazy is your husband, and that'll only happen when you inform him how much it cost.

So yeah, I'm not the best perfume saleswoman, and it's a good thing I don't get paid on commission. But I will say one thing for the job—I have a great view of the mall courtyard. I can see halfway across the building. It's sort of like being a field observer on teenage life. I know who's on the prowl for new dating material. (They're the girls who dress up, do their hair, and come all the way to the mall to buy a Cinnabon.) I know who's depressed. (These are the girls who buy something in every store.) And I know who's depending on winning the lottery to get by in life instead of going to college. (These are the girls who come to the mall every single day. I mean, do they not have homework to do?)

In between spritzing people with perfume, I imagine I'm writing my doctoral thesis on the subject. You know, the psychology of shopping and what your purchases say about you. Someday I'll write a long, impressive paper about everything I've learned from my time in Bloomingdale's and entitle it: "It's a Mall World After All."

Hey, the fragrance business can get pretty boring at times.

The most exciting thing that happens is, occasionally a guy will come by and pretend to be interested in perfume just to flirt with me. I flirt back if he's not from my high school. It's not that I'm a snob or anything. It's just that all the guys from my school are immature jerks. Really. I see enough of them to know.

I used to think it was just a girl thing to go and hang out at the mall. My dad, for example, hates to set foot in department stores. He'd probably resort to wearing bath towels cinched together with rubberbands if my mom didn't buy his clothes for him. But a lot of guys from my school hang out here. I see them wandering by on a regular basis.

I wasn't surprised when I saw Bryant Anderson or Colton Taft by the fountain in the courtyard between Bloomingdale's and the escalator. Bryant is Brianna's boyfriend; but it's not like they spend every waking moment together, so I didn't think anything of him being at the mall without her. Colton has been Bryant's best friend since freshman year, so they hang out a lot.

In between trying to entice customers with the spicy and exotic smell of Midnight Star, I watched the guys sit down on the benches by the fountain. Bryant's letterman jacket stretched across his shoulders, and he surveyed the expanse of the mall like a king looking out on his domain. His blond hair was mussed, as though he didn't care enough to comb it; but Brianna says he uses styling gel to get it to stay that way, so who knew how much of his I'm-so-good-looking-I-don't-have-to-worry-about-my-looks attitude is just an act.

Sitting beside him, Colton fiddled with his watch. Colton is just as handsome as Bryant, but in a more sophisticated way. Colton's dark brown hair is never out of place. His clothes look like he irons them before he puts them on. He doesn't have the strut of the typical jock but the smooth walk of an underworld spy. Brianna has told me more than once I should go out with Colton. She thinks we would make a great couple because (1) he is her boyfriend's best friend, (2) we're both in honors classes and occasionally study together, and (3) we both have names that start with the letter C and so are destined to be together. Bryant and Brianna. Colton and Charlotte. How cute, right?

I have to keep reminding her, she is absolutely not to play matchmaker based on the letter of my first name, and besides, I have a policy of not dating guys from our high school, even if Colton is the only person in our study group who remembers I like diet soda, but not Diet Coke. Whenever we meet at his house, he always has diet root beer for me. You gotta give a guy bonus points for buying your favorite soda.

But still, it wouldn't work out between us for many reasons. First of all, I haven't forgiven him for beating me in the National Honor Society presidential election, and second, he never pays any attention to me.

At least not in *that* way. When he wants to rub in

the election results, he'll smile over at me and suggest I call him Mr. President; and when he doesn't understand some concept from our microeconomics homework, I'm the first person he calls. He says I do so well in the class because I'm a girl and am therefore predisposed to understand the intricacies of shopping.

I'd love to be able to tell him no, I'm just smarter; but about twice a month I have to call him for help on some calculus problem, which ruins any possible gloating.

So despite all of Brianna's suggestions, Colton and I weren't likely to ever be a couple. If she wanted to have some sort of best-friends double dates, she'd just have to find a new boyfriend. Which, in my opinion, wouldn't be a bad idea.

Colton took off his watch and held it up to his ear as though to check to see if it still worked. It brushed against his hair. I absentmindedly sprayed Midnight Star onto a woman whose hands were too full of shopping bags to ward me off.

And that's when two girls came and sat down next to Colton and Bryant. Not just sat down, mind you, but sat down close and started up a conversation. From all the way across the courtyard, I could see Bryant smiling at them, leaning close, taking in their miniskirts and tight tops. For several minutes the air around me remained Midnight Star–free as I stared at Bryant and these girls.

They didn't go to our high school, and each of them carried a Gucci purse. This meant they had enough

money to spend hundreds on an accessory that did
nothing but beg thieves to steal it. Most likely they
went to Leland Prep, the local school whose unofficial
motto was, "Do we have to apply to Stanford—I
thought we owned that place?"

I've been to a few Leland Prep parties, and I tried to
remember if I'd ever seen these girls before. One had
bleached-blond hair; the other, red hair so bright it
had to be out of a bottle. I couldn't place them.

Did Bryant know them, or was this just a chance
encounter in the mall during which he had momentarily forgotten he already had a girlfriend?

Surely, any minute now Bryant would remember
Brianna, then he and Colton would stand up, give the
girls the brush-off, and leave.

Only they didn't. They stayed there talking and
smiling. At one point Bryant even reached over and
flipped the blond girl's hair away from her face—a blatant flirting move.

I held the perfume bottle limply in my hand. What
a two-timer.

They kept talking, and I wondered how well Bryant
knew "Blondie." I wished I could hear what they said.
I mean, it was possible, wasn't it, that the girls were
just asking for directions to, say, Bath and Body Works,
and Bryant was merely saying, "Here, miss, why don't
I move this hair out of your face to help you see
better."

The group stood up and walked two by two to the escalator. Colton and the redhead stood in front, while

Bryant rode up the escalator with his back to the railing so he could continue to look at Blondie.

I watched them till they moved past my line of sight. Once they got to the upper story, would they split up, walk around together, or perhaps even head to the food court or the theaters? It might be a double date, after all.

And if it was, Brianna had a right to know about it.

Still gripping my perfume bottle, I walked to the store's elevator. The Bloomingdale's shoppers would just have to do without Midnight Star for a few moments while I secretly spied on my best friend's boyfriend and the shameless blond hussy he escorted up the escalator.

Once I made it to the top floor, I hurried through Women's Sweaters and reached the front of the store. Bryant and his group had just exited the escalator and walked over to a jewelry store next to Bloomingdale's.

Colton handed his watch to the man behind the counter. Apparently to have it checked, or fixed, or something. I stepped behind a rack of blazers and peered out at the four of them.

And then someone tugged on my shirtsleeve. I turned to see a little boy, maybe six or seven years old, holding out a pair of women's black shoes. Not the elegant ones, but the type that resembled nurse shoes, only black. Like your nurse didn't have any confidence in the doctor's ability to save you, and was saving herself the trouble of changing shoes for your funeral.

"Do you work here?" the boy asked me.

My white lab coat–looking smock and name tag had given me away. "Yeah," I said.

"Can you help me with these shoes?" he asked.

"I don't work in that department," I told him.

He continued to hold the shoes toward me. "But you're a lady, and you know about shoes, right?"

I glanced back at the group by the jewelry store. Colton turned away from the sales counter, so I knew the group was about to leave. I didn't want to miss where they went. "What do you want to know?" I asked the kid.

"How do I tell what size to get my mom?"

"Have her try them on."

"I can't. They're a surprise for her."

I pulled my gaze away from Bryant and really looked at the kid. Although his black hair was neatly combed, he wore a faded yellow shirt under a stained jacket. His jeans were nearly worn through at the knees, and his own shoes were done up with laces that had broken and been knotted together. He didn't carry anything that indicated he had money on him.

"You want to buy shoes for your mother?" I asked him.

"For Christmas. Only I don't want to make her wait for Christmas to give them to her, because her feet hurt when she comes home from work." He held the shoes up for my inspection again. "So how do I know if these fit?"

I set my perfume bottle on the top of a rack of blazers and took the shoes in my hand. Size seven. The price on the sticker read $69.99 I didn't have the heart to ask him how much money he had. "How tall is your mom?"

"Shorter than you," he said.

Which was almost a given, since I'm five nine.

He held his hand up as far as it could go. "She's about this tall." Well, only if she was a dwarf. His hand didn't go up very far.

"These might fit her," I said, "but they're kind of expensive. Have you looked at the other pairs?"

He shook his head. "They have to be black. Her work says so."

I glanced back out at the mall. Bryant, Colton, and the girls sauntered across the hallway in my direction. I took another step behind the blazers and lowered my voice. "Well, if the shoes don't fit, she can bring them back and exchange them for another pair."

"Really?" His face lit up like he'd never heard of this aspect of shopping. And maybe he hadn't.

I peeked over the blazers. Bryant, Colton, and the girls had come into Bloomingdale's. They walked right past me. I kept expecting one of the guys to look over and see me. I actually held my breath for a moment.

I shouldn't have bothered. Both Bryant and Colton were too busy with their conversation to notice me. They stopped in front of a display of women's wallets, and one of the girls picked through them. If I had been a bit closer, I could have heard what they said. "Good luck with the shoes," I whispered to the kid; then when I was sure the group wasn't looking at me, I slunk from one clothes rack to the next. And then to the next. I pretended to straighten the sweaters on the rack while I strained to hear the conversation.

"Everything in department stores is so gauche," the redhead said. "But it's not like my tutor will be able to tell the difference anyway. 'Les prolétariat ne feront pas la différence.'"

This caused both Blondie and the redhead to laugh. Definitely Leland Prep girls.

"Get her this one." Bryant held up a green wallet. "Because nothing says Merry Christmas quite like fake crocodile skin."

Another tug on my shirtsleeve. The kid had followed me over to the new rack. "Will my mom need the box to exchange the shoes?"

Since I didn't work in the shoe department, I wasn't sure, but I figured anything could be returned with the receipt. "I don't think so," I whispered.

"Why are you hiding over here?" the boy asked.

"I'm not hiding," I said.

"Then why are you whispering?"

"I'm not." Okay, I was. "Sore throat," I told him.

Over by the wallets, the blond girl took the box from Bryant's hand and swatted him playfully in the arm with it. "You're too funny," she purred. "But no goofing off at Candice's party. Everyone has to be on their best behavior or her parents won't let her rent out the club again."

He grinned. "I'll use my best club manners the whole time."

Which pretty much answered the question of whether he was cheating on Brianna.

Jerk.

I turned my back to them and half leaned against the sweater rack. Poor Bri. How was I going to tell her about this when I knew what it would do to her?

I ought to walk right over to the group, snatch the crocodile wallet from Blondie's manicured hands, and smack Bryant with it. I ought to—

That's when I noticed the kid walking toward the back exit. He glanced from side to side. One of his hands held on to a lump underneath his jacket.

And then I understood. He had never meant to buy the shoes. He'd planned on stealing them all along.

I hurried after him, not calling out because I was afraid it would make him bolt outside. Just before he opened the door, I reached him. I grabbed hold of his jacket and yanked him backward. "What are you doing?"

He turned and looked at me with wide, frightened eyes. "Nothing."

"Nothing? You're shoplifting. Don't you know it's against the law?"

His eyes, still just as wide, filled with tears. "Her feet hurt really bad when she comes home."

"Where is your mother right now?"

The tears spilled out onto his cheeks. He didn't answer.

"Is she here at the mall?"

He shook his head.

"Who's watching you?"

He shrugged as though he didn't know. I suspected he didn't want to give me any more information than he had to. "Do I need to take you to mall security so they can find out who's supposed to be watching you?"

He looked down at the floor and mumbled. "I told my grandma I was going over to T.J.'s, but I rode my bike here instead."

There weren't any homes close to the mall. I wondered, but didn't ask, how far he'd ridden to get to the mall. "Listen, I don't think your mother wants you stealing things, even if you're doing it for her."

He didn't move or let go of the lump under his jacket. I'd either have to call security or wrestle the shoes away from him myself, and suddenly I knew I couldn't do either.

I bent down to be closer to his eye level. "What's your name?"

"Reese," he said.

"Look, Reese, if you want to earn those shoes, I'll buy them for you."

His gaze shot up to my face, the tears at once stopping. "How would I earn them?"

Yes, how? I glanced around the department store in search of something for him to do, but there wasn't anything. I mean, if I made him squirt perfume on people with me, both of us would get in trouble. "Um, you could pick up trash from inside the mall and put it into garbage cans."

"And then you'll buy the shoes for me?"

"Right."

He pulled the shoes from under his jacket and handed them to me. "And you'll give me the box for the shoes?"

"I'll get you the box and the receipt. That will come in handy if she needs to exchange the sizes." I tucked the shoes under my arms and looked over at the shoe department to see if anyone was around who could retrieve the box for me. "I'll buy these now. You come back when the trash is picked up from the mall. I'll be downstairs in the cosmetics department spraying perfume on people." Assuming, that was, the manager hadn't noticed I'd gone AWOL, and was just waiting for me to come back so she could fire me. Which was another reason to use my employee discount now, while I still had it.

The kid took off across Bloomingdale's without another word from me, and I walked over to the shoe department. Once I had bought the shoes—box and all—I went back downstairs with my bottle of Midnight Star. Bryant and friends were nowhere around, but I didn't care where they'd gone. I had enough information to bust Bryant. He had met another girl at the mall, flirted with her, and made plans to go to Candice's party.

Candice. I repeated the name to myself as I took the elevator back downstairs. I knew a Candy who went to Leland Prep. Could it be the same person? Maybe everybody else called her Candice. I only knew

her as Candy because that's what my ex-boyfriend Greg,
called her when we used to hang out together. Although come to think of it, Greg had been friends
with her since they were little, so that might just have
been his nickname for her. After all, Greg had called
me Char the entire time we'd gone out. This caused
Bryant and several of his football cohorts to also call
me Char, with an added snooty accent. From there
they've progressed to calling me Shar-Pei, Charlatan,
and Chardonnay.

Brianna kept telling me they were just teasing, which
is like flirting, so I should have felt complimented.
Like yeah, it's really flattering to be called after a dog,
a cheat, and booze.

You see what I mean about the guys from my
school?

I tucked the bag with the shoes behind the Estée
Lauder counter, took my spot in front of the cosmetic
aisle, and tried to forget about Candy and Greg. That
was the nice thing about Greg dumping me for Candy.
I no longer had to think about either one of them
again.

No one seemed to have noticed my absence or
missed the cloud of Midnight Star I kept spraying. I
stood there for the next fifteen minutes pushing perfume, but all the time I kept one eye on the mall.
Every now and again I caught sight of Reese running
back and forth across the hallway to the garbage cans.
It wasn't like there was all that much trash lying
around to begin with. The maintenance crew kept the

inside of the mall pretty clean. Still, every once in a while he held up his hand and waved an empty soda cup or dropped receipt like it was a piece of treasure.

I had to smile at his enthusiasm.

And then Bryant, Colton, and the girls showed up again. They must have been to the food court because Colton and the redhead carried soda cups while they walked. When they came to the benches by the fountain, they sat down with their backs to me.

Bryant sat close to Blondie with his arms spread out across the back of the bench, so he almost had his arm around her.

As I spritzed passersby I squeezed the perfume bottle so hard, several women probably smelled like Midnight Star for a week.

Reese ran up to me, breathless. "I'm done now. Can I have my shoes?"

"Sure." I walked to the Estée Lauder counter and handed the bag to him.

He looked in it as though he didn't quite trust me and had to make sure the shoes were really there.

"Let me give you some advice," I said. "If you tell your mother a stranger bought these shoes for you, she'll probably come down here and give them back to me. If you want her to keep them, tuck the receipt in the box, put them on your doorstep, and pretend you don't know anything about them."

"Okay." He clutched the bag to his chest and gave me a smile. "Thanks, Perfume Lady."

"Thanks for picking up litter. Now the mall is trash

free." I looked back over in Bryant's direction. He leaned over to tell Blondie something, and their shoulders brushed against one another. "Well, almost trash free."

Reese followed my gaze to where the group sat, then zeroed in on the soda Colton had plunked down on the bench between him and Bryant. "Oh. I didn't see that cup before. I'll go get it now."

"You don't have to," I said. "I think it still has soda in it, and if you were to accidentally spill some on Bryant, he might melt like the Wicked Witch of the West."

Reese blinked at the group. "Really?"

I smiled at Reese's amazed expression. "No, not really. He's not quite as bad as a wicked witch, so he'd probably just fizz a little."

Reese nodded slowly. "I've never seen a person fizz before."

"Neither have I, but at this moment I'm seriously considering conducting an experiment."

Now Reese blinked at me. "You want to throw soda on one of those boys?"

"Well, actually both of them, but I don't suppose there's enough in the cup for that. Besides, my boss wouldn't like it if I left my perfume spot to throw soda on people. Bosses are totally unreasonable that way." I took a quick look around the cosmetic department in case anyone was watching me talk to a little boy instead of spraying perfume on passing women. "Which reminds me, I'd better get back to work."

Reese tucked the box underneath his arm and turned away from me. "Okay. Bye. I'll do it for you."

I thought he meant he'd go so I wouldn't get in trouble. I really did. It never occurred to me that little kids take everything you say so literally. I mean, all right, so I might have told him Bryant would fizz if you threw soda on him. Certainly Reese ought to have known I was joking. Aren't they teaching basic scientific laws in elementary school? Evaporation. Condensation. And the fact that you can't actually melt people with soda.

While I watched, Reese walked up behind the group, took the cup of soda, and dumped it down the back of Colton's shirt.

I let out a gasp, which thankfully no one paid attention to because everyone was too busy listening to Colton yell. He jerked forward in surprise, then jumped up as though this might help him escape from the soda dribbling down his neck. Which, judging by the way he pulled at his shirt, didn't work.

Reese dropped the cup—which technically he shouldn't have done, since I'd just paid him to pick up the litter in the mall—then sprinted down the hallway toward the exit. Colton followed Reese with his eyes, debating, I suppose, whether to go after him, but the kid was fast. In another moment he was lost among the flow of shoppers.

The girls and then Bryant stood up. As they walked away, the girls flanked Colton, fussing over him and his dripping shirt.

I watched them leave with my fingers pressed against my lips. I berated myself for not telling Reese I was just kidding about the soda. And then I berated myself for not making it clear which guy to throw soda on.

two

I called Brianna as soon as I got home from work and told her everything. Well, minus the whole Reese incident. Partially because he'd aimed wrong, and partially because I knew Brianna would start to feel sorry for Bryant and Colton if she knew I'd sicced a soda-throwing six-year-old on them. And I was not going to give Bryant even a little advantage in this issue.

By the end of the phone conversation, she was crying, which almost made me cry too. "How could he do this to me?" she asked. "After six months of telling me I was the best girlfriend in the world, how could he"—her sniffling blotted out a good portion of the sentence—"and I was just sitting here working on his Christmas present."

I knew what the Christmas present was. A blue and green afghan she'd started at the beginning of November.

Crocheting. Yes. I felt partially responsible for this because she'd learned the skill from my mother. Mom is an interior designer, which means she can do all sorts of artsy-craftsy things, like sew curtains, dye lampshades, and faux paint walls to make them look like slabs of marble. She's known how to crochet since shortly after yarn was invented, but she only does it now for special occasions.

One day while Brianna was over, she caught sight of Mom working on a baby blanket, and Mom told her she was making it because she wanted her gift to be unique and something her friend would treasure forever. When Brianna heard the words *treasure forever,* you could almost see the idea settle into the folds of her mind. She had to learn how to crochet. It didn't matter how many times I pointed out to her that Bryant was a guy and thus wouldn't see the difference between a fleece blanket you could buy at a department store for twenty bucks and a crocheted afghan that would take you like a million hours to make out of balls of yarn. Brianna wanted her Christmas gift to be sentimental.

She spent the next hour sitting beside my mother, a string tethering her hand to a skein of yarn while she struggled to make her loops the same size. When she'd finally mastered this task, she learned the blanket pattern. When I say "learned," what I really mean is she would crochet a row, wail about it being all wrong, and then pull the whole thing apart. Half the time she looked like a yarn explosion had gone off around her.

Now after three weeks of working on it, she had only begun to leave in more rows than she pulled out. And I could just imagine her slouched over the afghan as she talked to me.

"I'm so sorry," I said. "But you can give it to someone else. I mean, your dad likes blue and green, doesn't he?"

"I need to talk to Bryant," she said, and hung up without saying good-bye.

I didn't hear from her the rest of the night. I thought about calling. I thought about going over, but I figured maybe she needed time alone.

When I got to school the next morning, I went straight to Brianna's locker. She stood there with her arms wrapped around Bryant in a way that indicated "time alone" wasn't high on her priorities. He saw me, stiffened, and sent a surly look in my direction.

Which probably matched the look I gave him.

Brianna pulled herself away from Bryant and smiled at me warily. "Now don't you guys start fighting. It was all just a misunderstanding."

"A misunderstanding?" I asked.

"Yes," Brianna said firmly.

Bryant bent down and gave her a kiss on the cheek. "I'd better get ready for class. See you later, Bri."

Meaning he didn't want to stay here and talk with me. He threw me another dark look in case I hadn't clued in to his attitude, then left.

Brianna watched him walk away, then turned to me with a dark look of her own. "Charlotte, you really ought to get your facts straight before you accuse people of things. You upset me so much last night I probably cried for a half an hour before Bryant came over." Brianna spun her combination and flung her locker door open. "Those girls at the mall were just Colton's friends. Colton is interested in Olivia, so when Bryant and Colton ran into Olivia and her friend Shelby, they all hung out for a while together. That's all it was."

"Bryant flirted with the girl."

Brianna sifted through the clutter in her locker until she found a math book. "Her name is Shelby, and he didn't flirt with her. He was just being nice to her for Colton's sake."

I gripped the books in my hands. "I saw Bryant. He was . . ." But I didn't know how to put it. How exactly do you describe flirting? He hadn't done anything blatant. It was just the little things you can't describe and yet know when you see them. The smile. The look. The way he leaned close to her. Flirting.

Brianna pulled a notebook from her locker. "You know, I hate to say this, Charlotte, but I think Bryant is right about you. He's told me since we started going out that you'd do something to try to break us up."

"Me?" I sputtered out. "So his flirting with other girls at the mall is my fault?"

She turned to me, eyelids fluttering with emotion. "See, that's exactly what I mean. You're trying to make me fight with him. I might have broken up with him if it hadn't been for Colton."

"Colton?"

"Yeah, he came over with Bryant to explain the whole situation and, you know, vouch for Bryant."

I gripped my books harder. By now I'd probably left fingerprint indentations on my calculus notebook. "Colton is Bryant's best friend. Of course he told you nothing went on. How come you're willing to listen to Bryant's best friend, but not your own?"

Brianna shut her locker with a thud and turned to me with exasperation. "Colton is right. You're too suspicious. You have it out for the guys at our school."

"This is not about the guys at our school," I said.

"You've never liked Bryant," she said.

Which is not entirely true. There was a time, say fourth grade, in which I held no ill will toward Bryant.

"What about the party at Candice's?" I asked. "You think it's okay for your boyfriend to go with Shelby?"

She rolled her eyes at me like I was being childish. "He's not going to that. Only Colton is. To see Olivia. Bryant is going to a wedding reception this Saturday with his family."

How convenient for Bryant.

Brianna let out a long sigh. "Look, Charlotte, we've been friends for a long time, and I don't want to fight with you, but you can't keep attacking Bryant this way."

Can't keep attacking? I repeated the words in my mind like they'd been spoken in a different language and I was trying to interpret them. *Can't keep attacking?* She thought I'd hurt him?

"You have to get over junior high," she went on. "So some guys were mean to you. So Bryant was one of them. That was a long time ago. We've all grown up since then."

Can't keep attacking. Maybe she meant the way I went silent when Brianna and I were talking together and he walked up to us. Or the way I winced whenever he called her "Babe."

"It's not healthy to hold grudges for so long. Colton even said so, and he's your friend."

Apparently not.

I'm not sure why this thought hurt so much. I shouldn't have expected any of Bryant's friends to take my side in an argument. But still, by taking Bryant's side, Colton had made me look like a suspicious, bitter busybody. Right there and then I swore to never drink another diet root beer at his house.

"Bryant is my boyfriend and I love him," Brianna went on. "Just don't make me choose between the two of you, all right?" She said the last part softly, like it was a plea and not a warning, but that didn't matter. She'd said the words, which meant she'd already chosen.

She smiled at me then, a consolation prize, I suppose. "Are you ready to go to class?"

Nope. I couldn't walk through the hallway with her now, making small talk as though nothing had happened. I shook my head. "I have some other stuff to do before first period. I just stopped by to see if you were okay." And then I turned away from her before I could say anything else. Not that I knew what else to say. At the moment my brain was only producing one sentence, and that was, *Are you insane?*

But that phrase got a lot of mileage in my mind.

How could she believe him and not me?

He was the one who had something to hide.

And hadn't I been incredibly forgiving to even speak to Bryant after the way he'd treated me in junior high?

Okay, maybe I had laughed and not believed Brianna when she'd first told me they were going out, and maybe I had even said the words, "Are you insane?" out loud at the time, but you couldn't really hold that against me. It was the obvious question and had apparently turned into her life's theme song.

I hugged my books against my chest, hard. Yeah, you learned all sorts of things at the mall. The first chapter of my doctoral thesis will be entitled "Why girls believe good-looking guys, and other marketing strategies in life that simply aren't fair."

I walked into AP calculus and saw Colton sitting at his desk. I tried to set fire to him with my eyes. Who was he to judge me and any grudges I might carry? He wasn't even around in junior high. He'd transferred to Hamilton High freshman year. He didn't know what I'd gone through.

First of all, despite what Brianna said (and where had she shelved her memory, anyway?), it wasn't just a few guys who were mean to me. It was most of them—Bryant being the supreme leader in this cause. And the guys who weren't mean didn't do anything to stick up for me, so they were jerks too.

You see, Charlotte is an unfortunate name to have if your sixth-grade class puts on a school play based on *Charlotte's Web* and you happen to be tall with sort of spindly arms and legs.

I heard every spider joke on earth. Every day for the rest of sixth grade. In junior high it progressed to insect jokes. After all, I wore glasses, so I already had four eyes. Spiders have eight eyes. Dung beetle larvae have six. Ants have two compound eyes, each made up of smaller eyes. I heard all the statistics just like I heard the speculations that I caught flies in my braces. People buzzed as they walked by me in the hallway.

Sometimes boys tease girls they like—you know, act all goofy to get a girl's attention. Let me assure you, this was not what I'm talking about. Using animal kingdom comparisons, this wasn't peacocks ruffling their feathers. It was wolves picking off the weak deer in the herd. These guys were going in for the social kill.

Even other girls distanced themselves from me— like talking with me would tarnish them by association. All in all, the whole experience was like hell, with the added perk of a bus ride to and from home every day.

At the end of eighth grade, my family took a two-year sabbatical to Argentina. I was still taller than everyone else, but the Argentineans thought I was cool anyway. They called me Charlotta, told me I had beautiful green eyes and exotic red hair. It isn't really red. It's auburn, but I guess in a country full of brunettes, it looked red.

In those two years I got rid of my glasses, braces, and fear of the junior high wolf pack. I stopped grow-ing and my figure filled out. My face, well, let's just say when you place my eighth-grade photo next to my sophomore photo, they look like before and after pic-tures in some ugly duckling contest.

When I came back to California at the beginning of my junior year, most of the class didn't even recognize me. A lot of the popular guys tried to hit on me. Like yeah, I was going to forget about the two years of hell they'd put me through.

So am I carrying a grudge? Maybe. Do I have it out for the guys in my school? No. I just have no use for them. Apparently Brianna didn't see the finer points of this philosophy; but still, she ought to know I could tell whether her boyfriend was flirting with another girl or not—after all, he'd been one of the popular boys who'd tried to hit on me.

In calculus class Mr. Hermansky handed back our last test. I got a 96. Colton got a 100. Normally he would have flaunted this fact at me at least once dur-ing class, but he didn't even look my way today.

I guess guilt takes all the fun out of gloating.

As I walked out into the hallway after class he came up next to me. "Hey, don't forget about the NHS meet-ing tomorrow before school."

I didn't turn my head. "Are you speaking to me,

Colton? I mean, even though it's obvious, I wouldn't want to be accused of jumping to the wrong conclusions again."

He let out a sigh. "Yes, I'm speaking to you."

"Well, it's too bad then that I'm not speaking to you."

Even though I walked quickly, he kept pace beside me. "Don't be this way, Charlotte. It's not like Bryant and Brianna are married. He's allowed to talk to other girls."

"Is that what you told Brianna—that Bryant is allowed to talk to other girls? Funny, when she told me about the conversation, it sounded more like, 'Charlotte is trying to break Bryant and Brianna up.'"

"Aren't you?" he asked, as though a denial from me would be a surprise.

"No, I just thought she should know the truth about Bryant."

"And you know the truth about him? I'm amazed you could tell that from your vantage point in the cosmetics aisle at Bloomingdale's."

This is what I call Colton's disdainful-intellectual defense. Just the lift of his eyebrow said, I'm thoughtfully considering not only the black and white of the issue but also every spattering of gray in between, while you, my friend, are a conclusion-jumping dolt.

I had seen him act this way too many times during history debates to be intimidated by it now. "Brianna can believe all of your convoluted excuses if she wants, but you and I know what really happened."

He shrugged, and it was the easy shrug of victory. "Yes, but you and I don't decide anything about Brianna's relationship with Bryant. She does, and she wants to believe my convoluted excuses." With a parting smile he added, "Try not to be late for tomorrow's NHS meeting. We're forming committees for the winter holidays dance." Then he turned and walked down a different hallway.

I watched him and his smooth underworld spy walk until he disappeared from sight. He thought I had no choice but to accept that he'd won.

Which was just one more thing he was wrong about.

Colton would be at Candice's party on Saturday. I was willing to bet Bryant would be there too. And so, one way or another, I was crashing that party. If a picture is worth a thousand words, one picture from my cell phone had to be worth a whole bucketful of Bryant's excuses.

By the time I reached home, I had second thoughts about catching Bryant. In order to snag an invitation to Saturday's party, I would have to call Candy. There is something pathetic about begging favors from an ex-boyfriend's current girlfriend.

It's not that I was mad at Candy for dating Greg. Really. Greg had just been an aberration on my part. We met while my mother was working on an interior design project for Greg's father's office. He liked me because I was tall and pretty. I liked him because he was rich.

That probably sounds wrong. I mean, it wasn't that I thought he would buy me expensive gifts, or marry me, or something. He just seemed so different from me. Stepping into his world was like visiting some exotic country. I wasn't a gold digger. I was a tourist.

Our relationship didn't last long. I discovered rich people aren't a premium version of everybody else. They're the same as everybody else, only with egos that quickly get annoying. He acted like he was doing me a favor to bring me to his club or out sailing with his friends. He would translate parts of their conversations as though I couldn't possibly know what a DeLorean was or why Martha's Vineyard was chic. He actually told me what fork to use at dinner. Is that necessary? I mean, if by chance you use your dessert fork for the salad, does it matter? Forks all do the same thing, don't they?

I usually ignored his instructions, hoping he'd get the hint, but he never did. He tried to change my nonelitist ways right up until he broke up with me. And he didn't even do that well. He brought Candy with him to tell me that—without malice or intent on either of their parts—their lifelong friendship had blossomed into something more. It wasn't anything I did. Greg thought I was a wonderful person and wished me the best in life.

So just like that, I was out of the three-forks-to-eat-one-meal world. I didn't miss it much.

While I got ready for work I vacillated back and forth: first talking myself into calling Candy, then talking myself out of it. She might not be the one throwing the party, and besides, how do you gracefully invite yourself to your ex-boyfriend's current girlfriend's party?

But this was for Brianna.

Finally I looked up Candy's number and called before I could change my mind again. She picked up on the second ring.

"Hi, Candy. It's Charlotte."

"Ohhh, hi." Her voice took on the tone of a person who'd found a lost puppy. "How are you doing, Char?"

"Fine. Really good. Hey, I know this is a request out of the blue, but are you throwing a party any time soon?"

"This Saturday," she said. "I'm having a Christmas party at the club."

The club. Bingo.

I moved the phone from one ear to the next, trying to get a better grip. "I heard some guys from my school talking about your party, and I wondered if there was any way I could swing an invite . . ."

There was a pause on the line, then Candy's voice sounding hesitant. "I'd love to have you, of course. I mean, I constantly told Greg how darling I thought you were, but do you think it's wise? Greg will be there, and I wouldn't want any awkward scenes between the two of you . . ."

Awkward scenes? Did she think I was going to beg for him back or something? Maybe throw a goblet at him and tell him he was a swine for leaving me? "Oh, it wouldn't be awkward," I said with forced cheerfulness. "Things are totally cool between Greg and me. I mean, you two are meant to be together, even I can see that. Besides, I'm interested in this other guy now—the one who's going to your party."

Candy's voice perked up. "You are? That's so wonderful. You've moved on with your life. What's his name?"

"His name?" I had to tell her something, and the only two guys I knew who were going to the party were Colton and Bryant. I didn't dare say Bryant. What if it somehow got back to Brianna that I'd told someone I was interested in him? She'd think I was just bad-mouthing him so they'd break up and I could snatch him. "Colton Taft," I said.

"Colton?" Candy let out a squeal. "I know Colton!"

Great. Terrific. I should have said Bryant.

"Colton used to go to the academy with me." She let out a sigh. "He's cute, Char. I'm so happy for you."

"It's not like we're a couple or anything," I said quickly. "I just, you know, kind of like him, but he, um, doesn't really know."

"Well, we can work on letting him know at my party."

No, no, no. This was not going at all the way I wanted it to. "Oh, I don't want to do that," I choked out. "I mean, I want to be low-key about the whole thing. You know, just hang out and see if anything interesting happens." Interesting between Shelby and Bryant, that was.

"Do you need something nice to wear? I just bought some pashminas that are to die for."

Pashminas? I was not about to admit I didn't know what part of your body you put a pashmina on. "Thanks," I said, "but I have plenty to wear."

"Are you sure? You know, the right outfit could accentuate your assets while concealing your figure flaws."

Figure flaws? I was afraid to ask what she was referring to. "I'm really okay as far as clothes go." At least I was until two seconds ago, when I started worrying about my figure flaws.

Another pause. "All right." I knew Candy didn't believe me. Still, she gave me directions to the club, told me they would serve hors d'oeuvres at seven, and then would have dancing until midnight.

I thanked her again, said good-bye, and hoped I wouldn't be the only one at the party without a pashmina draped over my figure flaws.

❧ three ❧

That evening when I walked into the mall, one of the first people I saw was Colton. He stood in front of the jewelry store strapping his watch onto his wrist. He didn't see me. I slunk down the escalator before he could.

He couldn't possibly have known about my conversation with Candy; still, I felt awkward even being in the same building with him—like he might glance at me and see the inner workings of my mind.

I walked to the cosmetics counter; picked up today's sample, Sweet Mystique; and dutifully spritzed people. My gaze kept drifting toward the escalator, just in case Colton appeared. Fifteen minutes passed. Then thirty. He didn't come down. He was either shopping upstairs, had left, or was just spending a really long time at the jewelry counter. With Colton's money, that may have been the case.

Colton's father is a Silicon Valley bigwig. Colton

only goes to Hamilton High because we have one of the best wrestling programs in the state. Personally, I don't know why people like the sport. I mean, it's just a bunch of guys dressed up in outfits that could pass for trapeze-wear who roll around and try to push each other through the floor. There are no exciting home runs, no across the court baskets, no holding your breath as you wait to see if the receiver catches the pass. Just two men who look like they're in the middle of cardiac arrest.

Colton's parents must be loaded because they let him drive whatever car he wants as long as he keeps a 4.0 grade point average. So he drives a dark blue BMW convertible.

All I get from my parents for straight A's is a smile and a "Good job!" I occasionally get to borrow the family minivan. Yeah, I'm cool.

I kept spritzing Sweet Mystique on people. Colton never came downstairs. After a while, Reese showed up with a blond kid.

"Hi, Perfume Lady." He waved a hand at me even though he stood only three feet away.

"Hi, Reese. Who's your friend?"

The blond boy, who was taller, skinnier, and probably a little older than Reese, spoke up. "I'm T.J. We came to pick up trash for you."

"Trash?" I repeated.

Reese tucked his thumbs in his pants pockets as though getting ready to take down a steer. "T.J. needs a pair of jeans, and I need shoes for my mother."

"Wait a minute, Reese. I bought shoes for your mother yesterday. What happened to them?"

His eyebrows furrowed together, and he frowned. "I did just what you told me to do. I put the shoes on the doorstep, box and all. When my mom found them, she was real happy. But then she returned her shoes and went to Wal-Mart and bought me and my sister shoes and stuff." He lifted his running shoe—a fresh black with silver stripes—for my inspection. "See?"

"Very nice," I said.

"So I need to buy her shoes again, but this time without the box."

I wished I could buy him more shoes. I really did. But I couldn't keep spending that much money on someone else's feet. I didn't even own a pair of seventy-dollar shoes myself. "I'm sorry guys," I said. "That was a one-time deal."

Two faces looked up at me blankly.

"If I keep buying shoes for your mother, I'm not going to have any money left."

"Please," Reese said. "Just one more time?"

T.J. held one leg up for me to see. "My jeans are too small, and when I pull them up, they give me a stomachache."

"Pleeeease," Reese added.

Great. I'd done a good deed and created two miniature panhandlers.

"Have you tried the people at Sears? Maybe they have some trash for you to pick up over there. Ask some nice-looking older woman. They like kids."

Reese and T.J. exchanged a glance. Then they sighed and their shoulders slumped. "Okay," Reese said. "C'mon, T.J."

I felt like Scrooge as they slowly walked away.

Chapter two of my dissertation: "You Can Meet All Sorts of Interesting People at the Mall." Don't talk to them though, as this just encourages them to talk back to you. Talking leads to trouble. Most wars, divorces, and political elections happen after a lot of talking. When at the mall, it's best to pretend you're mute. Or from another country. A country of mutes, for example.

Stray children should especially be avoided. Like ducks and seagulls, if you feed one, you will shortly be swarmed by an entire flock. Only children are more expensive to make happy, and also messier.

I continued to spray people with Sweet Mystique. One woman even bought a bottle. I wanted to tell her, "This perfume costs more than a pair of black working shoes and a new pair of jeans. You don't really need it."

Never once did I look out into the mall courtyard. If Reese and T.J. were going from store to store asking for help, I didn't want to see it.

An hour later they trudged back into Bloomingdale's. "Hi, Perfume Lady."

"Hi, guys."

Reese thrust his hands in his jacket pockets and sighed. "Sears doesn't have a perfume lady. And the shoe lady said no."

T.J. took a step forward. "The pants lady said no too."

"Really? I'm sorry."

The boys exchanged a glance, as though building courage. T.J. fiddled with the zipper on his coat. "So we picked up trash for you anyway. Did you see us? I kept waving, but you didn't wave back."

"Oh, sorry. I wasn't looking. That's nice of you boys to pick up trash and everything, but—"

"We even threw soda on that guy for you," Reese said brightly. "You know that one from yesterday."

"You . . . you . . . what?"

"He was upstairs buying stuff at Radio Shack," Reese said.

"We waited till he got outside though," T.J. clarified. "'Cause we didn't want the Radio Shack man to yell at us."

"You followed Colton outside and threw soda at him?"

Both boys nodded happily.

I felt sick one moment and wanted to laugh the next. I couldn't help myself—I wondered if it was a diet root beer.

Hmmm. Maybe I would have to buy Reese and T.J. something.

I shook off the thought as soon as it came to me. I couldn't help every little kid who threw soda on Colton. I mean, weren't there organizations that did that sort of thing—help kids, that is, not throw soda on arrogant teenage boys.

I bent down to be closer to their eye level. "Listen, guys, I'd love to help you, but you're asking the wrong person. Don't you have counselors at school that can help you?"

My question earned blank looks.

I tried again. "Where do you go to school?"

"St. Matthew's Elementary."

St. Matthew's. I should have known. It was a Catholic school downtown that took in a lot of poor kids. When I was younger, my elementary school used to do a clothes drive for them every year.

"Have you asked your teacher if there's someone who can help you?"

Reese's brown eyes blinked at me. "I asked Santa."

T.J. swatted his arm. "You know there's no Santa."

"Is too," Reese said. "Last year he brought me UNO cards and underwear."

T.J. put his hands on his hips and tilted his head. "That was your mom. Santa don't bring no underwear. Besides, you asked for a remote control car."

T.J. turned to me as though to prove the point. "Santa isn't real, is he?"

I stared back at them. My throat felt dry. It broke my heart. All of it. That Reese's mom didn't have work shoes. That T.J. didn't have jeans, and that Christmas would disappoint them again.

Two faces looked up at me, waiting for my answer. "Well, the thing about Santa is . . . you see . . . it's really the spirit of giving that's important . . . and well, you should really talk to your parents about Santa."

Reese's eyebrows drew together. I could tell he didn't understand. "And then will he bring my mom shoes?"

"Yes," I said, because at that moment I couldn't say anything else. "This year your mother is going to get her shoes." I nodded at T.J. "And you're going to get some jeans that fit."

T.J. cocked his head at me. "How do you know?"

"I work at the mall. Santa comes here all the time. Sometimes we talk."

The boys looked at each other, then back at me skeptically. "You know Santa?" T.J. asked.

"Sure. I sold him a bottle of perfume for Mrs. Claus last week. Come back here on the twenty-fourth and see if Santa hasn't left something for you."

"Promise?" Reese asked.

"Promise," I said.

T.J. gave me a hopeful smile, then just as suddenly narrowed his eyes. "Are you just saying that to get rid of us?"

"No. Well, yes. You guys have to leave so I can get back to work. You wouldn't want to get me in trouble, would you?"

Both boys shook their heads.

"Good-bye, Perfume Lady," Reese said, and then they disappeared in the crowd.

For the rest of my shift, I wondered how I was ever going to save up for college if I kept handing over my paycheck to every little kid that came along. I wondered how many children like Reese and T.J. went to St. Matthew's.

The world just seems to be teeming with holes. Needs so big, they can't ever be filled. I couldn't help all of those kids. Not if I worked day and night drenching people with perfume.

And then I thought of NHS. We did service projects a lot. This was partially because Ms. Ellis, our advisor, believed it was our civic responsibility to improve conditions in the world, and partially because we all knew community service looked good on college applications. It was also partially because—okay, I admit it—everyone figured it was just easier to agree to hold a fund-raising car wash than to hear me lecturing about the poor and downtrodden again; but the point is, NHS did service projects.

Why couldn't we do a something for the kids at St. Matthew's Elementary? Granted, we'd sold fruit shakes in the cafeteria at lunch for the past month in order to raise money to put on a winter dance, so probably no amount of lecturing would get the group to agree to another fund-raiser, but perhaps we could do a project for the St. Matthew's kids instead of the dance.

After all, the student body council were really the ones who were supposed to put on the dances. NHS only agreed to hold the winter dance because it was tradition. Years ago, the school hadn't had a winter dance, and then some NHS president decided to have one as a fund-raiser—thus proving smart people aren't necessarily good with finances. The dance never did much more than break even.

Why not put the funds to a better use? Besides, Ms. Ellis would probably jump at the chance to do something that was less work. She'd gotten engaged in October and was trying to throw together some huge wedding in January. She'd done nothing for the last few meetings but flip through bridal magazines and mumble about the cost of embossed napkins and centerpieces.

The longer I thought about it, the more certain I felt it would work. We could go to St. Matthew's principal and ask for a list of a couple dozen of the neediest kids. Then we'd buy them gifts and have Santa deliver them personally. Seeing their faces light up would be much better than paying some overpriced deejay to play dance music. I mean, who needed another dance anyway?

All I had to do was convince the rest of NHS to see it my way.

As it turns out, the rest of NHS has serious problems when it comes to seeing things my way. Ms. Ellis was only there for the first five minutes of the meeting, and then had to step out in the hallway to take a call from her caterer. She at least would have listened to my idea without the pained expression that showed up on most of the club members' faces.

I told everyone about T.J.'s jeans, and how Reese had tried to steal shoes for his mother, but she'd returned them so he could have shoes instead. There had to be so many kids at St. Matthew's Elementary like T.J. and Reese. Kids we could help have a good Christmas. I finished my appeal holding my hands out. "What do you think?"

Colton studied me with unblinking eyes. "You want us to give up our dance to buy presents for a juvenile delinquent?"

"He's not a delinquent. He's a little boy," I said.

"You said he almost stole some shoes. He tried to break the law."

I let out a sigh. "Well, yeah, but that isn't the point. The point is he did it for his mother."

Colton rolled his eyes. "Fine. He's a terrific kid, and one day he can grow up to steal a Mercedes Benz for her."

The rest of the group laughed. Colton shot them a smile to let them know they were together in this, and I was obviously out of my mind.

"This wouldn't just be for Reese," I said. "It would be for all the needy kids at St. Matthew's. You know, a service project."

Colton leaned toward me across the table. "Yes, we know what service projects are," he said, "because you keep making us do them. This year alone we've bought books for the library, done a canned food drive, and volunteered at a soup kitchen, where—I might add—some homeless women tried to hit on me."

"She was a harmless old lady," I said.

"She told me I was the reincarnation of her dead husband, kept calling me Phil, and tried to follow me home."

I held up one hand. "So she liked you. Most people would take that as a compliment."

"Not if most people had a crazy woman running

after their car screaming, 'Phil, baby, I'm still here for you!'"

Harris, the NHS treasurer, tapped his pencil against his notebook while he looked at me. "And then there was the stint at the Esperanzo Centro de Los Ninos you made us do."

Colton nodded in agreement. "How could I forget about Los Ninos?"

I leaned back in my seat with a thud. "What was wrong with that? We gave out treats and taught little kids some games."

"All of whom spoke nothing but Spanish," Harris said.

"So?" I asked.

"Charlotte, you're the only one of us who speaks Spanish."

"That's not true." I turned to Colton. "You've taken Spanish class for four years."

"Yeah, and apparently they've taught me a completely different language because I couldn't understand a single thing anyone said that day." He let out a sigh and shook his head as though reliving the memory. "I kept telling those kids to quit jumping on me, but none of them knew what I was talking about."

"They knew," I said. "They just didn't want to listen to you."

Colton put his hands on the table. "Yes, well, that's just one more reason why I'd rather have a winter dance than do a service project, but let's put it to a vote to make sure."

Before everyone could completely vote down my idea, I tried to come up with a compromise. "Okay, let's still have the dance. We can do that. But do we have to spend so much money on it? I mean, couldn't we cut back on some of the things and still do a service project for the kids at St. Matthew's?"

Harris lifted up a list detailing our budget for the dance. "What did you want to cut?"

I held my hand out to him, and he grudgingly forked over the budget. I scanned it for areas to chop. "The decorations. We don't need to buy those. The theme is Walking in a Winter Wonderland, and we all have extra stuff sitting around at home. Between us we probably have enough Christmas trees to create a small forest. And the deejay—do we really need to pay a guy to pick out songs for us? We can do that ourselves."

"We don't have the sound system," Harris said.

"I bet we could find someone at school who does." I turned to Colton. "Don't tell me that a guy who drives a convertible doesn't have a good stereo."

"Yeah," Colton said. "And I'd be thrilled to haul it to the auditorium so half the school can mess with it."

"No one will mess with it. I'll personally guard it, okay?" I sent a pleading look to where most of the girls sat, especially Kelly. We sat at the same table at lunch and therefore she had to support me. "Don't you remember how excited you got about Christmas when you were little? Don't you want to give that to someone else who might never have the chance to experience it?"

"It is the season for giving," Kelly said.

"Giving to others," I added. "Not squandering on a deejay."

Colton glanced over at the guys at the table, silently prodding them into action. Ben, a guy so tall he'd be great at basketball if he could only master that dribbling thing, shook his head. "We can't let the rest of the school down by putting on a crappy dance."

Wesley shrugged. He was the silent type who hardly ever said anything, but when he did, Kelly hung on his every word. She has, as we say at the lunch table, been Weslified. "Don't they have the Paper Angels program to take care of the poor kids?" he asked.

The guys nodded in agreement. "We vote for the dance," a couple of them said in unison.

I turned to the girls at the table in a plea for support.

Kelly shrugged. Most of the girls just looked at the table. Preeth, who sat on my other side, grunted and said, "I never go to the dances. I don't care what we do."

Preeth is one of those girls with an attitude.

Colton smiled benevolently at me. "So it looks like we spend our money on the dance."

I didn't reply. I also didn't say anything while Colton organized committees. Colton put Preeth and me in charge of refreshments, and then added, "Make sure you okay the menu with me before you buy anything so I can approve it."

Like maybe I'd be tempted to hand out popcorn and water to save money.

Which, now that I thought about it, wasn't such a

bad idea. Popcorn was a holiday food. I mean, why else did people string it and put it on Christmas trees? And who liked drinking punch anyway? Punch is liquid sugar with food coloring. Water is refreshing, healthy, and free. Well, free if we got it from the cafeteria sink.

I smiled at Colton. "Sure. We'll let you know." In large letters in my notebook I wrote, "Popcorn & Tap Water."

Colton glared at me, but he didn't bring up refreshments again.

The meeting went on, but instead of listening, I thought of T.J. and Reese. I'd told them I knew Santa. I'd told them to come to the mall on Christmas Eve day. Would they tell their friends about this? I knew the answer to this question without even considering it. How many kids were going to show up at the mall, and how in the world was I going to find a way not to disappoint them?

After school on Wednesday, I went shopping with Brianna, which was good, since it gave us some time to be normal friends. Things hadn't felt quite the same since the "Don't-make-me-choose" speech, even though neither of us had mentioned it again.

We went to the mall look for a Christmas present for Brianna's older sister, Amanda—only Amanda had recently decided everyone should call her Trinity. Not because she was Catholic, but as a protest that had to do with an atomic bomb site somewhere. I didn't really understand her reasoning and didn't want to ask, because Amanda/Trinity could go on about those sorts of things way past the time you stopped caring.

Despite her request for a name change, half the time Brianna called her sister Amenity, which means "pleasantness" and which really ticked off Amanda/Trinity. I suggested calling her Enmity, which means "animosity" and actually fits Amanda's personality better, but in the end we both just called her Amanda behind her back and "Hey, you" when she was listening.

Brianna and I walked through the mall looking for gift inspiration, but we mostly just saw the latest fashions, which Amanda wouldn't wear anyway. She bought all her clothes at Goodwill as a protest against overseas sweatshops. Brianna and I went with her to a thrift store once and were both happily surprised to find designer jeans there. I mean, I just figured that anybody who paid that much for jeans would be buried in them; but apparently no, some people give them to Goodwill. Brianna and I both bought a pair, and then Amanda lectured us all the way home that we had missed the whole point of shopping at a thrift store and that designer jeans were a blatant sign of materialism.

So probably Amanda wouldn't want anything from the Gap, but we went in anyway because they had a killer sale going.

"You could just tell her you got it at Goodwill," I said while I took a shirt off a rack. "Probably all the people in sweatshops around the world wouldn't hold it against you."

Brianna tilted her head one way and then the other, looking at the shirt. "I don't know. I really don't. What do you get someone who hates capitalism?"

"A plane ticket to the third world?"

"Don't tempt me. I'd rather have her somewhere in South America than at home for Christmas."

I didn't answer, because I wasn't sure whether she was joking or not. Sometimes Brianna and Amanda fought long and hard over the silliest things. Brianna hadn't seemed sad at all when Amanda went off to college, which always bothered me. When I go to college next year, I expect my younger sisters to mourn for days before they start fighting over who gets to move into my room.

We left the Gap and wandered into a T-shirt shop. I flipped through a rack of shirts. "Maybe we can find one with an anticapitalism logo."

"Yeah, I'm sure they sell lots of those." She sorted through decals on a table, then held up some iron-on letters. "Hey look, if I buy these and a plain T-shirt, Amanda will be able to make her own statement. She can write something like, Nukes make me puke."

"Or, I shop at Goodwill."

"Oh, she doesn't need a sign to tell people that. They know just by looking at her." We both laughed then, even though we shouldn't have, since Brianna was wearing her thrift store designer jeans at the time.

"You'd better buy her more than one set of letters,"

I said. "You know how Amanda likes to talk. She'll never be able to stop at one sentence."

Brianna picked up a stack of the letter decals, a red T-shirt, and then two more red T-shirts. "You know, I could make matching shirts for Bryant and me to wear to the winter dance."

I stiffened at his name, but tried not to show it. "What kind of shirts?"

"Like they could say, Two Turtle Doves."

Which just goes to show you that Brianna can be delusional at times because even I knew there was no way you would ever get Bryant, Mr. Superjock, to wear a shirt that read, Two Turtle Doves.

"Cute," I said.

"Or his could say, Naughty, and mine could say, Nice."

Which at least would be truth in advertising.

"You might want to ask him about it before you buy anything," I said.

She put the shirts under her arm and turned toward the cash register anyway. She shrugged as she walked. "If he doesn't like either of those two sayings, I can come up with something else."

I followed her up to the register and didn't make any other comments. Suddenly I felt like I couldn't say anything about Bryant that she didn't want to hear.

Chapter three of my mall dissertation: "Relationships with guys are a lot like shopping." Your purchase might look good at first, but this is often because when you step into a mall, you start to delude yourself. You want to believe those pants make your stomach look flatter, but no. You still look like you're smuggling a punch bowl out of the store. Reality hits sometime after you've lost the receipt.

Likewise, the typical teenage girl doesn't buy a guy what he wants. She buys him what she wants him to have. For some whacked-out reason she thinks these two things are the same.

When Brianna and I left the store, we ran into another group of girls from school. They weren't my friends, but they were Brianna's—because she is way more social than I am—so we all went around together. We looked at jewelry and shoes, and assessed the winter fashions. Pure, thoughtless mall shopping. Female bonding time. Only, I guess I don't know how to do it right, because I kept wondering if any of the girls would have spoken to me if Brianna hadn't been around.

Probably not, because they didn't talk all that much to me while Brianna was there.

Yeah, come to think of it, I learn a lot of stuff at the mall, but it's not necessarily good stuff. I may become one of those depressed college students when I write my dissertation.

Finally, after we'd tried on way more clothes than there were days left in the season to wear them, we bought what we needed. I went home with a cashmere sweater to wear to Candy's party. It not only felt soft against my skin, it felt full of potential, like it knew what I had to do on Saturday and wanted to make me look good while I did it. Even though I'd have to work for two days just to pay for it, I couldn't return it to the rack. After all, you have to buy a piece of clothing that understands you.

And no, this purchase, or any thoughts about using clothes as courage will not make their way into my dissertation.

four

At school, Bryant sent me the occasional scowl and suddenly wanted to talk to Brianna privately whenever I was around. She'd giggle and go off with him. She couldn't even see he was just trying to drive a wedge between us.

It was enough to make me wish the Two Turtle Doves shirt on him. In fact, I started helping her come up with more cute Christmas sayings.

Brianna asked me if I wanted to do something together on Saturday night, but I told her I was helping my mother put up crown molding in a client's house. I couldn't tell her I was going to Candy's party without her realizing I was trying to catch Bryant in a lie. I was not about to put myself in that situation again until I had cold, hard proof.

It's difficult for me to keep things from Brianna, partially because I'm used to telling her everything, and partially because I'm lousy at keeping secrets. My mind just doesn't function in secret mode.

At Brianna's house after school on Friday, I helped her with her Spanish homework and nearly spilled the beans half a dozen times.

BRIANNA: So *dicho* is the past perfect tense of *decir*?

ME: Right. Hey, do you know what a pashmina is?

BRIANNA, *snapping her fingers like this will rally her brain cells into production*: Is it a tense of *pasmar*?

ME: No, it's not a Spanish word; it's a piece of clothing rich people wear.

BRIANNA: Then why do I have to know it for the vocab test?

ME: You don't. I just uh . . . never mind.

It was a relief when Saturday came and I knew it would all be over soon. I put on my new sweater and—in an attempt at chicness—brown leather pumps. I hardly ever wear high heels. It's not like I need the extra height, and wearing heels is about as comfortable as strapping two shovels onto your feet. Still, I shuffled out the door in them and followed Candy's directions to the club.

When I arrived, a valet insisted on parking my minivan—which I hadn't expected, and which did nothing to make his day, I'm sure. After all those Mercedes and Cadillacs he probably went into shock sitting in my minivan surrounded by Taco Bell wrappers and lipstick tubes.

I walked into the club. It was so ostentatious, it seemed to be a caricature of wealth. You know, the polished wood floor, gilded paintings of horses, and chandeliers so big that in a pinch they could be used as wrecking balls. A man in a suit—I'm not exactly sure what his official function was—directed me to the Condor Ballroom, where a hundred or so of Candy's close friends hung out.

In one corner of the room, a large Christmas tree stood decked out in as many lights as the Milky Way. On another wall an enormous bay window looked out over a golf course. I could see the dark shapes of couples walking across well-lit walkways. Everyone else stood around tables where fruits, veggies, and other unrecognizable stuff lay on large silver platters.

I didn't see Colton, Bryant, or, for that matter, Candy anywhere, so I wandered over to the tables. After picking up a few stuffed mushrooms and an artichoke heart that looked like a flower, I circulated around the room.

No one paid any attention to me, which was simultaneously nice and depressing. I hadn't come to make new friends or pick up guys or anything; but still, after a few minutes I began to feel like I had leprosy, or at least a serious lack of pashminas.

Brianna says my good looks intimidate others and so sometimes people are afraid to approach me, but I don't buy it. If this were true, movie stars would be the loneliest people on earth. People would shun them in droves. Plus, if Brianna's theory were right, unattractive girls would be the least friendly in high school because they'd be afraid to approach anyone. But it's the opposite. Plain girls are the most likely to say hi to you in the hallway. Just try to get the time of a day from the last homecoming queen.

I think it's more likely that people are friendly in direct proportion to how little money they have. This is why a panhandler is more than willing to relate his whole life story to you while simultaneously telling you that you look like Nicole Kidman. And rich people, well let's just say, right then I'd entered one of the unfriendliest places in California.

I picked up a cracker with some sort of bland chunky stuff on the top and tried to look natural while I waited for Bryant and Shelby to appear somewhere. The cell phone lay in my jeans pocket, and I kept fingering it to make sure it was still there. Everyone seemed to be in pockets of groups. The only single people in the room were me and the three waiters who kept swooping over to the tables to replace trays of food or take away used plates. They all wore black tuxedos, which struck me as ironic. I mean how often is your nicest outfit the one you wait tables in?

I peered out the window, trying to see if I could recognize any of the people strolling around outside. They moved about, too far away to see clearly. I dragged my gaze back inside and finally spotted Candy in a circle of girls. Greg was nowhere in sight.

Candy looked too busy to approach, so I stayed by the refreshment table deciding what to eat next.

The artichoke thingy had been a disappointment—too salty—and I've never been crazy about mushrooms. I mean, they have the same texture as used gum.

On either side of a punch fountain stood miniature pine trees covered with cherry tomatoes. They looked like ornaments on little Christmas trees. I popped one into my mouth while I considered the punch fountain.

Pink liquid ran over lighted crystal shelves until it fell, churning, into a frothy bowl. Very pretty, although I doubted it did anything to improve the flavor of the punch. I picked up one of the already filled glasses on the table and tried a sip. Nope. Still tasted just like punch. See, rich people spend far too much effort on frivolous details. Putting punch in fountains. Putting tomatoes on pine trees.

I ate another tomato, enjoying how good it tasted. Whoever discovered tomatoes knew what they were doing, but that mushroom thing should have been a passing fad.

I took another cherry tomato. Then another. After about my fourth, Candy and friends came up to refill their plates. She saw me and gave me a quick Hollywood hug—you know, the type you imagine movie stars give each other before they say, "Dahling, we must do lunch sometime."

"Char, so good to see you." Candy glanced at the tomato on my plate with a forced smile, then turned back to her friends. "This is Charlotte, one of Greg's old friends. From Hamilton."

Three girls smiled in my direction, but they looked

more incredulous than friendly. One of them giggled. Without ever letting her smile falter, a second girl elbowed the first to be quiet.

Candy turned back to me. "Greg is coming later. His flight from Honolulu was delayed." She gave an airy laugh. "You know how that is."

I didn't, but I nodded anyway. "Make sure he finds me to say hi."

Candy leaned closer to me. "Have you talked to Colton yet? He's looking especially good tonight."

"Colton? No." I peered around the room trying to find him. "Where is he?"

Candy gazed around casually. "He was here earlier. I think he went out to the golf course with his friends—oh, there he is." She nodded in the direction of the door. "He's coming in now."

Colton walked into the room and it struck me—even though I saw him every day—how pleasantly tall he is. I appreciate tallness in a guy, since I'm only a few inches shy of six feet. I also appreciated his broad shoulders just on principle. Anyway, Colton looked nicer than usual, like he was both dressed up and casual at the same time. Like he fit in here with these people, which I suppose he did.

All three of Candy's friends and I simultaneously turned toward the door to look at him. It was the equivalent of waving a flag to get his attention. He glanced over, smiled at Candy, and then stopped when he saw me. The smile dropped from his face. He said something that I couldn't hear, but judging from his lip motions, he either swore or commanded an invisible dog to sit. I smiled back at him.

I waited for Bryant to come in behind Colton, possibly with a girl in tow, but Colton crossed the floor to us alone. He smiled again, but it lacked enthusiasm.

"Charlotte," he coughed out. "What are you doing here?"

"Talking with Candy and enjoying the appetizers." I took the tomato off my plate, holding it up as proof. "And you? Are you here with Bryant? Or Shelby? Or both?" I popped the tomato into my mouth, enjoying the feeling of victory.

His gaze traveled from my lips to the refreshment table and back. He took a step closer to me and lowered his voice. "Charlotte, those tomatoes are part of the centerpiece. You're not supposed to eat the decorations."

There is only one thing worse than being told you've just eaten the centerpiece, and that is choking on it. I gasped halfway between chewing and swallowing, and managed to breathe the thing in.

I stood there coughing. All eyes were riveted on my reddening face—watching, I suppose, to see whether I needed the Heimlich to recover.

All of the hacking made the punch in my glass swish around violently, and I knew I was one cough away from spilling it onto the club's polished floor. This would do nothing to enhance the moment, so I shoved my glass at Colton. He took it wordlessly, then smacked me on the back a couple of times. This didn't dislodge the tomato from my lungs but probably gave him a wicked pleasure anyway.

Candy's eyes grew wide. "Are you all right?"

I nodded, finally feeling like I could breathe again. "Sorry. I think I just need some fresh air." Because now I knew why Candy's friends were all smirking at me, and I didn't want to stick around and make small talk with them. Besides, Bryant was somewhere on the golf course, and I would bet money he wasn't alone. My hand went to the cell phone in my pocket. "I'll see you guys later."

Colton grabbed my arm and handed me my punch. "You need to take a drink. It'll help clear your throat."

"I'm fine," I said.

He didn't let go of my arm but kept propelling my glass back at me. He was stalling. "You need to take a drink. I know about these things. My father is a doctor."

"Your father isn't a doctor, Colton. He's a CEO."

Colton didn't let go of my arm. "Okay, but he plays golf with doctors, so he still knows this stuff. Take a drink."

I took a drink of the punch just so he'd let me go. "There. See, I'm fine. I'll go outside now."

He tugged me back toward him. "I don't think you should. You're still flushed, and all that coughing makes a person light-headed. You can't go out by yourself. You might pass out or fall in the pool or something." He turned to Candy, "Don't you think she should sit down for a while?"

I tried to pull my arm away from Colton. "I'm not light-headed."

Candy tilted her head and gave me a playful smirk. "I don't know, Char. You do look pink, and you're short of breath. It must be hyperventilation or love, so either way you shouldn't be left alone. I think Colton should sit with you until you've completely recovered."

"I don't need to, I mean . . ." But I didn't get to finish before Candy and her friends waved good-bye to us. Colton pulled me off to the side of the room where a couple of chairs stood on either side of an antique Bombay chest. Not the comfortable kind of chairs that invite you to sit down on them, the ornate kind that are there purely as decoration. Even I knew this, despite the fact that I'd just eaten a portion of the centerpiece.

Colton guided me to a chair. I sat in it and glared up at him. From across the room I could see Candy talking with the same group of friends and glancing in our direction. All of them giggled. I simultaneously wondered what they said and didn't want to know. I wished I could just go home, but I had to get proof on Bryant's cheating first.

I smiled up at Colton. "Okay, I feel better. Thanks for your help. You can go now."

He stood in front of me as though ready to grab me should I make a break for it. "You still look pink."

"Maybe that's because I'm getting angry at you for making me sit in this chair."

"I'm thinking of your health."

"No, you're thinking of Bryant outside with Shelby and what's going to happen when I catch them together." I took my camera phone out of my pocket and held it up for him to see. "You'll have a harder time explaining away their meeting this time."

He threw up his hands and let out a grunt of frustration. "Why do you have it out for Bryant?"

"Oh. Let me think really hard about this one. Maybe because he's cheating on my best friend?"

"He's not cheating on Brianna."

"If you don't have anything to hide, then why won't you let me go outside and see for myself?"

Colton put his hands on his hips. His eyes glittered in that dangerous underworld spy way. "He's not cheating on Brianna. Can't you just believe me about that?"

"Believe you? Colton, you're the guy who just told me your father is a doctor."

He shook his head and took a slow step toward me. I could catch a faint whiff of his cologne. "You know, for someone who's so pretty, you're way too sarcastic."

"And for someone who's so smart, you're way too—" I snapped my gaze to a place behind Colton's shoulder, pretending to see something. "Oh, there's Bryant and Shelby now."

My words did the trick. Colton's head spun around, and while he searched the club floor I jumped out of the chair and dashed past him. "Gullible," I called over my shoulder. "Way too gullible."

Okay. There are many reasons why girls shouldn't wear high heels. One of them is that they slow you down when you race across a club floor or try to outmaneuver waiters who've brought in fruit trays. I just want to make it clear that bumping into the waiter wasn't really my fault. I would have made it past him if he hadn't suddenly changed directions to avoid me while I simultaneously changed directions to avoid him.

I slammed into his chest, and the tray flew out of his hands, sending fruit chunks sailing across the room like edible confetti. Some of it landed harmlessly on the floor and windows; but unfortunately, most of it splattered into a group of Candy's friends, who all started needlessly shrieking. I mean, it was pineapple, not live tarantulas. And okay, watermelon in your hair is never going to look attractive, but it's not like it doesn't wash out.

Somewhere between the time I smacked into the waiter and the time I lost my balance and rolled across the floor, my cell phone flew out of my hand. I didn't see where it went. At that point I was more interested in peeling myself off the floor and wiping raspberries off of my face.

Colton held his hand down to help me up, which would have been very gentlemanly if he hadn't laughed while he did it. "Are you all right?" he asked.

How do you answer that question when the entire room is looking at you and you have fruit chunks stuck on your sweater? "Probably," I said.

He held on to my arm as though I might try to dart off again. "Don't slip. The floor's wet." And then he chuckled under his breath again.

Candy walked over to us, a smile wedged onto her

lips despite the fact that she was clearly gritting her teeth. "Are you hurt?" she asked me.

"No." I ignored Colton, who'd started pulling fruit pieces out of my hair.

"Oh, good." Candy gripped the glass in her hand. The smile stayed on her lips, but her words came out in a tight rhythm. "I don't know what the waiter was thinking of, jumping in front of you that way. I mean, certainly he should have anticipated that you were suddenly going to pop up and tear across the room like it had caught on fire."

"Sorry," I said.

"No, no, it wasn't your fault. They're supposed to be trained to deal with anything. Even . . ." her words trailed off as though she didn't have the heart to tell me what "even" was. She let out a low sigh. "Well, I suppose it's time to move to the dance floor anyway. You might want to"—her eyes traveled up and down the length of my fruit crusted outfit and she grimaced—"freshen up a bit beforehand."

Which made me doubly glad I'd turned down her offer of a pashmina.

Colton picked the last of the fruit from my hair. "I think Charlotte should go home and change before the dance. I mean, no one wants to be sticky all night."

"I'm fine," I said.

"I can drive you home. It's not a problem," Colton added.

I swiped remnants of cantaloupe off my sweater. "Really. A few paper towels will take care of this." I scanned the floor for signs of my cell phone, but didn't see it anywhere.

"I insist," Colton said. "You don't want watermelon juice covering you. It'll make a mess of anything you touch in the club."

I knew he'd won as soon as he said this. After all, I couldn't eat Candy's decorations, hurl fruit at her guests, and then make everything that I touched sticky. Still, I didn't say anything. I stood there trying to think of some way I could borrow a camera phone and get outside before Colton had a chance to warn Bryant. I bet you every single one of Candy's guests had camera phones on them—if only I could think of a way to borrow one.

Candy's grip on her glass loosened. "Char, it's very sweet of Colton to offer to take you home. And if you get back soon, you can join us at the dance." She twirled the stem of her glass between her fingers, giving us a knowing look. "And if you find something else to do instead, well, I'll understand."

Colton raised an eyebrow like he didn't quite understand but was beginning too. "Thanks," he said.

I couldn't meet Candy's gaze, and I certainly wasn't going to look anywhere in the vicinity of Colton's face. I looked at the floor and the smashed fruit lying around. "I dropped my cell phone somewhere," I protested weakly. "I can't just leave it."

Candy gave my shoulder a pat, which almost immediately turned into a push in Colton's direction. "When the staff finds it, I'll have them return it to you. It's all right to leave."

I had no choice. I let Colton lead me out of the resort and into his convertible. Thankfully, he had the top up. I didn't want to add the windblown look to my already pathetic hair.

We drove silently for a few minutes, then he took his cell phone from his pocket and placed a call. "Hi, this is Colton." He glanced at me and lowered his voice. "Hey, I had to leave the party suddenly."

A pause.

"I'll be back. There was a little accident, and I have to take Charlotte home to change her clothes."

Another pause. His voice grew even softer. "Yes, Charlotte."

"Hi, Bryant!" I yelled, just to be obnoxious.

"I'll talk to you later," Colton said, then snapped the phone shut and slipped it back into his pocket.

"Nice way to warn him," I said.

Colton looked straight ahead at the road and didn't answer.

I gripped and ungripped the armrest. "How can you sit there and help Bryant cheat on Brianna? I thought you were better than that."

He said something under his breath, which I couldn't quite hear, but which may have been more commands to his invisible dog. He slowed the car down, pulled into a grocery store parking lot, and killed the ignition. Then he turned to me. "We need to talk."

"Fine." I pressed my back against the passenger-side door to put as much distance between us as possible. "Talk."

Even though the car no longer moved, he gripped the steering wheel with one hand. "Would you please stop trying to break up Bryant and Brianna?"

"Me?" I sputtered. "Me? Do you realize Brianna is sitting home right now crocheting a love afghan for your best friend while he's off sharing stuffed mushrooms with another girl?"

Colton let out a sigh like he couldn't believe how unreasonable I was being, and leaned closer to me. "Bryant really likes Brianna. He's crazy about her. When Bryant talks about his future, Brianna is always a part of it. Do you understand what I'm saying?"

"Yes. You're saying Bryant's the type of guy who wants to eat his cake and have his stuffed mushrooms too."

"No, that's not it." He threw one hand up in the air. "Look, if you want to be mad at someone be mad at me. This is my fault. I set up the meeting with Bryant and Shelby at the mall. I insisted he come with me tonight."

"Okay, so you're a jerk too, but that still doesn't change Bryant's behavior. Now can you take me home?" I ran my hand across the front of my new sweater. "Raspberry juice stains if you don't get it out right away."

The muscles in Colton's jaw tightened. "If you stopped accusing me long enough to hear what I'm saying, you'd see there's a perfectly reasonable explanation for all this."

I folded my arms and waited for him to continue.

"This is the way it is," he said. "Shelby's father is

one of the football coaches at Stanford. Bryant wants to go to Stanford and already has a spot on the football team as a walk-on, but he doesn't have the money to pay the tuition. He does have a chance at a football scholarship. A lot of colleges want him. A few have even made him offers. He wants Stanford to make him an offer. Shelby can help him with that." Colton held up a hand as though taking an oath. "That's all that's going on."

"You're trying to get Shelby to convince her dad to give Bryant a football scholarship?"

"Right." Colton leaned forward again. "We haven't actually asked her yet. I figure she has to get to know Bryant better before we hit her up for that. But you see, he isn't really cheating on Brianna at all."

"He's just using Shelby," I finished.

"No, it's not like that. He's not going to ask her out or lead her on or anything. He's networking. Bryant's just forming a friendship that will help his future and thus help Brianna too."

"And the flirting?"

"He isn't flirting with Shelby."

I rolled my eyes.

"Being friendly is not the same as flirting," he said.

"And I can tell the difference between the two," I said.

He let out a grunt of disbelief. "I don't see how you could, since you never do either."

Like he'd know. Like he even cared whether I flirted with anyone.

"Look," Colton went on, "Shelby is the kind of girl who likes to get attention from guys—"

"Meaning she's a flirt," I said.

"But she does that with everybody. It doesn't mean a thing. And Bryant is going to tell her tonight that he's got a girlfriend. There's nothing wrong going on."

I sat back against my seat and surveyed him. "You don't consider it wrong to use people to get money for college? You don't consider it wrong for Bryant to tell Brianna he's going to a wedding reception when he's really going to a party to meet another girl?" I didn't even mention the rest. I couldn't bring myself to tell Colton about Brianna's don't-make-me-choose speech or my fears that Bryant was pulling her away from me anyway.

Colton held out a hand as though trying to show me his logic. "He needs to get into a good college if he's going to be able to support himself, doesn't he? If he and Brianna ever got married, you wouldn't want her to have to live in some run-down ghetto, would you?"

And anyone who didn't go to Stanford would obviously be doomed to such a fate. I almost pointed out that neither of my parents went to Stanford, but then didn't. If Colton considered my neighborhood as proof he was right, I didn't want to hear about it.

Colton reached over and turned the ignition back on as though he'd won the debate and the conversation was over.

He pulled onto the road, and I watched buildings and streetlamps go by while his words swirled around in my mind. "So you think the ends justifies the means. Typical utilitarian thinking. Honesty doesn't matter. The action with the best consequences for you is the right thing to do. You're so . . ." The frustration slowed my thinking process, and the word I wanted remained filed away in the vocabulary section of my brain. I shut my eyes as though this would help. It didn't. "I can't think of the right word."

He leaned back in his seat. "Look, you're a smart girl. You realize people need quality education to get ahead in this world. You don't want to spend the rest of your life spraying perfume on people, do you?"

"*Condescending*. That's the word. Thanks for the help. You're such a condescending elitist."

Sitting with one arm draped across the steering wheel of his sports car, wearing a Rolex, he rolled his eyes at me.

"There's nothing wrong with my job," I said.

"Right, Charlotte. Can you even afford to buy any of that perfume you spray on wealthy women's wrists?"

I gritted my teeth. "I don't need to buy overpriced perfume to smell nice, Colton. I've discovered a magical invention called soap. It does a fine job of making me smell good."

He pulled up in front of my house and smirked at me. "Okay, why don't you go use some of that magical invention right now and see if it does the trick?" He held up a strand of my hair, and then let it drop again. "You're hair is crunchy."

I opened the car door and stepped out without

telling him good-bye. I'd walked halfway to my front porch before I realized he was coming with me. I'd expected him to wait in his car. Suddenly I had all sorts of anxiety about my house in general, my living room in particular, and which of my little sisters were roaming around dirty, half-dressed, or looking for trouble.

I have three younger sisters. I sort of think my parents tried for a boy, but they won't admit this to us. "We just feel so blessed to have four girls," my mom will say when questioned about the situation.

"None of whom like football, camping, or NASCAR," my dad will grumble under his breath until my mom swats him. Then Dad will put on a smile and tell us, "No, really, I look forward to paying for four weddings," and "I'm nearly immune to all the hormones."

Dad has a particularly trying sense of humor, which was just one more reason to be nervous about Colton coming into the house with me. He once told Greg— and this is a direct quote—"Don't take Charlotte anywhere they serve alcohol. I have a short temper, a gun collection, and friends on the police force."

Greg didn't laugh. Probably Colton wouldn't either.

I turned the doorknob, took a breath, and pushed the door open.

Good news. The house was relatively clean. No sign of Rebecca's latest sewing project, Julianne's Barbie doll kingdom, or Evelynn's homework—which she frequently spread over the floor like she was trying to paper-train a puppy.

Bad news. My dad sat in the recliner reading the newspaper, and Mom was out putting up crown molding. I had no one to rein in my family. As we walked in, my dad glanced over the top of the paper at us and offered a grunt in greeting. "New guy?" he asked.

"This is Colton, Dad. You know, from my study group. He gave me a ride home to change clothes."

Dad lowered the paper and glared first at Colton and then me. "And what were you doing that required a change of clothing?"

"Nothing, Dad. I just had a food accident. Look . . ." I pointed to my sweater and the now dried juice stains on it.

"A food accident?" Dad repeated, then after a moment's thought added, "Where's the minivan?"

I didn't want to explain any of it to him, so I pretended I hadn't heard the question and hurried to the stairs.

I took them two at a time and called down to Colton, "I'll just be a minute."

Behind me my father said, "Son, if you haven't learned girl-speak yet, 'I'll just be a minute' is code for, 'This will take half an hour.' You'd better sit down."

I didn't stick around to hear more.

five

Getting changed didn't take me half an hour. It took me twenty minutes. But only because I had to dampen large sections of my hair to get it clean, and then I had to blow-dry it. I wasn't about to go back to Candy's party looking like a drowned rat. Plus, I had to touch up my makeup and find my green sweater. The one that brings out the color in my eyes. Not that I wanted to look good for Colton or anything. I mean, I just needed the extra confidence to face all those people at Candy's party.

When I walked downstairs, all of my sisters were sitting in the living room surrounding Colton like he was Santa Claus about to hand out presents. Rebecca hung back, shyly twisting her fingers through her hair while eyeing him from lowered lashes. As a freshman at Hamilton, she actually recognized Colton. Evelynn and Julianne, at ten and seven years old, just saw him as an interesting specimen of manhood whom they could tease, flirt with, and generally bother.

I didn't hear the whole conversation as I came down, but it involved Julianne asking about the finer points of wrestling. "What if you had to wrestle some fat guy? Wouldn't that be gross?"

"They put you in weight divisions so you only wrestle guys your same weight," Colton said.

"Do girls wrestle?" Evelynn asked.

Dad glanced over the top of his newspaper. "Only while shopping."

"I'm ready," I said.

Colton looked up at me. For a moment I thought I saw something register in his eyes. Surprise? Approval? I told myself it didn't matter.

He stood up. "All right. I guess we'll go back to the party then."

"Have fun," Rebecca cooed.

"Bring him back afterward so he can teach me to wrestle," Julianne said.

"Will you?" Evelynn asked. "None of Charlotte's other boyfriends know how to wrestle."

"I bet Colton could've whipped Greg," Julianne said, and then both girls giggled.

My father lowered his paper again. "Now girls, don't use all your pestering on this boy, or you'll have nothing left for the next one your sister brings home."

"Who are you bringing home next?" Julianne asked.

"Time to go," I said, and headed to the door. "Don't wait up for me." I opened the door, stepped outside, and didn't relax until the door shut behind us.

Colton walked beside me to the curb, and although I didn't look at him, I knew he was smirking. After we'd both climbed into his car, he turned to me. "So who's Greg?"

"Greg MacNelly. Candy's—I mean—Candice's current boyfriend."

Colton nodded. "Oh yeah, I remember Greg." He snapped on his seat belt and started the ignition. "Well, at least I have the distinction of being your only wrestling boyfriend. Is that because you usually go for the wimpy types?"

"No, I just don't generally date wrestlers, because it's a silly sport."

"Is it?" Still smirking, he eased the car out onto the street.

"When does anyone use wrestling skills in real life?"

"I'll use them."

"Yeah. I can just see you at some stockholder board meeting now. One of the CEOs gets out of hand, so you grab him by his Ralph Lauren tie and wrangle him to the ground."

Colton smiled over at me as he drove. "You look nice in that color."

I smiled back at him. "Thanks, but I'm still telling Brianna that Bryant came to Candy's party."

"Has anyone ever told you that you have a barbed demeanor?"

"Just you. I'll post it on my Live Journal with all the other compliments you've ever given me."

Colton looked straight ahead at the traffic, not at

me. "You want compliments? I might give you some if you stopped snapping at me all the time."

I bit my lip, refusing to snap at him. One minute ticked by, then two. Out of the corner of my eye, I saw him glance at me. I looked out the window at the car in front of us.

"I admire your intelligence," he said.

"Thanks."

"I also admire your compassion, your sense of humor, and the way you willingly help people with their homework."

"What about my inability to be bought off by compliments?"

"Okay, that I don't admire as much."

I laughed, a real laugh for the first time that night.

"Listen, Charlotte, you'll just cause needless pain if you go upsetting Brianna with talk of Bryant and this party. Nothing is going on between Shelby and him, I promise."

I didn't answer him.

"I'll chaperone them the whole time if that will make you feel better."

Oh yeah. I'd seen the stellar job he did with them at the mall. I still didn't answer him.

"What do you want from . . ." He stopped talking and leaned back in his seat. A slow smile spread across his lips. "I think we could strike a deal, Charlotte."

I waited for him to continue, and he did, slowly, confidently, as though he already knew my answer. "You want to help all those kids over at St. Matthew's Elementary. You want NHS to do a service project for them. I think I could arrange that. Of course NHS could only afford to give a hundred bucks or so. That's not much. It would only help a few kids. My dad's company, on the other hand, contributes to needy causes every once in a while. It's good for the company image, and a tax write-off. I bet I could convince him to throw in another five hundred dollars. That would help more."

I hadn't decided to take him up on his offer. I hadn't even begun to think about it. Still, I heard myself say, "Make it a thousand dollars and throw in a pair of women's black work shoes." I don't know where the words came from. Maybe I said them because I didn't think he'd agree.

His smile grew. "Done. A thousand and a pair of shoes it is." Then he held out his hand to shake on it.

I looked at his hand and all I could think about was Reese and T.J. They'd be so happy. I lifted my hand and shook with Colton.

Maybe Colton knows me better than I think. I probably would have called off the agreement if I had stopped to think about what I was doing, considered the implications for Brianna, or pondered how withholding information from your best friend because someone gives you a thousand dollars is like selling your soul to the devil—or in this case, Colton. But Colton didn't let me think about it. He plunged right into the details of the NHS service project.

As we drove, he told me that on Monday he would talk to the principal at St. Matthew's Elementary and ask for a list of thirty of their neediest students. Thirty students and a thousand dollars from Colton's dad, plus another hundred or so that we could manage to trim off the dance budget, would mean we'd be able to spend almost forty dollars on each child. We might be able to help even more kids if we could get the merchants in the mall to donate some items, or at least give us a substantial discount.

We'd have the kids sign a parent permission slip, a toy wish list, and a clothing-size chart, then assign NHS members to shop for the children. The last day of school before winter break, we'd bus the children over to the mall, where Santa would hand out presents in the Bloomingdale's courtyard.

The more I talked about the event with Colton, the more excited I became about it. We nearly had the whole thing planned out during the drive back to the party. Even Colton seemed to get into the spirit of the thing, organizing who would hit up which store, and how.

At the time Colton won the NHS presidency, I didn't think he would take it seriously. But even I had to admit he had the knack for organizing events. "Santa always comes to my dad's office party," he said as we drove. "I can get the suit from him. Who should we make wear it?"

"Oh, definitely you," I said. "You're the jolliest guy in NHS."

"Right. I'm not being Santa."

"Why not?"

Colton looked at me with a tilt of his head. "Because I've already had a homeless lady try to chase down my convertible. The last thing I need is a bunch of elementary kids doing the same thing. If they find out where I live, I'll have first graders showing up on my doorstep and demanding presents until next Easter."

We pulled onto the palm-lined drive that led to the club. I looked out the window and grinned. "You're worrying about nothing. Kids never try to follow Santa home, because they know he lives at the North Pole. You'd have fun handing out gifts."

"Sure, because I've always wanted to dress up as an old, overweight, hairy guy who has bad taste in clothing."

"We can vote about it during the next NHS meeting. I'll nominate you."

Colton shook his head. "No vote. If I'm Santa, I'm forcing everyone into a vow of silence." Then he sent me a smile. "Plus, you have to wear the elf suit."

"Your dad has an elf suit too?"

"I don't know, but if I have to be Santa, you've got to put on an elf suit. I'll find one somewhere."

Colton parked the car by the curb for the valets, then we walked up to the club. As we came to the door Colton reached out and took hold of my arm, stopping me from going in. His expression grew serious. "Remember, Charlotte, your part of the bargain is you don't say anything about Bryant and Shelby to Brianna. Ever again."

I felt an actual pang in my chest, probably the devil ripping my soul from my body. But how could I say no to all of those kids? And besides, maybe Colton was right about the whole thing anyway. Bryant was just trying to get into Stanford; he wasn't cheating on Brianna. I mean, if he actually liked Shelby, there was nothing to keep him from breaking up with Brianna. But he hadn't. So that must mean he did care for her. Colton was right, and I just read too much into everything. Still, I stood in front of the door, Colton's hand on my arm, and hesitated. "You'll keep an eye on Shelby and make sure she doesn't throw herself at Bryant or something?"

"Of course. I don't want to put him in some awkward situation. That's part of the plan."

"He's really crazy about Brianna?"

"Insane."

I let out a sigh. "All right then, it's a deal."

Colton smiled at me, and it may just have been my imagination, but it seemed a long time before he finally let go of my arm and opened the door.

We went through the lobby and into the Condor Ballroom. When my eyes adjusted to the darkness, I saw Candy and Greg standing nearby talking. They turned toward us, and Greg waved. Candy gave me a wary look. I didn't blame her. She probably wondered what I planned on destroying next.

"Char!" Greg stepped over and gave me a half hug. "We were just talking about you. I hoped you'd come back to the party so I could see you." Apparently finished seeing me, he turned his attention to Colton. "Hey, it's been a long time, Colton."

"Eighth-grade English," Colton said.

"You transferred to Hamilton for some sport thing."

"Wrestling," Colton said.

Greg nodded at him vaguely. Greg wasn't into sports, unless you count sailing as a sport, or maybe golf. "And how's wrestling going?"

"I took second at State last year."

Greg shook his head. "Too bad. Well, there's always this year." Which pretty much sums up why I wasn't all that heartbroken when Greg dumped me.

Colton smiled at him, but it was one of those smiles that indicated he was assessing Julianne's prediction that he could whip Greg.

Candy looped her arm through Greg's in a possessive manner. Probably so I wouldn't use any of my feminine wiles on her boyfriend. "Well, you two didn't come all the way back here just to stand around talking to us. Why don't you make use of the dance floor?" She gave Colton a conspiratorial wink. "Char's a great dancer. You'll have to work hard to keep her all to yourself."

Uh, yeah, could you be more obvious when you're trying to set two people up? It's a good thing I didn't really like Colton, or I would have been completely mortified. I was mortified enough as it was already.

Colton placed a hand on my shoulder, more as a way to get my attention than as an actual gesture of affection. "Right, we should dance, but first I have to make a phone call. You know, tell Bryant I'm back so he doesn't think he needs to get another ride home." He pulled out a phone from his pocket and looked around. "It's a little loud in here, so I'll step outside for a second." He took a couple steps toward the door, then walked back over to me and handed me the phone. "This one is yours. I forgot to tell you, I found it on the floor."

"You had my phone this whole time?"

He didn't answer, just stepped out. I let out a sigh, shook my head, and slipped the phone into my pocket. I should have known he'd been hiding it.

Candy let go of Greg's arm and took hold of mine. "Can we have a girl talk for a minute?"

"Sure," I said.

She waved Greg off with an "I could use some Evian, honey," and he obediently went off to get it. Once we were alone, Candy tilted her head at me. Her smile was the kind you give to small children. "You were a bit sharp with Colton just now."

"Oh that . . ." I said, and couldn't say more. I mean, I was not about to explain the whole Brianna, Bryant, Shelby, Colton-hiding-my-cell-phone-and-buying-my-soul story.

"Now, I know you never went through finishing school or anything," Candy went on, "but there are some basic things you should know about attracting a guy."

"I don't think you really need to—"

"I'm doing you a favor telling you this, trust me." Candy gave my arm a squeeze. "If you want Colton to ask you out, you'll have to talk to him in an attractive, alluring voice. That was not the voice I just heard. You sounded like a nagging, old housewife."

"There was more to it—"

"I know it doesn't take any sophistication to get attention at Hamilton High, but Colton has better breeding than those guys, which means you'll have to apply some finesse to get him." She took hold of both my shoulders with utmost seriousness. "That means no running across the room without looking where you're going. That means no eating—well, it might be easier to put it this way—don't eat something at a social function unless you see one of the other guests eating it first. In fact, that's excellent advice all around. Just watch the other guests and pretend you're like them. All right?"

"All right," I said, mostly so she'd let go of my shoulders.

She released me with a sigh. "Now, when he comes back in, I want you to take him by the arm and apologize for your sharpness."

"Right," I said, because I knew he wasn't coming back. He'd gotten me to agree to his terms, and most likely that whole phone call business was just a polite way to make an exit. I mean, why would he want to stick around and dance with me? Besides, he'd told me he was going to keep an eye on Bryant and Shelby, who, as far as I could see, weren't in the ballroom.

Of course when Colton didn't come back, Candy would think her opinion of me as a troglodyte who couldn't attract a boyfriend was justified, but oh well. There were worse things in life. You know, like having to apologize to Colton in front of her.

Almost as soon as the word left my mouth, Colton came up behind me. "I'm back."

My glance went from Colton to Candy, and then back to Colton. "Oh. Hi," I said.

Candy waved her hand at me in a go-on motion. I ignored her at first, but her go-on wave got bigger, and she added a *tsking* noise to the procedure.

"Sorry for snapping at you," I told Colton.

"Which time?" he asked.

"Take your pick." This answer apparently didn't please Candy, who started shaking her head. "I mean, I'm sorry for all of them," I said, and I even used an attractive, inviting voice just so Candy would be happy and leave me alone.

Candy didn't leave me alone. She made sort of a swirling motion with her hand. I had no idea what that meant. It must be one of those things they taught in finishing school, that I missed out on. I looked at Candy to try and figure it out, which made Colton glance over at her to see what I was looking at.

Candy immediately ran her hand through her hair like this was what she'd been doing all along, and gave a lilting laugh. "You two make such a cute couple. You should dance."

Oh. So the swirling motion was code for dance.

She could have picked something a little easier to figure out.

"Let's," I told Colton.

"Right," he said, and led me out onto the dance floor. A slow song played, so he wrapped his arms around my waist and I rested my hands against his shoulders. I could tell he was looking past my head. "So, what was that all about?"

"What?" I asked.

"You know, those things Candice keeps saying. Why does she seem to think we're a couple?"

"I have no idea."

"Liar." He bent lower to my ear. "She's over there with your ex-boyfriend talking about us right now. Why is that?"

"Well . . ." Now that I was officially no longer trying to trap Bryant, there was no reason for me not to tell Colton what I'd done, but I still didn't want to. "Candy sort of feels obligated to set me up, since she, you know, swiped my last boyfriend."

"Uh-huh." He glanced at Candy, and then back at me. "Any particular reason why I'm the chosen target?"

"Oh, well . . . it's obviously because you're the best-looking guy here."

"If you don't want to tell me the truth, I can always ask Candice, you know." He took a step away from me, but I took hold of his hand and pulled him back. Once we were in dance position again, I nervously fiddled with the collar on his shirt instead of looking in his eyes.

"Okay, I might have invited myself to Candy's party on the pretense I wanted to spend time with you when I really wanted to take a picture of Bryant and Shelby together."

His head snapped upward. "You lied to Candice about liking me in order to spy on Bryant?" I could feel him stiffen. "And you accused me of using people to get what I wanted?"

"That's different."

"Yeah, that's different. I'm using people to help Bryant get into college, and you're using people to get him in trouble. Don't try to take the moral high ground on this."

My gaze shot up to his. "Oh, you're right. Faking you like someone to get into a party is much worse than faking you like someone to get into Stanford."

"And speaking of your taste in men—"

"We weren't speaking about my taste in men."

Colton pulled me closer to him. "Well, we are now, and I'd like to commend you on your choice of Greg as boyfriend material. It's obvious you've found a much better class of men by refusing to date guys from Hamilton."

"Greg's not a bad guy. He's just—"

"Condescending?" Colton supplied. "Elitist?"

The sway of the music brought us closer together, and I felt myself being distracted as I noticed little things about Colton. His straight jawline. His broad shoulders. The fact that his hands were on my waist. Did I mention his broad shoulders? I tried to snap my mind back to the conversation. "Well, okay, I admit Greg is sort of an elitist, but he has other redeeming qualities."

"Like his checking account?"

"I didn't date him just because of his money," I said, which wasn't entirely true, but now that I'd sold my soul, I could lie without compunction. Besides, I wasn't about to admit the truth to Colton.

Colton peered over my shoulder at Greg again, shook his head, then leaned closer to me. "Explain this to me. You dislike me for being an elitist but dated Mr. Snob over there. What's the difference between the two of us besides the fact that I'm taller, better looking, and can actually bench-press more than my own weight?"

"Well, he asked me out and you didn't."

Colton let out a grunt of disbelief. "I don't ask out girls who have a policy of not dating guys from my school."

"Well, there you have it," I said.

"Have what?"

"Your explanation."

"What explanation? Are you saying you'd go out with me if I asked?"

I was not about to answer that question. If I said yes and then he never asked me out, it would be totally humiliating. Besides, if I said yes, it would make me sound like I just went out with anyone who had enough money. But I didn't want to say no. Standing there with my hands resting on his shoulders and looking into his eyes, well, dating Colton didn't sound like such a bad idea. And okay, I was beginning to see an advantage to the whole wrestling thing because I could feel the muscles in his shoulders. Wrestlers are totally buff.

"Well?" he asked.

"Are you actually asking me out on a date, or is this a theoretical question?"

"Are you saying you'd make an exception to your dating policy if I did?"

"Maybe," I said.

"Then maybe I'm asking you out."

"Well then, maybe you should tell me a date and time so I'll be ready."

"Maybe we could do dinner and a movie next Friday. Around six o' clock."

"I might be ready then."

He laughed and pulled me closer. "It was a stupid policy anyway, Charlotte."

"I'm just making an exception in your case. Besides, if I really like you, then that means I didn't lie to Candy, so I still have the moral high ground."

He laughed again. "You just want the moral high ground, don't you?"

"Maybe." Over Colton's shoulder I saw Bryant and Shelby come into the room. They stood close together, but his arms were folded—perhaps so she wouldn't take hold of his hand. In a moment Colton would notice them, and then he'd leave me. After all, he'd told me he was going to keep an eye on them. I'd told Colton I wanted him to keep an eye on them. Only, just now

I wanted Colton to keep dancing with me and totally ignore them.

See how quickly a person can go from being a good friend to a totally soulless individual?

For a moment Colton's gaze traveled in their direction, and then he pulled me closer. "It's kind of hot in here. Do you want to walk around outside?"

And then I knew he'd seen them too, and would rather be with me than babysitting them. I smiled back at him. "Yeah, let's go outside."

❧ *six* ❧

The grounds of the club looked the way I'd always imagined the Garden of Eden looked, only with putting greens. Manicured grass lay across the sloping hills. Bougainvillea bushes lined the walkways like giant fountains of flowers. Not a single leaf lay out of place on each perfectly formed tree. Across the grass a lake shimmered in the darkness. By its side half a dozen swans slept on the banks. You know your club is nice when it can double as a habitat for swans.

Colton and I strolled on the sidewalk and talked more about the Santa project. Then we talked about Mrs. Merrick, our physics teacher, and wondered what kind of husband she had. Mrs. Merrick has no patience with anyone and will snap your head off if you happen to ask her what page the next day's assignment is on. I speculated her husband was either deaf or constantly drunk. Colton insisted he was buried in her backyard.

Then we talked about other teachers, our favorite restaurants, and whether *Phantom of the Opera* was a good movie or not. Colton apparently has no appreciation for fine music or hunky guys who wear masks. Somewhere along the way, Colton took hold of my hand as though it were a perfectly natural thing to do. I let him, intertwining my fingers with his as we walked. I wondered how in the world I could start the evening angry with a guy and then two hours later hold hands with him. How is it that there is such a fine line between animosity and, say, walking around a golf course wondering if a guy will kiss you?

I guess I already knew the answer to this question, which was that I'd liked Colton all along. I'd just never thought of him as boyfriend material, because he never seemed interested in me. Plus he's friends with Bryant.

It's not that I really blamed Colton for being friends with Bryant. After all, Bryant was outgoing and popular. He was smart and athletic—so similar to Colton in the outward ways that maybe both of them overlooked the inward ways.

But still, as I walked around with Colton I didn't have the faintest idea how I should handle things. I mean, Brianna would be thrilled to hear that Colton and I were going out. It would mean that she'd been right all along and that there was some cosmic magnet pulling Colton and me together because both our names started with C. She'd want to double all of time. I couldn't even imagine how weird that would be.

I shivered in the night air and wished I'd brought my jacket with me.

"Are you cold?" Colton asked.

"Just a little," I said, because I still didn't want to go inside.

Colton took off his jacket and draped it around my shoulders.

"I can't take this," I told him, but I didn't take it off. "You'll freeze without it." After all, I had on a sweater. He only wore an oxford shirt underneath his jacket.

"I'm fine," he said. "Let's walk over by the pool and sit down."

I slipped my arms through Colton's jacket, then moved my hair so it lay outside the coat. The jacket smelled like Colton, and I wondered what aftershave he wore and if Bloomingdale's carried it. If they did, I might be tempted to grab a bottle during my break and take big whiffs of it.

Colton took my hand again and pulled me toward the pool area. There were actually two pools: one with some of those huge twisty slides hovering over the water, and a milder version with swimming lanes. Patio chairs, huge fake boulders, and planters surrounded both pools.

"Are you sure we're allowed to go here?" I asked, even though a dozen or so other kids milled around the pools. "Isn't it off-limits this time of night?"

"I don't think security cares. It's not like we need lifeguards. It's too cold for swimming."

"Are you getting cold?" I asked him.

"No," he said.

"Tell me if you do."

"I'll tell you." He gave me a mischievous grin.

Right then I knew he planned on kissing me. We would sit down somewhere secluded, talk for a while, and then he would tell me he was getting cold and did I want to warm him up?

I let the idea sit in my mind, debating whether I should let him kiss me tonight. We weren't even officially on a date, and usually I avoid kissing guys right off.

Colton led me to a bench a few feet away from the pool. It wasn't secluded at all, unless you counted the fact that anyone behind us couldn't see us, because the bench sat right in front of a low wall/planter with all sorts of ferns flowing off the top. It created a walkway between the club and a small building that wasn't open at that time but probably served food during the day. The wall did nothing to shield us from everyone else who stood around the pool. So maybe I'd been wrong about his intentions.

As we talked—the topic turned back to school—I kept glancing at his lips as if I could read the future from them. He had asked me out on a date for the following Friday; could he have meant he wanted to go out as friends?

But there was all that hand-holding earlier, and the mischievous grin, and was it just my imagination or did he keep moving closer to me?

Colton told me about his Thanksgiving trip with his family down to Rocky Point, and how Bryant had come along. Apparently, Bryant hadn't mastered the intricacies of Spanish and at one restaurant told his waiter he wanted *dinero*. Although the word sounds like *dinner*, it means money. Luckily, the staff was used to Americans who regularly butchered their language, or they might have assumed he was holding up the place, called the police, and left Bryant to rot in some Mexican jail.

Like that would have been a tragedy.

I must not have laughed enough at the story, because Colton tilted his head at me and said, "How come you don't like Bryant? Is it just the spider thing?"

"Just the spider thing? Isn't that enough?"

"So he called you some names in junior high. Everybody was called names in junior high. It's a prerequisite to high school."

"Were you called names?"

He shrugged. "Sure."

"What?"

Another shrug. "The usual: Jerk. Loser. Condescending elitist—oh wait, that wasn't in junior high."

I folded my arms. "I'm serious."

"Okay, okay." He looked upward as though consulting his memory. "I was called a jerk, a loser, and a sadistic, little pyromaniac-delinquent."

I raised my eyebrows at him.

"Okay, I made up that last one," he said, "but it fits a lot of junior high boys, so who knows." He unfolded my arms and took my hand in his again. "Actually, Charlotte, I don't remember what I was called, because

I didn't carry around each name in a personal grudge-bag for the rest of my life. Most people forget about these things and move on."

"Most people didn't have it flung at them every day. Bryant used to catch spiders and put them in my desk."

"So Bryant was mean. He was what—twelve at the time? Don't you think he's changed by now?"

But that was the point. I didn't think he'd changed. I thought he'd just grown more mature in his methods.

I held Colton's hand tighter because I was afraid in a moment he would stop holding mine. "There are two kinds of people in this world, Colton. The kind who understand how other people feel, and the kind who don't care. Junior high doesn't create people's personalities; it just reveals which kind they have."

"And people can't change?"

"Bryant never even told me he was sorry," I said.

Colton shook his head. "It's hard for guys to tell their friends they're sorry. It's nearly impossible to say it to people who already dislike you. Guys just aren't good with apologies." Colton pulled me closer to him so he could put his arm around me. "It doesn't mean he isn't sorry."

I rested my head against Colton's chest, feeling secure with his arm draped across my shoulder. Had I been too harsh on Bryant? I mean Colton liked him, and Brianna adored him. I respected the opinion of both these people. Maybe Bryant wasn't worse than anybody else; maybe I just judged him more severely.

Colton fiddled with the ends of my hair against his

jacket. "I know I'm sorry for the things I said in junior high, and I've never actually apologized to anyone."

I turned to look at him. "What did you say in junior high?"

He tilted his head back as though he had to think about it. "Oh, I don't know, just the normal stupid stuff. Like once during a girl's volleyball game I yelled out that trained seals could hit the ball better, and had better figures to boot."

"You yelled that to the opposing team?"

"No, I yelled it at our team. They stank."

"Colton . . ."

He held up one hand as though pledging. "I was joking, and I'm sorry I said it."

"They probably all went home and cried. You should apologize to those girls."

"I don't know where any of them are. Well, except for Kayla Taylor. She's standing over there talking to Candice."

I looked across the pool for the first time and saw Candy talking with a group of girls. She caught my gaze and flashed me a grin—I suppose because Colton had his arm draped across my shoulder. I gave her a little wave back.

"Which one is Kayla?" I asked Colton.

"The tall one with the short blond hair."

She stood beside Candice with a soda in her hand, poised, pretty, and with a figure that more closely resembled Barbie than a trained seal.

"You ought to apologize to her," I told Colton.

"Now? She's surrounded by all of those other girls."

"What's the point of being sorry if you don't let her know? You'll both feel better about it if you apologize."

He shook his head. "She probably doesn't even remember it anymore."

"Trust me, she remembers it. She went home, put your name in her journal, and then drew a thousand slashes through it."

Colton looked at me, then back at Kayla. "I can't just walk up to her out of the blue and apologize for a comment I made four years ago. She'll think I'm weird."

I lifted my face toward Colton's ear and whispered, "If you want to kiss me, you really ought to apologize to that girl."

"All right then, I'm going." He stood up and walked around the pool without another glance in my direction. Unfortunately, halfway to Candy's group Kayla and another girl left the others and headed in the opposite direction around the pool. Colton continued to follow them, but got waylaid when Candy stopped to talk to him. He nodded at her, smiled, and watched as Kayla walked away. Then he looked back at me, said something hurriedly to Candy, and pulled away from the group.

Kayla was almost gone. She walked behind the planter wall on her way toward the club. I didn't think he'd catch up with her, but he broke into a jog, and then I heard him call her name.

Somewhere behind the wall footsteps stopped. I heard another set of footsteps catch up.

"Kayla," Colton took a deep breath. "How are you doing?"

A girl's voice, tentative, said, "Fine."

"Do you remember me? We went to junior high together."

"Oh yeah, Colby, right?"

"Colton," he said.

"Colton," she repeated.

There was a pause. I bit my lip, anxious for him. Did he realize how close I was, that I could hear everything he said? I was sorry I'd made him do this and at the same time proud of him for doing it.

"Um . . . so . . . uh . . . do you remember how you used to play volleyball?"

"Yes," she said, her voice friendlier. "I still do."

"Great, great. That's really . . . um . . ., do you remember that one game back in junior high where our team was losing and I yelled out that trained seals could hit the ball better?"

Her voice grew instantly cold. "No."

"Oh. Well, I just wanted to tell you I was sorry I said it. You know, just in case you remembered me yelling it."

"Thanks," still cold, "but I already have a boyfriend."

"I wasn't trying to hit on you," Colton said loudly enough to make me realize he knew I could hear him.

Two sets of footsteps walked on. I put my hand over my face. She hadn't remembered after all, and I'd just made Colton make a fool of himself. "I was not hitting on you," Colton called again, probably for my benefit.

Okay, I owed him a really good kiss after this.

"Who weren't you hitting on?" I recognized Bryant's voice coming toward Colton on the walkway. "That girl who just passed? Dude, what's wrong with you? She was gorgeous."

I stiffened. A breath of night air lodged in my lungs and refused to come out.

"She's not my type," Colton said loudly. "And besides, I'm busy."

I heard a noise, like a slap on the shoulder. "Yeah, thanks for keeping the bloodhound off my trail tonight. I really owe you one. Olivia was looking hot, and instead you had to put in time with Miss Freezer. Maybe next time—hey, where are you going?"

I didn't care where Colton was going. Although had he asked, I would have offered some suggestions. I had been so stupid to think he cared about me, to think he saw me as anything other than a bloodhound and a bother. All his flirting—the way he'd held my hand and stayed with me all night—it had just been a lie to keep me away from Bryant.

I slid out of his jacket, left it on the bench, and walked toward the pool. I was leaving, but not by the walkway. I'd hike around the entire building if it meant avoiding Colton.

I made it halfway around the pool when he caught up to me.

He kept his voice low. "Charlotte, wait."

I didn't turn around, and I didn't glance over my shoulder. I just kept walking.

He grabbed my arm to stop me. "That wasn't what it sounded like."

Right. How many ways are there to interpret the phrase, "Thanks for keeping the bloodhound off my trail tonight"?

"Let me go." I tried to pull my arm away from him, but he held on to my elbow.

Then, as though he didn't want to make more of a spectacle than we were already making, he lowered his voice even more and pulled me a step closer. "Would you listen to me for one minute?"

Why? So he could tell me more stories? Or worse yet, so he could tell me that the ends justified the means—and I had just been part of the means of the whole scheme. I didn't want to hear it. With one last burst of energy, I said, "No!" and pushed him away from me.

It didn't occur to me until afterward how close we were standing to the pool, or how unexpectedly pushing someone could cause them to lose their balance.

Colton took a step backward. His arms flailed for a moment, but in the end gravity won out. A splash shot up that instantly drew everyone's attention. A moment later Colton's head popped out of the water, his hands already scooping his way to the side of the pool. He said something that resembled, "Aaaayyaaaeeeeaa!" but with a lot more exclamation marks.

"Your jacket is back on the bench," I told him. "Just in case you're cold now."

Then I walked away—well, technically, I walked past Candy and her friends, who all stared at me open-

mouthed. As I left, I heard Candy, her voice full of res-
ignation, speaking to one of the other girls. "I'm afraid
Greg was right about her all along," she said. "Some
people just can't be taught social graces."

I turned my cell phone off as I drove out of the club. I
didn't want to talk to anyone. It wasn't that cold out,
but I sat shivering anyway. It's amazing how in one instant you can transform from a confident senior into a
skinny junior high geek with braces and glasses. I
mean, I actually peered into my rearview mirror to see
if I looked the same.

I did, but apparently the geeky kid still lived inside
me somewhere, visible to all those who looked at me.
Because they all knew I was a loser.

Why had I ever thought someone like Colton,
who'd always been handsome and popular, could be
interested in me? His last girlfriend had been Hamilton's head cheerleader. Hello, you just don't go from
dating Miss Holds-the-School-Record-for-Jumping-Up-
and-Down-in-a-Miniskirt to dating Miss Holds-the-
School-Record-for-Most-Bug-Insults-Flung-at-Her.

Of course, it had all been a joke to him. He and
Bryant probably had a good laugh over the fact that I'd
been so easy to buy off. I must have seemed so desperate. All Colton had to do was throw a little charm my
way—well, that and a thousand dollars—and I'd turned
my back on my best friend.

Because that's what I'd done.

I gripped the steering wheel until my fingers hurt. Sure, Bryant was only interested in getting a football scholarship to Stanford. Nothing was going on between him and Shelby. That story was about as likely as the other one Colton had tried to sell me—the one about him wanting to date me.

I turned the van toward Brianna's house. I'd tell her the truth. All of it. Even the truth about what I'd done. It would mean she'd be mad at me, and the kids at St. Matthew's would have a lousy Christmas; but hey, that's the way life worked out a lot of times. The rich and the popular people of the world called the shots, and when you didn't do things their way, you ended up with underwear and UNO cards underneath your tree.

I slowed the van until it came to rest at a four-way stop. No other cars waited at the intersection, but I still didn't move forward. I just sat there thinking how unfair everything was.

Finally, I tilted the rearview mirror until I could see my face again.

I wasn't that skinny kid anymore, the one who let the popular guys harass her. And I didn't have to let down all those kids at St. Matthew's. After all, Bryant and Colton weren't the only ones who could play this game underhanded.

Colton and I had made an agreement that he'd come up with the money for our service project, and I wouldn't rat on Bryant. Fine. So I wouldn't rat on

Bryant. But that didn't mean some of Brianna's other friends couldn't, say, check up on Bryant's activities and discover the truth about him themselves. Maybe Kelly and Aleeta, who sat with us at lunchtime. I wouldn't tell them anything. I'd just point them in the right direction.

And then we'd see who was eating her cake and having her service project too.

I put the van into drive and headed back to my house. Finally I stopped shivering.

When I came through my front door, Julianne walked up to me, toothbrush in hand and her mouth half full of toothpaste. "Colton called you twice. He wants you to call him back."

I put my purse in the coat closet. "Does he?"

Rebecca waited for me at the top of the stairs, leaning across the banister. "What happened between the two of you? He sounded upset."

"Really?"

Evelynn popped her head out of her bedroom, still slipping her nightgown on as she spoke. "Are you going to call him back?"

"No."

She secured her last button and smoothed down her nightgown. "Why not?"

"Because I've given up on guys. They're all condescending elitists." I walked into my bedroom and shut the door, but I could still hear my sisters out in the hallway.

"What's a condescending elitist?" Julianne asked.

"Someone who upset Charlotte," Evelynn said.

Footsteps, and then my father's voice. "Is Charlotte home? Good. Now she can answer her own phone calls."

"I doubt it," Rebecca said. "She's given up on men."

My father grunted. "Well, that's one down, and three more weddings to talk you girls out of." He tapped on my door in passing and called out loudly, "Carry on, Charlotte, carry on."

❧ seven ❧

As I walked to second-period calculus on Monday I saw Colton waiting in the hallway by the door. I knew he was waiting for me. I also knew I couldn't avoid him forever. In fact, I couldn't avoid him at all, since we had three classes together.

When he saw me, he walked up. "Can we talk?"

"Sure." I kept my voice light, as though Saturday hadn't mattered at all. "Did you talk to your dad about our fund-raiser?"

"Yeah. He's cutting a check today. But that's not what I wanted to talk to you about."

"Then what? Our trip to St. Matthew's Elementary? I can do it by myself if you don't want to go."

"I'm going." He took my hand and pulled me farther away from the classroom, down to where the hallway spilled open to an alcove with benches. Neither of us sat down. I pulled my hand away from him as soon as we stopped walking.

"About Saturday," he said. "I know Bryant said some things that upset you."

"Are you talking about when he called me Miss Freezer, or when he said you only spent time with me to keep me away from Shelby and him?"

"It wasn't like that."

"He also called me a bloodhound. I remember that, of course, because I keep each insult tucked away in my personal grudge-bag."

Colton folded his arms. "Bryant didn't know you were listening."

"And that makes it better because it's okay to talk about people behind their backs."

Colton rolled his eyes. "You, of course, only compliment Bryant when he isn't around, right?"

"I . . ." I didn't know how to answer that accusation. "This isn't about Bryant and me. This is about you using me, which I suppose shouldn't surprise me, since that's how you get what you want, isn't it?"

Colton looked up, consulting the ceiling momentarily before he spoke. "I didn't use you, and you might be able to see that if you didn't have such a big chip on your shoulder."

"A chip on my shoulder?"

"Not just a chip," he said. "Stalactites. Stalagmites. Entire rock formations. No one can get close to you for fear of an avalanche."

I didn't know how to even begin to defend myself. He'd been in the wrong on Saturday. I was sure of it. How had he turned this around so it was my fault? I folded my arms, although more to keep myself from trembling than as an act of defiance. "You know what—I think we should call Friday off. I wouldn't want you to worry about getting buried beneath an avalanche or anything."

"Fine." Colton's voice turned businesslike, erasing our argument with a change in tone. Which just made me think he had never really wanted to go out on Friday and was glad to have the whole thing called off. "About St. Matthew's Elementary," he said, "I called this morning, talked with the principal, and faxed over a wish list and clothing-size questionnaire. They'll send home the wish lists today, along with permission slips for a Santa field trip to the mall. I'll pick up the wish lists Thursday after school."

"You have wrestling practice after school," I said. "I can pick up the lists myself."

Colton shook his head. "I've already cleared it with the coach. Besides, I should be the one to talk to Sister Mary Catherine, since I'm in charge."

Which, I suppose, was Colton's subtle way of telling me he was calling the shots as to how to run the Santa service project.

Man, you supervise one activity where a homeless lady chases someone's car and people no longer trust your judgment. Still, I wanted to make sure that both Reese and T.J. made it to the field trip. "I'll go with you," I said.

"Great. I'll meet you there." He turned around and walked back to the calculus room.

I stewed about Colton's accusations all through class. At lunch I didn't even try to keep up with my table's conversation. Kelly mostly talked about Wesley, who had flirted with her during honors English again, but still never asked her out. This caused a lot of speculation at the table as to whether he was shy, a player, or so used to liberated women, he expected Kelly to make the first move. I refrained from saying that since he was a guy and therefore basically evil, he might be trying to torment her. I didn't think the others at the table would consider my viewpoint as helpful.

Besides, it was too hard to pay attention to what Wesley had or hadn't said when what Colton had said kept running through my mind.

Like he had any right to comment on my shoulders.

"What do you think?" Aleeta asked me.

"Think about what?" I said.

Brianna gave a grunt of disbelief. "About Bryant and my matching shirts. I've almost decided on the phrase, 'All I want for Christmas is you.'" She returned her attention to a piece of notebook paper in front of her. "Or maybe not. Which do you think is best?"

Kelly leaned across the table to get my attention and mouthed the words, "They're all hokey."

"Which one does Bryant like best?" I asked.

Brianna shrugged. "I haven't talked to him about it yet. I figured I'd do it today, but I haven't seen him yet."

He was avoiding her now. Or maybe not. Maybe

that was my suspicious nature cropping up. "Don't you usually see him by this time?"

"Usually." Her eyebrows drew together. "Do you suppose he's sick?"

I wanted to say, "Definitely," then blink a few times and add, "Oh, did you mean absent?" But I didn't, because I'm actually nicer than Colton thinks I am.

Kelly leaned sideways to see around Aleeta. "There he is. He's walking over here right now."

We all turned to look at him, you know, to make it extra clear we'd been talking about him. For a moment his gaze flickered to mine, then it trained in on Brianna.

Brianna waved him over to her in her usual open fashion. "Hey, hunk. Guess what—I've been thinking about making matching shirts for you and me to wear to the winter dance. You know, something with a cute holiday phrase." She handed him the piece of notebook paper she had written on. "What do you think of these?"

He read the list silently, then raised a questioning eyebrow at Brianna, "Who needs reindeer when I have you, dear?"

"Charlotte thought of that one," she said.

I smiled over at Bryant.

"But right now I'm leaning toward 'Sugar Plum' for me and 'Sugar Daddy' for you," she said.

His smile twitched. "Um . . ., that's really cute and all . . . but I don't think I want to do matching shirts."

She blinked, taken aback. "Why not?"

"How about we both just wear red? That would be matching enough."

"Oh. Well, I guess if you don't want to . . ." She took the list back from him and looked it over again with a sigh. "Have you decided where we're going Saturday?"

"Saturday?" he repeated.

"Yeah. You canceled our date last Saturday to go to that wedding reception, but you promised we'd do something fun this Saturday."

Recognition flooded his face. "Oh, that's right. Listen, about Saturday, I totally forgot that my aunt is coming into town, so we're all going out to dinner as a family. My parents won't let me get out of it." Bryant shot me a hurried look, which because of my skeptical, grudge-holding nature, I interpreted to mean he made plans with Shelby on Saturday. Before I could sufficiently glare at him, his gaze snapped back to Brianna. "Let's do something Friday. A movie. You can choose."

"All right." She smiled up at him and scooted her chair over. "You want to sit with us?"

He glanced at me again, and I knew what would come next. Apparently it was time to prove, once again, that he could make Brianna pick him over me. "I don't want to crowd you," he said. "Besides, I have some stuff to do, but if you're done with lunch . . ." His voice trailed off into an invitation.

She'd only eaten half of her lunch, but she stood up anyway. "Sure. I'm done." She picked up her tray, said good-bye to the rest of us, and didn't look back as she walked away.

Bryant did though. Over his shoulder he sent me a gloating smile.

"Jerk," I said.

"Who?" Aleeta asked.

"Bryant. He just smiled at me."

"Well, I can see why that would upset you," Kelly said, and then she and Aleeta both laughed.

I took a sip of my milk and tried to think of a way to rephrase my last statement. Then I decided not to bother. Instead, I said, "Do you guys think I have a chip on my shoulder?"

"What?" Aleeta asked.

"A chip. A grudge. An attitude like a stalagmite."

Kelly and Aleeta glanced at each other. Which wasn't a good sign.

"Not really," Aleeta said.

"Well . . .," Kelly said.

"Not one as big as a stalagmite," Aleeta added.

I set my fork down on my tray. "But you do think I have a chip on my shoulder?"

"About some things," Kelly said.

"Like what?"

More glances between Aleeta and Kelly. Aleeta spoke first. "The whole Spiderwoman-refusing-to-date-anyone-from-our-school thing."

Kelly nodded. "Remember how you went on and on about the irrationality of voters after you lost the NHS election?"

I picked up my fork and stabbed my lasagna before cutting it. "Fine. But just because I have a chip on my shoulder doesn't mean I'm wrong about certain people."

My friends watched me silently for a moment, then Aleeta spoke. "So who told you that you had a chip on your shoulder?"

"Never mind." I shoved a piece of lasagna into my mouth so I couldn't answer.

"It was a cute guy, wasn't it?" Kelly said. "Those types of statements only bother you if cute guys say them."

I didn't answer, and I didn't look at them.

"Must have been a *really* cute guy," Aleeta said.

Kelly leaned forward. "Who was it, and do you like him?"

I took another bite of lasagna.

"She likes him," Aleeta said with a smile.

"Ryan Geno?" Kelly asked. "Arnold Carrillo?"

"Colton Taft," Aleeta said as though sure she was right.

Kelly nodded. "Which means we're really talking about Bryant, aren't we?"

Aleeta leaned closer to the table and lowered her voice. "Charlotte likes Bryant?"

"No," I said quickly.

"No," Kelly repeated, "She doesn't like him, which is why Colton thinks she has a chip on her shoulder." She turned to me then, wearing a triumphant smile. "I'm right, aren't I?"

I shuffled pieces of lasagna around on my plate. "I should stop hanging out with smart people."

"You could always try getting along with Bryant, you know." Aleeta said this like the thought might have never occurred to me before—which, I suddenly realized, it hadn't.

I pushed my plate away. "You don't actually believe his aunt is coming to town on Saturday, do you? Bryant blew off Brianna, and she doesn't even see it."

Kelly nodded over in the direction Bryant and Brianna had gone. "He's holding her hand right now."

I looked. The two of them stood at the foot of the stairs talking, with their fingers intertwined.

"That's because he's doing it slyly."

Aleeta stole one of Kelly's fries and took a bite. "It's good to see you're working on that chip-on-your-shoulder problem, Charlotte. I can tell your attitude about the guys at our school is improving."

"I can't say anything else to Brianna about Bryant, because she thinks I'm attacking him. But that doesn't mean you guys couldn't, say, stake out his house on Saturday and see where he really goes."

Aleeta took a fry and swirled it in ketchup. "Yeah, because we'd like Brianna to think we're attacking her boyfriend too. Hey, why don't we save ourselves the trouble and just make matching 'We Hate Bryant' T-shirts?"

I sat my fork down on my plate with a clang. Why was it that no one else could see what was happening? "Don't you guys care about Brianna?"

Kelly let out a sigh and shook her head. "When you

get in the middle of other people's love lives, it always comes back to bite you. You should have learned that by now, since you're still wearing teeth marks from the last time you helped Brianna."

Well, yeah, she had a point. Maybe even a good point. Still, it bothered me. Bryant apparently could do anything to anyone and always get away with it. It was his right because he was popular, good-looking, and could chuck a football around. Worse yet, I, who should have known better, had helped him by making that agreement with Colton. Almost to myself, I said, "When Bryant hurt me, no one even tried to stop him. How can I stand by and let him hurt Brianna?"

Kelly shook her head again. "You're looking for revenge."

"I'm looking for justice."

"Well, sometimes you can't have justice and friendship. So you'd better make up your mind which you want more." She picked up a french fry and ate it as though this closed the matter.

She didn't understand. She couldn't.

I leaned across the table toward Kelly. "If you spy on Bryant for me, I'll do something for you."

"Justice or friendship. You're not listening to me."

I spoke slowly, using my most enticing voice. "I'll take over the decorations for the winter dance."

Kelly stopped eating midbite. Half a french fry dangled from her fingertips.

For the last few days I'd heard Kelly complain a

lot about the fact that she only had a budget of fifty dollars and the whole gymnasium to transform into a winter wonderland. "And how are things going on the decoration committee these days?" I prompted.

She bit into the french fry, chomping it angrily. "Right now all I've got is a bunch of streamers and a glow-in-the-dark Frosty the Snowman. Harris is supposed to help me, but I've seen how he dresses, so I'm not sure I should actually trust him to decorate anything. He may, in fact, be color-blind."

"No," Aleeta said with a smirk. "While the rest of you NHS members have wasted your intellectual abilities, Harris constructed a time machine and went bargain shopping in the nineteen eighties."

Kelly popped the rest of her fry into her mouth. "Well, that would explain a lot."

"We've got tons of Christmas stuff," I said. "I'm sure my mom would let me empty out the house for one night."

Kelly sighed. "Ms. Ellis agreed to a couple of artificial Christmas trees, but beyond that, she doesn't want anything that can be broken, stolen, or thrown across the room like a football." Kelly raised both hands upward in a gesture of frustration. "What does that leave?"

I nodded. "Guys can throw anything across the room—including each other—which is why you ought to spy on Bryant and leave the decorations in my hands."

Kelly didn't say anything for a moment, then sent me

a skeptical look. "You're the one who keeps threatening to serve popcorn and tap water for refreshments. Besides, it's not right to spy on people. Plus, Brianna would be furious if she found out I did." More swishing. She looked as though she was about to take up french fry painting. "Which means it's going to cost you extra. You take over the decoration committee, and you get Wesley to ask me out."

I blinked at her. "I get Wesley to . . . How am I supposed to do that?"

"Believe me, if I knew, I would have accomplished it myself."

"But I never talk to Wesley outside of the study group."

Kelly smiled and bit into her fry. "You're still the perfect one to do it. You don't date guys from our school, so when you talk to him, he won't think you're hitting on him."

"Yeah, and if I talked to him," Aleeta said, her voice growing huffy, "I might be tempted to just snatch him up for myself."

"I didn't mean it that way," Kelly said. "You can talk to him too."

Aleeta took a sip of her milk and shook her head. "Never mind. I'll just wait until I need you to spy on someone for me. Charlotte can play matchmaker for you this time."

And then I knew I had no choice. "I can't promise anything," I said.

"Neither can I," Kelly said, and for the rest of

lunch, I split my time between devising a plan to talk to Wesley and figuring out how to decorate the gym for under fifty dollars.

As it turned out, the decorating was the easiest of the two to arrange. Maybe hanging out with my mom during her Martha Stewart moments has rubbed off on me, because by the end of the day, I had not only planned the decorations but given out the assignments. Rebecca and her friends agreed to wrap an assortment of large empty boxes with Christmas paper. Twenty helpful seniors (okay, people I cornered in my classes) promised they'd make two dozen paper snowflakes each. I would take batches of pinecones, glue them together in the form of Christmas trees, and then spray-paint them gold for the table centerpieces. I'd seen my mom do it before. They'd be pretty, cheap, and prickly enough to discourage being tossed across the room.

Talking to Wesley was harder. He took a couple of honors classes with me, but he sat across the room, so we didn't talk much. And now I was supposed to somehow walk up to him, smile, and say, "Hey, would you like to take out my friend?"

I stared at him all through English, hoping an idea would present itself. Right before class ended, one did. Specifically, our teacher told us we had a test on *Macbeth* tomorrow. Half the class groaned, but

I didn't. After the bell rang, I made a beeline to Wesley.

I caught up to him as he walked out the door. "Hey, Wesley."

"Hey," he said back.

"You ready for the test?"

He shrugged.

"You want to get together and study after school?"

"I've got wrestling practice after school," he said.

"Oh yeah." I'd forgotten he was on the team with Colton. Occasionally during our study sessions the two of them would lapse into wrestler-speech. We'd be talking about the driving forces behind the Civil War, and they'd be discussing the benefits of turks, guillotines, and other things we didn't understand but sounded sinister. "How about after wrestling practice then? At my house. I'll have plenty of celery on hand."

Celery may seem like a strange thing to lure a teenage boy to your home with, but throughout wrestling season wrestlers watch their weight in a way that would put anorexics to shame.

Wesley smiled over at me. "Celery would be great— just as long as you don't leave out any donuts to tempt me."

"No donuts," I said. "I'll see you at four."

After that, we went different ways in the hallway, and I let out a sigh of relief. That hadn't been so hard. Now if only the rest of my plan went as smoothly. I pictured the two of us talking about *Macbeth*. I would casually bring up the topic of Kelly. Subtly—so subtly he wouldn't notice my influence—I'd mention he ought to ask her out. In my vision he liked the suggestion. How closely my vision and reality would resemble each other remained to be seen.

❧ eight ❧

The nice thing about not having Wesley come over right after school was that it gave me time to straighten the house. Or rather, straighten what I could and yell at my sisters to pick up the rest.

"How come we have to clean the house every time you have a friend over?" Julianne said, moving her Malibu Barbie's beach party from the couch to her bedroom. "I don't make you clean when my friends come over."

"That's because your friends are seven years old," I said.

"And because your friends aren't cute guys," Rebecca added. "Who's coming over? Colton?"

"Wesley," I said.

Evelynn walked by me with her ballet shoes dangling from one hand. "When is Colton coming over again?"

I straightened magazines on the coffee table and

pretended the subject didn't bother me. "When he re-
alizes the truth about either me or Bryant."

Julianne's head popped up from behind the couch,
where Ken and a collection of tiny plastic picnic food
had fallen. "When will that be?"

"Oh, probably around the same time hell freezes
over."

"I thought Colton was your friend," Evelynn said. "I
thought you liked him."

"I do—well, I used to." It made me feel sad just to
say the words.

Rebecca gave me a long look. "But you're not going
to talk to him until hell freezes over?"

I straightened another magazine. "Well, anything is
possible. After all, Colton is in the same business as
the devil, so he probably has some pull down there.
Hell might be cooling as we speak." Then I went to
the kitchen to cut up celery stalks.

By the time the doorbell rang at four, the house was
clean and a vegetable platter lay on the kitchen table.
I'd also made popcorn—unbuttered for him and buttered for me. I grabbed ice from the freezer and dumped
it into two glasses. I felt as nervous as if it were me
who liked Wesley, and not Kelly.

"Can someone get the door, please!" I yelled, then
put a liter of diet root beer on the table. Footsteps ran
across the living room. The door swung open.

"Colton!" Julianne squealed happily. "You came!"

I stopped midstep. Colton? She must be mistaken. She had forgotten what he looked like and was now calling Wesley, "Colton," because they both had brown hair.

"Sure, I came," Colton said, and there was no mistaking his voice. "I still have to teach you how to wrestle, don't I?"

I headed toward the living room.

"Hey, Charlotte," Julianne yelled. "Hell must have frozen over!" And then in a quieter voice she added, "Charlotte was hoping it would."

"What?" Colton asked.

I sprinted the rest of the way to the door. As I rounded the corner I saw both Wesley and Colton in the entryway. Julianne stood in front of them transfixed, staring up at Colton with adoring eyes.

"Julianne, it's time for you to go to your room," I said. "Right now."

"Do you really know the devil?" she asked Colton. "Have you ever been to hell?"

"Sometimes I think I have," he answered, glaring at me.

Julianne started to ask more questions, which nobody heard because at that point I shoved her toward the stairs and hissed at her to never speak to my friends again. Then I calmly turned back to the guys. "Hi."

Wesley looked past me, his gaze traveling around the room. "Are we the first ones here?"

I stared at him blankly. I had absolutely no idea what he was talking about, why Colton was with him, or how to salvage my dignity after my sister's scene. "The first ones?" I repeated.

"From the study group," Wesley said, and then because I was still staring at him, he added, "That was today, right?"

"Yes, yes. That was today." Only apparently I hadn't made it clear I was just inviting Wesley, and so he had invited Colton along and was expecting the whole group to be here.

Okay, what was the best way to get out of this awkward situation?

1. Admit the truth and fess up that I'd just invited Wesley over. Of course, this would beg the question why. I could look like I was hitting on the guy my friend liked, or I could let them know I was trying to set him up with Kelly.

   Either of which would make Kelly hate me forever.

2. Play dumb and say, "Oh, I'm sure they'll be along any time now," then hope for some sort of solution to magically present itself within the next few minutes. Like maybe an angel would appear.

3. Faint, wait until the paramedics took my limp body away in an ambulance, and then, when questioned about the situation later, claim amnesia.

I was getting ready to faint when Rebecca walked out holding the platter of vegetables. "Did you guys want this in the kitchen or in the living room?"

Wesley walked over to her, grabbed a cucumber slice, and popped it into his mouth. "Great. I love cucumbers."

"You can put it in the living room," I told Rebecca. She laid the platter on the coffee table, and Wesley followed her, setting his backpack by the couch. Colton didn't move, probably because he hadn't finished glaring at me.

"There's soda and popcorn in the kitchen. Why don't you sit down, and I'll be right back with it." I turned, and when I was out of sight, I sprinted to the kitchen. Once there, I grabbed the phone, speed dialed Kelly's house, and bit a fingernail while waiting for her to pick up.

After three rings, she did. "Hello?"

"Kelly, it's Charlotte. Call everyone in our study group who's taking honors English. Tell them we have a study session over at my house right now, and they have to come. Tell them you were supposed to invite them earlier, but you forgot, okay?"

"What?" she asked.

"Don't ask questions. Just do it."

"What?" she asked again. For someone whose IQ is well within Mensa range, she was not picking up on the urgency of my plan very quickly.

"Just do it, and then come yourself. Wesley is here, and so is— Hi, Colton."

I hadn't noticed him come into the kitchen, but he stood in the doorway, arms crossed, surveying me.

"Bye," I told Kelly, and hung up the phone. Then I stood with a smile plastered on my face and wondered how much of my conversation he'd heard.

"I came to see if you needed help carrying things," he told me.

"Oh." I glanced over at the table where the popcorn, soda, and two glasses stood. "Thanks. You can carry the soda."

He walked to the table and picked up the glasses one by one. "When Wesley told me at wrestling practice that we had a study group at your house, I just assumed you hadn't told me about it because you were still avoiding me."

"I'm not avoiding you." I went to the cupboard and pulled out another glass.

"Right." He took the glass and added it to the ones already in his hands. "If I'd known you were setting up this study session as some romantic rendezvous between you and Wesley, I wouldn't have come."

"This isn't—" I lowered my voice just in case Wesley decided to come into the kitchen and help us. "This isn't a romantic rendezvous."

Colton raised an eyebrow in disbelief.

"This is just . . . I wanted to talk to Wesley about . . . you know, something." I had no reason to tell Colton about Kelly. No reason to trust or confide in him. He was, after all, the enemy. But standing with Colton in my kitchen, I felt like it was just another one of our study groups. Like he was the old Colton that I used to trust.

Besides, it's hard to think of a guy as the enemy when he's wrestler-buff, underworld spy good-looking, and has intense brown eyes that are gazing in your direction. Probably they teach guys in underworld spy school how to melt girls with that expression.

"So what did you want to talk to Wesley about?" he asked me.

"Kelly likes him," I said. "So I figured while we were discussing Lady Macbeth's insanity and Duncan's murder, I could, you know, casually find out if he likes her too."

Colton didn't blink. "He likes her."

"He does? How do you know?"

He shrugged like it was a silly question. "We talk sometimes. He told me on the drive over he hoped she would be here."

"Then why hasn't he ever asked her out?"

"He's shy. And we're in the middle of wrestling season, midterms, and Christmas." Colton picked up the liter of soda. "Have a little patience."

I reached for the bowl of popcorn, but didn't start out of the kitchen yet. "Well, can I hurry him along? Is there any chance he'll ask her out before this weekend?"

Colton shook his head at me, then walked toward the living room. "You're not quite grasping the nature of patience, Charlotte."

Which matched, I suppose, my grasp of the nature of guys.

Only Kelly showed up from the study group. She hadn't been able to reach a lot of the kids, and the ones she did talk to had other plans. Wesley didn't seem to mind, or notice, though. He and Kelly spent most of the time tossing popcorn pieces into each others mouth. I decided it would be a good idea to give them a little privacy, so twice I dragged Colton into the kitchen to help me with more refreshments.

The first time Colton just rolled his eyes and tapped his fingers against the countertop while I opened the freezer, "Very subtle, Charlotte. You needed two people to carry out fresh ice cubes. You could have at least invented a jar lid for me to open."

So the second time I did. I developed an insatiable craving for artichoke hearts and made Colton come along to the kitchen to open the jar. Once there, I went to the cupboard, took out a jar, then held it in my hands. "I think it ought to take you about five minutes to open this jar."

"Why? Am I supposed to be a wimp or something?"

"No. Some jars are just hard to open."

"Not for wrestlers. We have to have good wrist control." He held his hand out for the jar, but I didn't give it to him.

"All right then, we'll just say I had trouble finding the artichoke hearts—about five minutes of trouble."

"If you keep dragging me into this kitchen, it's going to look like you're doing it because you want to be alone with me."

"Hey, you're right," I walked over to the kitchen table, pulled out a chair, and sat down. "Which means we could be in here for ten minutes and Wesley wouldn't get suspicious."

Colton followed me to the table, but didn't sit

down. He folded his arms and looked at me. "And then what's Wesley going to think when we come back ten minutes later?"

I shrugged, "That your taste in women has improved? After all, you usually go for the cheerleader types."

Colton sat down, grudgingly. "I've only been out with one cheerleader. The rest of the girls surrounding me at that time were her friends. They come together, you know, like eggs in a carton or pairs of socks—squads of cheerleaders." And then he gave me a look that was a question all by itself. "Besides, as long as you hate my best friend, why does it matter to you what types of girls I date?"

For a moment neither of us spoke.

I knew he wanted me to apologize for my attitude about Bryant. He was waiting for it, in fact.

Which just goes to show you that getting slammed into a mat one too many times can turn a person delusional.

Bryant was using my best friend. And besides that, this was the guy who'd kept my desk well stocked with spiders throughout sixth and seventh grade. Even after all these years I still remembered the horror of finding them crawling over my things. It's not that I cared about spider footprints or anything, but you figure if spiders have taken up residence in your spiral notebooks, a few of them have probably ventured out of the dark and onto your person. Maybe some of the more adventurous ones are even spelunking through your hair.

Whenever I found one of Bryant's little gifts, I always had to stifle a scream and curb the desire to start swatting parts of my body.

Bryant thought it was so funny.

And now Colton wanted me to forget all of that and apologize for having a bad attitude about his friend? I couldn't. In fact, I was still counting on those stars I wished on in junior high to do their job. And when they did, Bryant would fall into a vat full of bloodsucking leeches.

I looked at the table instead of Colton. Neither of us said anything for a minute. Finally he reached over, took the artichoke hearts, and twisted the lid off. He placed the jar down in front of me with a thud. "I'm going to go study, Charlotte." Then he got up and walked back to the living room.

After that, the four of us went through the list of study questions, spewing off instances of symbolism, irony, and listing comparisons to other Shakespearean tragedies. Colton went through all of this with curt, formal answers in my direction.

Which was fine because I totally did not care.

When we'd finally gone over the entire list, the guys packed up their books, thanked me for the food, and left.

Kelly shut the door behind them, then leaned up against it with a sigh. "That went well."

I shut my book with a thud. "Good. Great. I'm glad. Of course, mostly I'm glad that I didn't have to fake amnesia, but the point is, I'm still glad."

It didn't make sense, but Kelly smiled at me anyway. She was too far gone in the Wesley zone to pay any attention to my ramblings.

"So you're going to spy on Bryant for me on Saturday, right?" I asked.

She gathered her books together, still smiling, "If Wesley asks me out before then."

"Oh, come on, Kelly. I got the two of you together today. You were alone for a while. You ate popcorn. That counts as a date, doesn't it?"

"Nope." She slid her books into her backpack and zipped it up. "But there's always tomorrow." Then she sighed happily and began planning out her wardrobe for roughly the rest of the year.

Let me say right now that when someone asks you what you want to be when you grow up, there's a good reason no one answers Cupid. This is mostly because being Cupid is a thankless job that often requires you to act like an idiot.

I didn't want to do it again tomorrow. I didn't even want to think about it. Between school, my job, all the holiday activities, Christmas shopping, and wrapping all those presents, I didn't have time to think about much beyond the fact that I can never find the Scotch tape when I need it. This is why, I suppose, it's called invisible tape.

And now, thanks to Kelly's stubbornness—or perhaps Wesley's stubbornness—I was going to have to put myself in some other impossibly awkward situation.

I picked up the popcorn bowl, dumped the rest of

the kernels into the trash can, and dropped the bowl
into the sink. Pursuing justice isn't as easy as they make
it seem in the movies. I gathered up our used soda
glasses and dropped them into the dishwasher, then
wiped off my hands and headed to my room.

At least I hadn't played the amnesia card yet. You
never knew when that might come in handy.

As hard as I tried—okay, I admit it, I didn't try that
hard—I never found an opportunity to talk to Wesley
about Kelly on either Tuesday or Wednesday. I did,
while passing him in the cafeteria lunch line, nod and
say, "Live dangerously. Try the meat loaf." But that was
it. And there's just not a lot of ways to introduce romance into a comment about meat loaf.

After school I went to work, where I thought of several more chapter topics for my dissertation. Like, just
because it is the season of brotherly love doesn't mean
shoppers are pleasant. This is especially true if your
store happens to run a special on SuperTeen talking
action figures and then runs out of them. In that case,
you get a lot of people complaining to you even though
you are just a lowly perfume sprayer and had nothing
to do with stocking action figures, running advertisements, or whatever. I mean really, did these people
think I was stashing a supply of action figures in my
perfume smock or something?

After work I went to Brianna's house to help her

with Spanish homework. She let me in, then yelled toward the kitchen, "How about working as a marine recruiter? Then you could at least meet hot guys!"

"Shut up!" Amanda yelled back.

Brianna headed down the hall toward her room, and I followed. "Amenity is home from college," Brianna said. "I'm helping her decide what she wants to do with the rest of her life." Over her shoulder she yelled, "I think the SWAT team would take you. After all, you have the right sunny disposition and people skills."

"Yeah? Well, don't make me use any of my skills on you!" Amanda shouted back.

I walked into Brianna's room and set my purse on her bed, which was already cluttered with crocheting stuff. "And why does Amanda need your career advice?"

"She's supposed to be at school, but she's taking a week off—right before finals—to think about ways to make her life more meaningful. She's not sure if she wants to go back to college next semester, because she's just wasting time taking classes that don't interest her."

I pulled Brianna's Spanish textbook off her desk and sat down. "Let me guess, she wants to start a band, right?"

Brianna shrugged. "Surprisingly, no. She's hasn't made any announcements of joining a band, a protest group, or a cult. She's just not sure she wants to go back to college."

"It's probably a phase. You know, like the time she became a vegan every other week."

Brianna picked up the crocheting needle from her bed, pushed over Bryant's afghan, and sat down. "Every time she does something stupid, my parents look at me like I'm about to become Amanda-the-sequel. Remember when they caught my sister smoking? They still give me lectures about lung cancer. She dated a guy who thought he was a vampire, and now my parents interview anybody who takes me out. I practically have to have a Breathalyzer after every party I go to because Amanda used to get drunk in high school, and now she's quitting college. Any moment my parents will burst into the room, pester me about what I want to major in, and insist it's never too early to think about life goals."

I opened up Brianna's Spanish book, flipping through the pages until I found the review questions. "So what do you want to do with your life?"

"I have no idea."

"Hey, you have something in common with your sister."

Her gaze shot over to mine. "The only thing I have in common with my sister is a few chromosomes."

We studied Spanish for about an hour, and then went to the kitchen to get something to eat. Amanda was still there. She sat at the table with a plate full of nachos in front of her and a book in one hand.

Brianna opened the fridge and peered inside. "You could always be a refrigerator repairman. There's no shortage of appliances in America."

Amanda turned a page in her book, but didn't look

up. "There's no shortage of a lot of things in America, and it's *repair person*. The word *repairman* is sexist."

Brianna took out a block of cheese and set it on the counter. "Which reminds me. I thought you were all gung ho to graduate in Women's Studies. You were going to save women everywhere from oppression by doing important things like insisting people call you Ms. Whatever happened to that?"

Amanda lowered her book. "I don't want to just *study* women's issues. I need a career where I can actually do something about women's issues." The book went back up. "And also a career where I can actually make a living."

Brianna poured tortilla chips onto a plate and sliced cheese on top of it. "Do you mean to say you want a career where you can make money—that green stuff which is the root of all evil?"

Amanda didn't answer right away. She fingered the spine of her book. "I'm not becoming materialistic. I've just realized it's hard to make a difference when you have no resources. Money is a resource, that's all." She lifted her book up again. "I mean, have you seen how much hybrid cars cost?"

Brianna put our plate of nachos into the microwave to melt the cheese. She stood by the oven, her arms crossed, which made her look like her mother. "Well, if you want a good career, don't you think you should finish college?"

"Probably. But I need to figure out what degree I want to earn. I thought I'd come home, where I could have some peace and quiet and think about it. Thanks, by the way, for giving me so much peace and quiet." She picked up her glass and took a quick sip. "Why are you staring at me like that?"

I knew why Brianna was staring at Amanda. It was the same reason I was staring at her. These were the first words Amanda had said in years that actually made sense.

"I'm not staring." Brianna took the plate from the microwave and bumped the door shut with her elbow. "We're just taking a break from studying Spanish." She took a few steps toward the kitchen door, then turned back. "You could be a doctor, you know. You could work in one of those clinics for the poor."

"Yeah. Maybe," Amanda said.

"You'd be a good doctor." Brianna paused for a moment, as though she was going to say more, but Amanda had already turned her attention back to her book.

We walked out of the kitchen and went down the hall. Brianna was ahead of me. I'm not sure whether she heard Amanda's muffled, "Thanks," or not.

nine

Thursday morning I walked by Wesley's locker four times so I could accidentally run into him. I had it all planned out. I would talk to him about his position on the dance committee. He was on the cleanup crew, but I would pretend I didn't know that and ask if he was too busy to help out with decorations. From there, we'd make general small talk about the dance until I mentioned how fun it is to go with a date and suggest he take Kelly.

On my fifth pass through the hallway with no sign of Wesley, I leaned up against the row of lockers and tried to think of a plan B. Was there any way I could work the whole conversation into the brief time we saw each other during English class?

"Hi, Charlotte."

Wesley appeared before me unexpectedly, startling me so much I banged my shoulders into his locker. Then in an attempt to appear casual and not plotting,

I gripped my books to my chest and stared at him. "Hi, Wesley."

He didn't move. I didn't move.

He nodded in my direction. "Uh, can you scoot over so I can get to my locker?"

"Sorry." I slid out of the way, blushing. "Is this your locker?" A stupid thing to say because, hello, I'd passed him at his locker like a hundred times before. Despite this bad start, I launched into my plan. "What a coincidence. I was just thinking of you. I mean, I was wondering what dance position you're on."

His eyes narrowed like he couldn't understand me. "Dance position?"

Oh, this was going well. I'd just asked the guy his dance position. Like excuse me, Wesley, are you about to do a pirouette? I thought so. When you're done with that, perhaps the two of us could do a little waltzing in the hallway or something.

"I mean your dance committee position," I said. "What committee are you on?"

"Oh." He nodded as he opened his locker. "Cleanup crew."

"That's great." Where was I supposed to go with this? I suddenly couldn't remember. I only knew I had to work Kelly into the conversation. "I'm doing decorations with Kelly."

"I thought you were doing refreshments with Preeth."

"I am, but I'm helping Kelly too because, you know, she can use all the help she can get." Oops, not the thing you want to say to a guy to entice him to date your friend. "Not that she's incompetent or anything. She's very competent. And smart. Well, of course you know she's smart because she's in NHS with us. I just meant she's busy. Although not so busy that she doesn't love to go out. Because she does. And she likes to dance too."

There is a time in every plan when you know it's time to cut and run. I had long since past that point.

Wesley stared at me in that same way people stare at mimes. You know, just waiting to see what bizarre thing they're going to do next.

I took a step away from the lockers. "So the dance should be really fun."

"Yeah," he said.

I didn't wait around to see if he had more to add. Even a mime has a certain amount of pride.

At lunch Brianna filled us in on the latest gossip about who was going to the dance as a couple and where they were going before and afterward. "Colton asked Olivia," she said. "I've never met her, but Bryant says she's nice."

"Colton asked Olivia?" I repeated, and then because I knew I sounded disapproving added, "He's one of the people in charge. What's he going to do if there's a problem with the music or something?"

"Let the deejay take care of it?" Aleeta said.

I bit a carrot in half and crunched it into little pieces. "Olivia didn't strike me as that nice. She seemed egotistical, if you ask me."

"Well, I guess we'll get to meet her and see for ourselves," Brianna said.

Yeah. And with the way things were going, Olivia and Brianna would probably become great friends and then— My thought process stopped. If Bryant had any romantic designs on Shelby, he wouldn't want Colton to bring Olivia to the dance, would he? Olivia was Shelby's friend. Olivia would see Bryant and Brianna together and tell Shelby about it.

It didn't make sense.

Unless Bryant really did tell Shelby he had a girlfriend, and I was wrong about the whole thing.

I ate another carrot, slowly this time, and mulled it over in my mind. Had I jumped to conclusions about Bryant, like everybody said?

It suddenly seemed possible.

I should have been happy, or at least relieved, but I wasn't. It felt as though my thoughts had scattered up in the air and they didn't know where to land. Was I intuitive or suspicious? A busybody or a good friend?

I continued to eat my carrot sticks, pulverizing them into nothing.

It didn't help that I knew Colton and Olivia would spend the evening dancing together while I stood at the refreshment table passing out cookies to happy couples.

I could have been the one dancing with Colton—but

no, I'd placed my loyalties with Brianna, the girl who was now poised to become Olivia's new friend. I couldn't even skip out on the whole stupid event because I was stuck on the refreshment committee—and oh yeah, the decoration committee too.

It wouldn't have been so bad if I could dance with someone every once in a while. Then I could at least pretend to have a good time. But no one would ask me to dance. Not since I had a policy of not dating the guys at my school. They'd all branded me a snob.

A snob with a chip on her shoulder.

I thought back to my sophomore year, when I'd moved home to California. It had felt so good to rebuff the advances guys had sent my way. *You had no use for me*, I had thought silently, *and so now I have no use for you*. I'd celebrated my separation from them. Separation was better. Only right now it just felt lonely.

After school Colton and I went to St. Matthew's Elementary together. He insisted on driving me because he thought it would be faster that way.

Neither one of us talked much during the drive. My thoughts still hadn't landed—well, except for my thoughts about Olivia. I was squarely against Colton going out with Olivia, but I wasn't about to tell him that.

Finally we pulled into St. Matthew's parking lot, got out of his car, and walked into the office.

The principal, a nun whose desk sign read, SISTER MARY CATHERINE, greeted us with a firm handshake. "It's a great thing you want to do for these kids. Just great. A lot of their families struggle." She sat down behind her desk, then shuffled around piles of paper. "I sent out thirty permission slips, and I got all thirty back. That has to be some sort of record. Usually we have to remind kids and remind parents, and then still only half the kids turn anything in."

Sister Mary Catherine handed a stack of paper to Colton. "The bus will leave here after school and make it to the mall sometime between three and three ten. You'll have everything set up by then?"

Colton nodded. "The mall will let us use their Santa chair between three and four o'clock."

They went on to talk about other aspects of the field trip, and I realized that not only had Colton arranged details with the mall, but also he'd been in contact with the principal's secretary.

As the president of NHS, he had every right to or-ganize the thing; but still, it had been my idea, and I felt completely out of the loop.

Colton glanced through the contents of the wish lists. "We'll pass these out to our members so they can start shopping. I'll give you a call a day or two before the twenty-first to make sure everything is still on track."

"Wonderful," Sister Mary Catherine said. "The kids are looking forward to it already." She stood up, signal-ing the end of our meeting. I hadn't said one thing during the whole session.

Sister Mary Catherine glanced at her watch, then smiled back at us. "I'm supposed to meet with the grounds crew in two minutes. Why don't I walk with you outside."

Colton shuffled through the stack of papers, scanning the wish lists while the three of us headed to the door.

"Is Reese somewhere in all that paperwork?" I asked. "Is T.J.?"

Colton flipped through some more of the papers, searching.

"Reese Smith and T.J. Macintosh," Sister Mary Catherine answered. "Their lists are in the stack." She gave a small laugh as we walked. "I know those two well."

"I met them in the mall," I said. "They seemed like nice kids."

"Most of the kids here are." Sister Mary Catherine glanced around the walkway that led to the parking lot. "Reese is probably still around. His grandmother picks him up after school. Oh, there he is."

Up ahead of us on the walkway, Reese leaned against the school wall. His gray backpack seemed almost as big as he did.

"Do you want to go over and say hi?" Colton asked.

I knew I should let Reese know I was a part of his field trip to the mall on the twenty-first so he didn't come to Bloomingdale's looking for me on Christmas Eve, but I didn't answer. It seemed a risky thing to introduce Colton to the kid who'd thrown sodas on him twice.

Sister Mary Catherine glanced at her watch again. "This is where I leave you. Thanks again for putting the field trip together." She gave us a wave and headed in another direction.

We walked on slowly. Colton examined the lists. "I don't know if this was such a good idea. Half these kids want electric scooters and Xboxes. We don't have the budget for that. They'll be disappointed."

"They'll be even more disappointed if they don't get anything."

Colton mumbled something that I couldn't hear but which seemed decidedly lacking in the Christmas spirit.

"Look around at these kids," I told Colton in a lowered voice. "They're wearing hand-me-downs, and living on the free-lunch program. They need our help."

He glanced around, then back at the papers. "You can't tell by looking at them whether they're on a free-lunch program."

"Yes, I can. They're skinny. Malnourished."

"They're little kids. They all look that way."

"Perfume Lady!" Reese called out. I looked up to see him running toward me. His backpack shook up and down with every step. "What are you doing here?"

"I just came by to talk to the principal about the field trip to see Santa at the mall."

Reese's eyes grew wide. "You really do know Santa?"

I couldn't help but smile. This was probably as close to famous as I would ever get. "I'm helping him out this year. And since you're seeing Santa during the field trip, you don't have to worry about coming to the mall on Christmas Eve. Santa wants you to spend that day with your family, so he'll bring your mom's present to you at the field trip, okay?"

Reese nodded, his eyes still wide. "Is he bringing me my other gift too? I asked him for enough candy to make me sick."

Colton looked up from his lists. "Why would you want that?"

Reese shrugged. "My mom always says if I eat all my Halloween candy, it will make me sick; but it doesn't—no matter how much I eat. So I figure it would take a lot of candy to make me sick. Maybe a whole sleighful."

"You want a sleighful of candy?" Colton said.

Reese shrugged again. "Santa gets goodies at every house he stops at. He's got to have a lot left over by the time he reaches California."

Colton made a notation on one of the lists. "Uh-huh."

Reese took a step toward me, and his brows pushed together as he considered Colton. He lowered his voice, but not low enough. "Isn't that the guy you asked me to throw soda on?"

Colton's head jerked up. He stared first at Reese, then at me. "You asked him to throw soda on me?"

"Of course not. The boy is delirious. That's what happens to children when they're malnourished. They start hallucinating." I put my hand against Reese's forehead as though checking for a temperature. "I'm afraid he has a serious case of it."

Colton folded his arms and continued to glare at me. "No, Charlotte, you have a serious case of it, and I'm not talking about malnourishment."

Reese stepped away from my temperature check and toward Colton. "She said you wouldn't melt like the Wicked Witch of the West, but you might fizz a little." Reese turned back to me. "He never did fizz."

"I'm about to," Colton said. "Just watch for a few more seconds."

"There's my grandma!" Reese said, and without another look at either of us, he ran to the crosswalk to meet her.

Colton didn't move. He stood with his arms crossed and clenched the wish lists. "Let me get this straight. You know, just in case we ever have another conversation about doing things you later need to apologize for. *You asked that kid to follow me around the mall and throw soda on me?*"

"No. I asked him to pick up trash." I took a step back from Colton. "Although I might have suggested it wouldn't be a tragedy if he spilled soda on Bryant in the process."

"On Bryant?"

"I can't help it if Reese doesn't follow directions well."

Colton shut his eyes. I took another step back from him. When he opened his eyes, he let out a sigh. "This has got to end."

I didn't want to ask what he was talking about. In fact, I didn't want to have any sort of conversation with him. I looked out across the parking lot toward the car. "You know, we should go home. I have homework to do."

"Oh no you don't." He took hold of my hand and pulled me to the crosswalk. "We're going to fix this right now."

"Fix what?" I let him lead me across the parking lot toward his car. I wished he'd just yell at me about the soda and be done with it.

"We're going to see Bryant and work things out between you once and for all."

"I don't want to see Bryant." I tugged at my hand, but he held on tighter.

"I know you don't want to. You'd rather just hate Bryant for the rest of your life, but I'm getting sick of it."

"You?" I asked. "What do you have to do with this?"

We reached his car, and he opened the passenger-side door for me. "I've been drenched by misguided sodas and shoved in pools because of it. Not to mention that you showered Candy's guests with fruit dip because of it."

He motioned to the seat, and I reluctantly slid in and folded my arms. "I'm sorry about the sodas."

"And Bryant is sorry about the spiders."

"No, he isn't." I wasn't trying to argue with Colton. I just didn't understand how Colton could be Bryant's friend and not realize certain facts about him. Bryant didn't care how other people felt. I didn't think for a moment he regretted anything he'd done to me.

Colton pulled out of the parking lot and drove away

from the school. His speed picked up the farther we went. "What do you want from Bryant? An apology? Fine. He'll give you one."

"He hasn't changed," I said.

"What you mean is, you don't want him to change, because you enjoy hating him too much."

He didn't understand. He'd never been unpopular, ridiculed, or pushed to the fringes of school life day in and day out.

I didn't say anything else to Colton. I couldn't. If I spoke, I would either start yelling or break into tears. I knew I'd regret either of those things, so I sat silently in his car and held my hair in a ponytail so the wind wouldn't whip it around my face into uncontrollable tangles.

We drove through the city, and then to Bryant's neighborhood. "You're taking me to his house?"

"Nope. To the park. He and some of the guys are playing basketball."

We drove past a row of houses, then pulled up to the curb. I could make out a group of guys running back and forth on a court behind the playground equipment. Colton turned off the car, got out, and came around and opened my door for me. Not because he was being a gentleman, but because I didn't get out of the car. He bent forward, closer to me, and turned on his intense girl-melting gaze. "Come on, Charlotte, you've wanted an apology for a long time. You're finally going to get it."

"It doesn't count if you make him tell me he's sorry,"

I said, but I pulled myself out of the car anyway. To tell the truth, I couldn't imagine Bryant would apologize to me, even with Colton there forcing the issue. He'd do something obnoxious like laugh or tell me he no longer thought of me in spider terms because I'd graduated to hound-dog status.

Which would be awful, but at least Colton would finally see I was right about Bryant.

We walked across the grass, then stood at the corner of the courtyard—Colton looked for Bryant among the crowd. I looked for a possible escape route.

After a moment someone sunk a basket, and the group relaxed its pace from run to shuffle. One of the guys walked the ball back to midcourt. That's when Bryant noticed us. He looked from Colton, to me, and then back at Colton. He said something to one of the other guys, and then they paused the game. Most of the guys went to the sidelines to grab a drink from their water bottles. Bryant picked up a Gatorade and walked over to us. As I watched each footstep I thought of all the other places I would rather be than standing here—like, say, having several teeth extracted or being attacked by wild dogs.

Bryant wouldn't apologize, and I was going to recruit several more elementary children to throw sodas on Colton for dragging me here and making this happen.

Bryant finally reached us. He took another sip from his bottle, then wiped away the sweat from his forehead. "Hey, what's up?"

Colton glanced at me, then turned to Bryant.

"Charlotte and I were just talking about junior high, and she's still upset about a lot of stuff, so can you just do me a favor and apologize for all the spider crap?"

I held my breath and waited for what I knew would come next. Bryant would smirk, tilt his chin mockingly, and say, "Spider crap? Is that what they did in your desk? Gee, if I'd known, I would have provided you with a tiny roll of toilet paper."

Bryant did tilt his chin, but it was more with disbelief than in a mocking manner. I suddenly felt like a three-year-old who'd thrown a tantrum and so was being given my way.

"Uh . . . sorry about all of that." Bryant shrugged as though it didn't take any effort to pluck the words from his mouth. "I was just joking around."

And that's when I realized Colton was right about me. I felt no satisfaction. In fact, it disappointed me that Bryant could apologize so painlessly. What did that say about me?

"It's all right." I shrugged, matching Bryant's nonchalant stance even though my insides trembled. "So do we have a truce?"

"Sure. Truce." He smiled, but I wasn't sure if he meant it.

Then we stared at one another awkwardly while Colton beamed at the two of us like a marriage counselor who'd just made a major breakthrough. I didn't know what to say next or how to suddenly bridge into small talk, so I was glad when one of the guys yelled, "Bryant, are you in?"

With a quick good-bye he jogged back to the game.

Colton and I turned back to his car. "Well?" Colton asked. "Well?"

"Okay, you were right. He apologized."

"And?"

"And maybe I did have a chip on my shoulder about him."

Colton nodded, smiling. "See, I told you Bryant wasn't such a bad guy."

I didn't answer. I didn't know if Bryant was a bad guy or not, but for the first time, I was willing to try to give him the benefit of the doubt.

On the way home Colton and I talked about the winter dance. Specifically whether or not I had refreshments ordered. Which I didn't. "It's in a week from tomorrow," he told me, as though the date may have slipped my mind altogether. Then he offered me ideas for "Winter Wonderland" theme refreshments I could buy, such as holiday sugar cookies and hot spiced apple cider. I kept wondering if he was suggesting things because he wanted Olivia to have a good time.

At last he pulled up in front of my house. "I'll call bakeries today and find something to order," I said just so he'd stop worrying about it. "Gingerbread or snowmen or something with red and green frosting. Whatever is cheapest."

"Cheapest?" he asked, as though he'd never heard of the word before.

"Yeah. If we have money left over from our dance budget, we can spend more on the Santa project."

He turned in his seat, considering me with skeptical eyes. "And you're in charge of the decorations too?"

"It will be nicely done," I insisted. "Just not expensive."

He continued to stare at me. I could tell he didn't think it was possible to do both of those things at the same time.

"Really, it will be fine," I said. "More than fine. Perfect. And everyone at school will love NHS and think you're wonderful because you're the president of such a cool group."

"Good." He leaned back in his seat as though finally relaxed. One of his hands ran across his hair, smoothing down where the wind ruffled it during the ride. I put my hand on the door handle, but instead of opening it, I found myself admiring the way the sun lay in golden patches across his hair.

Why hadn't I made up with Colton while I had the chance? Then instead of taking Olivia to the dance, he'd be taking me.

I opened the door and stepped out, but before I shut the door, I turned back to him. "As long as we're all apologizing, I probably should tell you I'm sorry for having Reese throw sodas on you."

"You probably should," he said.

"I'm sorry about that and, you know, pushing you into the pool."

He shook his head and laughed. "It's okay, Charlotte." He gave me half a wave, then drove off. I watched him go, my gaze jogging after the car. It wasn't okay. It wasn't okay, because he wasn't taking me to the dance.

✤ ten ✤

The next day at school Colton and I split up the wish lists and we each took half to hand out. Even though I wanted to shop for Reese and T.J., we decided the girls should shop for the girls and the guys for the guys. That way Colton wouldn't be forced to search the doll aisles for a Barbie Ballerina or fairy princess and the St. Matthew's girls wouldn't have to wear outfits that the NHS guys put together. I mean, even the poor have dignity.

As we walked to lunch I handed Kelly her list. She took it from me, but didn't read it. "When do you think Wesley will go shopping?"

"I have no idea."

"Why don't you find out, let me know, and then we can arrange to bump into him."

"Kelly—"

She lowered her voice and walked nearer to me. "You said you'd help me with Wesley. You promised."

"And it turns out I'm a lousy matchmaker. Besides, I've called a truce with Bryant, so—"

Kelly grabbed my elbow. "There he is—over by the drinking fountain. Go talk to him." She made a sharp turn and walked away, leaving me standing in the hallway.

I stood there for a moment while students flowed around me and locker doors thudded shut. I tried to think of a good reason—or actually any reason—to talk to Wesley. When I came up with a pathetic inkling of an idea, I trudged over to him. He finished taking a drink, saw me, and gave me a brief nod. I stood in his way so he couldn't leave.

"Hi, Wesley." I fingered the lists I hadn't given out yet and prayed he didn't know Colton and I had split up the papers by gender. "Do you have your list of stuff to buy for the St. Matthew's kids yet?" I flipped through my stack as though looking for a paper with his name on it.

Wesley tilted his head at me. "Yeah. Colton gave me mine. He has the guy lists."

Great. He knew.

"Oh yeah. Right." I held the papers against my chests and felt myself blushing. "So you already have your list. When are you planning on going shopping?"

His eyebrows drew together like he was trying to figure out why I was bugging him about it. "Soon," he said. "I mean, I just got the list today."

I fluttered one hand in his direction. "I wasn't implying there was a hurry, or you wouldn't get it done, or anything. I know you're really responsible. I was just . . . you know . . . shooting the breeze."

"Oh." He nodded. "I don't know. Maybe I'll go sometime after wrestling practice."

"You mean today? Today after wrestling practice?"

Instead of looking at me, his glance darted around me as though he wanted to sprint down the hallway. "Uh, maybe."

He took a step forward, but I scooted over so I still stood in front of him. I couldn't let him get away now, because there was no way I could corner him some other time today to find out the necessary information.

"Bloomingdale's said they'd give us thirty percent off. And of course Wal-Mart always has a good selection. I'm not sure where I'll go. How about you? Do you know where you'll go shopping yet?"

Wesley's eyes took on a look of panic. He was probably imagining me chasing him down the hallway throwing more questions at him. He took a small step sideways. "I don't know. I'll probably check the ads first."

Still no good. Kelly would no doubt insist I keep pestering him until I found out more details. By the end of the day, he would either think I was in love with him or psychotic.

Wesley took another step to try to get around me, but I reached out and grabbed hold of his wrist. "Wesley, can you do both of us a favor?"

The look of panic grew. "What?"

"Can you please just ask Kelly out so I don't have to follow you around all day like some stalker, trying to find out where you'll be and when you'll be there? I'm too busy to do it, and besides, I can't think of a reasonable excuse for the two of us to bump into you in the boys' underwear section of Bloomingdale's anyway. So I'm just not going to try. Okay?"

He relaxed, but not much. "Okay."

I let go of his wrist. "Great. I'm glad we've had this little talk." Then I turned around and walked to the cafeteria.

When I got to our table, Kelly, Aleeta, and Brianna all looked up at me.

"How did it go?" Aleeta asked.

"Good." I put my tray on the table and sat down.

"So did you find out where he's going shopping?" Kelly asked.

"Oh, well, not really." But he probably wouldn't issue a restraining order against me, so it was still good. I opened my milk carton and inserted the straw. "I'll keep working on it though."

I fully planned never to go out of my way to speak to Wesley again, but what Kelly didn't know wouldn't hurt her.

I spent Friday night and a good part of Saturday misting shoppers with the latest pop-star perfume. (Like any of us know what celebrities actually smell like anyway. Which just goes to show you another harsh truth about shoppers—they're gullible.) Then I walked around the mall buying stuff for my St. Matthew's girls. As irony would have it, I almost bumped into Wesley. I saw him heading to the electronics section at Sears and nearly had to dive through a vacuum cleaner display in order to get away from him.

I mean, after our talk I didn't want him to think I was following him around anyway.

Late Saturday night Kelly called me, sounding both happy and hesitant. "Wesley asked me to the winter dance."

I put the phone between my chin and my shoulder so I could wrap one of the outfits I'd bought that day. "That's great!"

"Did you really threaten to stalk him if he didn't?"

"What? No, I just suggested he ask you out, you know, so I didn't have to make up excuses for the two of you to run into each other."

Kelly let out a disgruntled sigh. "When you said you were a lousy matchmaker, I didn't know you meant it so literally. I mean, now I don't know if he really likes me or whether he's just afraid of you."

I folded a piece of wrapping paper around the box. "He likes you. Colton told me so."

"Colton?" Her voice rose in distress. "Colton knows I like Wesley? How many people did you tell?"

"Just Colton. Stop worrying. You'll have a great time at the winter dance."

She let out another sigh, this time resigned. "Since Wesley asked me Saturday morning, I felt obligated to spy on Bryant for you."

"You didn't have to do that," I said. "Remember, I called a truce with Bryant."

"Thanks for telling me that now. I spent an hour and a half sitting in my car down the street from Bryant's house. Luckily, I brought my cell phone with me so I could talk to Aleeta. Most of the conversation was about how paranoid you are."

"Thanks," I said.

"Well, sorry, but I was afraid one of the neighbors would see me parked out there and call the police. I made Aleeta check on the Internet to see if spying on someone was an arrestable offense. She never found out for sure, so I'm still half-expecting a police officer to show up on my doorstep."

I pressed a piece of tape against the wrapping paper. "Sitting for long periods in your car can't be against the law. People do it every day during rush-hour traffic."

"There wasn't any traffic. Just me, a couple joggers, and Bryant's dad painting the trim on their house."

The tape dispenser squealed as I pulled off another piece of tape. "Bryant's dad was painting the trim on his house?"

"Yeah. Not something you'd generally do when you have houseguests. I hate to say this, but maybe you were right about Bryant lying to Brianna."

Neither Kelly nor I spoke for a moment. Finally I said, "Maybe his dad wanted the house to look nice for company."

"Right. And maybe he's the type that isn't embarrassed to have guests see him splattered with paint. It is possible. Maybe that dinner they had with Bryant's

aunt was the really casual type you can wear your painting clothes to."

"Did you see anyone besides Bryant's dad?" I asked.
"Bryant or the aunt?"

"I never saw an aunt, but Bryant pulled out of his
garage at six and drove off."

I held the tape limply in my hands. "He drove
off?"

"Yes. I'm not exactly sure what he wore, since I had
to duck under my dashboard as he drove past, but it
looked like that green cardigan Brianna bought him for
his birthday. I think he was dressed up."

I didn't want to hear this. Not now. I had the irrational urge to tell Kelly to stop it, to tell her she wasn't
being fair. Instead, I let out a slow breath. I'd just go
through this conversation logically, without bias in one
direction or the other. It would all make sense if I
found out the details. "Did you follow him to see where
he went?"

"No."

"Well, why not?"

"Because I'm a teenage girl, Charlotte, not an un-
dercover agent. I figured Bryant would notice me trail-
ing him around town if I drove off after him."

I fingered a piece of tape, not paying attention to
where I put it on the wrapping paper. "It doesn't necessarily mean he lied to Brianna. Maybe his mom sent
him to the store for something for dinner, or he went
to the airport to pick his aunt up, or something."

"You don't get dressed up to go to the store or the
airport," Kelly said.

"There might still be a logical explanation. We shouldn't jump to conclusions."

A pause filled the line, then Kelly's voice sounding crisper. "Who is this, and can I please speak to Charlotte?"

"Very funny. I know it's not like me to give Bryant the benefit of the doubt, but I'm trying to have a better attitude about him." I folded the wrapping paper over the top of the box and added the last piece of tape. "Which at this moment is taking a lot of effort."

"So we don't tell Brianna anything about Bryant?"

I stared at the package and thought of Brianna, then Bryant, then Colton. "We don't have anything concrete to tell her. It's all just suspicions. We'd be spreading rumors if we said anything now."

"Okay." Kelly let out a relieved sigh. "But that means my part of the bargain is done, and you're still in charge of decorations, right?"

"Right." I wasn't likely to forget about that. Half my fingers were nicked from where pinecones had pricked me while I glued them into centerpieces.

It was just one more reason, and suddenly I could think of many, to never try to find out if your best friend's boyfriend is cheating on her.

The next week at school I spent a lot of time watching Colton, thinking of Colton, and finding reasons to talk to Colton. I talked with him about every detail of the service project and dance. No member of NHS had ever put as much effort into consulting with their president over upcoming events as I did. And he seemed to enjoy talking to me. He smiled when he saw me—a sly sort of smile, like he knew why I was suddenly so conscientious. He asked how my sisters were. He asked what my plans for Christmas were. He never, however, asked me out.

I wondered how serious he was with Olivia, and if he would look at her the same way he looked at me at Candice's party.

Thursday morning at breakfast I grumbled to my family that I had yet to receive any snowflakes from the seniors who said they'd make them for me, and I was bound to be up half the night cutting them out.

Dad spread butter on his bagel. "You don't need snowflakes for your dance. Just tell everyone it's a California winter, so you're decorating with tourists."

"Find the people who said they'd help and remind them," Mom said. "You need to study for your midterms, not make decorations."

Julianne spooned cereal into her mouth. "I'll help you make snowflakes. What color do you want them to be?"

"White," I said, and figured that anyone who had to ask was not going to be a lot of help.

After breakfast I rounded up every pair of scissors in the house, took them to school, and had Brianna hand them out. I figured people would actually make snowflakes if she asked, since she's Miss Socialite and has no visible chips on her shoulders. And of course, everyone made them for her. What started as a bit of surreptitious snipping turned into a fad by second period, and then a political statement at lunchtime. Half the senior class cut up old homework assignments and made them into snowflakes. I had unknowingly touched a nerve, a massive longing of the student body to purge their notebooks and cut holes into the things our teachers had forced us to study.

Brianna gave me so many snowflakes, I couldn't fit any more of them on my locker shelf. I had to stack the rest in Ms. Ellis's science classroom.

I didn't bring them home with me. What was the point when I'd just have to haul them back to school on Friday to decorate the gymnasium?

This turned out to be a good thing, since at dinnertime Julianne and Evelynn dumped an armful of paper snowflakes on the table.

"We didn't want you to have to cut them all by yourself," Evelynn told me.

"I made the pink ones," Julianne added, "because I wanted them to be snowflakes you see during the sunset."

Mom laughed. "I didn't have time to make you any snowflakes, but I didn't want you to miss studying, so I called a friend of mine who works at Party City and asked if they could donate anything. I've got a box of streamers in my car."

Dad sifted through the paper, moving it off the table and onto the countertop. "I'm surrounded by flakes."

I picked up a few that had fluttered onto the ground and put them on the counter. "No, you're surrounded by very nice people."

I stayed after school on Friday taping enough snowflakes onto the gymnasium wall and ceiling to qualify them for blizzard status. While I did this, Wesley and Harris lugged in artificial trees, a glow-in-the-dark Frosty the Snowman, and a small herd of light-up reindeer that I'd liberated from my front yard. I stretched the streamers from the middle of the ceiling to the side of the wall, and then let their ends dangle down behind the refreshment tables. I hoped to create a focal point so the eye would be drawn to the food, but when I was done, it just looked like I'd forgotten to decorate the rest of the ceiling.

So then I added more streamers, which connected from the ceiling to the opposite side of the room, where the deejay would be. We still had a ton of streamers left, so I added some more for balance, until Wesley looked at me and said, "I thought it was a winter theme. Why are you making the room look like some sort of huge Maypole?"

My mom makes decorating look so easy.

I went back to taping snowflakes on the wall. After putting up approximately two million, my arms ached, and then I ran out of tape. I still had snowflakes left over, and it was a shame to throw them away, since I'd insisted people make them for me. Plus, I had the irrational fear that everyone was going to walk around the gym looking for the snowflakes they made, and they'd be all ticked off if they found them in the garbage can. I laid the last few dozen across the tablecloth on the refreshment table.

After a quick dinner at home, I went to the bakery to pick up the cookies. Preeth was in charge of the drinks, which I was glad of while I was lugging boxes of cookies into the gymnasium—because I couldn't have carried them and gallons of hot spiced apple cider— but which I became less glad of when I saw her. She'd brought glass pitchers instead of insulated thermoses.

"You were supposed to heat up the cider at your house and bring it to school in the thermoses," I said as I brought in the last batch of cookies.

She shrugged and heaved a gallon jug of cider onto the table. "I decided it would be easier to use the microwaves in the school kitchen."

I picked up a gallon of cider, walked to the cafeteria, and tried the kitchen doors even though I knew they were locked. Ms. Ellis had told us during the first planning meeting that the school was very particular about who they let have access to the kitchen. Only the cafeteria ladies held the keys, and rumor was, you had to fight them gladiator-style in order to be considered a worthy key recipient.

I walked back to the gymnasium, hurrying so quickly the cider swished back and forth. "The kitchen is locked," I told Preeth.

She looked from me to the cider. "We can always serve it cold, then."

"We could if we had ice." I checked my watch. Six-fifty. "Where is Ms. Ellis?"

Preeth nodded toward the deejay. "She and her fiancé are looking at the music selection."

Over by the deejay, a tall, thin man draped his arms around Ms. Ellis's shoulders. He whispered something into her ear, and she laughed. I doubted this was a good time to request that she run to the store and buy ice for us.

I glanced at my watch again, as though it might change its mind and give me a few more minutes. "Maybe we can catch someone who's on their way here and ask them to bring some."

While I grabbed my phone from my purse Harris wandered up to the table. He picked up a cookie and chomped on it while he looked around. "By the way, what's with all the streamers?"

"They're decorations."

"Oh." He tilted his head up, considering them. "It's sort of like being in a circus tent."

I shot him a dark look and punched in Brianna's number on my cell phone. He quickly added, "Not that a circus tent is a bad thing. I mean, no one pays all that much attention to the decorations anyway." His eyes narrowed as he surveyed the room. "And what are those pink blobs on the wall by the DJ?"

"They're snowflakes my little sister made. She likes pink."

He nodded. "Oh. Well, we can just tell people those are the snowflakes tainted with industrial pollution." Harris picked up another cookie and popped it into his mouth, probably as an excuse to stop talking to me.

I turned away from him when Brianna picked up her phone with a "Hello?"

"Hi, Bri, can you do me a favor?" As I spoke, I ripped open a package of napkins and set them on the table.

"Sure. What do you need?"

"Ice for the cider. Can you stop by a convenience store and pick some up?"

"Oh." A pause. "Bryant and I aren't actually going to the dance."

Several napkins fluttered to the floor, and I bent down to pick them up. "What do you mean you're not going to the dance?"

"Bryant decided he wanted to go to a movie instead."

"A movie?" I stacked more napkins into a crooked paper tower. "You can go to a movie anytime. This is the Winter Wonderland dance. You made snowflakes for this."

"I know. He doesn't feel like dancing."

"Tell him we have both reindeer sugar cookies and double chocolate chip cookies." I'd ordered the reindeer cookies to match the theme, and the double chocolate chip because I was not about to watch Olivia and Colton dancing together unless I had chocolate. "Tell Bryant I'll save a chocolate chip one for him." I cast a glance at Harris. "Well, if you hurry anyway."

"Sorry, Charlotte, we're about to go into the theater. I have to hang up now. Bye."

I held the phone in my hand, completely forgetting about the ice. Bryant just decided he didn't want to go to the dance? Why? I could think of only one reason, and that was because he didn't want Olivia to see him with Brianna.

I hated having these suspicions, but they didn't seem to want to go away.

Next I called Kelly and Wesley. They didn't pick up. Aleeta was en route, but didn't have any money on her. It was nearly seven o'clock, and the deejay played the first song. People wandered into the gym in a steady stream, although none of them seemed to be dying of thirst just yet.

I dug through my purse for my car keys so I could get the ice, then looked up to see Colton and Olivia walking toward the refreshment table.

❧ *eleven* ❧

Olivia wore a silky red blouse and a pair of jeans, which even though they were made out of the same denim that mine had been constructed from looked ritzier. Maybe because she wore red high heels with them. Maybe because the expression on her face, the elevation of her chin, and the swing of her hips all made her look like a runway model coming down the catwalk.

Colton turned his attention to the spread of food. "Hi, guys. Got everything set up?"

"Just about," I said.

Olivia looked at me with a raised eyebrow. "You're in charge of refreshments? That's ironic."

As far as I knew, Olivia had no idea who I was, let alone whether I had any refreshment committee skills. I'd only seen her at the mall, and she hadn't seen me there at all.

I looked from her to Colton, and then back to her. "Oh? Why is that?"

She shrugged and a smile slid across her face. "Aren't you the one who had some refreshment problems at Candice's party?"

My cheeks suddenly felt warm, but I tried to keep my composure. I'd forgotten she'd gone to that party. "Yeah, that was me." And then because Preeth and Harris both turned to stare at me, I added, "I ran into a waiter and made him spill a tray of food."

"Not just spill—I think they're still cleaning watermelon fragments off of the walls. But that's not what I was talking about." Olivia forced another laugh and tossed her long red hair off her shoulder. "I meant when you ate part of the table centerpiece."

Harris puffed out an amused chortle. "Charlotte, you ate a centerpiece?"

"They were cherry tomatoes," I said. "I didn't realize they were there as decorations."

Olivia leaned closer to me in a confiding manner. "See those strings of popcorn on the Christmas tree? They're off-limits."

Harris and Preeth both laughed at this, but I couldn't muster more than a smile.

Harris elbowed me. "Hey, now I know why you wanted paper decorations. They're less tempting, eh?"

"Well, I have to do what I can to keep my weight down," I said.

Olivia picked up one of the snowflakes from the table and held it up. "Is that what this is? A decoration?"

"It's a snowflake," I said.

"Oh, right. I can see that now." She tossed it back on the table. "*Ars gratia artis.*"

"You speak French?" Harris asked in awe—like producing a phrase from another country was some exotic accomplishment and not something we all did every day in our foreign language classes.

"Yes, I speak French," Olivia said. "But that was Latin."

"Latin . . .," Harris murmured.

I folded my arms and staunchly refused to be impressed, because hey, no one speaks Latin anymore. It's only used to describe medical conditions, to say the occasional Mass, and apparently to impress smart guys.

"I speak Spanish," I said to no one in particular. "Fluently."

Colton picked up a couple of the chocolate chip cookies and held one out for Olivia. "Do you want something to eat?"

"Too messy." She waved off his hand and picked up a sugar cookie instead. "With my luck, I'd get chocolate chips on my shirt. And you know how awful it is to get chocolate out of silk."

No, actually I didn't.

Olivia giggled as she nibbled on the edge of her cookie. "It's a Juicy."

Harris looked at her blankly. "Your cookie is juicy?"

"No. The shirt." She tossed her hair off her shoulders so we could get a better look at her blouse. "It's a Juicy Couture."

Preeth nodded. "Oh, you mean it's one of those brands with a silly name like Guess."

"It's not at all like Guess." Olivia took another bite of her cookie. "You can get Guess anywhere."

Colton picked up the pitcher. "Do you want something to drink, Olivia?" He poured juice into a Styrofoam cup without waiting for her answer. "Have some hot apple cider."

"Um . . .," I said.

"Be careful," Colton added. "You might need to blow on it."

"Actually . . .," I said.

Olivia picked up the cup and took a sip. She didn't spit it out, although her facial expression indicated she wanted to.

After she managed to swallow, she put the cup down on the table and looked at me. "That isn't hot. It's room temperature."

Colton had poured a glass for himself, and now he held it to his lips, sampling it like he was determining whether it had been a good year for apples. "Why isn't this hot?"

I opened my mouth to answer him, to explain I was on my way to get ice, but somehow looking at Olivia— who in the two minutes she'd been here had managed to insult me, the decorations, the food, and our knowledge of high-end designer brands—I just couldn't give her one more thing to be disdainful about. "We haven't had a chance to heat it up yet," I said.

Colton replaced his cup on the table. "Well, you should hurry. People are starting to come."

"We're working on it right now," I said.

The deejay put on a slow song, and Olivia took hold of Colton's elbow and leaned in close to him. "This is one of my favorite songs. Let's dance."

"Sure." Colton shot me a look. "I'll be back to check on you later. I mean, you know, the refreshments." Then he turned and let Olivia pull him out on the dance floor.

Preeth watched them go. "Why did you tell Colton we were serving the cider hot? I thought you said you were going to buy ice."

I picked up a chocolate chip cookie and bit off a piece. "Did either of you like Olivia?"

"Total snob," Preeth said.

"Yeah, but she's hot," Harris added.

Preeth glared at him. I smacked him in the shoulder. "Okay, your opinion doesn't count, Harris. Preeth and I didn't like her, and so we're not about to give her another reason to look down on us."

Harris cocked his head. "How does serving cold cider give her a reason to look down on us?"

"You're a guy. You wouldn't understand. The point is, we're serving the cider hot."

Preeth fingered the handle on one of the pitchers. "You just said we couldn't get into kitchen."

"True. But we're all National Honor Society members, so between the three of us, we ought to be able to figure out a way to heat liquid."

"Right." Harris nodded slowly. "Anyone got a bunch of magnifying glasses, flint, or a particle accelerator?"

"How about a cup warmer?" Preeth said. "Ms. Ellis has one of those in her class room."

I shook my head. "It would take forever to warm an entire pitcher."

"A Bunsen burner would do it fast enough," Harris said. "And there are plenty of those in the science room."

I considered the idea as I looked down at the refreshment table. "I think the room is still unlocked from when I got all the snowflakes out. We could heat up the pitchers there, then bring them back here. Well, if they didn't get too hot." I suddenly imagined myself rushing through the hallways carrying a heated glass pitcher while I tried not to spill scalding water on myself or the school floor.

Perhaps Harris had a similar visual because he said, "It would be easier to heat them up here."

"Except Bunsen burners work on natural gas, and we don't have any of that down here," Preeth said.

Harris shrugged. "I've got a propane tank out in my dad's truck. He uses it for welding, but I don't think he'd mind if we borrowed it."

"Do you know how to use it?" I asked.

Harris gave a small laugh. "I use it all the time when we're camping. It shouldn't be hard to rig something up." He took a set of keys from his pocket and jingled them in his hand. "I'll go get the tank while you guys grab a couple of Bunsen burners."

He walked away from us, still jingling his keys. Preeth turned to me. "You stay here and man the table. I'll get the Bunsen burners."

It did occur to me after she left that we should have gotten Ms. Ellis's okay on this venture—only I knew Ms. Ellis wouldn't okay it. I mean, this was the woman who didn't want any decorations that could be thrown by teenage boys. She wasn't going to let us have anything in the room that had flames shooting out of it.

I glanced at the dance floor. Ms. Ellis was obliviously dancing with her fiancé. Oblivion is a good mental state to keep teachers in. Hopefully, she wouldn't notice the Bunsen burners at the refreshment table— or if she did, it would be after we'd heated the cider.

I ate a cookie and then another one while simultaneously tracking Olivia and Colton dance across the room. They looked like every other couple out on the dance floor, but I watched Colton intently anyway, as though I could determine how much he cared for her by the position of his elbows.

After a few minutes Harris came back and then Preeth. They set up the makeshift cider heater behind the refreshment table so it wasn't visible unless you leaned over the table to look for it. While we waited for the pitchers to heat up, I handed out cookies to everyone who walked up. I explained about the cider, always checking to see if Colton and Olivia were on their way back.

With my luck they wouldn't return. They'd never know we were able to pull off a decent holiday drink, and therefore I'd continue to remain the girl who wasn't competent enough to serve food.

Colton moved easily on the dance floor, as confident there as he was in an NHS meeting or wrestling match. Olivia, however, didn't dance well. She hardly put any effort into it, like she was just too cool to be enthusiastic.

Why did he even like her? Well, I mean besides the fact that she'd never pushed him in a pool, or anything.

A guy named Josiah from my calculus class walked up to the table. I handed him a cookie, then made a bit of small talk—stalling—while I waited for the cider. After a minute I figured he was probably really thirsty and just too polite to demand a drink, so I made my standard disclaimer about the temperature of the cider and asked if he wanted some anyway.

"Oh, I'm fine," he said, looking out at the dance floor and not at me. "I don't know why I'm here anyway. Some friends said I should come with them; but of course, they're all out dancing, and I have nothing to do."

Which is an example of how smart people can really be stupid sometimes. "It's a dance," I said.

He gave me a look that indicated he was also pondering that smart people can really be stupid. I clarified my statement. "You're not supposed to just hang out with your friends. The whole point of coming is that you ask girls to dance."

"Oh yeah . . . right," he said. "Is the cider hot now?"

I had known before that Josiah was shy, but I hadn't realized how shy until now.

"Nope, sorry. Maybe in a few more minutes. Do you want to dance with me in the meantime?"

"Oh." He blushed, but didn't flee. "All right." And it was as easy as that. The guy who was too shy to dance and the girl who wouldn't be asked to dance because she'd offended all of the guys in her school had solved their problems. Well, at least for one song anyway.

I left my post at the table, assuring Preeth and Harris I'd come back in a while to relieve them so they could dance, which neither of them seemed very enthusiastic about doing. I figured this meant I didn't need to hurry back. After I danced with Josiah, I noticed some guys from NHS standing around talking, which they totally shouldn't have been doing, since NHS sponsored the event and did they not see all the girls flanking the sides of the gym? So then I had to go and ask each one of them to dance so I could give them a pep talk about the merits of socializing.

Which also gave me a better view of Olivia and Colton, even though I was not staring at them. Well, at least not all of the time.

Her stunning lack of rhythm did not improve.

After about half an hour the two of them walked back over to the refreshment table and got drinks. I watched them, happy to know Olivia could no longer complain about the cider's temperature.

Some other guys came up to the table and seemed to know Olivia because they all started talking and she kept smiling at them. As the minutes went by, I wondered if Colton would get jealous, but he talked with the guys too, and didn't seem bothered by the situation.

The song ended, and I wandered over to the refreshment table. I looked at Preeth and Harris so I didn't have to look at Colton.

"You finally came back to relieve us," Harris said, and then before I could reply, he added, "All the cider on the table is cool enough to serve. It stays at optimum temperature for roughly five minutes. The Bunsen burners are on their lowest setting, but the cider in the pitchers is still pretty hot, so let it cool down a bit before giving it to anyone." He stepped around the table. "Got that?"

"Sure," I said.

Preeth followed Harris around the table, which I hadn't expected. "You're leaving too?" I asked. "I thought you didn't like to dance."

"Harris is going to teach me how to do the country swing," she said, and then the two of them walked off without another glance in my direction.

Colton turned from his group to me. "I can help you for a few minutes." Without waiting for an answer, he put one hand on Olivia's arm. "You don't mind if I help Charlotte with the refreshments, do you?"

Olivia tossed me a look over her shoulder and feigned a smile. "Well, someone had better help her if food is involved." Then she turned her attention back to the other guys and giggled about something. Probably me.

Colton came around to my side of table, and Olivia and company threw away their empty cups. The group then strolled off in the direction of the dance floor without saying good-bye. Not that I cared.

Colton tilted his head and looked behind me. "What are the pitchers doing on the floor?"

"They're keeping warm."

"Bad idea. You'll knock into one and tip it over."

"No, I won't. I know they're there." I took a step away from the pitchers just so he'd feel better.

He let out a sigh that indicated he shared Olivia's view of my inability to handle the complicated nature of refreshments. "Wouldn't it be easier to put the pitchers on the table?"

"Well, Ms. Ellis might not appreciate us using her Bunsen burners to warm cider. Preeth thought we should keep them hidden."

Colton's eyes narrowed as he took a closer look at the pitchers. "You're using Bunsen burners as a kitchen appliance?" He let out a slow sigh, then surveyed me. "You know, you could have just told me you didn't want to be in charge of refreshments."

"Preeth was supposed to warm it at home and bring it in insulated containers. When she didn't, we had to improvise."

He looked out into the darkness of the dance floor and shook his head. "You know, Charlotte, when I said we could cut costs on the dance, this wasn't what I had in mind. Thank goodness I didn't put you in charge of music, or right now you'd be in front of a microphone with a harmonica, wouldn't you?"

"You don't have to help me if you don't want to," I said. "I can pass out cookies and man the cider all by myself, you know. I'm both capable and competent, so if you'd rather go hang out with Miss Look-at-Me-I'm-Wearing-a-Designer-Shirt, go right ahead."

He cracked a smile, and his gaze slid back to me. "You don't like Olivia, do you?"

I straightened a row of cups, rolling my eyes as I did. "And to think you questioned my taste in guys."

"Olivia isn't that bad. Well, she's not as bad as Greg anyway."

"Which is why I dumped Greg. Well, okay, technically he dumped me, but I wasn't sad about it, which counts as the same thing."

Still smiling, he leaned toward me. "You're jealous, aren't you?"

"Why would I be jealous of her?"

"Because she has what you don't."

"Which would be what? A bad hairdresser, poor rhythm, or a striking lack of financial sense when it comes to buying clothes?"

His smile grew. "Admit it, you're jealous."

"I'm not jealous." I straightened the napkins into a tall stack. "Rich people are so arrogant. You all think everyone just sits around coveting your wealth. Well, my happiness isn't dependent on my bank account numbers."

He gave a mock grunt. "I wasn't talking about Olivia's money. I was talking about me."

"Oh." It was suddenly hard to breathe.

Colton picked up a glass of cider and took a sip. "We're not a couple—Olivia and me. So if you want to flirt with me, it's all right." He was teasing, but there was also truth mixed into this game. Perhaps more truth than he knew, and I felt as though everything inside of me was stretched tight.

I didn't want to face him, so I kept my gaze centered

out on the dance floor. "I see. Should I bat my eye-lashes, or were you thinking along the lines of point-less small talk?"

"Actually, I like the way you keep looking at me."

"I don't keep looking at you."

"Yes, you do."

I didn't look at him, just to prove the point. If he had admitted he liked me too, this discussion would be much easier. But he hadn't said anything along those lines, so I didn't know if this was playful banter or some horrible exposé on my pitiful crush.

"If you're not a couple with Olivia, then why did you bring her to the dance?"

He shrugged and took another sip of his drink. "She asked if Bryant and I wanted to take a tour of Stanford and then go to a play on campus. I told her I couldn't, because I had to go to an NHS dance. Then she said she liked dancing, and the rest just sort of happened."

"Oh." I tried not to smile too much about this news, because I figured Colton didn't need more evidence of my crush.

He scanned the dance floor as though noticing for the first time his friend's absence. "Where are Bryant and Brianna?"

"They decided to go to a movie instead."

His eyebrow raised. "Really? I thought Brianna wanted to come."

"She did."

Colton took another sip of his drink as though it didn't matter, but with that one phrase my suspicions

not only popped up again but settled comfortably into
the corners of my mind. I was not trying to feed them,
but suspicions have a way of making themselves at
home and rummaging through your fridge without permission. "So it's strange that they went to the movies
instead of the dance," I said, even though Colton was
no longer considering this fact.

I handed out a couple of cookies and some drinks to
passing students; then when we were alone again, I
turned to Colton. "Did Bryant's aunt come to town last
Saturday?"

"Not likely. His aunt teaches at Oregon State.
They're probably having finals."

This was the equivalent of standing in front of my
hungry suspicions and yelling, "The pizza's here!"

I ran my fingers over the tablecloth. I'd been so
careful to get the right color of red, but in the dim
light it looked dark brown. Which was one more way,
I suppose, that I'd done a lousy job decorating the gym.
"Bryant told Brianna that his aunt came to dinner last
Saturday," I said. "He broke a date because of it."

Colton drank the last of his cider and tossed his cup
in the garbage. "Is this more Bryant-bashing? Don't you
remember how he apologized and you said you were
going to get along with him?"

"I am trying to get along with him. I'm just wondering why he told Brianna he couldn't go out with her
because his aunt was coming to dinner, when Kelly saw
him leaving his house dressed nicely while his dad
worked on painting the trim of their house."

Colton folded his arms. His jaw twitched. "Did you send your friends to spy on Bryant?"

He made it sound like such a bad thing. I didn't answer him.

"Charlotte," he said.

"Okay, yes, I did, but that was before he apologized to me, and I hadn't started trying to get along with him yet."

"And now you are?"

"Colton, you don't understand." I took a step toward him, making a sweeping motion with one arm as though I could explain it to him with hand gestures. I wasn't trying to accuse Bryant—I just wanted an explanation. I wanted Colton to suddenly remember that Bryant had several aunts, one of which liked to drop in and help people paint their houses.

All my gesture did was manage to do was knock over my napkin tower and send several fluttering to the floor. Colton took a step away from me. "I understand perfectly, Charlotte. If I hang out with you and I'm still friends with Bryant, then sooner or later I'm going to end up drenched again because you can't let go of the past. You're so sure that—" He stopped suddenly and straightened up. "What's that smell?"

"Smell?" I repeated, and immediately smelled the acrid scent of burning plastic. Turning, I noticed a cloud of smoke billowing up from the end of the table. I gasped, then yelped, "Colton, the tablecloth is on fire!"

I knew exactly what had happened. The napkins I knocked off the table had landed on the Bunsen

burner, started a flame, and now that flame was looking around to see what else it could consume. I had
thoughtfully provided it with not only a tablecloth but
dozens of paper snowflakes and a napkin tower.

Colton scanned the room, searching the gymnasium
walls. "Where's a fire extinguisher?"

"I don't know." But I did know where liquid was. As
the fire climbed to the top of the table, I picked up two
cups of cider and threw them in that direction. The
flames flickered for a moment, then continued their
march toward the cookies. I grabbed two more cups
and repeated the process.

Colton picked up cups to help me. He mumbled
several things under his breath, and I'm pretty sure he
fired me from the refreshment committee, but I was
too busy pouring cider on the table to answer him.

The thing about being in a darkened room is that
people tend to notice when there is suddenly a lot of
light, like say, a table lit up like a bonfire, and they
begin to swarm around you gasping and yelling, but
not really doing anything to help. I mean, someone
actually called out, "Stop, drop, and roll!" Which is
handy information if you yourself are on fire, but not
such good advice if you're trying to extinguish blazing
cookies.

I started to panic—not because the fire was so big,
but because I suddenly realized I'd spent all afternoon
taping kindling to the walls and ceiling. I'd also dangled
streamers over the table, which is just the sort of thing
you want hanging over flames. Then Ms. Ellis pushed

her way through the crowd with the fire extinguisher and sprayed down the table.

I don't think I breathed at all throughout the duration of the fire, so it's probably a good thing that it only lasted for about a minute—just long enough to draw everyone's attention to me pitching cider at the refreshments, to create a nasty cloud of smoke, and oh yeah, for me to slosh cider onto Colton's shirt.

This was an especially bad omen, since the last words he'd said to me before the fire were, "If I hang out with you and I'm still friends with Bryant, then sooner or later I'm going to end up drenched again."

I stared at Colton's shirt. "You're not that wet," I told him.

Breathing hard, he looked from the smoldering refreshments to me. "What?"

"You didn't get drenched," I said. "Just a little splattered."

His eyes narrowed momentarily like he didn't know what I was talking about, and then a flicker of understanding passed over his features.

He didn't have time to reply, however, because just then the smoke alarm and sprinkler system kicked on.

Usually I hate the shrill ring of the fire alarm, but tonight it was sort of nice, since it masked the shrieks of the student body as they went running from the gym. I mean, okay, so the sprinkler system is misnamed. It wasn't a light sprinkle, but more like a torrential downpour, but still, it was just water. Water is not going to hurt you, well, at least not unless you were stupid enough to pay a lot of money for a designer silk shirt. Then you may have a reason to pick up a folding chair and hold it over your head like an umbrella while you scramble across the room screaming. And I did feel bad for Olivia as I watched her do this.

But still, there was no need for everyone else to get hysterical. Especially not Ms. Ellis. Oh, she wasn't hysterical at the sprinkler part. She became hysterical later as Harris explained about the Bunsen burners and I explained how I'd accidentally knocked a couple of napkins off the table. She called us many names, none of which are usually associated with National Honor Society members. Then she made us clean up every single soggy snowflake in the room while she went outside to tell three fire trucks that we weren't in need of their services.

Colton and I were never alone together as we cleaned up, which was probably a good thing, since really, I didn't want to hear his assessment of the matter.

❧ twelve ❧

Brianna has a warped sense of humor. I know this because she wouldn't stop laughing when I called her Saturday morning and told her what happened. I mean, all night I worried about how I was going to face everyone at school when they knew I'd accidentally set the refreshments on fire. I also worried about the trouble I was going to get into with the administration for unauthorized Bunsen burner use, and whether or not the deejay throwing himself over his speakers in order to protect them had actually worked.

After the sprinklers shut off, the deejay carried the sound system back to his truck, cradling it in his arms like it was an injured child, and Colton shook his head and said, "I'm *so* glad I didn't let you talk me into using my stereo equipment." Then he didn't say anything else, and he left to take Olivia home.

He was mad at me, and I didn't know how to fix it.

Also, Olivia would undoubtedly tell everyone she knew what I'd done, and then I'd be forever banned from social gatherings and have to go to college in some distant state where they didn't know about my troubled refreshment history.

And was nearly setting the gym on fire something that showed up on your high school transcript?

See, a good friend would be concerned for you instead of laughing so hard that she had to keep gasping for air.

"Colton will eventually get over it," Brianna told me when she could finally talk. "He's only mad now because he's the president of NHS, so he'll get blamed for the fire too."

"Maybe," I said. I hadn't told her about our disagreement over Bryant right beforehand. "I'll be sure to let the principal and everybody else at school know he didn't have anything to do with it."

"And apologize to Colton again when you see him," Brianna said. "Be extra nice, and he'll forget all about Olivia."

Well, I didn't know if he'd actually forget Olivia. Probably the image of her hefting a chair over her head and swearing in three different languages was burned into his memory like it was into mine, but still Brianna had a point.

On Monday I got all sorts of abuse about the dance. People sang, "Raindrops keep falling on my head because I set off the smoke detector," and various versions of "Singing in the Rain." I also heard, "Hey, you sure made a splash at the dance!" "Next time the theme can be Noah's Ark!" and "What does NHS stand for? Nice Hot Shower? Not Highly Sensible? Never Heard of Safety?" And about three hundred other variations.

The principal called Harris, Preeth, Colton, and me into his office to lecture us about responsibility, liability, safety rules, and fire hazards. I didn't think he'd ever get tired of telling us about what could have happened and reciting every awful inferno story he'd ever heard. I mean, by the time he finished, I'd developed a firm paranoia of anything related to fire and might never be able to light a candle, use an electric appliance, or stand near a birthday cake again.

Since Harris, Preeth, and I had set up the Bunsen burners, we were given in-school suspension for the rest of the week, and then another week of suspension when school started up after winter break. Colton just had suspension for the rest of the week because he'd known about the Bunsen burners and hadn't alerted the teachers.

This, the principal assured us, was letting us off easy. He could have given us straight suspension and not allowed us in school at all. Admittedly, this would have killed my grades, but on the other hand, it would have been a simple way to avoid everyone until they stopped thinking of new meanings for NHS. As it was, I still had to see them at lunch. Plus, I'd have to sit in the study hall room for a week with Colton. I knew he'd do nothing but glare at me because I'd turned yet another NHS project into a disaster and gotten him suspended in the process.

Throughout the week when they let all of the in-school suspension delinquents out to walk to lunch, I went out of my way to talk to Colton. I apologized again. I tried to make small talk. It didn't get me anywhere. Any time I spoke, his expression took on a hunted look, and he kept looking over his shoulder as though something bad was about to swoop down and grab him.

Brianna found another use for the iron-on letters she'd bought. On Thursday, Preeth, Kelly, and Brianna all came to school wearing the matching shirts with the words, FREE CHARLOTTE on the front and COOKIES ARE BETTER FLAMBÉ on the back.

"I thought you were giving the shirts to Amanda," I said when I saw them.

"I decided to give her a book on finding the right career. Besides, she was the one who came up with the 'Free Charlotte' phrase."

Well, it was nice to know they found a cause they could agree on.

On Friday, NHS met in the school parking lot after school to coordinate last-minute details about the Santa project and to load all the presents into my van. Colton kept stealing glances at me.

Which meant something.

Of course it might mean he was keeping an eye out to make sure I didn't do anything stupid, dangerous, or that would leave him drenched; but still, it meant something.

I wished we could drive to the mall together, but I had to transport the presents, and Colton took a load of NHS members in his convertible. Harris and Preeth came with me, probably because they knew I was the one person who wouldn't offer them an opinion—pro or con—about the merits of burning down the school.

Once we all got to the mall, the other NHS members unloaded the presents from the back of my van while Colton disappeared into the men's room to change into the Santa costume. I went into the women's room, clutching the plastic bag that contained an elf suit.

Surprisingly, it was a real elf suit, at least in that it only used enough material to cover an elf. The skirt was way too short for a human being, and I kept tugging at it, trying to pull it down farther. Normally, nothing would have made me put on the bright green tights that were included with the outfit, but the skirt was so short, I had to. I mean, one wrong move and thirty elementary children would be telling their friends that they knew what color underwear Santa's elves wore.

Faux fur lined both the skirt and the red velveteen jacket. I'm using the term *fur* loosely, since it more closely resembled a strip of building insulation than any living animal. I put black, pointy elf slippers on, and then a red stocking cap with attached jingle bells. After this was done, I surveyed myself in the bathroom mirror.

I decided the only positive thing about wearing an oversized furry hat with jingle bells is that it might draw people's attention away from my bright green legs and nearly nonexistent hemline.

It took courage to walk out of the restroom. I mean, at least Colton would be disguised in his Santa beard and costume. Anyone who saw me—and I knew high school kids were walking around the mall—would recognize me.

When you've nearly burned down the school gym and you need a boost of credibility with your peers, it's probably not a good idea to show up in the mall in an elf suit; but still, I was stuck with the job. I stood at the restroom door repeating to myself, "It's for the kids," several times. When my feet still didn't move, I added, "It's Christmastime, and no one will think anything of it." They wouldn't make endless jokes about my fashion choices, career ambitions, or how my taste in men had improved now that I was hanging out with an older, overweight, jolly guy.

Yeah, just like they hadn't made jokes about how some girls would do anything to meet buff firemen.

I knew as I stood there in the doorway that I had done this to myself. I'd sent out the message I didn't need any of them. Now that people had a chance to make me eat humble pie, they were taking full advantage of the situation.

Which goes to show that even though you chose justice over friendship, it doesn't mean you'll get it—justice, I mean. It's more likely you'll spend your one break from suspension dressed like a Keebler Elf–hooker.

I could probably write a really in-depth chapter for my dissertation about this day. You know, sometime in the future—after therapy had recovered all the memories I was about to repress.

I mean, seriously, I was so starting to hate the mall and everything that had ever happened in it.

I took a deep breath and walked out of the restroom. Once I made it to the courtyard where the Santa chair was, things wouldn't be so bad. I would blend in with the rest of the Christmas decor. Probably no one would even give me a second look.

Three steps out of the restroom, I saw Bryant getting a drink at the water fountain. I resisted the urge to turn around and flee back into the bathroom. I wouldn't have made it back gracefully, considering I jingled every time I moved. I took a long breath, forced a smile, and kept walking forward.

Bryant looked up, saw me, and his head jerked back in surprise. He nearly spit out the water he'd been drinking. "Charlotte!"

"Hi, Bryant." I motioned toward my outfit, pretending I didn't feel stupid. "It's what all the well-dressed elves will be wearing this Christmas season."

His gaze traveled from my pointy elf shoes to my furry hat and back again. "Let me guess, Bloomingdale's is making you spray mistletoe-scented perfume today?"

I laughed, jingling as I did. "No, I'm helping Santa pass out presents." I nodded toward the men's bathroom. "He's getting changed in there right now."

Bryant looked blankly at the bathroom as though Colton had never mentioned anything to him about it.

"The Santa service project for the needy kids at St. Matthew's," I prompted.

"Oh." He nodded without a hint of recognition. "That's really cool of Bloomingdale's to do. Where are you going to be? Inside the store?"

I vaguely wondered why he asked. Was he actually volunteering to walk with me there? That was so sweet. So unexpected. "We're using the Santa chair out in the courtyard."

"How long will you be there?"

I shrugged. More jingling. "We're singing some Christmas carols, then handing out presents to thirty kids. I'm guessing about an hour."

"Maybe I'll stop by and see you." He took a step down the hallway. "Right now I've got errands in the opposite direction."

"I'll give you a candy cane when you come," I called after him. "It's one of the professional perks of being an elf."

He shot me a smile, then walked away.

I stood by the drinking fountain and let out a breath I hadn't realized I'd been holding.

That hadn't been so bad.

I'd been nice to Bryant, and he'd been nice back. It seemed like a small thing and yet a big thing at the same time—a sign that the past was over.

As I stood by the water fountain, Colton came out of the men's room. He carried the Santa bag in his hand and wore his normal clothes. He saw me and did a double take. "Wow. You look really . . . um, elfish."

"I look like a trampy gnome with gangrene. You gave me this outfit as payback for getting you suspended, didn't you?"

He shook his head and laughed. "Actually, no. The elf outfit came with the Santa suit, but now that you mention it, it does seem a fitting revenge."

I pulled the skirt down again. "There's nothing fitting about this outfit. That's part of the problem." After adjusting my skirt, I gestured toward his bag. "So why aren't you decked out as Saint Nick yet?"

"I put the costume on, then realized I'd left the box with the wig and beard in my car. I can't go around the parking lot in half a Santa suit. I had to change back into my regular clothes."

"I can get it for you," I said, momentarily forgetting I was mortified of being seen in my own costume. "Or I can call someone else from NHS."

Colton looked down at his watch. "It's okay. We still have fifteen minutes till the bus from St. Matthew's arrives, and everyone else from NHS is probably busy arranging the presents. I have time."

He turned down the hallway, and I followed beside him, sounding like a one-elf sleigh as I walked. He glanced over at me, laughed, and said, "I need a picture of you like that."

"Thanks. Not only will you be unrecognizable in your costume, you didn't even tell any of your friends you were doing this, did you?"

He let out a grunt. "I don't need a bunch of them coming down here to bug me. It's bad enough I've got to do this at all. How much do you want to bet some kid gets so excited to see me, he wets his pants—while he's sitting on my lap?"

"That's not going to happen," I said. "Well, probably not, anyway."

He swung the bag slowly as he walked. "At least when I'm dressed as Santa, that one soda-throwing kid won't recognize me." Colton took a few more steps and added, "You better make sure he's not anywhere near a drink, just in case."

"I'll make sure," I said. "I'm really sorry about all that."

"Right," he said.

"No, really." We'd almost reached the mall exit, and I stopped walking. "Look, Colton, I'm sorry for getting you suspended, and for soaking you at the dance, and, you know, for making your date cry . . ."

He raised an eyebrow at me. "You're apologizing for making Olivia cry? Charlotte, you're the one who yelled, 'Now you look really Juicy!' as she ran out of the room."

"I was trying to lighten the mood of the situation. How was I supposed to know she has no sense of humor?"

"People who dash past you while hauling chairs over their heads generally don't have a lot of humor."

"Which is why I shouldn't have said it. And while I'm apologizing, I'm also sorry about Bryant. I've been far too suspicious of him, but you know him best, and if you say he's not cheating on Brianna, then I believe you."

Colton slowed his pace and smiled. "You're done Bryant bashing?"

"Absolutely." I took a step closer to him, not even caring that I was getting all sorts of stares from the shoppers who passed by. "In fact, I just talked with him, and we were very nice to each other."

"You just talked to him?"

"Yeah. Back at the water fountain."

"The water fountain at school?"

"No, the water fountain here. I talked to him right before you came out of the restroom."

The smile dropped from his lips. "Bryant is here at the mall?"

"Yeah," I said. "That's how I knew you hadn't told him about the Santa project. He had no idea why I was dressed as an elf."

Colton looked back down the mall hallway and the surrounding shops. "What's he doing here? He's supposed to be at a dentist appointment."

I shrugged, but Colton wasn't paying attention to me anymore. His eyes scanned the mall. "Brianna asked him to come over to her house and study for the English final, and he told her he couldn't because he had a dentist appointment."

"Oh." In a supreme effort not to be suspicious, I added, "Something must have come up."

"Yeah." Colton walked a few more steps in silence. "Which way did he go?"

I looked around and shrugged again. "This way, I think. He said he had errands in the opposite direction from Bloomingdale's."

"Errands," Colton repeated, then pulled his cell phone out of his pants pocket and speed dialed a number. A moment later he said, "Hey, Bryant, I just wondered if you want to go hang out or something." A pause, and then, "Oh, that's right. You're at the dentist. Well, happy drilling then. Bye."

Colton snapped the phone shut and thrust it back into his pocket. "He's right outside."

I looked out the door but was too far away to see anything except the shoppers coming inside. "How can you tell?"

"I could hear the Salvation Army bell ringer coming through his phone."

I took another step toward the door, but didn't want to get too close, as conspicuously dressed as I was. "Why would he lie about it?"

Colton looked past me, his lips pressed together in a flat line, and didn't answer. And then I saw someone I recognized. Not Bryant, but Shelby. She came from the parking lot and went across the sidewalk. As we watched, Bryant walked up to her, gave her a quick hug, then bent over and kissed her cheek. The two held hands, turned their backs toward us, and started off toward the movie theaters.

Colton stared after them. "I can't believe this."

I could, even though I didn't want to. I'd been right all along. Which is not to say it made sense to me. I mean, how could anybody be so stupid as to trade a girl who genuinely cared about him for . . . what? A flirt from another school who'd most likely forget about Bryant when the next wave of football players came through. I wanted to call him every swear word I knew, along with a few of the ones I'd learned from Olivia as she was fleeing the dance. Instead, I mutely watched the two walk by.

Colton took the phone from his pants pocket, opened it, and put on the camera function. Then he stepped out of the mall long enough to point it in Bryant and Shelby's direction.

When he came back inside, he looked at his phone and not at me.

"What are you doing?" I asked.

"Sending it to Brianna. What's her cell number?"

I told him and watched him punch the number in. After a moment he said, "There. Now Brianna knows what she's dealing with." He shut his phone and slid it back into his pocket. I could tell he was gritting his teeth. "I can't believe he lied to both his girlfriend and his best friend," he said.

I wondered which betrayal bothered Colton the most. For someone who was supposed to be jolly in a few minutes, he looked far too pale.

I'll admit right now that the phrase "I told you so" crossed my mind. About a hundred times. But I didn't say it. Maybe I'd finally learned to pick friendship over justice after all. Instead, I put my hand on his arm. "I'm sorry, Colton."

He shook his head. "I'm the one that didn't believe you. I should be apologizing."

"Yeah, I guess, but I've gotten so used to apologizing, it's become a habit."

He gave me a half smile for my attempt at a joke, then stared out at the parking lot. Like if he looked at it long enough, he could find a way to undo what had already been done and Bryant would come back and tell us he didn't really mean any of it.

Finally Colton glanced at his watch and said tonelessly, "I'd better go get the rest of my Santa suit. Why don't you check on everyone else and make sure the presents are set up."

I nodded, and without a word of good-bye, he walked out of the mall doors. For a moment the Salvation Army bells grew louder, then softer again when the door shut.

I walked across the mall to the Bloomingdale's courtyard, jingling. I'm sure most shoppers who pass Christmas elves expect a certain level of cheerfulness, and I probably should have at least tried to smile for the benefit of the little kids I passed. But I couldn't. I kept wondering what Brianna would do when she saw the picture. Would she need a shoulder to cry on immediately, or would she be too busy destroying everything Bryant had ever given her to need me for a while?

And what would Bryant do next? What would Colton do? Another question tapped away in my mind even more incessantly than the jingle bells. I heard it with every step I took: Where would Colton and I stand with each other after the fallout?

✤ thirteen ✤

When I got to the Santa station, I checked over the piles of presents, even though the other NHS members had already arranged them in orderly stacks. Each child would receive two boxes, one with an outfit and another with a toy. Everyone but Reese, that was. He had an extra shoe box for his mother and a note explaining that Bloomingdale's would happily exchange them if they didn't fit.

I ripped open the packages of candy canes and took out the first dozen so they would be ready to hand out. Had Brianna already seen the picture? Had she called Bryant to yell at him yet? Probably not. Bryant and Shelby had headed toward the theaters, which meant they were most likely going to a movie—although there was an ice-cream place next to the theaters, so they might have gone there. If Bryant went to the movies, he'd turn his cell phone off, and Brianna wouldn't be able to reach him until later.

I heard the kids before I turned around and saw them. A chorus of "There it is!" and "Look at all of those presents!" and "Are they for us?" filled the air. Then a small herd of children and the two teachers who tried to control them poured into the courtyard. "Where's Santa!" several of them called as they swarmed around me.

"He'll be here in a minute." I glanced around the mall looking for Colton. "He's checking on the reindeer in the parking lot."

"I didn't see a sleigh in the parking lot," one girl said.

"I did," another chimed in.

"You did not," the first girl said.

"Did too," the second insisted. "It was red." She looked up at me for confirmation. "Wasn't it?"

Actually, it was a dark blue convertible. "Right," I said.

Both of the teachers kept telling the children to sit down, but the children ignored the teachers and hovered around the Santa chair, throwing glances at the packages.

"Santa will be here in a minute," I yelled over the noise, and wondered how long it took to put the costume back on. I couldn't hold off an elementary school mob forever.

At last the teachers got the majority of the kids to sit down—although some kept popping up to switch places. Then one of the teachers, a woman who looked so old she could have been a childhood friend of St. Nick, started the group singing "Santa Claus Is Coming to Town."

A real elf would have known the words to this song, but I didn't and had to fake my way through by singing things like, "He knows when you are sleeping. He knows when you're awake. Because he works for the FBI and has all your phone lines bugged."

I didn't sing the last part loudly.

Right before we started in on "Jolly Old Saint Nicholas," which I only knew the first line of, Reese noticed me, jumped up, and gave me a hug. I took him a few steps away from the group so I could talk to him without disturbing the singing. "Hey, Reese, good to see you."

"Perfume Lady," he said, "did Santa bring my stuff?"

I bent down to be closer to Reese's eye level while simultaneously trying not to bend at the waist, so my skirt would stay put. "Well, I'm not sure about all the candy you asked for, but I noticed one of your packages is the shape of a shoe box."

Reese let out a slow breath. "Santa brought the shoes." And then as though he doubted his own statement, he added, "Where are they?"

"Over with the other presents. Santa will give them to you when it's your turn."

He looked around me at the stacks of packages, his eyes scanning for a shoe box. "Santa is giving them to us now, right?"

I nodded. "It's an early Christmas stop."

Reese turned slightly and called over his shoulder to the rest of the group, "See, T.J., I told you we didn't have to go to sleep first. He's giving them to us now!"

I smiled at the image this provoked—thirty elementary kids sacked out in the Bloomingdale's courtyard in an attempt to help Santa with his routine.

Reese turned back to me. "Can I be the first one to see Santa? I want to give the shoes to my mom right away."

"Your mom isn't here. You'll have to wait until you get home to give them to her."

"She is too here. She works over there." Reese pointed to Ruby Tuesday, which was a few stores down from Bloomingdale's, then cocked his head at me. "I thought you were supposed to know everything."

"That's only Santa, not the elves."

I hadn't noticed Colton walk up behind me until I heard his voice—deep and booming in a Santa imitation. "Yes, Reese," he said, "Santa knows everything, but most of the time my elf friend here is frighteningly clueless."

"Thanks, Santa," I said.

Colton clapped his hands together and addressed the audience, "All right, I'm ready to see some good boys and girls. Who's ready to see me?"

Every child immediately yelled, "Me!"

The noise and pleadings from the audience drowned out Reese's "Can I be first?"

Colton—probably because he didn't want to admit he didn't know the children's names individually—reached down to the stack of presents, picked up two, and called, "Marissa Pond, meet me at the Christmas chair!"

A girl shot up from the audience and nearly leaped all the way to the chair. I squeezed Reese's arm. "Don't worry. You'll get to talk with Mr. Know-it-all in just a few minutes."

Colton cast me a glance over his shoulder. "Elf-girl, why don't you come pass out the candy canes?"

I gave Reese a wave good-bye, then followed Colton over to the chair. Marissa jumped up on Colton's lap the second he sat down. They exchanged a few words about whether she'd been good, then he gave her the gifts. I handed her a candy cane, and she ran happily back to the audience.

I picked up another set of gifts and handed them to Colton. He ho-ho-hoed a bit, then called the next child up.

It was sweet to watch Colton—his voice a forced baritone—talking with the children. They were all so excited, clutching their gifts to their chests as though they held something precious. One girl wrapped her arms around Colton's neck as she left, gave him a hug, and solemnly declared, "I love you Santa. You're my favorite holiday."

The next boy whispered into his ear, "Say hello to Rudolph for me."

I wished I had a recorder with me. I wished we'd brought them more gifts.

Finally Colton called Reese's name. For a moment no one answered. I scanned the audience but still didn't see him. Then he ran from the back. I hadn't seen him before, because he'd been standing behind the group

with a woman. She must have been his mother because she had the same dark hair and large brown eyes.
She wore a white shirt, black pants, name tag, and—I
noticed—a pair of flimsy black dress shoes.

I wondered if she knew what Santa was bringing her
son or whether she'd just come out to see him receive
his gifts.

Reese hopped up onto Santa's lap and, without being asked, said, "I've been real good this year, Santa.
Didn't tease my little sister or nothing."

"Is that so?" Colton asked.

"I did my homework too, even when I didn't know
the answers."

Colton shifted in his seat. "It's good that you're trying, although perhaps you should ask for help when
you don't know the answers."

Reese nodded in agreement. "That's what my teacher
keeps saying."

"And while we're on the subject of behavior, it's
very naughty to throw soda on people."

Reese hung his head, and I kicked Colton's chair.
"Santa knows you're not going to do that anymore,
right Reese?"

Reese nodded quickly. "Right."

Colton held his hand out to me, and I handed him
the stack of Reese's presents. After handing the first
two to Reese, Colton held up the shoe box. "It seems I
brought a present for your mother to the mall. Do you
think you could give this to her?"

Reese let out a yelp of a yes, then grabbed all the

boxes and was off of Santa's lap and running toward the back. Another child climbed onto Colton's lap, but I barely paid attention to what they talked about. My gaze followed Reese across the courtyard. He held out the shoe box to his mother. She laughed, shook her head, and pushed the box toward him. These are your presents, she seemed to say.

So she didn't know about the shoes.

I watched as Reese held them out to her again, and again she shook her head. After another minute of this, Reese finally set his other boxes down, ripped the wrapping paper off the shoe box, and handed it to her.

The smile dropped from her face. She stared down at the shoes, picked up the note, then took one shoe out, holding it up in disbelief.

I couldn't hear their conversation, but it ended with Reese's mom bending down to hug him.

I felt the tickle of tears rolling down the corner of my eyes. I tried to wipe them away before anyone noticed, but wasn't fast enough. The boy on Colton's lap looked up at me and cocked his head. "Santa, how come your elf is crying?"

"Hormones," Colton answered. "The elves get very emotional around this time of year." Colton leaned closer to the child and lowered his voice. "That's what Santa needs all the chocolate chip cookies for."

The boy nodded at me as though watching a Discovery Channel documentary. "Ohhhh."

I kicked Colton's chair again, but laughed as I did. I was even able to watch Reese's mom slip off her old shoes and put on the new ones without starting up again. She took a few steps in them, smiled, and tousled Reese's hair. After a moment she put the shoes back in the box, gave Reese another hug, and walked into Bloomingdale's. I suppose because I'd gotten her size wrong and she wanted to exchange them.

At least I hoped that's what she was doing. If she returned those shoes again, and I had to keep rebuying them for her, I would be a seriously disgruntled elf.

I kept one eye on the store while T.J. climbed onto Colton's lap. "Are you the real Santa?" T.J. asked.

Colton ho-hoed a bit and answered back with a vague, "What do you think?"

"I don't believe in Santa, 'cause I didn't get nothing but some ratty old stuffed animals last year. If you're the real Santa, how come you only brought me ratty old stuffed animals?"

Colton shot me a desperate look, and I could already see him adding this moment to my other service project disasters. The homeless lady who'd chased after his car, the flaming refreshment table, and now having to look a little boy in the eyes and take responsibility for ratty stuffed animals.

"You always give the most stuff to the rich kids," T.J. went on. "And they don't even need it. How come that is?"

"Well, . . . T.J." Colton drew out the words, and I could tell he was stalling while he tried to come up with an answer. "You see . . . there are many complicated things about Christmas that are hard for me to explain . . ."

"The gift isn't what's important," I said. "What's important is the love behind the gift. You're just as loved as the rich kids."

For a moment T.J. said nothing; his face remained emotionless. "Does that mean I get stuffed animals again?"

"No," Colton said with relief. "I think my elves made you Lego this year."

"Lego?" T.J. sat up straighter. "The Star Wars kind I asked for?"

Colton took the boxes from my hand and placed them in T.J.'s. "You'll find out when you open it."

I didn't hear what T.J. said next. My attention swung to my side, specifically to Bryant striding up to the chair. He scowled at me, his eyes narrow and his face a blotchy red. In a low voice he said, "You just can't mind your own business, can you? You're some kind of freaking stalker who follows me around and sends pictures to my girlfriend. I bet you think you're real smart, don't you?"

I smiled back at him, refusing to be rattled. "Smarter than someone who doesn't notice a stalker dressed in a bright red and green elf outfit."

"You think you've taken Brianna away from me? This isn't over."

Colton turned to Bryant and still using his Santa voice—although not quite so jolly at the moment—said, "This is over for right now. My elf is busy. Why don't you go home, cool down, and we'll talk about it later."

Bryant threw a disgusted sneer at Colton. "Don't tell me what to do, fat boy. This doesn't concern you."

Then without another look at Colton, he turned back to me. "What did you say to Brianna when you sent her that picture? What have you told her?"

I heard his question, and yet it almost didn't register. My mind was still back on the fact that Bryant had just told off his best friend without even recognizing him.

Colton prodded T.J. off of his lap, stood up, and faced Bryant. He lowered his chin to let Bryant get a better look at his face. "Stop yelling at the elves," he said with forced humor. "Or Santa will put you on the naughty list."

Bryant took a step toward Colton, squaring his shoulders. "Yeah, I'll tell you what list you can put it on. You can put it on the list that you shove—"

"Bryant," I said, "will you please just go away. You're upsetting the children."

Out in the audience every single eye was riveted on us. The kids had completely lost interest in their presents, and all stared at the guy who was yelling at Santa. Harris and Preeth took off in a fast pace for—I'm not sure where. They hurried into Bloomingdale's and away from us. Maybe to call for mall security, or maybe just to avoid the ensuing bloodshed.

The two teachers walked slowly toward us, but since both were women—one who didn't look much older than us, the second who looked so ancient she seemed to be in need of a Boy Scout to help her reach the front of the courtyard—I didn't think either of them would intimidate Bryant.

"Oh, you're worried about upsetting people?" Bryant flung at me. "Too bad you never worried about upsetting me. You're nothing but a self-righteous, two-faced, piece of—"

Colton put his hand on Bryant's shoulder. His baritone voice had a growl to it. "Go. Home. Now."

Bryant shrugged off Colton's grip. "Don't touch me. You don't own the mall. I'll say whatever I want to you and your little ho-ho-ho."

"Bryant," Colton said, and it was almost his normal voice. Bryant should have recognized him, but still didn't. Bryant took a step toward me, but before he could reach me, Colton took hold of his arm and pulled him backward.

That's when Bryant yelled a few words that weren't appropriate for a room full of elementary students and swung at Colton's face. I heard a smack and saw Colton's head jerk back. He took a staggering step backward. His Santa hat nearly fell off, but remained attached to his wig at a drunken angle.

A collective gasp went up from the children, along with two or three shrieks from the girls sitting in the front.

And then in the next moment Colton convinced me that wrestling is not such a useless skill after all. He grabbed Bryant's elbow, threw his right arm over

Bryant's head, and in one swift movement pulled Bryant over his hip and to the floor. Bryant struggled to get up, but Colton stayed on top of him, keeping him headlocked and on the ground.

Next to me T.J. let out slow breath. "Santa rocks!"

The girls in the front row clapped, and the kids in the back row all started cheering at once.

Colton said something to Bryant, which made him stop struggling, but I couldn't hear it for all of the kids applauding. One girl said breathlessly, "I don't care what my parents say. I'm staying up to see Santa this year."

"Wait till my mom hears what Santa does to the people on the naughty list!" her friend replied.

Okay, so this was another service project that didn't turn out like I planned. Probably there would be some concerned parents calling the school to question why Santa was wrestling passing shoppers to the ground. Ms. Ellis would most likely ban NHS from doing any more extracurricular activities, but it wasn't my fault this time. Colton had taken the picture of Bryant and Shelby and sent it to Brianna, so he couldn't blame me for this.

Two burly guys wearing mall security badges hurried down the hallway just as Colton let Bryant up off the ground. The four of them stepped away from the group to talk, and Ms. Ellis joined them. She kept speaking excitedly and waving a hand in Bryant's direction. I wondered if she could give Bryant in-school suspension for punching Santa at the mall.

Yeah, he was pretty much the last person I wanted to be stuck with in study hall all day.

About this same time Harris and Preeth walked out of Bloomingdale's and up to me. "What do we do now?" Harris asked.

I looked around at the rest of the NHS members. They all stared back at me as though I should know what to do next.

I took another glance in Colton's direction. He and Bryant seemed quite busy yelling at each other, plus Colton kept touching his cheek and wincing, so I had a feeling he was in no mood to sit through the last few children. I picked up the next stack of presents and called out, "While Santa is busy . . . um . . . giving a deposition to mall security, I'll hand out a few of the presents, okay?"

A wave of grumbling rippled through the audience, followed by the chant, "We want Santa! We want Santa!"

Suddenly Colton had become Elvis, and a poorly dressed elf wasn't going to cut it.

I cast another glance in Colton's direction. He'd stopped talking to the security guards and watched as the crowd called his name. From beneath his slightly skewed beard, he smiled.

"All right," I said. "We'll wait for Santa."

A cheer went up from the audience, and they didn't stop cheering until Colton came back to the chair. As Bryant walked into Bloomingdale's with security guards—I assumed they were escorting him out of the mall—a girl jumped onto Colton's lap. "I love you, Santa," she said.

"I love you too," he said.

She reached over and gave his biceps a squeeze. "For a fat guy you're really buff."

"Well, Santa has a lot of time to work out between holiday seasons."

Colton tried to hurry the last five kids, probably because his cheek was swelling, but it was all he could do to interest them in their presents and get them to leave. The last two kids wanted his autograph.

Finally I told the group Santa really had to go because Mrs. Claus needed him to shoo away vagrant polar bears from the toy workshop. I guess after seeing Colton take down Bryant, they believed the story, and I was able to lead him away into Bloomingdale's. A round of applause followed us as we left.

As we went up the elevator in the store Colton leaned against the wall and touched his cheek. "How bad is it?"

"It's red and swollen."

"Where are we going? Harris has the bag with my clothes."

"We'll get those later. The refrigerator in the break room has an ice machine. I think you need that more." The elevator door opened. I led him down the hallway and past the manager's office. Once we got to the break room, Colton sat down on a plastic chair and pulled off his hat and wig. I grabbed some paper towels and ice from the freezer.

I pushed another chair next to his, but instead of sitting on it, I knelt on it, leaning over to him so I could hold the ice against his cheek. He winced, but didn't move away.

"The kids loved you," I said by way of consolation. "You did a great job."

"Yeah. Now they all think Santa Claus is a jolly old fat man who brings them presents and tackles people in the mall. Someday they'll tell their therapists about this afternoon."

"No, they won't. They thought you were wonderful. Didn't you hear them all chanting, 'I believe in Santa!' as you left?"

Colton leaned his head against the back of his chair as though this thought brought him no comfort. "I can't believe Bryant actually punched Santa in front of a bunch of little kids."

I didn't answer.

"Go ahead and say it," Colton said. "You were right and I was wrong."

I turned the paper towel over because that side was getting too wet. "I'm not happy I was right."

He let out a sigh. "Yeah, neither am I."

"What did he say to you?"

A muscle twitched in Colton's jaw, and I knew he was gritting his teeth. "He said I was on your side instead of his."

"What did you say to him?"

"That the next time he wanted to lie to someone, it had better not be me."

I turned the ice, moving it slightly on his face. He seemed so tense, so miserable. I wished I could make it all go away. Neither of us spoke for a few moments. I wondered if Bryant and Colton's friendship was over.

Colton reached up and peeled the beard from his face. A sticky adhesive had kept it in place, and when Colton pulled it from his chin, it sounded like tape ripping apart.

"Did that hurt?" I asked him.

"I can't tell. My cheek is too busy throbbing for my face to register pain anywhere else."

I put the ice back to his cheek. Some of the water from the ice cubes drizzled down his face, and he reached up a hand to wipe it away. "You're getting me wet." He looked me in the eyes for the first time, and the corners of his mouth turned upward. "Although I suppose I shouldn't complain about that, since it's like your trademark or something. If we're going to hang out together, I'll need to start wearing my raincoat."

"Are we going to hang out?"

He tilted his head and considered me lazily. "I've always wanted my own elf."

"Oh, have you?"

"And if you remember back to Candice's party, I apologized to Kayla, which means you owe me a kiss."

"I remember that." I knew I was blushing, so I shrugged and smiled. "I'll keep my eyes open for mistletoe."

Colton took my hand from his face and held it loosely intertwined with his fingers. "Mistletoe wasn't part of the agreement." Then he bent toward me and gave me a kiss, which made me realize I should make him apologize to people more often. On a daily basis, in fact.

As I thought about what a good thing apologies were, and once again wondered what kind of cologne Colton wore, the door to the break room opened. I pulled away from Colton so quickly, I almost fell off my chair.

I looked over and saw Harris and Preeth grinning at me from the doorway. "Man Charlotte . . ." Preeth said. "What exactly did you ask Santa for this Christmas?"

Harris held out a large plastic bag. "You guys ready to change?"

"Yeah," Colton answered. He stood up, walked over, and took the bag. "Are the kids back on the bus?"

"Yes. The teachers were all worried about you. They wanted to make sure you were okay. Ms. Ellis had to keep telling them she would see to it that you got the necessary medical attention—which reminds me, Ms. Ellis is getting a first aid kit, and she wants you to meet her outside the restroom in your normal clothes. You know, just in case you have to go to the ER or something. She doesn't want to traumatize any kids in the waiting room by making them think Santa has been out brawling before Christmas Eve."

"I wasn't brawling," Colton said, "and I don't have to go to the ER."

Harris shrugged. "You could just tell the little tykes you fell off the roof. Occupational hazard and all that."

Colton flung the plastic bag over his shoulder like it was Santa's sack, then turned to me. "Elf-girl, are you ready to go back to your secret identity?"

"I'm ready," I said, following him out the door.

But really, I knew there was no going back.

❧ fourteen ❧

After the service project ended, I drove some of the NHS kids home, then went over to Brianna's house. Kelly and Aleeta were already there, sitting on her bed. Together the three of them had almost managed to unravel all of Bryant's afghan. It took my breath away—the sight of all that blue and green yarn lying in a heap on the floor. As I stared at it the words, "But you spent so much time on it!" leaped from my mouth.

Brianna looked up at me with red-rimmed eyes. "That's the whole point. I spent so much time on him, and it was all for nothing. Just like this stupid blanket." She gave the yarn a tug, and a row of the blanket disappeared. "You were right, and I never should have made it. It's all for nothing."

I sat down beside her and took what was left of the blanket out of her hands. "It wasn't for nothing," I said. "You learned how to crochet. And you learned things from your relationship with Bryant." I struggled to think of something to use as an example. "Like now you know what kind of guy to avoid."

"Tell me exactly what happened," she said. "I talked to Colton on the phone for a little while, but I'm not sure he told me everything. He lied to me about the whole thing at the mall, so now I'm not sure."

"He didn't lie. He just didn't realize what was going on. He's as upset about this as you are."

She took the blanket out of my hands. "No, he's not. He wasn't in love. He never sat around planning what B names he would call his children. I was going to name our son Brady, our daughter Brandy, and our dog Brawny."

Which is just one more proof that things really do work out for the best.

"I'm sorry, Bri," I said.

"Did he really kiss her? Colton said he kissed her."

"Just a little one on the cheek."

She fingered the blanket, twisting the yarn with her fingers. "Colton didn't make it sound like it was just a little one."

"Maybe he saw something I didn't. He went outside."

Kelly leaned in closer. "Or maybe Colton was talking about some other time. He's probably talked to Bryant since their fight. He might have found out more details."

I glared at Kelly because saying this sort of thing wasn't helping Brianna feel any better.

Brianna gave the yarn a particularly vicious tug.

"When I'm done, I'm taking this pile of yarn and leaving it on Bryant's doorstep."

"He doesn't deserve it," I said. "You should crochet something new. For yourself. A sweater maybe."

"I only know the chain stitch," she said.

"You could learn," Aleeta said. "And then you could teach me. We could have matching sweaters."

Which apparently was the wrong thing to say because Brianna teared up again.

The doorbell rang, but none of us moved. We were too busy shoving Kleenex in Brianna's direction. "You'll find someone better," Kelly said.

I nodded. "I see a lot of guys at my perfume sprayer post. I'll start interviewing them."

From out in the living room we heard Amanda yell, "Bryant's here to see you!"

For a moment Brianna remained perfectly still. She clenched the wad of tissue in her hand. Then she stood up, dropped the Kleenex on the bed, and wiped her face with the back of her hand.

"You don't have to talk to him if you don't want to," I said.

"I want to," Brianna answered. "He owes me an explanation."

Kelly, Aleeta, and I exchanged glances, but none of us said anything. Brianna walked out the door and shut it firmly behind her.

Brianna's house isn't very big. It's just three bedrooms with a kitchen and living room. So no matter where you are, there isn't a lot of privacy. Amanda sat in the living room reading a book and apparently had no intention of leaving, because Brianna and Bryant went into the hallway to talk.

"I'm really, really sorry," he said.

"Then why did you do it? You cheated and you lied to me." For someone who'd been crying, her voice sounded surprisingly even. "I believed in you when my friends said I shouldn't. You made a fool of me."

Silence. Then his voice sounding pained. "I didn't mean for any of it to happen. Look, I was just trying to be her friend. She knew I had a girlfriend. The first time she came on to me, I stopped her."

The first time? Exactly how many times had there been? And if he knew what she was like after the first time, why had he allowed there to be any other times?

Brianna didn't say anything to him, and he went on. "The second time it just sort of happened. I didn't want to totally brush her off and be rude, you know?"

"So what you're telling me is you made out with her to be nice?"

Aleeta leaned over and whispered, "I didn't know Bryant offered that service to lonely high school girls. He should advertise in the school newspaper."

Out in the hallway Bryant raised his voice. "Look, I'm trying to work things out with you. Don't you even care about us?"

"Me? You're the one that cheated."

"And I said I was sorry. But I don't consider it

cheating, because it didn't mean anything to me. At the mall today she told me she wanted me to break it off with you, and I told her, 'Shelby, I'm sorry but I don't have those kind of feelings for you.' It would have all just blown over once I got on the Stanford football team."

I wished I could see Brianna's face so I knew what she was thinking. "Don't take him back," I whispered.

It wasn't Brianna who spoke next though, but Amanda. Apparently she'd come down the hallway to interject herself into the conversation. "Excuse me, Bryant, are you asking my sister to trust you when you've just shown by your actions that you're completely untrustworthy?"

His voice softened, "I think I deserve a second chance."

Amanda spoke again. "No one deserves trust. You have to earn it."

"Look," he said. "This is between Brianna and me. I wasn't talking to you."

I stood up and walked to the door. I'm not sure why. I suppose just in case Brianna needed my help, I could fling open the door and yell at Bryant or something.

I shouldn't have bothered. Amanda never backs down in an argument.

"Shall we go over the facts of the situation and see what they reveal?" she asked. "Fact one: People don't usually come on to you unless you encourage them. Fact two: You're perfectly capable of giving a woman the brush-off if you don't want her attention, which leads us to fact three: You wanted her attentions. Fact four—"

"I don't have to listen to this," Bryant said. The sound of his footsteps went down the hallway. "Call me when you want to talk, Brianna."

"I'm not calling you," she said.

More footsteps. "Fine."

Then Brianna opened the bedroom door and nearly ran into me. Her face was drawn tight as though each step hurt. I put my arms around her, and she covered her face with her hands, sobbing. I held on to her. Kelly, Aleeta, and Amanda all joined me until we looked like a football huddle of emotional women.

"It'll be okay," I said.

"We're here for you," Kelly said.

"I've decided to become a divorce lawyer," Amanda said.

Well, we all have our own ways of showing we care.

On Saturday afternoon while I did the dishes I called Colton to see how his face was. He said the swelling had gone down, but it was still red. I told him Santa was supposed to have red cheeks, which I'm sure he totally appreciated, even though he didn't laugh. We talked for a while, and then he told me he had Christmas shopping to do and asked if I wanted to come along.

"Who are you shopping for?" I asked.

"You," he said.

"Me?" I fumbled with the cup and half dropped it into the dishwasher. "Shouldn't you do that while I'm not around?"

"Maybe, but this way you can tell me what you want."

I picked up some spoons and slid them into the silverware rack. "That's sweet, Colton, but you're missing the whole point of gift giving. You're supposed to guess what I want."

"Like use my psychic powers?"

"Right."

"Hmmm. Do you want some perfume you can spray on your own time?"

"Nah."

"An umbrella?"

"Nope. That's what I'm getting you."

He let out a mock grunt. "I thought you were done drenching me?"

"Well, in theory . . . but in theory I'd never planned on drenching you in the first place."

"How about one of those Martha Stewart books on refreshments?"

I put the last of the silverware into the dishwasher and shut the door. "Okay, you've made your point. I'll go with you to pick something out for myself."

As it turned out, this took most of the day. Partially because when he came over, Julianne and Evelynn commandeered his attention and made him take them for a ride in his convertible. After that, Colton and I drove to the mall, but we went there to eat dinner at Ruby Tuesday.

Colton requested a table in Reese's mother's section. He didn't explain why, but I knew without asking it was so he could leave her a big tip.

After we sat down, she came to our table carrying a water pitcher and wearing the black shoes. She ran through the standard introduction, the specials, then kept snatching glances at me as she filled our glasses. Finally she said, "Did you come to the mall yesterday with a school group?"

Well, I guess it had been too much to hope that she wouldn't remember the tall girl in the tacky elf suit. "Yes," I said, "our NHS group passed out presents."

She smiled above the water pitcher. "It was so kind of you." She hesitated then, as though she hadn't made up her mind whether to say more. At last she said, "How did you know I needed shoes? Why did you buy them for me when I'm not a child?"

I opened my mouth, but didn't know what to say. Colton, however, answered without hesitating. "Because your son asked for them for Christmas. We had all the children fill out a wish list, and he wrote that he wanted black shoes for his mother."

She nodded, smiling, but not looking at us. The water pitcher trembled in her hands. "He has a good heart—and now I have good shoes. Thank you. My feet feel much better today."

I smiled back at her. "We were happy to do it for you."

She left then so we would have a few minutes to look over the menu.

I watched her go, then leaned toward Colton. "See, aren't you glad we did that service project now?"

"Yeah, I'm glad," he said, but the look he gave me made me wonder whether he was actually thinking of the service project.

I reached across the table and took hold of his hand, very carefully, so I didn't knock over my water glass in the process.

After dinner we walked around the mall, talking. I bought a Barbie doll convertible for Julianne, since she'd liked riding in Colton's. He suggested I get her an I'm-a-cool-wrestler Ken doll to go along with the car, but apparently through some oversight of Mattel's, those don't exist.

After some more walking, Colton decided I shouldn't see what he picked out for me after all. I had a good idea what it might be though, because before he left, he held up my wrist, sized it with his fingers, and then asked if I liked gold or silver better.

We agreed to meet back in front of Nordstrom in half an hour. I'd already bought presents for the rest of my family, and I really had no idea what to get Colton. That's the problem with shopping for rich people. They already have everything they need, and what they want is out of your price range.

I wandered around the mall for a while, then thought

about getting him some more of the cologne he wore. You know, just to ensure he never ran out.

I walked over to Nordstrom men's cologne section and sniffed every bottle until I found it. Then I held the bottle pressed against my face for several moments, until the saleslady came over and asked if I needed help. I assume she meant help in purchasing the cologne. I gave it to her to ring up.

As I walked out into the mall I ran into Candy and one of her friends.

"Char." Candy's brow knit together in worry when she saw me. "How are you holding up these days?"

"Fine," I said, "How about you?"

She whispered something to her friend, then took hold of my arm and pulled me a few steps away. "There's no need to pretend with me. I already know how you got kicked out of school for arson." Her lips pinched together, and then she let out a sigh. "I blame myself, really. You were fragile when Greg broke up with you. All this has just been a cry for help, hasn't it?"

"No, the fire was an accident, and I'm only suspended. Besides, I'm going out with Colton now, so you don't need to feel guilty. Really."

Her eyes narrowed as though she didn't believe me. "Colton? Colton Taft?"

"Yes." I looked behind her and saw him walking toward us. "There he is now."

She turned, gave him the once over, then stepped even closer to me. "What happened to his cheek?"

"Oh that. He was dressed up as Santa Claus for an NHS project, and well, he sort of got in a fight, and Bryant punched him."

I didn't have time to explain anything else before Colton reached us. He switched his shopping bag from one arm to the other so he could take hold of my hand. "Hey, Candice, out doing some shopping?"

She smiled but shook her head sadly. "Colton, you should have gone to Leland Prep with the rest of us. You know, wrestling simply isn't worth it." Then she called to her friend, and the two of them walked past us into Nordstrom.

Colton watched them go. "What was that all about?"

"Apparently I'm a bad influence on you."

"Yeah, probably."

I elbowed him but kept hold of his hand.

As we walked away from Nordstrom I told him the whole conversation, then added, "I'm never going to be able to face any of those people from Leland Prep again. Now they all think I'm some sort of fragile person who sets things on fire when she's upset."

He shrugged. "Look on the bright side. At least they've forgotten about you eating that centerpiece."

"Oh, right. I feel much better."

"Come on, you don't really care what the people at Leland Prep think about you, do you?"

"No, actually I'm still too worried about what the people at my own high school think about me."

He squeezed my hand. "Some of us think you're pretty great."

And then I smiled, because I did feel better.

I guess some of the stuff you learn at the mall isn't so bad after all.

Take a journey to faraway lands in search
of the perfect . . . prom date?

My ~~Fairy~~ fair
Godmother

Janette Rallison

Read on for a sneak peek at
Janette Rallison's new
romantic adventure

For Master Sagewick Goldengill

Dear Professor Goldengill,

Thank you for allowing me to raise my semester grade through this extra-credit project. First off, let me say that I was a little worried about the whole thing. When I went into the Fairy Godmother Affairs office to get my assignment, the lady behind the desk wouldn't even tell me which of the sisters, Jane or Savannah, was supposed to get the wishes. She gave me a condescending look and told me that as a fairy godmother my first task was to figure that out. Then she handed me this huge report to read and said, "I do hope this mission is more successful than your last."

Personally, I think the main problem I had with my last assignment was the leprechaun assistant FGA gave me. I mean, I know we have a lot of free time during these projects, but halfway through the job, he wandered off to play poker with card sprites and I never saw him again. So I told the lady that I wanted to work with, you know, some really hot elf guy, or at least a unicorn, but she flipped through her papers and said, "You've been assigned Clover T. Bloomsbottle."

Which is the same leprechaun I had last time.

I asked the lady, in a very calm manner—despite what she might tell you—"What in the world is FGA thinking?"

She told me, "FGA is aware of Mr. Bloomsbottle's shortcomings on the last mission. That's why he's been relegated to twenty-first century America until he can prove he's willing to use his magic in accordance with the Unified Magical Alliance guidelines. FGA believes in giving everyone a chance to redeem themselves."

So let me say right now that this would have gone a lot smoother had I been given an assistant who actually assisted in something.

I will send you a fifteen-page report I put together about the troubled teenage souls involved, so you can see how I used my magic to solve their problems, thus proving I have mastered the magic necessary to pass apprentice level and pursue my education at God-mother University. Where, I might add, I will totally apply myself.

I've also added side notes to this report in order to show you how much I've already learned about human culture.

Sincerely,
Chrysanthemum Everstar

From the Honorable Master Sagewick Goldengill
To Mistress Berrypond

Dear Mistress Berrypond,

I am in receipt of Chrysanthemum Everstar's report, yet it seems quite a bit has been left unsaid about her time as a magical godmother for the mortal Savannah Delano. Can you please have the Memoir Elves elaborate so that the academy and I can more accurately assess her project?

Yours,
Sagewick Goldengill

From the Department of Fairy Advancement
To the Honorable Sagewick Goldengill

Dear Professor,

As you requested, we sent Memoir Elves to the mortal Savannah Delano's home. Madame Bellwings, Memoir Elf Coordinator, was not at all pleased with this request, because elves who write the memoirs of teenage girls have the unfortunate habit of returning to the magical realm with atrocious grammar. They can't seem to shake the phrases "Whatever" and "No Way," and they insert the word "like" into so many sentences that other elves start slapping them. They also pick up the bad habit of writing things in text message form (i.e., R U going 2 the mall?) and for no apparent reason occasionally call out the name Edward Cullen.

Currently the Memoir Elves who delved into Savannah's mind while she slept are in detox. They are doing well in their recovery process, although one still occasionally stands in front of the mirror and asks, "Do you think I look fat in this?"

Savannah is none the wiser and the elves were able to compile a thorough report. You should be able to find out exactly what part Chrysanthemum Everstar played in granting wishes and whether she did indeed follow all fairy/mortal protocol.

The memoir report follows as told to the elves by the subject Savannah Delano:

Chapter 1

Here's my definition of a bad day: your boyfriend of four months—who until 12 seconds ago, you thought was the most perfect guy to set foot on earth—breaks up with you.

My definition of a truly horrible day: the aforementioned boy dumps you for none other than your sister.

The definition of my life: he does all of this right after you inform him that you blew your last dollar buying your dream prom dress. He asks if you can get a refund. It turns out he'll be taking your sister.

• • •

I stared at Hunter across the restaurant table, so many thoughts shooting through my head that I didn't know which one to pick first and aim in his direction.

"I'm sorry," he said. "Jane and I didn't mean for this to happen."

"Really?" How do you not mean to ask your girlfriend's

older sister to prom? Do the words just trickle out by themselves? Was someone else in charge of your lips when this happened? I didn't say any of this, because there wasn't a point. What he meant was: I didn't mean to like her better than you.

I wanted to ask him why he did—like Jane better than me, that is—but somehow I couldn't bring myself to ask the question. The answer would hurt more than not knowing.

Almost as if he'd read my mind he added, "It's just that Jane and I have more in common. We're both more..." He moved his hand in a rolling motion as though trying to catch the right word somewhere over the tabletop.

During the pause, I thought of my own adjectives. Smart? Talented? Good-looking? No, it probably wasn't looks. Jane and I looked too much alike for that. She's pretty, true, but I always got noticed first. Jane always has been content to be known as the quiet, studious one. The quiet, studious one who had now stolen my boyfriend.

"Organized," Hunter said.

"Organized?" I repeated. "You're dumping me because I'm disorganized?"

"I guess 'responsible' is a better word," he said.

"So I'm disorganized and irresponsible?"

He leaned toward me but his eyes distanced themselves. "Don't take it the wrong way. You have lots of great qualities: you're fun and you're pretty, you're just"—more hand rolling, as though this somehow unwound his tongue—"always late for everything."

I stared back at him, stunned. This was how guys chose girlfriends—based on their punctuality?

"I'm not late for everything," I said, even though I hadn't been ready when he came to pick me up tonight. But I'd had a good reason. One of Mom's hair clients had needed an updo for a fancy night out and Mom hadn't finished with her perm appointment, so I'd stepped in to help out.

I nearly pointed this out, but then stopped myself. It hadn't been tonight's ten-minute wait that had decided my fate with Hunter. He'd only scheduled this date to break up with me. I should have sensed it by the way he'd hardly looked at me while he ate his dinner.

"Jane and I both want to go to college," he went on. "You don't even want to go to high school."

"What's that supposed to mean?" I have never said I didn't want to go to high school. I enjoy high school. Well, at least the socializing part. Geometry I could do without. Ditto for world history. And really, why should I care what the symbolism in *The Grapes of Wrath* stands for? Do employers ask those kinds of questions during job interviews?

He shrugged. "You don't take your grades seriously."

"I took us seriously," I said.

That made him flinch. "I'm sorry," he said.

I pushed my chair away from the table. "Take me home."

We drove back toward my house in silence. Inside my head a whole orchestra of thoughts played out, competed with each other, blared so loudly I could hardly think.

He drove looking straight ahead and I caught a glimpse of his profile. I hated myself for still thinking his wavy black hair had the perfect amount of gloss to it, that he looked more like a knight preparing for battle than a high school senior. A girl shouldn't have thoughts like that about the guy who just dumped her.

My throat felt tight and I willed myself not to cry. I wanted to point out all of Jane's faults to him. She was the most unspontaneous person in existence. She had no imagination, no creativity. When we were bored as kids, could she come up with a decent game using a box of macaroni, a tube of tooth-paste, and the kitchen table? I think not.

I didn't say anything though. I had enough pride not to beg him to reconsider. I just sat and listened to the orchestra in my mind playing loud and clear: your sister is better than you. Finally he pulled up in front of our house. Without a word I opened the car door, stepped outside, and slammed it shut.

I didn't walk across the lawn to our house; I walked down the sidewalk. I was not going inside. I didn't want to talk to Jane right now, or hear the same type of apologies I'd just heard from Hunter.

Instead of driving off, Hunter pulled up alongside of me and rolled the car window down. "Where are you going?"

"I don't see why that concerns you."

"If you don't go inside, it will look like I never brought you home. Your family will wonder where you are."

What he meant was, Jane would worry where I was. Heaven forbid she experience any guilt over this. "Well, you know me," I told him. "I'm the irresponsible one."

He kept following me. The car inched along beside me going about two miles an hour. "Come on, Savannah, don't be this way."

I wasn't supposed to have a reaction to this? I was just sup-posed to smile and wish them luck or something? I didn't answer. I looked straight ahead and kept walking. I had meant to go over to my best friend Emily's house but I couldn't go there with this one-car parade following me. When I came to the cor-ner of our street I walked straight instead of turning right.

Hunter leaned toward me, a mild reprimand in his voice. "It's dark and you didn't even look for cars before you crossed."

"I didn't have to. If a car was coming they'd have hit you first."

He let out a sigh. "Get back in my car."

I kept walking.

"I mean it, Savannah. I'm not going to let you run off and upset everyone at your house because they don't know where you are."

Which just goes to show you how arrogant he was. He just assumed I'd planned on turning the night into a big production where I disappeared and Jane got to worry that I'd run away from home or something. Well, okay, maybe that did sound like a good idea, but still, it was arrogant of him to assume that sort of thing about me. I didn't look at him. My purse thumped against my side in an angry rhythm.

"Savannah, get in the car."

The park came into view. I picked up my pace.

"You're being melodramatic about this."

Well, he could just add that to the list of my other faults he no longer had to put up with.

"I'm not leaving and I've got a full tank of gas."

Of course he did. Organized people always kept their tanks full.

I made it to the park and finally turned to him. "If you want to follow me, fine. Have fun driving through the swing sets." I left the sidewalk and walked across the grass. The park sat in the middle of our neighborhood, surrounded by houses, and more than a few streets ran up to it.

I didn't have to look back to know what Hunter would do. He would sit in his car and watch me walk across the park until I headed toward a street. Then he'd drive around and head me off on that street.

I strolled toward the first street opening on the right. Before I got out of sight I turned to check and see if his car had left. As soon as it had, I doubled back, walking the same way I'd come. Except that instead of walking home, I turned onto

Emily's street. Really, Hunter was almost pathetically easy to lose. Which just goes to show you that college bound doesn't necessarily mean street smart.

I stayed at Emily's for the next three hours. Not really long enough to worry my parents. My curfew on weekdays is 10:00 PM. If Jane knew I wasn't with Hunter anymore and worried about me—fine. If she thought I was out with her new boyfriend until past 10:00—even better. I sat with Emily on her bedroom floor, cried, and ate Oreos. The whole time Emily told me what a great catch I was and how I didn't need Hunter. What kind of jerk hits on his girlfriend's sister? What kind of sister steals boyfriends from family members? They deserved each other.

I nodded at everything she said but couldn't agree with any of it. It felt like the people who knew me best didn't care about me. In my mind, Hunter's list of my faults kept growing. All of my popularity was a sham. I didn't really have anything going for me. I was disorganized, irresponsible, and didn't take my classes seriously. Which probably showed a lack of ambition, talent, and dependability. Obviously there was something permanently wrong with me, something too huge to fix.

And on top of all that I had a cream silk and chiffon prom dress hanging in my closet that cost me three hundred and fifteen dollars. I didn't want to return it to the dress shop. How humiliating would that be?

Emily must have sensed that her pep talk wasn't working—probably because I kept making Oreo skyscrapers and shoving them in my mouth. She finally took the package away from me. "Savannah, someone else will ask you to prom. Someone better, someone who appreciates you, and then you'll see Hunter was wrong."

I nodded. I still didn't believe her.

When I walked into my house at 10:15, my parents and Jane

sat in the family room talking in harsh, subdued voices. I knew they were talking about me because they stopped as soon as I walked in. Three faces turned toward mine. My parents' expressions were concerned. Jane's showed a mixture of worry and defiance. She didn't speak. I knew she was waiting for my accusations; I could already see her lips poised in defense.

"You owe me three hundred and fifteen dollars for a prom dress," I told her, then walked upstairs to my room.

· · ·

I ate oatmeal without sugar the next morning as a sort of dietary penance for my Nabisco sins. I imagined the little oat flakes "tsk tsking" as they floated by blobs of fat that were headed straight to my thighs. It was the only reason I could think of to be happy that I now had to walk to school. I wasn't sure if Hunter would still drop by the house to offer me and Jane a ride, but there was no possible way I was going to get in the backseat and watch Jane sit beside Hunter. So it was just best to be long gone before he came.

While I ate, Mom tried to talk to me about the whole situation. She'd also tried last night, but I'd told her I was tired and just wanted to go to bed. Jane came into my room last night too and gave me her side of the story, which was pretty much like Hunter's side of the story, except that her eyes didn't look away from me as she told it. When I didn't comment she added, as though it should explain everything, "Hunter and I will both be going to George Mason in the fall. You didn't think that a freshman in college was going to keep dating a junior in high school, did you?"

Yes. But I didn't say that. I just added "immature" to my mental list and said, "Would you mind turning off the light on the way out? I've got to get up early in the morning."

She sighed and left.

So Mom gave me a concerned-parent pep talk as I ate my oatmeal about how she was disappointed in Jane's choices, but if it hadn't been Jane, it would have been someone else. Dating had its ups and downs. After all, at this point in my life I wasn't looking for a future husband. I should be dating for fun, to learn about relationships, to see what kind of qualities I liked in a guy. I would go through many more boyfriends before I found the right one.

Which, I can tell you, is not what you want to say to your daughter when you are trying to cheer her up. I wanted to say, "Really? You mean I get to feel like the bottom of my stomach has been manually ripped out with each relationship I go through? I can hardly wait to get back to the dating market."

But of course I didn't say that because none of this was my mother's fault, unless you count the fact that she gave birth to Jane.

Besides, I'd finished crying about it when I'd finished my last Oreo skyscraper. As Dad would say, I'd taken my losses, now I needed to regroup, rethink, and plan the next offensive. Which in this case involved getting someone even cooler to ask me to prom in order to show Hunter and Jane that I didn't need or care about them.

I nodded at Mom. "I'm fine. Really."

She reached over and patted my hand. "I know you will be. Just remember, boys come and go. Sisters are forever."

Jane swept into the room, walking by the kitchen table and scanning the counters. "Has anyone seen my chemistry folder? I left it on the coffee table and now it's gone."

I picked up my glass of milk and took a slow sip. "Nope."

She hurried out of the room, mumbling.

I ate my oatmeal. Mom watched me in silence. Finally she said, "Maybe after school the two of us can go out and do something. Would you like that?"

"I'm fine. Really."

Jane came back into the room, this time with her hands on her hips. "My brown shoes are gone too. They were in my closet last night and now they're not. What happened to them?"

I took the last bite of my oatmeal and shrugged. "Don't know."

She pulled her gaze from me and turned to Mom. "If I can't find my brown shoes, I'm going to have to change my entire outfit. They're the only shoes that match these pants."

I stood up to take my bowl to the sink. "Don't be too long. You know how Hunter hates to wait." Then I left the room.

Okay, so it was slightly evil to hide her stuff, but considering all of the things I could have done, I figured she still got off easy.

JANETTE RALLISON has been writing since she was six years old, although the quality of her work has improved substantially since then. She is the author of many books, including *Revenge of the Cheerleaders*. She lives in Chandler, Arizona, with her husband, Guy, and their five children.

Visit her Web site at
www.janetterallison.com
and check out her blog at
www.janette-rallison.blogspot.com

For other hilarious and heartfelt

high school tales, don't miss . . .

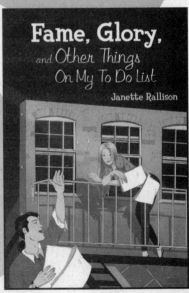